Praise for *What It Was Like*:

"My obsession with *What it Was Like* is identical to the one the story's wry, intelligent, and completely unremorseful narrator has for the beautiful, sexually intoxicating and mesmerizing Rachel Prince, with whom he begins a romance that we know from the opening pages is ill-fated. Once I started reading, I had to finish the book as fast as I could. Reading *What is Was Like* made me experience all the joys – and dangers – of teenage lust with an immediacy that I haven't felt since *Splendor in the Grass*."
– Stan Chervin, Screenwriter, Academy Award nominee for *Moneyball*

"*What It Was Like* is a story about all kinds of love – the obsessive first love of two unforgettable teenagers as well as the layers of love that can lie in tortuous wait between parents and children, a love as deep and hidden as an ominous quarry. If indeed you've ever wondered what kind of parents J.D. Salinger and Patricia Highsmith would have made if they had gotten together, then look no further than Peter Seth, their literary progeny."
– Kevin Sessums, author, *Mississippi Sissy* and editor in chief, *FourTwoNine* magazine

What It Was Like

Peter Seth

THE
STORY PLANT

The Story Plant
Studio Digital CT, LLC
PO Box 4331
Stamford, CT 06907

Copyright © 2014 by Peter Seth Robinson
Jacket design by Barbara Aronica-Buck

Print ISBN-13: 978-1-61188-190-5
E-book ISBN-13: 978-1-61188-191-2

Visit our website at www.TheStoryPlant.com

First Story Plant printing: September 2014

Printed in the United States of America

0 9 8 7 6 5 4 3 2 1

To, for, and because of Buffy

Editor's Note

This manuscript was discovered among the papers of the late Justice Thomas X. Jordan, who passed away in 1983 after serving on the Supreme Court of New York State, Appellate Division, from 1951 to 1979. Since then, it has circulated privately among psychologists, attorneys, judges, and mental health professionals, as a representative case study of a particular type of criminal mind.

The manuscript has received minimal editing, in order to preserve the writer's grammar, punctuation, spelling, capitalization, etc. It was deemed preferable to publish it with as little editorial tampering as possible, so that the voice of the perpetrator can be heard. There is no point in publishing a book with (*sic*) after every third sentence.

[This cover letter, on the letterhead of the firm of Bishop, Hosker, Finch & Mantell, LLP, was found with manuscript.]

March 5, 1970

The Honorable Thomas X. Jordan
Justice, Supreme Court of New York State
Appellate Division
Second Judicial Department
45 Monroe Place
Brooklyn, NY 11201

Dear Justice Jordan:

In accord with our conversation on February 3, I am sending you the document compiled by my client during his incarceration.

This exhibit is offered to the Court, in advance of the appeal, in the interest of justice. It opens a window into my client's state of mind before, during, and after the incident. It is meant as a supplement to the trial transcript, not a replacement for it. Previous counsel's decision notwithstanding, this is a truer account of the elements of the case than you will find anywhere. My many hours of consultation with my client have convinced me of this fact.

Needless to say, a copy has also been made available to Mr. Hackett in the district attorney's office as part of the pre-sentence investigation.

Please do not hesitate to contact me should you require any further elaboration or clarification.

Respectfully yours,

Lester J. Mantell, Esq.

LMJ:amb
enclosures
CERTIFIED RETURN RECEIPT REQUEST
P 562 631 873

Part I

The Summer

Record of Events #1 – entered Monday, 10:31 A.M.

~

My excellent new lawyer told me to write everything down exactly as it happened, so that's what I'm going to do. I didn't testify at my trial and that didn't work out so well, to put it mildly, so I'm going to write down everything that I wanted to say – and should have said – on the witness stand. I know people think that they know what happened, but I'm here to tell you that "the whole truth and nothing but the truth" has not been heard...until now.

All kinds of stories floated around for months, before, during, and after the trial, all kinds of lies. The whole Romeo-and-Juliet-Leopold-and-Loeb-Bonnie-and-Clyde thing that all the newspapers and TV stations made such a big deal over: most of it lies. On the one hand, I really don't care what other people say about me. So many people hate me now who don't even know me that it's already completely absurd. (I'm not saying that I'm the nicest person in the world; I am far from that. But I'm no monster.) On the other hand, deliberate fabrications and distortions have hurt my family. They've been through enough; they don't need any more pain. My life is already ruined; let's just leave them alone.

I'm going to try to tell things in the order that they happened, but I can't guarantee anything. Sometimes I'll have to move around in time. My intention is to be clear and to tell the full story, as it relates to the Incident. I'm going to try to leave out anything extraneous. Everything that I say here goes to what I've learned to call "state of mind at the time."

OK, I'm going to try to make this fast. It's really a very simple story. What happened was this: I met this girl and did a very stupid thing. I fell in love. Hard. I know that to some people that makes me an idiot and a loser. What can I say? They're right. I did some extremely foolish things; I'm the first to say it. And they've left me in jail and alone. What can I do? These things really happened.

It began with a pure and deep passion, and ended in obsession and violence. In heartbreak and shame and the personal destruction of many lives. But it wasn't like the James Dean movie or the epic rock-and-roll song that the newspapers made it out to be. (Some jerk *did* write a song about it.) It was simple, at least at the beginning, and personal and real. Let me say right now that I deeply regret my part in everything bad that happened. How what started so innocently became so ... un-innocent ... how things became twisted – even now, after so much time has passed, my mind can't quite grasp all the events; even over time. Time: which is what I'm doing now. We'll see what happens. My new lawyer tells me that I have reason to hope. Why am I suspicious of "hope?" All I know is that it's breaking my mother's heart for me to be in here. I can stand it; I don't know if she can.

Also, I don't know how much longer I'm going to be in my own cell, "for my own protection," so I'll try to finish this up fast. I know people have only so much patience with teenage angst, myself included. So my first rule is: No Whining. The last thing anyone wants to hear is some loser whining about how life and love all went wrong for him.

While I'm thinking about it, let me establish some other ground rules. As far as my parents, I'm not going to go into too much detail about them. It's not their story. They deserve their privacy after what they've gone through. It's one thing to go through some kind of difficulty yourself; it's quite another to have to stand by and watch someone you presumably love have to endure it. I shouldn't say "presumably." They *do* love me. That parental love; it's crazy. Crazy primal. Because, if you look at the people in this world, many of them couldn't possibly be loved by anybody *but* a parent. But I guess all kinds of people are loved. Serial killers on death row get marriage proposals all the time.

Also, I'm not going to use any curse words (though, God knows, my inner monologue is pretty much one continuous, indiscriminate stream of profanity). So once I start, I might never stop. So, No Swearing. And, to tell you the truth, I don't want to get bogged down in too much nastiness or put people off unnecessarily. There's plenty there already to put people off. Also, No Religion, No Politics, and as little as possible about The War.

I'm almost afraid to begin this. I don't know why. Nothing can happen to me that's any worse than what's already occurred, so why not just go ahead and say it all? Everything: just as it happened. It is deeply embarrassing and shameful that I have to do this at all. To be a justifier, a self-defender, an alibier: just another "innocent" skeeve in prison, looking for a way out. But circumstances have forced me to do this. I didn't think I'd have to take a last stand, this young. But let's face it: adults really have no respect for the thoughts and feelings of teenagers, so I pretty much didn't stand a chance from the get-go. I should be out living my life, not rehashing a few episodes from several months ago that happened to lead to some unfortunate consequences. Already I sound defensive, and I don't want to be. *"Unfortunate consequences??"*

It's noisy, even in this protected wing. Lots of slamming doors, metal-on-metal. Yelling, and then more yelling to stop the yelling. It makes it hard to concentrate. I won't lie and say that I'm not scared and lonely. I get visits occasionally and can make phone calls, but I know I'm in this alone. And I'm going to get through it, alone. Sure, my life is ruined, but maybe I can salvage something from this disaster. It's a terrible thing to admit, that one's life is ruined, especially because I'm still pretty young. But even if I ever get out of here, I'll always be that kid from Long Island, the Ivy League Killer, the Kid

Who dot dot dot. From all the newspaper and radio and TV coverage, everyone thinks that they know me. "Experts" were certain that I was "using" her; other "experts" were just as sure that she was "using" me. They were all fools who knew nothing about love and how it works. But, in a way, it doesn't matter anymore – everyone now knows my name (which is precisely why I'm not going to use it anywhere in this testimony). So let me tell you right now, right up-front: *no one knows me.*

There's this guard in my section who lets me write under the covers after lights-out. I think he has a son my age. He looks at me with that "what a jerk" expression that I sometimes get from my Dad. He knows that I shouldn't be here. Everyone knows that I shouldn't be here. So how did it happen? How did I get here?

~

I can tell you when it started. It was the summer before my first year of college, the summer of 1968. (You remember "Mrs. Robinson" and "Tighten Up" and Janis Joplin's "Piece of My Heart" and "This Guy's in Love with You"? See, it really wasn't so long ago.) And if I was smart enough to get into Columbia with a decent scholarship, I was smart enough not to stay home living with my parents all summer. Oh, we got along fine and all, but after my mother suggested that I work another summer in her rich cousin Ralph's printing company and my father offered to get me a job in the stock room of the furniture store where he worked, I knew that I had to find a better way.

My solution was not too imaginative, I admit – a job as a counselor at a sleep-away summer camp in Upstate New York, taking care of a bunch of kids – but it fit my requirements: it got me out of the house and into a decent job that would give me a good chunk of money by the end of August. And it was two months in the country – that had to be a good thing. I was used to spending my summers at home, working at the printing company and taking some extra courses. So there was nothing wrong with having an easy summer before starting Columbia.

"Energetic, positive young people needed" said the flyer on the bulletin board in the student union at Hofstra where I had gone with my friend Paul to see this bad band his cousin was in and to futilely try to meet some college girls. *That could be me*, I remember thinking, looking at the little pictures of happy, healthy summer people on the flyer – water-skiing, playing baseball, sitting around a campfire. It was already April, and I had to make a decision soon. So the next day I called the number on the flyer and set up an interview for that very evening.

That was when I first met Stanley Marshak, one of the three Marshak brothers who owned Camp Mooncliff, near the town of Boonesville in the mountains of Upstate New York. Two of the Marshak brothers were doctors, but Stanley was the brother who ran the camp. He was the person who interviewed me at his home in Roslyn in an office that he had in his basement. The house was a nice split-level in a very nice neighborhood. Evidently, owning a camp was a good business.

Stanley welcomed me at the front door with a firm handshake, as if he were testing my character or something. He was a tall man, broad and balding, with a bushy moustache that curled a little at the ends. I smiled and held his grip, just as firmly. He walked me downstairs to the basement, all done in green and white: Camp Mooncliff's colors. Stanley told me all about the camp and its illustrious three-decade history, how he and his brothers founded it, and how he, Stanley, a life-long bachelor, was "married to Mooncliff." It was sort of amusing, how enthusiastic and how proud of the place he was. (I had never been to a sleep-away summer camp like Mooncliff before, only some local day camps when I was little, but I kind of knew how things worked.) But I liked that he liked the place so much.

Stanley showed me an endless carousel of slides of Mooncliff, projected on the white basement wall, and told me what the job entailed: watching/babysitting/counseloring a bunch of ten- and eleven-year-old kids for all of July and August for X number of dollars. (I don't really want to say how much I made. My mother always told me that it's vulgar to discuss money, and she's probably right. But I'll say it was good money and would help set me up for the fall.) My job was Junior Counselor in the Intermediate group, which meant that there would be an older counselor in the bunk who was really in charge, so my responsibilities would be limited.

Stanley and I talked for about forty-five minutes, an hour tops, and he hired me on the spot. I signed a contract right then and there. In those days, I could impress adults fairly easily.

The night before I was to leave for Mooncliff for the three-day Counselor Orientation, I made a last-minute check of everything I was going to take on the bus. I had sent a trunk full of clothes and other stuff up to the camp two weeks before, as directed. I'd used my Dad's old army trunk, which he got a big kick out of. You need a lot of clothes for two months, plus it apparently got really cold up in the mountains at night, so I had to pack all kinds of clothes. To carry on the bus with me, I had one small suitcase with some extra clothes and toiletries, and a little thrift-store knapsack I used to carry books and other things, figuring that maybe I'd have some time to read and hang out. I made sure that I had the packet of information for incoming freshmen that Columbia had sent me. And I took my address book – not that I had anyone in particular to write to – just in case.

"You have everything?" asked my Mom, who was washing dishes when I came downstairs to the kitchen for my last dinner at home. "Did you take extra Q-Tips?"

"Thank you, but I *have* Q-Tips," I said, controlling my annoyance. "I know how to pack."

"Those mountain lakes can be very chilly, and you don't want to get a cold in your ear."

"A cold in my *ear*?"

"Don't laugh," she said. "You have to be careful in the mountains."

"You have to be careful *everywhere*," I teased, grabbing her around the waist and pulling her playfully away from the sink.

"Hey, I'm all wet!" she cried, grabbing a dishtowel and trying to dry her hands as I roughhoused with her.

"Stop!" she giggled, twisting away from me. "What are you doing – !"

I let her go, making sure that she wasn't hurt or anything.

"You can't wait until tomorrow to get rid of your mother?" she gasped as she composed herself, drying her hands and smoothing the front of her housedress.

"Oh," I said, changing subjects. "Did you remember to do that last blue pinstripe shirt I asked you – ?"

"It's hanging in the hall," she said, having turned back to the sink.

"You're the best," I said, giving her a little kiss on the back of her head. She was smaller than me now – I was eighteen and an "adult" – but it still felt kind of odd to be kissing *down* at my mother.

The next morning, I was up at 5:30 a.m., woken by the sound of my Sony clock radio set to WNEW-FM. Too early for Hendrix. I clicked it off.

"You up?" my father asked as he cracked open the door in the dark.

"Yeah," I grunted.

I had told my Dad that I would take a cab or get a friend to drive me since it was so early in the morning, but he wouldn't hear of it. ("It's my job to take you," he'd said simply, without any resentment. "No big deal.") It wasn't just saving me the cab money; he wanted to do me one last favor before I left. He even had fresh coffee made when I got downstairs.

It was still pretty dark when we got into my Dad's old gray Chrysler and drove to meet the Mooncliff bus.

"If you need anything," my Dad said as we drove along in the very light traffic, "call."

"I will," I said. "It's not like I'm going a million miles away."

"You wish," he joked back. My Dad likes to joke and tease, but in a gentle way. Sometimes we fight, like all fathers and sons, especially since I'm an only child and fairly strong-willed anyway, but I don't think there's a mean bone in his body. Of course, he could be tight with a buck. We weren't the richest people in the world, but still, in winter, he would refuse to turn on the furnace until you could almost see your breath. Mom and I would tease him, calling him "*Heat*-ler." He did not like that one bit, but we still called him that because it was funny. All through everything that's happened to me, through every horrible downturn, he has been my rock.

The meeting place for the counselors was the parking lot of the Holiday Inn on Hempstead Turnpike. Fair enough. It was centrally located and convenient if anyone had to stay over the night before. When we turned into the parking lot, I could see a big silver bus in the corner past the hotel by the curb with a whole lot of people and luggage next to it.

As we drove closer, I said to my Dad, "You can drop me here."

"I can get you nearer," he offered.

"No," I said. "That's OK. It's crowded over there."

My Dad pulled the Chrysler over to the curb and stopped the car.

"Don't worry," he said. "I don't have to meet your new friends."

"It's not that!" I protested, but he just chuckled and got out of the car to get my stuff out of the trunk. But I got out faster.

"I've got it," I said, pulling the old Samsonite out with a wide swing, almost hitting him.

He waited for me to clear away and then slammed the trunk hard.

"Good," I said, glancing over to the bus and the growing crowd near it.

"Well," my Dad said. "You made it."

"Thanks," I said. I stepped forward and gave my Dad a good hug. "Take care of Mom. And the Mets."

"I can't guarantee anything!" he shouted as I picked up the suitcase, slung the strap of my knapsack onto my shoulder, and walked toward the crowd. "Especially the Mets!"

I was glad that he drove me, that we'd had a last good moment together. But he was right; I didn't want to have to introduce him to all these new people, people I didn't even know myself.

You should know that I'm not the most outgoing person in the world. I am, generally speaking, cautious. I like standing back and watching things, but I can get by in most social situations. So as I walked toward the bus and all the people, quite a few dressed in green-and-white Mooncliff uniforms, I felt mildly optimistic about my prospects for the summer. All these people seemed excited and enthusiastic to begin the summer, even at 7:00 a.m. "Energetic, positive young people," indeed. I approached the group and dropped my suitcase next to all the other suitcases that were being loaded into the open belly of the bus. People were all talking, chattering excitedly. Most of them seemed to know each other, and they appeared genuinely happy to see each other. The girls all seemed to be pretty and bouncy, the guys all tall and jockish. I wondered just how I was going to fit in with all these cheerful, upbeat people.

"If you haven't checked in, please check in with Susie at the front of the bus!" some guy bellowed, and I obeyed.

I walked up to a round-faced, freckle-nosed woman in a Mooncliff baseball hat and sweatshirt with "Susie" stitched on the front, standing near the open bus door with a clipboard in her hand and introduced myself. She welcomed me with such enthusiasm and sheer niceness that I thought she was joking. But she wasn't.

"Marcus!" she yelled. "Come 'ere and meet a new guy! He's gonna be your next-door neighbor!"

When I said that all the guys were tall and jockish, I should say that there were exceptions. One was a blondish, heavy, sheep-doggy kind of guy who was walking toward me with a big smile and an extended hand.

"Marcus Miller," he introduced himself. "So I guess you're in the Inters?"

"I guess I am," I said.

"Well, don't worry," he said with a hearty snort. "I've been going to Mooncliff forever – since I was a kid – so I can tell you everything."

"Where all the bodies are buried," added Susie with a secret smile for Marcus.

Marcus grunted and guided me away from the bus, "She's just kidding. There are no bodies." Then he let out with a deep, macabre Dracula-type laugh that surprised me. Maybe there would be some nice, smart people to hang out with this summer.

One thing: this Marcus could talk. As we waited for the bus to load, Marcus started a running commentary on the camp, the owners, the campers, the quality of the bus we were riding, the box lunch they gave us, everything. I found out that Marcus had to have either something going into his mouth (food) or coming out of his mouth (talk) at all times. But I was happy to let him chatter on – it was really too early in the morning for me – and I learned a lot about Camp Mooncliff and the summer that awaited me.

"That's Jerry Mays, the H.C.," Marcus muttered, nodding in the direction of a tall, sharply crewcut man in a Mooncliff varsity jacket and pressed chinos. "Boys' head counselor. He's basically . . . OK." Marcus said "OK" grudgingly. "The Marshaks love him 'cause he keeps a lid on spending, so we all have to learn to live with him, as long as we're living in the Moon-shak."

"I can do that," I volunteered. I wanted to seem eager and agreeable, and I *was*. Looking around at all the other counselors, I judged that most of them appeared to be a couple of years older than me. (I was, after all, hired as a "Junior Counselor.") They all seemed very wholesome and alert and well prepared for the summer. I was going to make every effort to be likewise.

I am no fan of long bus rides, and if you add in a soggy tuna fish sandwich and warm orangeade, you get some idea of my inner/outer circumstances on the almost-three-hour trip to Mooncliff. Marcus sat next me and talked, almost non-stop, the whole way. I must have dozed a little during the ride – in fact, I'm sure I did – but I learned more of Marcus' inside tips about being a counselor at "the Moon-shak": how to manage my free periods when I got them; what the best bars in Boonesville, the town nearest to Mooncliff, were; how to bribe your waitress, who was a "Boonie" (the Mooncliff word for "townie"), in the Mess Hall for better service and seconds; where the best place was to take a girl if you wanted some privacy – the Quarry. All during the bus ride, the girl counselors did a lot of singing and clapping. Camp songs, college songs, Beatle songs, Motown songs, Byrds songs, folk songs. From "Michael, Row Your Boat Ashore" to "Puff, the Magic Dragon" and some songs I didn't know.

"Get used to the singing," Marcus whispered. "That's Mooncliff spirit."

"Spirit" turned out to be a big thing at Mooncliff. People were always being encouraged to get or get more of or get the right kind of "Mooncliff spirit." I found out later that "Mooncliff spirit" meant different things to different people.

Not quite three hours later, including a quick bathroom stop at the Red Apple Rest on Route 17, the big bus wheeled slowly off the narrow two-lane blacktop road in a wide turn. Crunching gravel, the bus drove through the front entrance to

Camp Mooncliff, marked by a huge green-and-white painted sign, in a frame made of real logs. We were there, at last. Everyone cheered, including me, as the bus rambled down the long entrance road through the dark forest. I was very ready for this bus ride to end.

When I finally stepped off the bus onto Camp Mooncliff soil, it felt like I was stepping onto the Earth for the first time. It took me a moment to get my balance and it was bright so I had to shade my eyes, but the ground under my black Keds felt good and solid. Squinting, I stood away from the bus as the swarm of counselors who knew what they were doing sorted the luggage from the bus's lower storage compartment.

I had seen the slide show in Stanley Marshak's basement, but there is nothing like the reality of *being there*. And, to honor reality and be completely accurate, Camp Mooncliff was spectacularly beautiful. I'm not a nature freak or a Boy Scout or anything, but I know beauty when I see it: the bluest, clearest sky; a large hourglass-shaped lake surrounded by lush, green hills; long, graceful lawns; green grass and trees everywhere, with flowers of different colors all along the neatly tended gravel pathways; lots of white buildings, trimmed with green shutters and doors, spread out over the rolling campus like big, new toys. Even the air was clean and beautiful.

A bunch of us guy counselors grabbed our luggage and walked together down to the Boys' Campus. The bunks were arranged in circles – Junior Circle, Inter Circle, etc., for each group – and Marcus showed me where Bunk 9 was, next door to him in Bunk 10. They were nice, tidy little buildings, with cute front porches; everything had obviously been repainted recently. When we were walking down to the bunks, I saw a crew of workers putting clean, fresh sand into the sandbox in the little kids' playground and laying flowers in a pattern around the giant flag pole, spelling "CM" in white petunias. (At least I think they were petunias.)

"Our kids –" Marcus told me, "Inters – ten-, eleven-, and twelve-year-olds – they're much easier to deal with than the real little kids, who can drive you completely bats. Some of those kids are barely *toilet-trained*. But the teenagers, the Seniors, they're even worse. They'll give you lip if you let them. Some of 'em have beards thicker than mine! Our kids, you can still scare."

"Well," I said. "That's good."

As soon as I walked into Bunk 9, I could tell that another guy had already moved in. I assumed it was my co-counselor, the Senior Counselor to my Junior Counselor. (Some people, those with cars, drove up on their own.) He had taken the bed in the far corner of the big, rectangular room. His bed was all made up neatly, with two plump pillows at the head and a perfect bedroll at the foot. His end table, this big, green-painted cubby, was already set out with his belongings, and he had a Boston Patriots pennant thumb-tacked to the bare wooden cabin wall. And he was, from the sound of it, in the shower.

"Hello!" I called out loudly, even though I was fairly sure that he couldn't hear me. But it just seemed polite.

The rest of the main room was taken up by a dozen or so unmade army cots, soon to be occupied by the campers, in two rows against the walls, with a big green cubby for each bed. I took the bed in the opposite corner from my co-counselor, all the better to keep an eye on the kids. Plus, having a corner gave me two walls, some extra places to put my stuff, and my own window. I needed that: I like to breathe.

I walked from the big main room out to the back porch. I could still hear the shower going full-blast in the bathroom. (Now I could hear my new partner *singing*.) On the large, screened-in back porch, just as Marcus told me it would be, was my father's old army trunk that I'd had shipped there two weeks before. Taking up the other two non-screened walls of the porch were two rows of empty closets, so everybody had a good place to hang clothes. More and more, it looked like Mooncliff was pretty well organized.

I dragged my trunk back to my corner of the room, undid the combination lock, which I remembered on the first try, and

started to unpack my squashed clothes. I opened the cubby
next to my bed and checked the inside for cleanliness. Not
bad, but I still dusted out all three shelves with my hand and a
tissue from my pocket. I started to transfer piles of my clothing from the trunk to my bed, trying to maintain the order of
the stacks, when I heard the slap of wet footsteps behind me.

I turned and saw this lanky guy wearing nothing but a
towel – around his head. He was dripping water from everywhere, and I mean *everywhere*.

"Yo!" he said, drying his hair roughly. "I thought I heard
somebody, but I had soap in my ears. Good shower!"

"Hey," I tossed him a wave.

He took the towel off his head, wrapped it around his
waist, and came toward me with an extended hand.

"Hi," he said, still talking rather loudly, still with soap in
his ears. "I'm Stewie Thurman. I guess the bus got in?"

I introduced myself as he re-wiped his hand on his towel.

"Glad to see another human being," he said.

"I can pass for that," I replied, and he laughed easily,
which I was happy to see.

"I drove down yesterday morning," he continued, looking
me over, checking out my stuff. "It wasn't so bad."

"From where?" I asked.

"Massachusetts. Western Mass."

"Cool," I said, never having been there, but it seemed like
the right thing to say.

"There are closets in the back; they even have some wood-
en hangers," he said, walking back toward his bed and dropping his towel to get dressed. "This place is pretty nice. I used
to be a counselor at this camp near Burlington – Camp Manitopa. All boys. Ever hear of it?"

"No, but I don't know that much about camps. This is my
first time."

"Oh, I guess that's why they put you in here with me. I've
done this before."

"At Manitopa."

Stewie paused again, "I thought you said you never heard of it."

"Never mind," I said, seeing that Stewie was no rocket scientist. But then again neither am I, and he seemed like a sweet, laid-back, loosey-goosey guy. He looked older than me by a couple of years, but he acted younger. I could see where we might be a good combination.

As I unpacked and Stewie performed his post-shower rituals, he talked about a lot of things: his beloved car –"the Super-Coupe" – which turned out to be the 1961 Plymouth Belvedere with a custom light-blue paint job that he'd driven down from Massachusetts; his vast experience as a counselor ("That was a real camp, man – we just had *tents* and *outhouses!*"); his excellence as a wide receiver on the junior varsity football team at the local state college he went to, and his slim hope of moving up to the varsity that fall; and his grandparents' cranberry farm. All summer long I learned about the whole process of cranberry farming from Stewie. Up until that time, I did not know that there were two different ways to grow cranberries: dry and wet. At every Thanksgiving dinner for the rest of my life, as long as it lasts, Stewie Thurman and his grandparents' cranberries will probably cross my mind.

As he dowsed himself with cologne, powdered his underarms, and dabbed his acne with some kind of pencil, I got my things unpacked and organized. While Stewie kept up his free-flowing monologue, I carried my hanging stuff into the best remaining closet in the back porch, placed my toiletries in the best remaining cubby in the bathroom, and made my bed. With all these new people around me, I made a conscious decision to be a good listener this summer.

"I'm great with kids," he said, looking into a round shaving mirror he had set up on his dresser. "So don't worry about anything. Just follow Uncle Stewie."

As he talked on, I set up my Sony clock radio. After some fiddling with a straightened wire hanger I attached to the antenna, I found, amid the static, "Louie, Louie" on WABC-AM.

"Yo!" shouted Stewie. "Turn it up, dude!" He danced around, trying to step into his underwear while still looking in the mirror. "Louder!"

I was glad to oblige. Stewie was a big, happy guy, and I knew that the kids would probably like him a lot; he was like a big kid himself. Which was going to make my job a lot easier. So I counted myself lucky and turned up the crackling volume.

"'Ohhh, baby! . . . Me gotta go now . . .'"

∾

If I was expecting a fairly easy summer in the country, which I confess I was, I was quickly disabused of that notion by those first three days of Counselor Orientation. They worked us from morning until night, like Marine boot camp trainees, schooling us in the Mooncliff way of doing things. From morning 'til night, it was Mooncliff routine, all signaled by bugle calls like in the army: "Reveille" at 7:00 a.m., "Taps" at 9:00 p.m., and a bunch of other calls in between, for meals and changes of activity, telling everyone what to do and when. They showed us how each bunk was to be run and how to handle the weekly laundry: whites in the white bag, colors in the striped bag, socks in the net bag. They showed us how to make sure the bunk stayed clean by setting up a cleaning schedule for the kids to perform each morning before Inspection. They showed us how to make the required "hospital corners" with the bedsheets. I was impressed.

They showed us all the athletic fields and facilities, and demonstrated how they liked to teach the campers how to play baseball and basketball, not to mention volleyball and soccer. I hadn't picked up a baseball glove or bat in years, but some of the guys were real jocks – you could tell just by looking – who took this stuff very seriously. But I acquitted myself decently during these sporting sessions. (I was always just good enough at sports not to embarrass myself, but guys are always worried about things like that. Especially in a new situation.)

We hauled *all* the campers' trunks – that's more than three hundred trunks – to their proper bunks, in teams, in four pickup trucks. We laid down white chalk lines on Mooncliff's baseball diamonds with little wheeled carts and hung the nets on the *eight* tennis courts, and the volleyballs courts too. We trimmed the greens and raked the bunkers on the pitch-and-putt golf course. There were several sessions on safety: what to do when your kids got sick, how to keep the bunks safe – like not keeping food outside the bunk that might attract bears. (*"Bears?" "Yes, bears! Especially at night."*) They taught us all these camp songs and cheers; I think I still have the sheets with the words someplace. At the waterfront – there were two separate swimming areas across the lake from each other: Boys and Girls – they taught us "the buddy system" and how to keep the kids safe during both Swim Instruction periods and General Swims (morning and afternoon). We counselors were tested to see if we could swim, and let me tell you, mountain lakes in the morning are *cold.*

There was a super-serious safety session at the rifle range, led very slowly, almost phonetically by Gil, the hillbilly riflery counselor.

"They let *our* kids – *ten-year-old kids* – shoot guns?" I whispered to Marcus.

"Only BB guns," he whispered back. "They *love* it! The bigger kids get twenty-twos. Single-shot, bolt-action Marlins."

"Nice," I said, not exactly sure what that meant.

Some of the training sessions were conducted by Jerry the Crew Cut, and some were with his opposite and rival, Harriet Wyne, the Girls' H.C., a big blonde with a big voice in a perfect Mooncliff green-and-white track suit. Dale Buckley, the Inter Boys Group Leader, who was technically my immediate boss, ran some meetings for just his Inter counselors – Marcus, Stewie, me, and a bunch of other seemingly nice guys. There was Sid, a chunky guy with glasses who was the other guy in Marcus' bunk; needle-nosed, sarcastic Brian, who taught archery of all things; Alby, a big quiet guy built like a body-builder; Eddie from the Bronx, who was a real jock but nice, not aggressive; and a couple of other guys whose names I still didn't know, but, all in all, they were like the guys you'd meet in an average gym class.

Dale had been the Inter Boys Group Leader for a couple of years now and took his job pretty seriously. He was a beefy PE teacher from somewhere in Ohio, bull-necked and sandy-haired. He didn't live in one of the bunks, but in a separate building called The Staff House. The Staff House housed all kinds of "extra" people: Doctor K., the fat camp doctor who spent the whole day tanning himself; Captain Hal, a Navy veteran and head of the boating program; Estelle Davis, the tall, stringy Inter Girls Group Leader and Dale's opposite; Esther, the sour little gray lady who was the secretary in the Main Office; Sal, the head of the Boys' waterfront – special people like that. Stanley Marshak was smartest of all: he had his own separate little green-and-white house, on a pretty little hill behind the Main Office. I guess it pays to be the owner.

From the beginning, Dale seemed to be a fair guy. He sat us down in the middle of Inter Circle, on the circular bench under this enormous tree, and told us what he expected of us Inter counselors this summer.

"This is the fourth year I've been doing this," he said, chewing on a piece of grass. "And I'm here to tell you that the Marshaks are good people to work for. Most of you guys are new, but a couple of you know me. Marcus. Sam."

We new guys looked at the two veterans, who nodded positively, then back to Dale.

"This is how I work: you play by the rules, you don't make me ride you, you watch your kids, you don't call attention to yourself . . ." Dale paused to let that sink in. "Then you should have a good time this summer. I can't be fairer or plainer than that."

Fair and plain: that was my first impression of Dale, and it stood up for the entire summer. No matter what, he tried to be a good employee for the Marshaks, a good boss to us counselors, and was a good leader for the Inter boys – all at the same time. All in all, Dale was super-fair to me later after the difficulties started, but I'm getting ahead of myself.

On the night before the kids were to arrive – K-Day – there was a big campfire in the field out behind the Rec Hall, and a barbeque with burgers, hot dogs, and this fresh-from-some-nearby-farm yellow-and-white corn-on-the-cob that tasted like candy. They were letting us relax on this last night of freedom. One of the guys brought a guitar, and the girls started singing folk songs as the fire grew and sparks flew up into the black night sky. I thought I had seen stars before, but the night sky at Mooncliff was like the Hayden Planetarium times ten. You could actually see the milk in the Milky Way: so many stars behind stars, behind more stars.

That's when the Crew Cut gave us one last pep talk.

"I just want to say one last thing –" Jerry started to say when Harriet wisecracked, "For *now!*" And everybody laughed: by now, we all knew that Jerry liked to hear himself talk.

Jerry shot a look at Harriet – they would needle each other all summer, but never in front of the campers – and continued, "One *last* thing."

He looked with one long sweeping stare at all us counselors, sitting or lying on blankets around the glowing fire, and pronounced, "This summer – these next eight weeks – can be the best summer of your lives." He paused for dramatic effect. I could hear the crickets all around us.

"I mean that," he said. We were all listening with complete attention because we all, me included, *wanted* this to be the best summer of our lives.

"You can make it whatever kind of summer you want it to be," he continued. "*Provided* you remember that this summer is, first of all, about responsibility. And children's *lives*."

I looked around at everyone listening, concentrating on Jerry's every word.

"Safety and protection is your Job Number One," he raised his voice even higher. I don't think anyone but me knew or cared about his bad grammar.

"Six years ago," he continued. "A little seven-year-old girl named Susan Factor drowned at Camp Indian Trails, just outside of Honesdale. During a completely normal General Swim, on an ordinary afternoon, in the middle of August. And, mind you, this girl was a good little swimmer. And today? . . . Camp Indian Trails does not exist, and their owners are bankrupt and living in disgrace!"

He paused, then repeated, "Job Number One."

As Jerry talked on – I mean he was saying good, positive, helpful things, but my mind couldn't help but wander – I looked around at the other counselors in the big circle, their faces illuminated by the campfire. They were all paying strict attention to Jerry, taking in every syllable. Over the three days of Orientation, I had checked out all the counselors, by which I mean to say, all the *girl* counselors. Already some couples had started to pair off. You could see the quarterback-types pursuing the cheerleader-types. Marcus and Stewie had kept up a steady commentary about the quality of "this year's crop" (I am quoting Marcus) for the past two days. All the guys lusted after the ultra-blonde Sharon Spitzer, the aloof goddess-like girls' swimming instructor, whose body "did not quit." I just kept my mouth shut. It's generally the ugliest, fattest, least attractive guys who are hardest on girls' appearances.

But truthfully, as I looked around that campfire, I did not see any girl for me. I was younger than most of the girl counselors, and I just didn't *feel* anything from anyone I had seen. Which was OK. If I just did a good job, had a low-key summer, and saved my money for Columbia, that would be enough – more than enough. I didn't need fireworks or excitement; I didn't need anything special to happen.

I'm just saying that I went into that summer at Mooncliff with the purest of intentions. Before that summer, I never had trouble with any authority figure – not my parents, or anyone else's parents, or any teacher or principal. I was/am a good kid. What happened happened, not by any great, nefarious scheme of mine, but by Fate. Or something like Fate, or Love, or Destiny. Or maybe it was the Fate Within Us. In any case, it was both the luckiest thing that ever happened to me and the beginning of the end.

Record of Events #2 – entered Tuesday, 5:31 A.M.

~

I remember we were all very ready the next day for the kids to come up. All this talk about the campers-this and the campers-that, camper safety, camper letter-writing, camper *nutrition;* it was time for the little buggers to arrive. The buses had left collection points in Manhattan, Brooklyn, Connecticut, New Jersey, and several places on the Island early that morning, so we were expecting them to arrive at Mooncliff shortly after lunch.

The Moon-shak, as I said, was very organized. We had been given the names of the campers in our bunks and were now aligned in rows on the baseball field. We stood next to big, colorful signs that the girl counselors had made for each bunk with Magic Markers and glitter on oak tag, mounted on big sticks. When we finally saw the first of the big silver buses rumble down the entrance road onto the main campus and into the sunlight, we all cheered – the real work was finally about to begin.

"Let's get this show on the road!" I said, standing with Stewie and Marcus and the rest of the Inter Boys' counselors as the first bus rumbled onto the baseball field.

"Be careful what you wish for, kid," someone behind me muttered.

I turned around quickly and saw Jerry standing there, winking at me, his crew cut bristling in the sun. I smiled reflexively, but I was surprised by how easily he managed to

sneak up on me like that. He clapped me on the back – hard
– and walked away.

Marcus nudged me in the side and said, "They're always
around."

"Who?" I asked, watching Jerry as he worked his way
down the line of counselors, pep-talking different guys.

"Some supervisor or other," said Marcus. "There's no privacy here. Someone is always watching you."

"Great!" I said sarcastically. "Who needs a private life?"

Marcus snickered as the first bus rolled to a halt at the
far end of right field. The air brakes hissed, the front door
opened, and the bus began disgorging children. One by one,
they stepped off onto the grass, kids in all sizes, each one met
by some helpful Mooncliff person.

"Say goodbye to paradise, guys," said Stewie, as he
scanned the list of our campers. "Which bus is this?"

"Connecticut!" someone yelled out.

We didn't have a kid on the Connecticut bus, but, as the
full assault of buses filled the ball field, it wasn't long before
we would have a bunch of them. I watched as the kids, some
of them already in green-and-white, swarmed off the buses
like insects. In no time, the field was buzzing with people and
noise as bus after bus emptied.

"Inter Bunk Nine!" Stewie yelled through cupped hands.
"Anybody for Bunk Nine? . . . We need some kids! We got
zilch here! We'll take anybody!"

Everyone near us heard Stewie and laughed. By now, I
had gotten used to the fact that Stewie was a goofball. He
liked to laugh and make other people laugh. He liked to have
fun. In that, we were alike. But Stewie liked to call attention
to himself, which was the very opposite of me. But that made
me hopeful that we would be a good team, controlling this
bunch of weird-looking and rowdy ten- and eleven-year-old
boys gradually filling the row behind us.

The semi-controlled chaos spread across the field as hundreds of kids streamed off the buses. Some of the kids were

really young: five and six. A couple of the little boys were crying. One little girl wandering around was carrying a big teddy bear. What kind of parent sends a teddy-bear-carrying kid away from home for eight whole weeks? And some kids were – well, they weren't really kids. The Senior boys, some of them, were bigger than me. One kid practically had a full beard. And the girls? The Senior girls? A couple of them – at sixteen – were model-tall and model-pretty. Some looked more mature than the girl counselors. But I really didn't have time to look: Stewie and I were, little by little, being overrun by the growing mob of Bunk 9 kids growing restless and rambunctious behind us.

"Why don't I take this bunch back to the bunk and get them started?" I said to Stewie. "You wait here for the other three."

Stewie thought for a moment. I don't think that he expected me, as the Junior Counselor, to make any suggestions, much less a good one. But he saw the wisdom in my idea and agreed, "Good idea."

So I turned and saw seven little faces looking up at me, waiting for orders. I had to act.

"OK, guys," I announced. "Let's move!"

With a collective cheer, they turned and ran toward the Boys' Campus, arms, jackets and knapsacks flying, a pack of wild, clumsy animals. I had no choice but to fast-walk after them – who knew what trouble these kids could get into?

By the time I trotted up the steps and into Bunk 9, the free-for-all was in full swing. Kids were fighting other kids for – well, for everything: who would have the two remaining corner beds, who would sleep next to whom, who had the right to which closet in the back porch, who had claim to the few wooden hangers that were left, who would sleep on the mattress that had "cooties." In other words, madness.

At first, I tried to talk sensibly to them. I reasoned with each pair of kids who had a conflict, looking for a fair way to arbitrate their disagreement. But eleven-year-old boys are not interested in fairness; they are interested in getting their way, no matter what. Finally, I had to yell at them. In fact, I used the voice that my Dad used for yelling at me, the voice that used to scare the hell out of me when I was eleven.

"Stop what you're doing right now and FREEZE!!!" I bellowed in my best once-removed-Brooklynese.

It worked. They stopped what they were doing and froze in place, their eyes wide with surprise and a little fear. Thank goodness that Marcus was right: they were scare-able.

Just then, Stewie came in with the three other kids.

"Hey, man," he said. "Looks like you got things under control. I got the three other guys. You won't believe it: the driver on the South Jersey bus went into diabetic shock and almost crashed the bus!"

"Cool!" said a couple of the kids as the three stragglers who entered with Stewie spilled out their story of near death on the New Jersey Turnpike.

Stewie came over to me as the other boys all converged on the Jersey kids.

"How you doing?" Stewie said to me in a low voice.

"OK," I sighed. "But why do they fight all the time?"

He looked at me as if I were a moron and said, "They're *kids*." That, I guess, was the best explanation for a lot of the behavior I was going to deal with for the next eight weeks.

But we managed to get the kids unpacked without too much drama and down to a General Swim at the Boys' waterfront to cool everybody off. During General Swims, the counselors stood on the wooden docks surrounding the swimming areas, holding long bamboo poles and watching the kids swim. Presumably, we'd be there to hold a pole out to save a kid who was drowning, or at least help a kid who was struggling. A lot of that time was spent looking across the lake to the Girls' waterfront to see if Sharon Spitzer was wearing a bikini that day.

We got the kids out of the water, into clean clothes (green-and-white camp uniforms for this first Line-Up), and up to the flagpole area where the whole camp was assembled. Everyone gathered in a big circle around the newly painted flagpole before every breakfast and every dinner. That let Jerry make announcements, reward bunks and individuals who did something noteworthy, and bring the entire camp together at the beginning and the end of the day, not to mention actually saying the Pledge of Allegiance and raising and lowering the Stars and Stripes.

As Jerry welcomed everybody with a gassy speech about the event-filled, life-changing summer ahead, I looked at the big circle of people assembled around the flagpole. There were more than three hundred and fifty campers and over a hundred counselors. And that's not counting all the other staff: the kitchen workers, the waitresses, the maintenance guys, plus assorted hanger-on-ers like Marshak cousins, in-laws, and spouses. It was quite a little society plunked down in this beautiful forest, isolated with its own rules and customs. Standing alongside Stewie behind the kids of Bunk 9, I wondered if I was going to be a good counselor. I had never really done anything like this before. As the color guard lowered the flag to the recorded bugle call that was broadcast from Jerry's H.C. Shak, I put my hand over my heart like everyone else and wondered just how well I was going to fit in, this summer in paradise.

∿

On the first night, they broke us into groups: Juniors, Inters, Lads and Lassies, and Seniors. The bugle call sounded, and Stewie and I wasted no time in getting our campers out on schedule. We were the new guys and we didn't want our bunk to be late; certainly not on the very first night.

Some kids are just naturally slow, but a few of our kids seemed to be something's-wrong-with-them slow, so as we herded them across campus toward the Rec Hall, I started singing the theme song from *Rawhide,* the one about keeping those doggies rollin'. "Rollin', rollin', rollin." The kids all laughed and sang along. It made them act sillier, but at least it got them moving faster, and we were there on time. By the next morning, and for the rest of the summer, they were "the Doggies."

As we burst into the big, open basement of the Rec Hall, Dale was directing the moving of the benches and chairs.

"Let's have four rows – two on each side! Boys on one side, girls on the other!" he bellowed and pointed. All these excited kids, my Doggies included, went into action, dragging the wooden chairs and benches across the cement floor into the formation that Dale mandated.

On the other side of the room were the Inter girls, who were doing the same thing, only shriller and gigglier. The Girls' Group Leader Estelle Davis, a beanpole redhead, clapped her hands and shouted out orders in a raspy voice: "Come on, Inter girls! Let's beat those Inter boys!" Boys-versus-girls was always a big motivator around Mooncliff, but especially with this pre-pubescent age group. And so there was more chair-knocking and shouting and shrieking and stumbling than before. I just laughed and let it happen. Stewie, however, pitched right in, making sure all our chairs were aligned. He actually cared about helping our boys beat the girls.

Finally, to stop all this noise, Dale put his two index fingers in his mouth and whistled, so loud and so high (damn, I wish I could whistle like that) that everything in the room came to a screaming, screeching, whistle-controlled halt.

"Inter Camp! Please sit downnnnnn!" he ordered from the front of the room, and, as he let his "nnnn" die, everybody did just that. They might have been giddy and fidgety, but they all sat right down. I was impressed by Dale's command of the room.

My Doggies were in the second row, behind the younger Inters. Stewie was on one end, and I sat on the other, next to Bunk 10 and Marcus, who kept up a steady stream of low chatter as Dale called the meeting to order.

"Welcome, Inter Camp . . ." he shouted. "To the best summer of your lives!"

As if on cue, the kids cheered like mad. Dale and Estelle
beamed as they let the kids release some energy.

As Dale addressed the Inters, I looked around the big
room. The basement of the Rec Hall – the upstairs had a really
nice, professional-quality basketball court and a full stage for
doing plays and talent shows and things like that – featured a
large, all-purpose room with a juke box, ping-pong table, and
a big playing area for games and general hanging out. A few
steps up to another level, and there was the Snack Shak, the
Camp's canteen. (Did I mention that a great many things at
Mooncliff were named the something-Shak, in honor of the
Marshaks? There was the Snack Shak, the Nature Shak, the
Boat Shak, the Boys' Milk Shak, the Girls' Milk Shak . . . you
get the idea.)

My gaze wandered across the walls covered with green-
and-white pennants and black-and-white photographs of happy campers from earlier years. They seemed to have a nice
sense of tradition here. I guess that there is something timeless
about a place like this: time goes on, but the kids always stay
young.

Then it happened: I saw her. I caught a glimpse of this
older girl across the room, sitting with the Inter girls. She was
sitting on the end of the second row, as if she were a counsel-
or, but I hadn't seen her before. She had long, dark hair and
seemed to have a pretty face (it was a big room and she was far
away). But there was also something else. Just the way she sat
with her arm around the crying, probably homesick little girl
next to her, comforting her, she attracted me instantly.

"Psst!" I whispered to Marcus,. "Who's all the long, dark
hair over there?"

"Oh," he whispered back with a snort. "Forget it. She's
trouble. Totally spoiled. A Marshak cousin."

"Why haven't I seen her before?" I muttered.

"I don't know. She must be a C.I.T. this year," Marcus whispered back. (C.I.T.s were "counselors-in-training." They were seventeen-year-olds: too old to be campers, but too young to be counselors. Stanley charged them only half the camper rate for the privilege of being taught how to be a counselor.)

Dale coughed and shot a look our way. Estelle was talking about something.

"Come on, guys," hissed Stewie to our kids, snapping his fingers. "Pay attention!"

"As far as evening activities *off* campus," Estelle announced to the eager Inters. "We're going to be going bowling," which elicited *oohs* and *ahhs* from the kids. "And GO-karting!" B*igger oohs* and *ahhs*. "And if you listen to your counselors and play your cards right . . ."

Unable to take my eyes off the pretty girl across the room, I whispered to Marcus, "She really has this interesting attitude going on, and –"

"Don't even bother," muttered Marcus. "She teases a couple of guys to death every summer. It's really nuts. Nothing happens."

I grunted some acknowledgement, but I didn't stop looking at the girl. I like to think that I'm not easily impressed, but there was something undeniably appealing about her. Even from across the room.

"What's her name?" I whispered.

"Rachel . . . Prince," he intoned softly, and I heard, for the first time, the name that would be forever linked with mine.

Record of Events #3 – entered Wednesday, 8:01 P.M.

~

That was the first time I saw her. I saw her several times more before I actually spoke to her. It wasn't a question of my not having the courage to go up and speak to her – well, it *was* that – but it's mainly that there was no opportunity. I saw her twice a day, at morning and evening Line-Ups around the flagpole, in those first couple of days. She looked as if she were in her own perfect little world, standing quietly with two or three adoring girls around her. Once I saw her at the pay phone outside the Main Office, twirling the phone cord around and around her forearm as she talked intensely to someone on the other end. I looked at her, and I think she looked at me, but we didn't really meet until the fourth night. I suppose that I could have just walked up to her at any time and struck up a conversation like a normal person, but that's not me.

The first time we talked – the very first time – it was the night of the fourth day, and the Doggies, along with the rest of the Inter Boys, had their first Evening Activity with just the Inter Girls: square dancing. Now this was a pretty hardcore-sissy, squirm-inducing activity for a bunch of nine- ten- eleven- and twelve-year-old boys. But it was the first real icebreaker with the Inter Girls, something that had to be done sometime.

So Stewie and I herded the Doggies – all of us dressed like cowboys, or as close as we could come – to the upstairs of the Rec Hall, all the way fighting their reluctance to do anything that combined girls and dancing. But I have to hand

it to Jerry or the Marshaks or whoever at Mooncliff found
these square-dancing people; they had this old geezer (I guess
that's redundant, but he was so old, redundancy in this case is
simply the correct emphasis) named Pecos Pete, and he called
one helluva square dance.

"Honor your partner! Honor your corner!" Pete's charming, rinky-dink combo of bass, banjo, guitar, and kazoo/ap-
ple-cider-jug/washboard/spoons/Adam's apple, played by
what must have been his family (the whole bunch looked like
the Joad family, but with sequins), got even the shyest kids up
and dancing. Oh, sure, some of the kids were goofy, but the
music eventually worked its honky-tonk magic. We circled
right and circled left; we dozy-doed this way and that way.
I'm not the greatest dancer, but this I could do.

I don't remember exactly what songs they played as I tried
to "dance" and keep my kids in line. But I do remember those
glimpses I had of Rachel, all night long, as she danced.

How she danced! She was two squares away from my
square, but as I circled right and circled left, as I allemanded
left and allemanded right, I could see her, her dark hair flying,
her eyes sparkling, graceful hands reaching out to help the
little kids in her group or whipping them around the square,
their feet barely touching the floor. She was having such fun
that it made *me* have more fun. The drive and good humor
in the music, the dancing, and the general tone of just-bare-
ly-controlled confusion (kids giggling, beaming, sweating)
made the night fly by. Swing by, really.

The square dance ended in a big, yahoo circle, and the
boys who until recently couldn't stomach the thought of dancing or even *holding* some girl's hand for more than a second
had to be dragged out of the Rec Hall bodily.

Coming out of the wide back doors into the night air,
herding my sweaty Doggies, is when I literally ran into Rachel . . . well, almost. This was the first actual moment of
contact, under the pool of floodlight, right outside the doors.
She, stumbling over her girls; me, counting my kids, strug-

gling still to recall their names, and tangle-footed too. And then, there we were, face to face.

She smiled at me. There was a slight pause in the Universe.

I said, "It's hot."

She said, "It's summer," looking me right in the eyes. Her eyes were very blue. *Blue*-blue. Right then, *right then*, I felt that something was going to happen between us. I didn't know exactly what, but I knew it was going to be something . . . significant.

The path back to the bunks from the Rec Hall divided – Boys' Campus, one way; Girls' Campus, the other way – but for a while, before the split at the big baseball backstop, girls and boys could walk together. That's where the older campers, the boyfriends and girlfriends, could get one last kiss before being separated.

So Rachel and I, with the other counselors, walked the kids back down the path toward the big backstop, all together. This is when we talked for the first time, introducing ourselves carefully. At least I was being careful.

"You're new," she said. That was a good sign; it meant that she had noticed me.

I didn't say anything. (Did I freeze, or was I just being smarter than usual by *not* being me?)

"You'll like it here," she added, with an easy certainty in her voice.

"I believe you," I said. Not sure if she was being sincere or condescending.

We walked for a moment in tantalizing silence.

"I've been coming here, to the Moon-shak, forever."

"I didn't see you at Orientation," I replied, feeling what it was like to walk next to her. I was just tall enough for her.

"They made me come up with the campers. In the *buses*," she said, reliving the unpleasant memory. "But at least I'm a C.I.T. now – *finally*."

"So now you get the best of both worlds."

"Or the worst; my curfew is an hour earlier than you counselors, *and* I can't go off campus."

"Oh, that's not so bad. I'm sure you'll find a way around that."

Which made her laugh, once. Good. That was a start. The laugh, and a look. As we walked and talked, I was listening not only to her words but also to the sound of her voice. Her voice was *musical*, the way she ran her words together or lingered over individual syllables. She played her voice like it was some instrument: she was quick to laugh, quick to darken everything; one moment celebrating the smallest detail of something, and the next, condemning something or someone else with a surprising, full, throaty ferocity. She had this insolent, confident manner, so relaxed about her beauty that as she walked next to me, talking to me, I felt myself being *drawn in*.

"I like my girls, the girls this age," she said. "They're very honest and pure, before all the *teenage* drama begins."

"You don't like teenage drama?" I asked.

"Only my own," she said. Which made *me* laugh.

"But this is definitely my last year here," she went on. "So I want to try to be a good counselor."

"Why is it your last year?" I asked.

"It just is," she said, with a simple finality that made me ask nothing further. At least for the time being.

"They put me in with Sara Molloy," she went on. "Who is a very good counselor. They call her Serious Sara, but I like her anyway."

"Well, I'm sure *you're* going to be a very good counselor too," I said.

"How would *you* know?" she shot back to me.

I was a little stung by her sharp response but didn't show it. I liked how she talked, her quick words and her sly smiles, how she didn't simply accept my cliché of a compliment. I liked how she was playing with me.

"I just have this feeling," I said, completely casual.

She smiled when I said that.

"I saw the way you danced back there," I said. "Tossing those kids around like rag dolls."

"I'm very strong . . ." she smiled. "For a girl."

"I bet you are," I answered right back, trying to keep looking in her eyes and not down to her upper arms and the rest of her body.

With a twist of her mouth, she was about to say something flirtatious (I think) when Estelle, standing guard at the big backstop, stopped us all cold.

"OK, boys! Back to Boys' Campus nowwwww!" announced Estelle. "Girls – you know where to go!"

Rachel moved away from me, gathering her campers. "OK, Bunk 8 – you heard Estelle!"

I had to say something to her before she got away.

"So, that was fun," I said, indicating the Rec Hall and the square dancing.

She paused, turned on me, and purred, "I approve of any activity where you honor your partner."

The formality of her diction and the direct way she looked at me stood me still for a moment. I laughed, and she liked that I laughed. Then she turned with a smile, knowing that she had almost certainly conquered another male heart.

She looked great, walking away bouncily, quickly hugging one of the girls to her side and joining in their song or game or whatever they were doing. I stood there for a moment, watching her go. When she walked away, it was as if the world had dimmed. Everything was a little darker, a little less exciting, a little less alive. I noticed that the very first time she left me, and it was never, ever really any different.

I was snapped back to the present world by the Redheaded Doggy, pulling at my arm. I had promised to read them a story after Lights-Out if they cleaned up the bunk a little before Evening Activity, and kids unfortunately never forget a promise. So I walked with Stewie, herding the Doggies and the other Inters back to the Boys' Campus, all the while thinking of Rachel. Marcus caught up next to us, falling in step through the damp night grass.

"That's where *you'll* have to break up the boyfriends and girlfriends, later in the summer."

"Boyfriends and girlfriends?" Stewie said. "But these kids are only eleven!"

"Are you kidding?" Marcus squawked. "These horny little suckers! Summer is all about raging hormones. Besides, some of 'em are almost twelve. All they whisper about is 'cuppies.' *This* girl's got cuppies, *that* girl's got cuppies."

"What's 'cuppies'?" I asked.

"Oh," he said. "That's Mooncliff slang for 'breasts.' I don't know how it started. Did you see: Mazlish? That little twerp has this poster of Nancy Sinatra in his closet that *I* want!"

I laughed and said, "I bet your boots are going to walk all over *him*."

"I, uh, saw you talking with Prince back there," said Marcus.

"Yeah," I said neutrally.

"So . . . ?" he demanded some elaboration.

"So what?" I said. I didn't owe him any explanation. There was nothing to explain at this point.

Marcus laughed and shook his shaggy head. "Oh, boy. She's gonna chew you up and spit you out! A girl that pretty, who *knows* she's that pretty? You sure she isn't too much for a regular dude like you?"

I grunted out a "ha" and let him have his laugh. I had better things to think about. And how did he know I was a "regular dude?" I certainly didn't feel regular, walking alongside Rachel Prince.

We got the Doggies back to the bunk, and with about the expected amount of chaos from getting twelve little boys into bed – *with* toothbrushing, please! (What is it about young boys and hygiene?) – I settled back on my bed and thought of Rachel, how she looked when she was dancing, how she looked walking next to me, how she looked when we were face-to-face. I mean, I was watching and counseloring and shouting at the Doggies who were screwing around and not getting ready for bed, but in the back of my mind, I was thinking of Rachel. The seed had been planted: real events that I could then relive, re-imagine, and spin into fantasy. Even when I got them into bed and was reading them the story of *The Tell-Tale Heart* (I'm a huge Poe fan) in the dark by flashlight, I was still thinking of Rachel, seeing her in my mind's "vulture" eye as I read them Poe's tale of madness, obsession, and murder.

Looking back on everything now – with *my* vulture eye – I can't even begin to describe Rachel Prince in a way that would do her justice. It wasn't just her physical beauty (the hair, the eyes, the perfect nose); it was her restless, intense attitude and the way that she used her beauty and charm and wit almost as weapons, but *selectively*, that made her different from any girl I'd ever met. After all, there are a lot of medium-height, nicely shaped, moneyed, long-dark-haired beauties from the Island and in this world, but none of them had the Life Force that Rachel possessed. If she was selfish and moody sometimes, she could just as easily turn gentle and almost angelic in a moment. If that made her difficult for some people to take, it made her attractive to me. Some people say that Rachel was self-centered. I guess that was true, but if you had a self like Rachel Prince's, you'd be centered on it too. But there was no objective, external reason for my feelings. Love is not logical, and a great, all-consuming love, which is what we had, creates its own *super* logic. Only It matters; only It makes sense.

Record of Events #4 – entered Thursday, 5:15 A.M.

~

The next morning – the mornings in the mountains were shockingly cold – we tramped the kids through the dew-soaked grass to Line-Up around the flagpole before breakfast. I was tired: this getting up at 7:00 reminded me too much of school, not summer vacation, and now *I* had to be the enforcer, getting slugabed kids out on time when I was the one who wanted to stay in the sack. Stewie was always the last out of bed, throwing his sneaker at any Doggy who was slower than he was. Through gritty eyes I looked across the big circle of the whole camp – all yawning and toeing the ground, listening to Jerry drone the announcements, saying the Pledge of Allegiance – and looked for Rachel. There she was, standing behind her girls, calmly keeping them in line and quiet. I watched her for a long while. She wore this big coat with a hood that almost hid her face. She didn't look at me, or even look my way.

Which was fine with me. Just because I was looking at her didn't mean she had to look at me. After all, she was much better to look at than I was. Of course, ascribing good motives to questionable actions became something of a habit with me, later on.

So I went into breakfast and brooded all the way through the meal – if she wanted to ignore me, fine. Oh sure, we were attracted to each other last night, but I was also sure that a lot of guys were attracted to Rachel, came on to Rachel, fantasized about Rachel. So if she was wary, perhaps she was right. She didn't know me from Adam. I would have to be patient . . . and have some kind of a plan.

The meals in the Mess Hall were a lot of things: loud was one of them. Four hundred-plus people eating in one huge, barn-like building make a lot of noise. Kids are noisy, and counselors trying to control noisy kids are noisy. Add to that the clanking of glasses and silverware, the drumming feet of the hustling waiters and waitresses, the mind-numbing inanity of eleven-year-old boys in deep discussion, and you get the idea. Especially first thing in the morning.

"You shouldn't eat that. They put saltpeter in the food."

"What's saltpeter?"

"It's this stuff they put in the food so we can't have sex."

"You can't have sex anyway! You're eleven, you dork."

"But even if I wanted to."

"Who would want to have sex with *him*? He's eleven *and* ugly!"

"*And* mental."

"Look who's talking? The human zit!"

"Peter *who*? From Bunk *Twelve*?"

Then Stewie finally yelled for all of them to shut up so we could all eat just one meal in peace.

And the food itself? Well, let's just say that every meal featured a fruit punch they called "bug juice." Pitcher after pitcher of bug juice. Sometimes it was red, sometimes orange, sometimes even green (lime, a/k/a "Mooncliff Moonshine"), but it was always bug juice.

Sometimes I wish I could get lost in those silly memories. My memories of Camp Moon-shak and the trivialities of life there that seemed so . . . trivial, now seem so significant and precious. They are my refuge. So if I might be, shall we say, unsure of myself right at this moment, as I sit behind bars, on that particular morning after the first night we met, when I walked out of breakfast onto the sunny flagstone porch of the Mess Hall, in the clear, warming air of morning, and saw her waiting for me as if it were the most completely natural, inevitable thing to do, that's when I knew that *she* felt the same way too; something *was* going to happen between us.

She was sitting on the low wall on the Girls' side, with two of her campers sitting beside her, but her eyes were on mine as I came out the Boys' door. She had a smile that said: *What took you so long?*

I walked over to her, as Steve McQueen as I could. Which wasn't much, I admit, but I didn't scare her away.

"Hi," I said to her, trying to keep my voice normal. "How did you sleep?"

She hesitated. I don't think she was expecting me to say that. "Oh . . . I had crazy dreams."

"All dreams are crazy," I said.

"Some more than others," she answered back. I liked this flirting.

"What do you have this morning?" I asked. Her eyes were even bluer during the day.

"We have kickball!" she said, faking enthusiasm for my amusement. Or was she really enthusiastic? I liked trying to *read* her.

"A *girls'* sport? I've never played a girls' sport."

"You don't know what you're missing," she said archly. "Girls' sports are the best. How about you?"

She squinted in the sun, looking up at me, tilting her head.

"Arts *and* crafts!" I intoned.

"Both of them at the same time?" she laughed. "That *is* a challenge."

"Hey, I'll make you a lanyard," I offered.

She smiled and shot back, "I'll see your lanyard, and raise you an ashtray." Which made *me* laugh. I liked that she liked to play. But as if on cue, she was called by a chorus of her loving campers –"Rayyy-chlllll!" – waiting for her at the bottom of the steps, down from the porch.

I just looked down at her, and she looked up at me, and we smiled. We said nothing because we didn't have to.

"Later," I mouthed.

She let herself be dragged away by her girls.

"Save me!" she yelled back to me as they pulled her in the direction of the Girls' Campus.

"I will," I said, knowing that she probably couldn't hear me. But perhaps she could *feel* me. In any case, I should have learned right then that I'd have to, as my Mom used to say, *"make do."* Make Do with the amount of time, whatever it was, that I had with Rachel. Something or somebody always seemed to be pulling us apart. That was a hard lesson to learn, and one that I always fought against. If only they had just left us alone. . . .

So as I walked back to the bunk to watch the Doggies clean up for Inspection, I thought about Rachel, and I could think about her all morning. Of course, through this whole thing/experience/ordeal, I spent much more time thinking about Rachel than actually being with her. The ratio is pretty alarming when you think about it, but really, what we do most during our waking hours is talk to ourselves continually, back and forth, remembering and imagining and reliving, all the stupid/monumental/trivial/tragic things in our lives: this inner monologue *is* our life.

～

From then on, my goal for the summer changed. Oh, I still wanted to be a good counselor, have a hassle-free summer in the country, and walk away with a decent chunk of change at the end – all those things – but suddenly my life became all about seeing Rachel. Nothing else really mattered. I mean it was the *obvious* thing to do.

I learned her bunk's schedule so I could make it my business to run into her at various times during the day. (All of the bunks' schedules for the week were posted in the Main Office.) Fortunately, because she and I were counselors for the Inters, our paths could cross more often "naturally," whenever our kids had a co-ed Evening Activity, like that first square dance.

But that wasn't enough for me. There was never "enough" for me: I had to see her more.

I had a free period that next afternoon and devised a plan to cross Rachel's path "accidentally." (Yes, counselors occasionally were treated like actual employees, with some of the benefits of real workers, so we had a free period each day and a day off each week. Mine was Wednesday.) I found out that Rachel's bunk had boating first thing that afternoon, right after Rest Period. So during the Rest Period, I signed out a rowboat from Captain Hal, the old, beer-bellied head of the boating program, who really didn't care if I *ate* the boat, as long as I checked it out properly. Under the supervision of his suspicious red eyes, I moved the colored tag for Rowboat #4 on the Big Board from one hook to another hook, and stepped uneasily into Rowboat #4. I got control of the oars and pushed myself away from the other boats along the dock. Carefully, I rowed out to the far end of the lake. Then I stopped the oars and waited.

I brought a book with me, but I couldn't concentrate on it. My mind kept wandering, going over every word Rachel and I had exchanged and every look she had given me, even going so far as to imagine how she might be as my girlfriend. I know it might have been premature, but I couldn't help thinking what I was thinking. I mean I had had girlfriends before, in high school, but no one very serious. The girls I really desired never seemed to like me (except as a "friend" or homework helper), and the girls who liked me just didn't seem to be all that desirable. If that sounds borderline silly and frustrating and futile, all I can say is that most human relationships are that way, so far as I've seen. That's why this sudden spark with Rachel seemed so promising, so surprisingly real.

I pulled my Mets cap down over my brow, reclined carefully across the rowboat's seat so that I could prop my feet up, and I drifted. As I settled in, the up-and-down movement of the water rocked me uneasily. I thought of Rachel's dark hair swinging and bouncing as she square-danced, how she radiated joy and vitality. Marcus said that she teased a couple of guys every summer, but I didn't pay too much attention to that. He was probably just jealous; no girl as fine as Rachel would ever show any interest in him, that's for sure. No, I could tell from the way that she looked at me, with those x-ray blue-blue eyes of hers, that she definitely liked something in me. It wasn't just my imagination. I definitely felt something from her. Definitely . . . something . . . definitely . . . something. So many scenarios to imagine . . . so many possibilities.

"Hi."

I guess I must have fallen asleep, but I don't think I flinched too obviously when I heard her voice. I sat up quickly and saw Rachel in a rowboat with two of her campers at the oars, bobbing on the lake, right next to me. They were all wearing these huge orange life preservers and had big grins on their faces.

"Oh, hi," I stammered out, trying to retain my cool.

"Looks like you fell asleep," Rachel said with a sly smile.

"No!" I lied, trying to salvage my dignity. "I was just lying there, thinking –"

"Thinking with your eyes closed?" she asked sharply.

I regained my balance in the boat and shot back, "I do *lots* of things with my eyes closed." Which made her snicker and made the little girls giggle.

Rachel looked at me for a moment, x-raying me, and said, "I thought it was you out here."

"No," I said coolly. "I simply *drew you* to me." And, for a change, she didn't know if I was serious or not; *she* was the one who was stopped in place. The little girls giggled louder, whispering to each other, and rocked their boat a little.

"Stop it!" Rachel snapped at them. "Remember what Captain Hal said about moving around in a boat?" The girls stopped moving, obeying her instantly, gripping their oars.

"What *did* Captain Hal say about moving around in a boat?" I asked her.

"I have no idea," she whispered to me. "But probably not to do it too much."

I liked the way she joked. I liked the way she looked, even in a life preserver over a Mooncliff T-shirt over a bathing suit. She had nice, smooth thighs.

"What are you reading?" she asked me.

"*Gatsby*," I said simply, and waited.

She said nothing at first, but the pleased look on her face said everything. *Gatsby* was the perfect bait *and* the perfect hook.

"I've read it," she said. "Twice."

"Try the short stories," I said.

"I *have*," she said.

"Can we go now??" one of the little girls whined, but before the words were out of her mouth, Rachel turned on her and spat out, "Be quiet, brat!"

Both little girls were instantly silent, with wide, scared eyes.

"After the stunt you pulled," continued Rachel, sounding very adult. "You shouldn't be allowed out of the bunk at all!"

She let them sit and listen to her words ring out on the open water. I was quite impressed by her command over the girls – I wished the Doggies listened to me so automatically – *and* by the quickness of her temper.

Rachel turned to me and winked.

I played along, saying, "Oh, come on, Rachel, be nice to these girls. They've been rowing so hard, you can see the beads of sweat on their poor little foreheads."

That really made the girls giggle.

One of the girls, a pudgy one with a mischievous smile, said, "Rachel said that 'boys are toys.'"

This made both little girls burst into laughter as Rachel objected.

"Hey, you two!" she said. "Did I tell you you could talk?"

"'Boys are toys'?" I repeated thoughtfully. "You think that's true?"

"It is for some boys," she said back with that sly smile. She was very pretty, and, yes, she knew it. It was going to be a challenge to get close to her and yet not give her the upper hand.

"How about if I race you lovely young girls back to the dock?" I offered, and they accepted faster-than-instantaneously as I knew they would. With a shriek and a clatter and a big push of their oars, the little girls started to row vigorously.

"Row! Row fast! Come on – before he's ready!" Rachel cheered them on as I hustled around in my seat and took up my oars. They splashed me and splashed themselves as they rowed like demons away from me and across the lake. As soon as I began, I had to stop rowing to keep my copy of *Gatsby* from sliding off the seat and into the bilge water in the bottom of my rowboat, but then I started rowing medium-hard.

"Don't let him win!" shouted Rachel as I started to catch up to them.

"Here I come!" I yelled, pulling hard on the oars, getting my back into the stroke. I probably splashed more water than I should have, rowing furiously, but I could barely keep from laughing.

"Keep rowing!" Rachel yelled. "Pull together! Now – pull!!"

Over my shoulder, I could see Rachel urging the little girls on. They were churning up the lake with their rowing, but not moving too straight.

"I'm gonna catch ya!" I hollered fake-menacingly. "I'm an irresistible force!"

Of course, at the end, I let them win and let them tease me –"*Nyah-nyah-nyah! Slow poke!*" – when we got onshore. We were all soaking wet, exhausted and laughed out. But Rachel knew that I had let them win. (It was a good move on my part; girls love it when you're nice to little kids or animals – and don't say, "Same thing.") And for the rest of the summer, all the girls in her bunk loved-loved-loved me; that is, up until things started to happen.

Unfortunately I was late for archery with the Doggies, which annoyed Stewie who couldn't go on his free period until I got there. And in my rush, I forgot to move my boat tag on the Big Board, which led to a perpetual evil eye from Captain Hal for the rest of the summer. But it didn't matter when compared to the sense I had that Rachel and I were on a good path, a good trajectory. I had just left her, and I couldn't wait to see her again.

～

After dinner every night there was Free Play for about an hour, when they let the kids roam around and do pretty much what they wanted until Evening Activity. One night I was assigned to supervise the distant volleyball courts. Not that I knew anything about volleyball; it was just my turn. I didn't even have time to tell Rachel where I was going to be after dinner.

Jerry and Dale were watching me as I waited on the front porch of the Mess Hall for her to come out. Dale reminded me, "You're on volleyball, right?" so I couldn't just stand there and not move.

"Right," I said. "Volleyball," and walked down off the porch. She and her bunk still hadn't come out. Fortunately, a couple of the Doggies – the Fat Doggy and the Doggy With Braces – liked to follow me around, and they could occasionally prove useful. Like at this moment.

"Wait by the Girls' door," I ordered them. "And when Rachel Prince comes out with her bunk, you tell her that I'm covering the volleyball courts, OK?"

"We know who *Rachel* is," the Fat Doggy said. "You don't have to say her last name."

"Just go!" I yelled, and they took off. These two kids couldn't find their own underwear if it was wrapped around their heads – which it sometimes was, courtesy of the Doggy Bully – so I didn't hold much hope for their finding Rachel and giving her my message. I went to Jerry's H.C. Shak where the volleyballs were kept, filled a duffel bag with balls, and made my way to the courts.

Sunsets were especially beautiful at Mooncliff. No matter how hot it got during the day, things cooled off in the mountains by dusk. The light seemed to soften everything, and the mountains seemed lusher and puffier. In all this lovely nature, it seemed a waste of time, not being with Rachel.

I sat down on the bench next to the volleyball courts and unzipped the bag of balls. No one, not one kid, had come down to play. Of course, the volleyball courts were in a fairly obscure part of the campus, but still, I felt stupid being there. I wanted to be with Rachel, period. It was something I had never felt before, like a force building within me. I recalled saying to Rachel on the lake that *I drew you to me,* and how she reacted to that. Maybe I *did* draw her to me. I had always used my brain for schoolwork and abstract things; maybe I could use my brainpower in the service of something for my real *inner* self.

And no sooner did I concentrate, no sooner had the thought formed in my mind, than there she was, walking with the two Doggies and a few girls from her bunk too. She had a big smile on her face, a princess with her escorts.

"You sent your slaves to fetch me," she said. "Did I have any choice in the matter?"

"Not really," I said cheerfully.

"May I sit down then?" she said formally.

"Yes," I said, standing up and making a sweeping gesture to the empty space next to me. "By all means! Simon says you may sit down."

"I'm sorry they exiled you out here," she said taking her place on the bench as the kids fought for the duffel bag at my feet. They pulled out all the balls, which went bouncing across the court.

"I'm not . . . not anymore."

"You know I would have found you, eventually," she said moving right up next to me, as she dodged one of the volleyballs that came our way. I reached out and deflected the ball away from us, and her arm touched my arm. I didn't move as our skin touched; neither did she. I felt like our first kiss could happen at any time, that I could just turn, put my arm around her, and kiss her, but I held back. I actually should have kissed her; she was so beautiful, and *right there*. But it wasn't the right time, not with all these kids around.

"I couldn't wait for 'eventually,'" I said.

So instead, we sat there and talked. I got her to tell me about herself, about past summers at Mooncliff, and about her life at home. I let her talk because it seemed to relax her, and I liked to watch her – she was so animated and engaged, so lovely even as she was grieving about her situation.

"I can't believe my parents actually forced me to come back here again," she said. "I was supposed to go on a teen tour this summer. To Europe! After they promised I could! But because they're going through this *divorce* I had to be nearby. I am once and for all finished with the Moon-shak. I feel so trapped! You cannot believe how I'm just bursting to get out of here."

"Well, *I'm* glad you came back," I said.

"Yeah," she said, looking away from me into space, then looking down. "Well . . . you never know what's going to happen."

I took her hand, making her look at me, and said, "I know one thing that's going to happen."

She drew a slight breath.

"Don't you feel it?" I continued. "That you and I are –"

She put her finger up to my lips to sssshh me. "Don't let's get ahead of ourselves," she said softly.

I took her hand away from my lips and held onto it. "That's OK," I said, agreeing with her. "I'm not worried." I don't know why I was saying such things to her. Looking back, I guess I said them because I was able to . . . because I *felt* them. Before my brain intervened with its usual doubts and second thoughts, I just said what I felt.

The outside world had pretty much disappeared. We had moved into what we later came to call The Zone: everything except the two of us faded away into some kind of out-of-focus, irrelevant unreality. The only real thing was Rachel-and-me, together-as-one, in The Zone.

"You're not like most of the guys that Stanley hires," she said. "You're not –"

"A dumb jock?" I finished her sentence.

"I wasn't going to say that," she said, pushing her arm against mine. "I was going to say that you were different, but there's also something very familiar about you."

"I'll take that as a compliment," I said.

It seemed like the most natural thing in the world, to open up to each other.

"Some people say that I'm spoiled," she said, looking down, playing with one of her fingernails. "And they're probably right, to some extent. But I don't really care. They don't have to live *my* life: *I* do. Everyone expects me to be one way, this perfect princess way, but I'm not that way at all. I just want to live the way *I* want to live. Is there something wrong with that?"

"No," I said. "Not at all," encouraging her to continue.

"I am a very good daughter," she insisted. "At least I try to be. But my parents expect me to go to college and marry some nice, rich doctor and live in the suburbs and have babies and join a country club, and I'm just not going to do it. Does *everybody* have to be the same? I mean, is that some kind of *rule*?"

"Not if you don't want it to be," I said. "If that's what you want."

"Finally, what other people say really doesn't matter all that much," she said, carefully brushing an ant off the bench. "People will say just about anything, so you have to be ready to ignore everybody and just listen to yourself."

Our conversation opened up, just like a flower in one of those time-sped-up films.

"Go on," I urged her.

"People expect you to be one way when you're really another way inside," she said.

"Some people have to put up fronts," I agreed. "To *hide* what's really inside."

"Because they're secretly ashamed of who they really are, and that no one would ever fall in love with them, or care about them."

"So everyone is, on some level, pretending to be someone they're really not," I added, following her train of thought.

"The potential for misunderstanding is incredible, isn't it?"

"It's a miracle any two people get together at all!"

"Yes," she smiled bitter-sweetly. "An absolute miracle."

She was so lovely and fragile even as she was trying to seem strong and self-assured. She was certainly beautiful and confident, but I couldn't help but see something wounded, something secret inside her, deep inside her. Something a little dark and vulnerable that I thought I could reach. I wanted to say the right thing and keep her interest.

"My parents fight some," I said, trying to sympathize with her. "But I don't think they'd ever divorce each other." I didn't say: *Who would ever want either of them if they left each other?* But that's what I was thinking.

"*And*," she said. "It's a bigger deal, kind of, because I'm an only child –"

"Me too!" I practically shouted.

That was a very big moment of connection for us.

"So you understand," she said, clutching my arm.

"The tug-of-war?" I said. Which made her nod her head vigorously.

"It's hard to think that they were once in love," she said. "The way they treat each other."

"People do stupid things all the time," I said. "I want no part of it. I believe in *negative learning*."

"'Negative learning'?" she repeated.

"Yeah," I said. "Learning what you *don't* want in life is as important as learning what you do want."

"And what *don't* you want?" she asked me.

"Right now? Anything that keeps me from getting closer to you," I said. With no fear or embarrassment. I just said it. And she looked back at me, dreamily, in The Zone. I don't know why I was so relaxed with her. Speaking to a girl this pretty, normally I would have frozen up or tried to be too clever. Instead, I was just myself, my ordinary self, but that seemed to be enough for her.

The bugle call ending Free Play sounded from the P.A. system, startling us back to reality.

"So," she said, "I'll see you later tonight, and we can –"

Her words instantly pleased me until I remembered something.

"No!" I interrupted her. "Dammit! My kids have something tonight with these Eagle Scouts from town, knot-tying or something, and then I have O.D. right after that." ("O.D." was short for being "on duty" which meant that a counselor had to stay on duty outside the bunks in Inter Circle, or wherever they put me, and make sure that the kids were all safe and sound until midnight when their actual counselors came back for curfew – 1:00 AM on Fridays and Saturdays. The average counselor had O.D. every three or four days, and we were always trading O.D.s, depending what you had going on any particular night.)

"You're right," she said. "I forgot. We're doing this pajama party with the Lassies. Estelle had us doing party favors all afternoon. And you're really on O.D. tonight? That means I won't see you until tomorrow."

The thought really seemed to displease her; I liked that.

"That's OK," I said. "We have tomorrow."

"But I want to talk to you more *now*!" she said.

I liked that she had that slightly unreasonable streak in her. Rachel wanted what she wanted more than most people did. Some people might call it being willful, or self-indulgent.

But in this case, since what she seemed to want was me, it was perfectly fine.

But before we could say or do anything else, Harriet was right there, at the edge of the courts, ordering everyone back to their bunks.

"Let's go, campers!" she shouted in a husky voice. "Back to your bunks!" She clapped her hands and looked straight at me.

"Boys!" she narrowed her gaze and ordered. "Let's take it back to your side!"

Just then the Fat Doggy grabbed the duffel bag of volley-balls and ran away with it, only to be chased by the Doggy With Braces and a couple of Rachel's girls.

"Hey! Wait!" I yelled at them, torn between having to go after my kids and wanting to stay with Rachel.

"Uh, Rachel," rasped Harriet. "Wanna collect your girls?"

"Time to go," Rachel said softly and got up from the bench.

She took a couple of steps away and turned back to me.

"Why didn't you kiss me?" she asked, making slits of those blue-blue eyes.

Before I could answer, she quickly turned and was gone with her girls.

She left me speechless – which is very hard to do – and falling in love too. Which had never happened before.

Record of Events #5 – entered Thursday, 9:01 P.M.

~

The Evening Activity that night with the local Eagle Scouts from Boonesville was, on the one hand, very easy. We counselors just basically sat there and let these Eagle Scouts, who were almost my age but seemed more like goony teenagers, entertain the Inter boys, going on about knots and scouting and what they did for their merit badges. Dale helped guide the session; Stewie helped demonstrate the knots by letting himself be tied up; Marcus made sarcastic comments to me about the Boonie Scout leaders under his breath virtually without pause; and I spent the whole time frustrated, thinking constantly about Rachel. Why was I wasting my time *in here* when there was this fantastic, exciting girl *out there*?

I thought about what I had learned during our talk at the volleyball courts. I already knew that she was pretty and clever, but there was definitely something complex and maybe a little dangerous about her. I knew that I would have to "handle" her carefully if I was going to get anywhere with her.

Also, she was rich. I could have known that just because she had been going to Mooncliff all these years: all these kids were basically from rich families. Two of the Doggies' parents were doctors. But from the town Rachel lived in and the way she talked about her parents' fight over their divorce – how much alimony Mrs. Prince was entitled to, who was going to get the *new* Cadillac, and who was going to get the condominium in Fort Lauderdale – and the casual way she talked about money, made me think that she might be *rich* rich. That thought both excited and worried me.

I wound up having to get the Doggies into bed by myself that night. Stewie had a "very sure thing" set up with Marcy, this bouncy semi-blonde from the Midwest, who was in the bunk next to Rachel's. He was going to meet Marcy at the Main Office, where you had to sign out anytime you left the camp, and take her to Bailey's, the best bar in Boonesville. I told him to go, no problem. Just after he left, a nasty fight between the Redheaded Doggy and the Very Fat Doggy broke out over the order of possession of this much-passed-around Classics Illustrated *Count of Monte Cristo* comic book, and I had to break it up, yell a lot, and punish both of them. I dumped both their beds over onto the floor – the frames, the mattresses, everything: a traditional Mooncliff punishment. Then, they had to pick up their beds and make them themselves, in silence. This was after repeated warnings. I *hated* getting that angry at the kids. First of all, I am not, by nature, a violent person. (I know that may seem like a ridiculous thing to say, writing this from a jail cell, but it is the absolute truth.) It just seemed like a lot of wasted energy.

When things quieted down, Doggy tears all dried, I turned out the bunk light and went out with my book, blanket, and flashlight into the cold night to take up my O.D. post on the bench in the middle of Inter Circle until midnight. I also borrowed a bag of Doritos from the Fat Doggy, which I told him I would replace. I set myself up on the bench, putting out my stuff for the couple of hours in the cold. Occasionally, there would be something to do on O.D. Sometimes, a kid would get sick, or some kids would start a ruckus (say, a "raid" on another bunk, using wet toilet paper or water balloons or squirt guns as the weapon of choice). Then you'd have to get off your butt and go deal with the situation. But mostly, it was quiet.

All the counselors who weren't on O.D. were usually hanging out in the bottom of the Rec Hall at the Snack Shak, or were at the Main Office, making calls on the pay phone outside, or had gone into town like Stewie in his Super-Coupe with his Very Sure Thing, to Bailey's or, if they really got lucky, the Quarry, the old abandoned stone quarry that served as the local lovers' lane. But for me, there was nothing to do but stay at my post in the middle of Inter Circle, reading my book by flashlight until midnight.

I had brought some Hemingway stories with me, figuring that they would be easy to read and the print was big. But I just couldn't concentrate. There I was, alone in the night, wrapped in a blanket on a hard bench, wasting time. Right then, Rachel was probably hanging out at the Snack Shak (as a C.I.T., she wasn't allowed off campus), so some guys were probably talking to her, trying to get somewhere with her while I wasn't around. Obviously, she knew how to handle guys; all pretty girls learn how to do that. But still, I didn't like the thought of guys – Marcus, for instance – talking to her and looking at her, ogling her body and all. I know what guys think about when it comes to girls, and it's not pretty.

I heard a coyote howling – crying, actually – in the distance, and it sent a shiver through my shoulder blades. Surrounded by forest, there was life all around me in the dark, and I was really defenseless. I hadn't seen any coyotes, but other people had. And there had been bears until a few years ago when they found a better way to secure all the kitchen garbage. But here, at night, with everything so dark and exposed to nature, all I had was my flashlight.

Just then, something rustled and screeched in the woods, right in the bushes at the edge of the Circle: some animal, or something. I jumped about a mile off the bench, throwing off the blanket, the book, and the bag of Doritos, which went everywhere. I shined my flashlight into the bushes and yelled out –

"Who goes there?"

Instantly I felt silly for using such a movie-type cliché, but that's what I said. My heart was pounding, remembering the warning during Counselor Orientation about the bears, knowing that I had Dorito-scented bear bait all over my hands. But I felt even sillier when I saw that it was *Rachel* peeking out from behind one of the thick bushes, with a big smile on her face.

"Hi!" she shout-whispered, waving at me. When she saw that I recognized her, she ducked back down behind the bushes. I don't have to tell you that girls were strictly forbidden on Boys' Campus, and *at night, after "Taps,"* it was an even worse infraction. In fact, it was just the kind of thing that I, as an O.D., was there to *prevent*. And, of course, I was absolutely, blindly thrilled to see her.

Checking to make absolutely certain that no one was around, I fast-walked toward where she was hiding, keeping my flashlight beam on the ground in front of me.

"What the hell are you doing here??" I whispered.

"Aren't you glad to see me?" she said.

"Of course, I am," I said, trying to keep my voice down. "But you'll get us both into trouble!"

"So?" she smiled, pulling me down behind the thick hedge. "We weren't finished before. I didn't get my kiss."

There was a little bit of light, thrown by a flood lamp on a big pole between Inter and Junior Circles, and I could just see Rachel's face. She was dressed in all dark clothes, with the hood of a sweatshirt drawn tightly, framing her almost-perfect features.

"You're right," I whispered, surprised in two ways. Not only was she here to see me, but she had come for a kiss.

"I'm really not usually this forward with boys," she said.

"That's OK," I said, gently loosening and moving the hood of the sweatshirt back from her head, letting her long hair free. She might have been lying a little, but I didn't care. "You can be any way you want to be."

That seemed to be the right thing to say because she closed her eyes dreamily and tilted her head back just so, and I moved in for that kiss. That perfect first kiss. Not too soft, just warm and close and deep and long and –

"What are you doing?" she said when I stopped for a moment.

"Letting you breathe," I said softly. "But I don't have to."

She giggled sweetly.

"I can't believe you actually came here to see me."

"I have this habit of getting what I want."

"I believe you," I said. I mean, who would deny her anything, especially a kiss? "Wait a second," I whispered.

I turned away from her, sprinted to the bench in the middle of the circle and, making sure that nobody saw me, picked up the blanket and ran back to her.

"Good idea!" she whispered, rubbing her hands together. The grass was already soaked with dew, and the ground was cold.

"This is really dangerous," I said as I spread the blanket out. "We could get thrown out of here."

"Oh, that's impossible," she said. "They can't throw me out of here: I'm *related*. My Aunt Penny is married to Bernie Marshak."

"But what about *me*?" I said. I was the one on duty, and technically not doing my job. "*I'm* the counselor. *I'm* supposed to control things and make sure the rules are obeyed. This is in direct violation of Mooncliff rules and regulations. They could fire me at any –"

She laughed, putting her hand gently over my mouth, and said, "Oh, I wouldn't let them do anything to you! You're completely innocent."

Which made me laugh. Me, in the dark, on O.D., with an illegal girl.

"I can't help it, Rachel," I said. "I have a terrible tendency to overthink things."

"Well . . ." she said in a plain, sweet whisper, "Stop it."

That was when our gazes locked; I took her hand and guided her down to the blanket. And we kissed again, much more deeply. It was cold on the blanket on the ground – cold and dangerous and fairly uncomfortable and foolhardy. It was wild and rushed and unforgettable, and we didn't even nearly finish.

Right in the middle of things, there was a loud cracking noise from Inter Circle. We stopped instantly, not breathing. I peeked out from behind the bush. I recognized a couple of Senior counselors walking through the Circle on their way back to their bunks. It looked like they had gone to Bailey's like Stewie, and gotten drunk because of how loudly they were talking and trudging. They didn't even notice that no one was sitting O.D. on the bench in the middle of the Circle as they walked past. Barely twenty yards away from them, Rachel hid behind me as I hid behind the bush. She pulled the blanket up around us and we huddled there, not making any noise and trying not to move.

One of the counselors stopped short. Did they hear us? Were we caught?

Rachel inhaled, making a tiny frightened noise. I winced, wondering if they heard her. Of course, there were crickets and all kinds of forest sounds all around us, but we had made human sounds. A moment passed when I heard nothing but my heartbeat, Rachel's breathing, and the crickets.

"What'sa matter?" said one of the counselors.

The other guy paused for a long, aching moment, and said, "Nothing . . . I farted."

Rachel and I held each other tight, trying not to laugh. The other counselor – I recognized them by now: Jeff and Warren, the guys from Bunk 15 – swatted the farter on the arm, and they walked on, laughing and crunching through the wet night grass and out of Inter Circle.

We breathed again, but it was a close enough call for us to start getting ourselves together.

"We better go," I whispered, and she nodded in agreement.

"It's cold," she said.

"Sssh!" I said, pulling on my shirt as I helped her. "More guys'll be coming back soon."

"I know," she said. "Jerry is kind of insane about making curfew."

"Great!" I said to myself. I stood on one leg, putting on my shoe, and Rachel, unable to resist a mischievous urge, gave me a little push, and I fell over, right into the bush.

A ripple of her musical laugh just came out of her. I'm sure I was funny, falling over, but it wouldn't have been funny if somebody had heard us.

"Are you completely crazy?" I whispered harshly, as I pulled myself up and out of the branches.

She giggled, "Only when absolutely required," helping me get my balance.

And she kissed me again before I could say anything else. And since kisses are better than words, I forgot what I was going to say. When we came up for air, I pulled the hood of her sweatshirt back up over her head and tucked in her soft, long hair.

"You *are* insane," I said. "To come here to see me." She looked so pretty and proud of her dangerous mission.

"No, I'm not," she said. "Wasn't this fun? Sometimes the right thing to do is just right there in front of you."

"I absolutely agree," I said, and I drew her back to me for one more, strong kiss. She was cold, and we were both shaking, but it didn't matter.

"Be careful going back," I said.

We held on for one last moment, and then I let her go.

"Don't let anyone see you."

"Don't worry," she said, blowing me a sweet, soft kiss. "I'll *fly* back!"

Then she turned and disappeared into the woods toward Girls' Campus, down a path through the trees that I didn't know existed. I guess that, from coming to Mooncliff for so many years, she knew some short cuts. I watched her until she disappeared into the forest, knowing/hoping that she'd make it back to her bunk safely.

I picked up the blanket, shook it out, and folded it up as best I could as I walked back to my bench. Remarkably, there wasn't a sound coming from any of the bunks. Not one kid cried out, no one made a fuss, the whole time that Rachel was there. No other counselors were walking by; there was still a little time until curfew. It was as quiet and peaceful as night should be. I sat down on the bench, leaned back against the trunk of the tree, and ate the rest of the Doritos. How, I wondered, did I suddenly get to be the luckiest guy on the planet?

Record of Events #6 – entered Friday, 6:17 A.M.

~

We weren't caught that night. We got away with it cleanly, just as Rachel said we would. At Line-Up the next morning, Rachel stood behind her girls across the big circle, cheerful and happy. She only looked at me once, but her Mona Lisa smile said, *Didn't I tell you we'd get away with it?*

After breakfast, she was waiting for me, sitting on the low wall in the corner of the front porch.

"Nice morning," she said to me as I approached her.

"Nice night," I said back to her.

We couldn't really talk because she had a couple of her girls around her, and I had two Doggies in tow. But our eyes connected.

"What do you have this morning?" I asked her.

Her eyes, even bluer in the morning light, never left mine. "I have no idea," she said. She seemed really happy to see me, her co-conspirator.

"Riflery!" her girls brayed. Which made us laugh.

"Who *are* these kids?" I asked Rachel, trying to find The Zone through the chaos of our campers pulling at us.

"We're the campers you *love*!" said the Smart Doggy who was pulling on my arm along with the Doggy With Braces.

I shook them off with a laugh, "I'd love it if you'd clean up the bunk for a change! Instead of Doggies, we should call you 'Piggies' instead!"

Rachel's girls laughed at that and started making pig noises at the boys who retaliated with noises of their own.

"Let's go, campers!" Harriet shouted from the front steps. "And *Inter counselors!*" – she looked right at us –"Everybody back to the bunks for c*lllll*lean-up!"

I don't know why Harriet seemed to single us out. We weren't the only people hanging out after breakfast; there were lots of counselors getting in one last smoke or one last joke. Who really wanted to go back to the bunk and watch a bunch of kids clean toilets badly? But we waved our goodbyes as our campers dragged us back to our respective bunks.

But before we went our separate ways, one of her campers, the pudgy one with frizzy hair from the rowboat, shouted to me, "She's still in love with Eric! . . . She gets letters from Eric!"

I turned to see Rachel swatting at the little girl who darted laughingly away, just out of her grasp.

"You little snoop!" screamed Rachel, chasing her, and not in fun.

I watched as Rachel caught up to the little girl, twisting her T-shirt in her grasp and holding her tight. She marched the little girl away, obviously giving her a good talking-to. Rachel didn't take any lip from her kids. Good for her.

But that name couldn't stop reverberating in my mind: "*Eric.*"

~

I got Sid from Marcus's bunk to cover for me at Swim Instruction, and I surprised her at the rifle range, which was on the far, far side of the baseball fields.

"You sweet thing!" she cried when she turned around after I had snuck up on her and put my hands over her eyes. She had been standing with her back to me, watching with her girls as Gil, the riflery counselor, loaded a BB gun.

All the girls turned and looked at us.

"You girls watch Gil!" Rachel ordered. "*Now!*" Instantly, all their heads swiveled back to face the BB gun demonstration.

Delighted by the automatic obedience she commanded, I took Rachel by the hand and led her away from the rifle range toward a flat boulder nearby.

"I can't believe you came to see me!" she said.

"It seemed like the right thing to do," I said. "Right?"

I checked to make sure that all her girls were watching Gil before I pulled Rachel into a deep, warm kiss.

I released her and whispered, "That's for last night."

She smiled dreamily and kissed me back, even more deeply.

"And that's for right now," she said.

I tried to pull her into even another kiss, but she turned away.

"We should stop," she said.

"We should *never* stop!"

But she laughed, pushing me away with both hands, and I let her. It really wasn't the right place, or the right time. She giggled that musical little laugh as I took her by the hand and sat her down on the flat boulder in the sun. I sat next to her, very close.

We didn't say anything for a while. We just sat in the sun, feeling its warmth like that great Beach Boys song, our shoulders touching. And it was OK, being silent together. It was surprisingly . . . comfortable.

I whispered to her, "I can't believe they let these little girls shoot guns."

"They're only BB guns," she said. "And it's really fun. And it teaches them gun safety. I've been doing it my whole life here, every summer."

She jumped up from the boulder and demonstrated. "'Load, cock, aim, fire. Load, cock, aim, fire.' I'm actually a great shot. I have medals."

"So let me get this straight," I said. "You're strong, *and* you can shoot a gun?"

"You don't think I can shoot?" she said, her voice rising once challenged.

"I bet you're Annie Oakley," I said with a smirk that I just couldn't keep off my face; she was so damn cute.

"*Better.* My father has a couple of guns," she said. "He says it makes him feel safer, in our neighborhood. Besides, he says a girl like me has to learn to take care of herself."

"Oh, I have no doubt that you can take care of yourself," I cracked, which made her smile and poke my arm. "My parents are not what you'd call '*gun* people,'" I said, thinking of my father with a gun. "They're more like . . . Formica people. Linoleum people."

Which made her giggle out loud, earning us a disapproving cough from Gil.

"Can we have a little quiet back there?" he twanged. "We are dealing with a dangerous firearm here!"

The Inter girls all turned as one and looked at us with dark accusatory looks.

"Sorry," I said. "We'll shut up."

I got up from the boulder, took her hand, and walked her a little ways away from the rifle range.

"C'mon," I whispered.

"Y'know, I got a big fat earful from big fat Harriet this morning," she said. "About spending too much time with you on the Mess Hall porch after meals. The old bag. She's just jealous. She only wishes a man would look at her without gagging!"

"What did she say?" I asked.

"Oh, just the regular control thing," she said with a dismissive twist of her mouth. "'*You must consider your priorities more caaarefully, Rachel.*' She's always hated me, hatchet-faced old –"

I had to smile, so fierce was her condemnation of Harriet and so dead-on was her imitation.

"What?" she said. "You don't think people want to control you? Everyone wants to control someone! My parents want to control me."

"But no one controls you," I teased her.

"Not unless I want them to," she flirted back, but I could tell that she really didn't like the idea of *anyone* controlling her.

It was as good a time as any to ask the question that had been eating away at my brain.

"So," I said. "Can I ask you a question?"

"You can ask me anything you want," she said, looking straight into my eyes without a hint of fear.

"Who is Eric?"

I think the name made her flinch just a little, but she kept her eyes locked on mine.

I waited until she spoke. I wasn't going to let her off the hook.

"Eric?" she said with a slight stammer. "Where did you get that? Eric is . . . nobody."

I didn't say anything else. I let her talk.

"That's just something from home," she said haltingly. "Oh, I know what it is! I have this big reputation around here as a tease and everything, but that isn't me anymore. Don't listen to anybody; I'm really not the same person I used to be."

She paused and her eyes narrowed as she thought of something that troubled her.

"I've learned a lot of things lately," she reflected. Then she took my hand in her two hands.

"And," she said, pausing for just a second. "I've been developing certain plans. Things that I've been thinking about seriously, for a long, long time. You want to know them?"

"Go on," I said.

"OK," she said in a lower voice, choosing her words carefully. "What I feel is . . . that . . . you don't have to live the way that other people live; you can make different choices. We can live different lives."

"I know we can," I smiled back.

"No!" she said sharply. "I'm serious."

I saw that she was and said, "Keep going."

She got quiet for a long moment, and I saw that she was telling me something that obviously meant a lot to her.

"So you know I'm going to be a senior this year at Oakhurst High."

This, I did know. The little town of Oakhurst was about a twenty-minute drive from my house, but a world away, income-level-wise.

"And this is the year I'm supposed to be applying to colleges and all that," she said.

"I know," I said, coaxing her to continue. "So?"

"Well," she said, her eyes fixing on me. "What if I didn't do all that? What if I didn't go to college like everyone else? My grandmother left me some money that I inherit when I turn eighteen, which will be next January."

"Well, happy birthday to you," I said, impressed.

"No, listen to me!" she said fiercely. "I've decided. I'm going to take that money and move into the City and get an apartment and just live for awhile. I am *finished* with school, at least for now. And I am finished with unhappy, hostile people telling me what to do. Why should I listen to my parents? They're *miserable*! I don't want to be like them. And so if I refuse to be put into a mold –"

"I won't put you into a mold," I said, but she went on, ignoring me.

"Some people say I'm selfish and naïve and everything, but I don't care what people say. I'm going to get this money and do what *I* want to do with my life. At least for now, while I can. And now with you going to *Columbia*" – she pointed at me, her two index fingers aimed directly at my heart – "it's like it was *planned*. I *so* didn't want to come here again this summer, but now I see it was for a reason. It's like Fate brought you here, to the Moon-shak, so that we would meet.

And now I'll have you in the City, waiting for me, when I make my move. It's like it was meant to be!"

She smiled, hopeful and a little uncertain, wanting me to respond.

"Well?" she asked me. "What do you think?"

I admit it: I was a bit dazzled. I had been flash-daydreaming about her virtually from the moment we met, fantasizing about how I could make this girl mine – and there she was, two steps ahead of me, making plans for us to be together in the fall *and beyond*!

"Wow," I said. "When did you think all this up?"

"I don't know," she said. "It all just came together. I've been thinking about this for a long time, about doing something with my grandma money –"

"Your 'grandma money'?" I repeated with some amusement: I mean it did sound funny.

"But meeting *you*" – she leaned forward, ignoring my wisecrack, and poked my thigh, right above my knee – "crystallized everything. It's like a sign that I'm doing something right."

"But –" said the Realist/Puppet in me. "Don't you *want* to go to college?"

"No!" she shot back. "Not right now! I'm *sick* of school, aren't you? Oh, I used to get all As, but then after a while, I decided what's the point? I used to sit in the front row and flash my teachers a big, big smile and get all As. So then one day I stopped smiling and started sitting in the back row and all the As magically disappeared. It's all just a big game, and I stopped caring about it a long time ago."

"I'm sorry . . . I never really thought about it that way," I said, realizing that I sounded a little foolish. "College was always such an . . . an inevitability," I continued. "It's all that anyone ever expected of me. *And* it beats going to 'Nam. I mean I need the student deferment, or I'm gonna be face-down in some rice paddy somewhere."

"OK," she conceded. "You're right about that. At least I don't have to think about going into the army."

"Maybe you could join the WACs," I joked. "You look great in green." But that was the wrong thing to say.

She grabbed my wrist tightly and said, "No, I'm really *serious* about this. I want something *different* out of life."

I could see that she was more than serious. The intensity in her eyes stood me still. This was no idle thought with her: this was a long-contemplated, life-or-death escape plan.

"Do your parents know about this?" I asked.

"My parents have totally screwed up their lives," she said. "Why should I take their advice? . . . I'm not saying anything new; I'm just going to be the one to *do* something about it."

"OK," I said, nodding, trying to show that I understood her. "I hear you."

"But do you *believe* me?" she asked, her blue-blue eyes burning into mine, asking me for the truth.

"I believe you."

I hustled down to the Boys' waterfront, my head spinning with thoughts of Rachel. I'm such a "good boy," with hardly a rebellious bone in my body, and here was this girl who seemed to have everything (looks, brains, money, confidence), everything the typical suburban princess possessed, and yet she wanted something different out of life, something *more*. Rachel was becoming more and more interesting by the moment.

～

By the time I got down to the Boys' waterfront, I had missed the big hoopla of the Redheaded Doggy passing his swim test to get into Area #3, the deepwater area. He was the last Doggy to pass into Area #3, which removed from his head the social stigma of having to buddy up with a lowly Junior during General Swims. I was sorry I missed his triumph, but made it up to him and the rest of the Doggies that night. I gave them a pizza from the Snack Shak after "Taps" and the long-postponed recitation of *The Raven* in my best fake-Boris-Karloff accent, postponed "nevermore."

Record of Events #7 – entered Friday, 9:12 P.M.

⁓

I was/am an extremely private person. Maybe it's because I'm an only child who had his own room all his life, but I have never liked being the center of attention of a group. I think that if by magic I were to be offered any superpower, it would be invisibility. But that was not the case at Mooncliff because it wasn't long before the whole camp knew that we were "going." Rachel was well known at Mooncliff not just because she was related to the Marshaks and had been going there since she was seven, but because she was one of the prettiest girls there. She was conspicuous. I, on the other hand, am nothing to look at, but since I was the new guy who had "got Prince," I became an object of curiosity and some admiration too. And after I kicked butt in an Evening Activity of Counselor *"Jeopardy"* – at Dale's urging, for the sake of the Inter Boys' team – as Rachel cheered openly for me, it was impossible to hide our relationship. (I think that was the night that she really fell in love with me.) At first, I didn't care what anyone else thought. I could take any number of "Beauty and the Beast" jokes. Not that I'm that ugly; it's just that she's that pretty. And what did it matter anyway? I had Rachel.

Of course the Doggies immediately became my "assistant boyfriends" to Rachel (in the words of the Smart Doggy). They glommed onto her wherever she was, followed her around, and did her all kinds of unnecessary favors: things designed to curry favor with her and to annoy me. I didn't like the extra attention they brought to us. I wanted "us" to be a secret, living in The Zone, and strictly minding our own business. (You see how that turned out.) But I understood. The

Doggies liked being around this very pretty, very interesting, very charismatic girl. Everybody did.

I think the Doggies really fell in love with her at an Inter picnic, night swim, and long session of "The Hokey Pokey" when Rachel said that she could out-arm-wrestle my entire bunk. I intervened to save her the effort and embarrassment (I mean, *my* embarrassment), but she was determined to prove her point. Hell, I could never stop Rachel from doing something once she decided that she wanted to do it.

So with the entire Inter nation – all the boys and girls – watching, Rachel put the Doggy Bully's arm down – (he was designated as the Representative Arm for the entire bunk) – onto the surface of the picnic table in two perfect, steady, agonizing seconds. The girls cheered, and the boys jeered.

"You let a girl beat you!" they shouted. "A *girl*!!" as the Inter girls danced and twirled in victory.

Another battle between the sexes won, another battle lost, I took the Doggy Bully aside and comforted him.

"It's OK, kid," I told him. "It won't be the last time that happens, that a girl beats you." But he still cried in my lap like a baby.

When I saw Rachel later that night at the Snack Shak after we got the kids into bed, I felt her upper arm through the softness of her must-have-been cashmere sweater.

"So you *are* pretty strong," I said.

"I told you I was," she said. "I don't lie."

I reached out to touch her arm again, but she shrugged it away.

"And it's not my arm that's strong, silly," she said. "It's my will power."

I had to smile at that. She looked so tough and cute at the same time.

"Your will power is fantastic!" I whispered, leaning in to her.

"Why don't we get out of here?" she said. Which was exactly what I was going to say.

∿

I couldn't see her enough. (As I said, I'm not stupid: I *know* what's good.) And fortunately Stewie cut me some slack so I could get extra time with her. In all other cases, I tried to fit my schedule around hers. Why? So we could be together. After dinner one night, I switched my Free Play coverage of the baseball diamonds with Big Alby who was on waterfront duty and wanted to play baseball anyway. Rachel and I sat by the lake all Free Play as the sun set over the lush mountains, golden flecks dappling the water. Kids came and went, pestering us, but what did it matter: we were in The Zone again.

"I talked to my mother on the phone," Rachel said. "Which was a huge mistake."

"Why did you call her then?" I asked.

"I had to get her to send me some medicine," she replied.

I decided not to ask *what* medicine.

"But we got into a fight, of course," she said.

"Over what?" I asked.

"Nothing. Her same nonsense. It's the middle of summer, and she's trying to tell me a million things I have to do the moment I get home. It's just so unnecessary. And now with the divorce becoming final, I'm supposed to feel sorry for her because *she's* the victim! *She* got walked out on. Poor baby. I would have walked out on her too! I know she grew up poor in Brooklyn, and her mother beat her, and her father walked out on her family when she was little. All that is awful; I know. But on the other hand, who cares? That doesn't give her permission to ruin *my* life just because *she's* unhappy and screwed up!"

No question that she was extremely passionate and precise about her situation, about everything around her, really. I watched her face, her gestures, her body movements; I didn't say that she was beautiful when she was angry, but I thought it. I also thought that I would not like to be on the receiving end of her anger, but I would be willing to risk it. A girl as strong as Rachel needed a strong boyfriend.

She said that she really didn't like her mother's new boyfriend, a lawyer named Herb, who was helping her mother in the divorce proceedings.

"By 'helping,'" I said. "You mean 'making things worse.'"

"Exactly!" she said. "There's something very creepy about this guy. I've met him a couple of times. He pretends to be nice, but it's that *creepy* kind of nice. I'm pretty sure he's the one who insisted that I come here, back to the Shak, all in the name of trying to keep things *normal* for me. But I know it was because he wanted my mother all to himself. Yuck. But he'll be sorry – super sorry. He shouldn't go up against my father. My father is someone you do *not* want to go up against."

"I'll remember that," I said, wondering how screwed up Rachel's family actually was. Lots of money and a nasty divorce going on. Difficult mother, frightening father, *and* the mother's creepy boyfriend? I could see that getting involved with Rachel would mean, to some extent, getting involved with these people. I still remember another thing she said that chilled me to my insides: *"How many times do you have to be told that your parents would never have gotten married if only your mother hadn't gotten pregnant before you believe it?"* What a thing to say to a kid, I don't care what the circumstances are. But, looking at her, I knew that all that didn't matter. I would go a long way for this real live beautiful, emotional girl.

"I *really* don't look forward to going back to school," she said cheerlessly. "I've cut off most of my friends, or former friends. Or rather, I've allowed them to cut *me* off. I guess that's the way I'm *supposed* to see it. *I'm* the outcast. But you can imagine what the kids in Oakhurst are like: fairly shallow, fairly stupid. I guess it's good that I like to be alone."

"Good," I said, touching her hand. "I like to be alone too."

"Well," she said with a sweet, shy smile. "Then just possibly we can be alone *together*. Right?"

The bugle call sounded Retreat, echoing around the campus from the P.A. system, ending Free Play.

"Time to go and be responsible," I said, standing up.

"What's the Evening Activity tonight?" she asked.

"Campfire *and* hootenanny. I'll toast you a marshmallow," I said, bringing her to her feet for a last kiss until the next time I saw her.

~

The one place where we felt semi-safe was the Quarry. Around the Moon-shak, there were always campers and other counselors and all the various supervisors watching us. But whenever we could steal an hour, the *same* hour, we would meet at the Quarry. It was this huge, abandoned bluestone quarry that was actually off Mooncliff property, but a short walk from the end of the pitch-and-putt golf course through state land on this old abandoned trail. Over the years, the Quarry had filled up with water and was now an enormous swimming hole/dumping ground/lovers' lane for the kids of Boonesville. Rachel and I would go there to be away from Mooncliff and the world, and sometimes it worked.

"This is huge!" I said the first time I laid eyes on the Quarry. "I see why people come here! This is truly cool!"

The surface of the water must have been as big as a football field, and the walls on all sides were tall and sheer. The drop from the edge of the rock face down to the water must have been a hundred feet. It took about a good ten minutes from the end of the last golf hole, walking down a weed-trampled trail through the forest, to get to the Quarry, but it was worth it.

Pointing across the water to the other side, Rachel said, "That's where the Boonies go to park and make out."

"That's what Marcus said," I replied. "But we can make out right here."

I took her in my arms for a long kiss. It felt great to hold her, knowing that no one was around to see us. We could really relax.

"It's so peaceful here," she said, after the first round of kisses. "I wish we could stay all day. No Estelle, no Harriet –"

"No Serious Sara?" I added.

"She's not so bad," Rachel said. "But I just want to be with you. Not those bratty kids. Am I right? . . . Do you not *agree*?"

After that, we kissed more. I don't know for exactly how long, but I, being older and supposedly wiser, stopped us before things went too far. We had to be back at camp soon, before too many people missed us.

"Look!" I said, breaking the kiss.

There, about thirty yards away from us munching on the leaves of a bush, was a very large deer – a beautiful deer with a completely white, almost albino face.

"Sssshhh!"

We both looked in absolute silence as the deer looked back at us with an almost *human* disdain. We had invaded the deer's domain, and she didn't mind us as long as we behaved ourselves, kept our distance, and didn't make any sudden movements.

"Bambi's mother," Rachel whispered.

"It's her turf," I whispered back. "We're privileged to be here."

Rachel held close to me as we watched the deer eating leaves and watching us at the same time. Her eyes never strayed from us as her jaws kept chewing and chewing.

"She must hate Mooncliff," Rachel murmured. "She must hate *all* people. She's probably right. Think of what we do to Nature –"

Just then we heard two loud popping noises, like gunshots, from *across* the water. All of us – Rachel, Bambi's Mother, and I – swiveled our attention to the far side of the Quarry. There, at the top of the rock face was a large truck that was backing up to the very edge. Its engine backfired loudly as it inched backwards until it was on the verge of falling into the water far below.

Then, the whole bed of the truck slowly tilted up and all this junk that was in the back spilled out and tumbled in an enormous clatter down the sheer rock face. I saw what looked like an old stove, a floor lamp, at least a half dozen tires, some wooden crates, and a bunch of stuff I couldn't identify crash into the water with this huge splash that echoed around the Quarry for a good five seconds.

"That's disgusting!" Rachel said. "They're littering!"

"I thought the Boonies used this as a swimming hole," I said. "How stupid."

"Well," said Rachel. "Apparently they also use it as a garbage dump. . . . Trash dumping trash."

Some of the junk sank immediately, but some of it floated on top for a while. The truck drove right away, but we watched until all the junk had finally disappeared under the surface, in a pool of bubbles that finally popped and resolved.

"What idiots," I said.

"They don't deserve a place like this," said Rachel. "*She* does."

But when we looked over at the bush where Bambi's Mother had been standing, the deer was gone.

"She got out while the getting was good," I said.

"Smart girl," said Rachel. "We have *got* to come back here!"

And we did.

Record of Events #8 – entered Saturday, 4:47 P.M.

∼

"Hey! Kid!" someone called me.

It was Dale, walking my way on a hot afternoon. I was coaching the Inter C softball team – the kids who really couldn't play at all – in advance of a big intercamp game against hated rival Camp Tioga. He had been across the wide playing field at the "good" baseball diamond, with the A team, coaching the kids who actually could play.

"Come here a minute," he said, sitting down on the bench in the shade and leaving room for me. "Let 'em play catch for a while."

I walked toward Dale, shaking my head, saying, "They're *trying* . . ." I plunked myself down next to him heavily. "We had 'em shagging some flies. You should have seen the collisions."

"As long as there was no major damage," he said. "But you might want to consider putting Dornfeld over there in a crash helmet before he kills himself."

I stifled a laugh as we watched one of my prime klutzes miss another one.

"They're very good at the 'Two, four, six, eight, who do we appreciate' cheer," I offered, which got a chuckle out of Dale.

He was a pretty easy-going guy and seldom made fun of the campers, at least not the way we other counselors did. (We weren't really mean about the kids, but jokes are jokes, and guys are guys.)

"You know," he said, spreading his arms out on the back of the bench behind us. "I like the way you handle your bunk. I've seen how you talk to your kids, even the pain-in-the-ass ones. You're a natural counselor."

I couldn't believe that he said that. I thought that I was actually a pretty ordinary, if not downright mediocre counselor. I really didn't *love* being with the kids the way I thought I was supposed to, the way guys like Stewie did. I did my job and wasn't a completely unfair jerk to the kids, but that was about all. Stewie was the one who gave them wedgies and went on "Noogie Patrol," play-terrorizing the Doggies at bedtime to their giggling delight. He's the one who helped them break their baseball gloves in with neat's-foot oil. Stewie was the one forever organizing games of two-hand touch football for the Doggies and lots of kids from other bunks, where they could try out the elaborate trick plays and double-reverses he would concoct, plays that "humiligrated" the opponents of his junior varsity team at Dumpville State in Western Mass or wherever he went. I mainly wanted the kids to leave me alone.

"Thanks, Dale, but –" I started to say, but he cut me off, pivoting around to look straight at me.

"But don't be *stupid*, boy," he said right into my face. "People have eyes."

I am seldom accused of stupidity (except by myself, of course), so I was a little taken aback by Dale's words. I really didn't know what he meant. When I didn't respond immediately, he leaned into me and whispered harshly

"*The girl*! You've got to watch yourself around the Prince girl," he continued. "I'm saying this for your own good. I know she's pretty and everything, but people are watching the both of you. And there is some . . ." he paused, "*concern* about her."

"'Concern'?" I said to myself. "Concern about what?"

"You really want to get involved with a girl like that? A loose cannon? And related to the owner?" he asked, rapid-fire.

"Come on, be smart boy. I don't care how pretty she is. Believe me, life is complicated enough."

I knew that I should say something, but I didn't say what I wanted to say, which was: *Mind your own business, Dale! I'm entitled to see whomever I want to see, as long as I'm doing my job!*

Instead, I let him talk.

"You know me. I just want the summer to go smooth. When I get heat from above, well," he said as he stood up. "I don't like heat."

Heat from above? I thought. Who did he mean? Jerry? The Marshaks?

Instead, I just said, "OK, Dale. Thanks for the heads up. I appreciate it."

"No problem," he said. "You're just young, the both o' you, and you're going much too fast. That's all." He picked up a bat from the ground as he got up from the bench. "As I said, I just like things to go smooth. Trouble for my counselors makes trouble for me, and I *despise* trouble. Especially on a beautiful day like this."

He looked down on me, to make sure that I got his meaning, and tossed the bat back on the ground, clattering against the other bats loudly.

"I hear you," I said as simply as I could. I didn't say that I agreed with him, or promise him anything. I just said that I heard him.

"For a smart guy, you certainly know how to piss a lot of people off," said Marcus as we herded the kids back to the bunks after baseball.

"What did I do?" I shot back at him. "I'm a good counselor. I do my job. Dale just said so."

"You know what I'm talking about," he said. "Every spare moment, you're with Prince. After meals, during Clean-Up, before dinner. I know how many activities you skip out of to go hang with her."

"Yeah," I said. "But he doesn't know that unless someone tells him."

Marcus didn't say anything. Which made me wonder if he was ratting me out to Dale and/or Jerry.

∾

I wanted to talk to her after dinner about what Dale said, but I couldn't. Jerry pulled me away at the beginning of Free Play to go with Stanley Marshak to talk to some big-shot doctor from Boonesville who went to Columbia a zillion years ago. Mooncliff liked to maintain good relations with the locals. After all, most of the kitchen and grounds staff came from Boonesville and the surrounding white-trash towns. Sorry to be so blunt, but that's what they were.

I talked – or rather this old Boonie doctor talked – almost all Free Play about his good old days at Columbia (the College *and* Physicians and Surgeons) and taking a course with Lionel Trilling (which is what everybody at Columbia says) while I stood by and nodded politely, occasionally chuckling at one of his bad jokes. Stanley Marshak was there next to me, grinning with fake pride, rocking back and forth in his shoes and patting down the wiry ends of his moustache nervously. All I wanted to do was get away from them and see Rachel.

That afternoon, all during a long, humid, gnat-attracting nature hike, I thought about her and her plans for us. I had little patience for the Doggies who were screwing around as Stewie and I herded them along the forest trail, trying to keep things orderly for Norm the Bug Guy, Mooncliff's elderly and revered nature counselor who was at the head of the line. The Doggies were in an especially rambunctious mood. They were in the middle of this week-long laughing mania over the word "groin." ("Hello, Mr. Groin!" . . . "Stop looking at my groin!" . . . "Would you like some groin on your salad?" . . . and calling Stewie and me "The Groinmaster" and "Assistant Groinmaster" respectively.) For a while, it was funny. After a couple of days, I and especially Stewie wanted to strangle them.

"There is no such thing as a private life in places like this," Stewie lectured me as we walked behind the last and slowest of the hikers. "Everybody knows everything about everybody, and what they don't know, they make up."

"Great," I said. "People don't know everything or *anything* about me. People are, for the most part, ridiculous."

"You're just finding this out?" Stewie said.

"No," I said. "But when they start to affect your life –"

"What are you gonna do?" said Stewie. "They *have* you. You're an employee."

"Yes, I'm an employee," I said. "But they don't *own* me. I'm still a free human being."

"Now who's being ridiculous?" said Stewie.

I didn't like to think that Stewie was right, but, in this case, he had a point.

∾

As it turned out, I never found Rachel during Free Play. I took as hasty an exit as I could from the chat with the doctor from Boonesville and Stanley, but I never tracked her down. I did catch up to her later that night after Evening Activity (the Lads and Lassies assassinated *The King And I.*) As everyone was going back to their bunks, with kids rushing everywhere and clouds of moths all around the floodlights outside the Rec Hall I went looking for her. Instead, she found me.

"I can't believe it!" she said, pulling me aside. "First, they force me to help with the make-up before the show so that I can't see you. And now they want me to sit O.D. tonight!"

"But C.I.T.s aren't supposed to sit O.D.," I said. Which was the truth.

"Harriet said it would be good 'counselor training' for me," she said, her mouth twisting sarcastically on the offensive words.

"But I thought you were such a terrible person, with wrong priorities," I said. "Now they want you to sit O.D.?"

"They say they want to give me more *responsibility*," she said. "Of course, there'll be another counselor there with me, so it's all completely a farce. But there was . . .something else."

"What?" I asked. I could tell it was something that embarrassed her.

"… I slapped one of my kids," she said.

"And you got in trouble for it?" I exclaimed, thinking how the boy counselors regularly abused their campers, if only to keep them in line.

"Well," she admitted. "It was across the face."

"Oh, that's not good, I guess," I muttered.

"Hey," she shrugged. "I've been slapped across the face plenty of times. The girl was *completely* out of line."

I let that pass, but I didn't like to think of Rachel being slapped across the face, or the fact that she was so casual about it.

"Are they gonna make any of the *other* C.I.T.s sit O.D.?" I asked.

"No!" she said. "I asked Harriet about just that, and she said that I –"

"*Rayyy-chllll!*"

Her kids called her, and Serious Sara was standing right there with an impatient look on her face, so I had to let her go.

"You should go," I said.

"This is completely unfair!" she said.

"I know," I comforted her.

She moved closer to me and whispered with a wicked smile, "You want to come visit me?"

Her look excited me, I admit, and from that close I caught a whiff of her fresh, perfume-y self, but I said, "Uhhhh . . . I better not. You *know* they'll be watching you, waiting for you to screw up."

"You're right," she said glumly. "You're being good. Ugh."

"I want to keep us out of trouble as much as possible. That's what a good boyfriend does, right?" I said.

"I guess so," she murmured adorably.

"So, I'll see you tomorrow?" I tried to sound positive and upbeat, which I think she appreciated. But even though she knew that people were watching, she kissed me firmly on the lips before she ran away through the crowd toward her waiting campers and Serious Sara.

She didn't look back, so there was nothing left for me to do but herd the Doggies back to the bunk with Stewie and get them into bed, all the while making alternative plans for the rest of the evening. Stewie offered to give me a ride in the Super-Coupe into Bailey's, but he was going with Marcy, and I didn't want to be a third wheel. Instead, I did what most of the counselors who didn't go into town did: went and hung out at the Snack Shak in the bottom of the Rec Hall.

There was a jukebox there, and a ping-pong table, and you could get food from the canteen. There was usually a poker game going, small stakes only. Occasionally, the ping-pong games, especially among the guys, could get a little heated. Stewie almost got into a fistfight with Billy something, one of the Southern guys. In any case, it was a place to unwind after a day of brat-watching/counseloring.

When I walked into the Snack Shak, I could smell the greasy hot dogs being grilled and hear the Young Rascals' "You Better Run" pounding out of the jukebox. If this were a normal night, I'd be walking in and I'd see Rachel there – either at a table with some of her friends, or by the jukebox – waiting for me. And I'd go straight over to her, and that was that. But it wasn't like that tonight. I was alone-alone and didn't particularly like it.

"What's with you?" said Eddie from the Bronx, who was at the counter, waiting for his jumbo dog and lime Rickey. "What are you doing here?"

"Rachel's got O.D.," I said simply.

He looked at me for a moment, then guffawed like a donkey for a couple of moments. I just stood there and endured it.

"Wait a second," he said. "Isn't she a C.I. – ?"

"Forget what you're gonna say," I cut him off. "You know rules are different for different people around here." I drummed on the counter, deciding if I wanted to waste my money on some junk food.

"Wow," he said. "Heavy." Nodding in agreement and turning to look up and down at the back of Edwina, the chubby Boonie in charge of Snack Shak who was preparing his food.

"Who is that, Harriet?" he asked, guessing who had changed the rules. "Bitch."

Which made me snicker. Everyone – or, let's say, a lot of people – hated Harriet. Rachel and I weren't the only ones.

"So why aren't *you* in town?" I asked him as we walked over to a little table and sat down. I decided not to get anything to eat. All they had was junk there: any candy I wanted I could always take from the Fat or Very Fat Doggies. They had plenty, and I was doing them a favor.

"And spend all my paycheck before I even *get* it?" he said scornfully. "Half a the guys've already been drawing on their paychecks, just so they can go into Bailey's and spend it getting drunk. I want there to be *something* left at the end of August."

"Square business!" I concurred with him. I hadn't completely forgotten that the whole point of this summer was to walk away with a nice chunk of money for college, which was only a few weeks away now. The summer was *flying* by. And now I had an even greater motivation to save money – to be able to *afford* rich Rachel Prince in the fall.

As I sat there, all my uncertainties about the fall were coming together: Who knew what was waiting for me at home? Starting college *and* keeping Rachel? Could I do both? I *would* do both! But what would be the cost? . . . And the competition?

Record of Events #9 – entered Saturday, 7:16 P.M.

♆

She wasn't at Line-Up the next morning, which was disappointing. I always liked to see what she was wearing each morning and try to catch her eye for a long-distance smile. But this morning it looked like one of her girls was missing, too, so Rachel could have still been back at the bunk, taking care of her. I didn't see her after breakfast either since I had to cover my bunk *and* Bunk 8 (a favor I owed Big Alby) before I could find out from Rachel's girls where she was. I knew that her bunk had swim instruction that morning, so I sent the Smart Doggy from our Arts and Crafts session down to the Girls' waterfront to check. He came back with the information that Rachel had a "personal emergency."

"That's it?" I quizzed him. "A 'personal emergency'? Nothing else? No details?"

"Very sorry, Assistant Groinmaster, *sir*! That is all they said, *sir*!" he reported, standing at attention, with a straight face, the little wiseguy.

"You're worthless," I said, dismissing him. "Go back there and grout."

I didn't see her at lunch either because, amazingly enough, the Doggies had won Inspection that week. I think that the inspector that week, Sal the head of Boys' waterfront, pitied them; we were the only Inter bunk that hadn't won a single week all summer. It was truly a miracle that they won at all. A couple of the Doggies could simply never master the technique of the hospital corner. One inspector actually found

M&Ms concealed in one of the Fat Doggy's hospital corners. Later, the humiliated Doggy actually defended his actions, saying, "Well, they didn't *melt,* did they, numbnuts?"

The Doggies were rewarded with a trip into Boonesville for lunch and a movie. This was a big deal for Mooncliff kids: lunch at the Kandy Kitchen and a real movie, in a real movie house, in the middle of the afternoon. The burgers were thick and fairly good, the famous Atomic Brittle was tooth-rottingly sweet, and the movie was (and I *swear* this is true) *"The Shakiest Gun in the West"* with Don Knotts. I liked him better as Barney Fife. And I missed Opie and Aunt Bee too. All through the movie, I wondered what kind of personal emergency Rachel could be having. I wondered if it was something with her health, or some kind of accident. But they would have said that. Maybe it was a female-type thing, and they were too embarrassed to tell that to the Smart Doggy. Maybe it was something with her parents, like another call from her impossible mother. I sat in the dark, my arms chilled, in the minty air-conditioned movie house air, turning these thoughts over and over in my mind, just waiting to get back to the Moonshak to find out what was going on.

We got back late. Our little bus broke down – you know, those short yellow buses – and Stewie had to walk to find a phone at a local farmhouse and call for help. By the time we got another ride back to camp it was late and hot, and the Doggies were cranky and tired. When we finally rolled in, Dale gave us the happy option of doing a quick swim just for the Doggies, even though it was close to dinnertime, as long as Stewie and I were on the docks *with our bamboo poles,* to make sure the kids were super safe. Dale was good about that; he stuck to the routine unless there was a good reason not to. And in this case, there was. But, meanwhile, it kept me away from Evening Line-Up and finding out about Rachel.

By the time we got the Doggies up to dinner, everyone else was halfway through their meal. When we walked in the Boys' side door, I looked across the Mess Hall to Rachel's bunk's table, which was almost against the far wall. No Rachel. There was Serious Sara at the head of the table, but no Rachel.

I tried to rush the Doggies through dinner, but it was Salisbury steak, their collective favorite.

"It's just regular hamburger," Stewie teased them. "Turd, swimming in liquid crud!" Even as they kept insisting on the superiority of Salisbury steak over ordinary hamburger.

"Mystery meat, in secret sauce! Would taste much better with *cranberries!*" he said in a funny voice that the Doggies loved. I couldn't wait to get out of there. By the end of the meal, I had to pull the Very Fat Doggy, who wouldn't believe that there weren't any more cupcakes, out of the Mess Hall by one of his skin flaps.

It took me a little while, in the chaos of Free Play, but I found Serious Sara on the good baseball diamond. She was a wicked softball pitcher, with a fast windmill-type motion, and I figured that she might be there.

"Rachel's been up at Stanley's house all day," Sara said to me when she walked off the field. Sara had become a bit, shall we say, frostier to me. "Or, most of the day."

"Stanley's house?" I asked her as she sat on the bench, throwing a ball repeatedly into her glove and not looking at me. "What happened?"

"You'll have to ask her," she said. "It has something to do with her parents, I think."

I could tell that I wasn't going to get any more information out of Sara.

"OK, thanks," I said. I decided to go directly to Stanley's house behind the Main Office, figuring that she must still be there.

I walked past the Main Office, where some people were waiting to use the pay phone on the wall outside. I made sure to stay wide of the line so that no one would talk to me. I didn't feel like chatting with anyone.

When I got around the Main Office, I saw Stanley's house up on its little rise, all by itself. It was a small house – painted white with green shutters, of course – with a front porch that had white wicker chairs and a table and pretty flowers all around. It wasn't all that big, but it was cool that Stanley had a whole *house,* with *air-conditioning,* to himself, all summer. I guess it's good to be an owner.

So that's where Rachel was all day? *All* day? Something wasn't right. I suppose that it was good that she was related to the Marshaks, so she could get this special treatment. On the other hand, I think that it was because she was related to the Marshaks that we were singled out, scrutinized, and ultimately persecuted.

I stood there for a moment, wondering if she was still inside. Could she be peeking out one of those little lace-curtained windows, looking for me? She must know that I would be worried about what was going on with her. It felt right, to be concerned about her. This is how a real boyfriend should behave. I *should* be there. But what if it weren't Rachel but *Stanley* who saw me out of one of those windows? I had already been warned by Dale to stay with my kids and not spend so much time with Rachel, at least during "work" hours. I knew that they were on my case.

I stood there for one more moment, weighing the situation. I suddenly felt stupid: What was I doing, just standing there, where anybody could see me? Rachel would find me when she could; she would *feel* me calling to her. I didn't need to be standing there. I realized that I had made a mistake, being there. I turned and quick-walked away from Stanley's house. There was no place else to go but back to my kids.

Evening Activity was an intercamp *counselor* basketball game against Camp Tioga. I didn't even to try out for the counselor team. First of all, I wasn't tall enough. But even if I were, it was very tough to get on the team. There were some serious jocks and seriously tall guys on the boys' staff. Stewie, who was over six feet, didn't even try out.

"I'm saving my knees for football. I have a shot at the varsity in the fall if I stay healthy," he said as we moved the Doggies into their row of seats; boys were on one side, girls on the other. I was glad to see that I wasn't the only person who was already planning for the future.

"I bet you're a great football player, Stewie," said the Doggy Bully as we sat down.

"When I get into the open field with the ball," Stewie said. "I am Lance Alworth."

"Cool!" said the Doggies.

I had to stifle a laugh at that one; I guess everyone has delusions. I looked across the basketball court, through the forest of enormous Tioga counselors who were warming up with show-offy lay-up drills, to the girls' side. Rachel's bunk wasn't there yet. I watched Harriet pacing around as if she were about to jump center herself. So the game began.

There was a lot of noise – cheering and yelling and the players running up and down the court, blocking my view of the girls' side. Right at the beginning, two kids got into a shoving match that required that I take them outside and yell at them. Kids can be so cruel. There was a kid in the next bunk who was born without one of his thumbs. Some kids used to call him "Niney" behind his back, and sometimes to his face.

When I got back inside and sat the kids back down, Rachel's bunk was there, across the Rec Hall floor in its proper row, with Serious Sara and the rest of their girls. But there was no Rachel. I was definitely surprised by that. I thought that, for sure, she'd be back with her bunk by now. I decided to tell Stewie to watch the Doggies so that I could check with Sara to find out what was going on. I figured that, with everyone so caught up in the game, I could walk outside the Rec Hall and around to the other side door, and no one would see me.

As I stood up to get Stewie's attention, I felt a tapping on my shoulder. I thought it was one of the Doggies, and I turned around, ready to snap – and it was Rachel. Right up close to my face.

"Hi," she breathed.

"Hi!" I said. "My God! How have you been?"

"Not so good," she said. Her face was puffy and her eyes were red from crying. "You think we can go outside for a minute?"

I spun out of my seat, and we were outside almost instantly.

"How have I been?" she said, her arms crossed, shivering in front of me on the balcony outside the Rec Hall. "I've been better, I can tell you that. I've been on the phone all day long, off and on, with my mother *and* my father. First, my mother; then, my father. Then, this *judge*! Then both of them again. It looks like the divorce is being finalized, and they're both being predictably, *almost perfectly* horrible. I *knew* this was going to happen. Fighting about all this alimony money and child support money and *this* little thing and *that* little thing, and then blaming it all on *me*! Like it's all my fault they hate each other's guts!"

"Oh, baby," I murmured.

I put my arms around her to stop her from trembling.

"Listen," she whispered urgently. "Take me to Bailey's tonight!"

"What?"

"I want to go to Bailey's," she insisted. "Take me there tonight. I'll meet you in the parking lot after 'Taps.' Borrow someone's car."

"But won't you get in trouble?" I asked.

"I. Don't. Care," she said, staring straight into my eyes. "All my life I've heard about Bailey's; now I wanna go. I've *got* to get out of here tonight. *Please?*"

I could tell that she had been through a heartbreaking day, and this was a kind of test to see if I would help her when she really needed it.

"OK," I said. "Sure. Of course." I could tell that was what she wanted to hear, what she *needed* to hear, and so I said it. "The parking lot. After 'Taps.'"

She turned and ran down the balcony, to go around the Rec Hall and back to the other side. I was instantly excited by the thought of taking her to Bailey's, even though C.I.T.s weren't allowed off campus, so the possibility of her/us getting into trouble if we were caught was more like a *probability*. Still, at that moment, with Rachel so unhappy, what she wanted mattered more to me than anything. So I decided to make it happen for her. Dale had called her "a loose cannon." Maybe she was. But maybe that's one of the reasons that I was so attracted to her. I was/am such a self-controlled, level-headed, take-no-risk kind of person. Maybe just what I needed was a loose cannon in my life.

Record of Events #10 – entered Saturday, 11:14 P.M.

~

We lost the counselor basketball game to Tioga by twelve points, which was actually a good thing. If we had won, there would have been a big Mooncliff celebration at Bailey's. After a loss, there was less of an impulse to leave campus and celebrate.

As Stewie and I walked the Doggies across campus and back to the bunk through the dew-soaked night grass after the game, I started to put my scheme into effect.

"Hey, man," I said, "you going into town tonight?"

"Nah," he said. "Marcy has O.D."

"So," I asked innocently. "What're *you* thinking of doing?"

"I dunno," he said. "Maybe go down to the Rec Hall and play some ping-pong. Beat the Munk's ass again, with his *fancy Chinese* grip."

"OK," I said. "Then how about you let me borrow your car?"

"Aww, man! . . ." he said, stopping in his tracks. "The Super-Coupe?"

I hadn't asked to borrow it all summer, but this was the time.

"Look, Stewie, I'm a great driver," I pressed my case. "And I'm only going into town."

"Awwww, mannnnn!" he repeated, and started walking again. I stayed with him.

"I haven't asked you all summer, and it's –"

"OK!" he said suddenly, before I had to push any harder.

"Great," I replied.

"What am I gonna say: 'No'? You're my dude."

"Thanks, man," I said. "You're the best."

"You gonna take, uh, you-know-who into town?" he asked in a lowered voice.

"Perhaps," I hedged.

"OK," he said with a note of doubt in his voice. "But take care," he continued. "I mean with the upholstery. No spills, if you understand my drift. There's a blanket in the trunk."

"Thanks, man, I owe you."

He snickered and said, "You are completely wacko . . . And I don't know *nothing* about this."

⁊

With the keys to the Super-Coupe jingling in my pocket, I hurried across the campus as the last notes of "Taps" played from the P.A. system. Stewie had said, "Get out of here!" and I was happy to oblige. I signed out at the Main Office and fortunately nobody was there to ask me for a ride into town. I don't know how I would have lied my way out of that one.

Thank goodness there were a couple of floodlights illuminating the parking lot because the rest of the night was pitch-black. Stewie told me that he'd parked his car at the far end under some trees to "minimize solar damage." I walked down the long, wide center row, wondering if Rachel was there already; hoping, really. I couldn't call her name: someone might hear me. But I didn't see anybody. Maybe she couldn't get away. Maybe Estelle or Sara or Harriet or somebody kept her back. I just had to trust that she would be there, as she said she would, just as I would want her to trust me.

There was Stewie's Plymouth – I have a hard time calling it "the Super-Coupe" with a straight face – right under the trees, just where he said it would be. I felt for his keys in my pocket. I would get the car and drive it toward the Main Office.

Maybe she would see me there: How could she miss this big, bright turquoise thing?

"*Hey!*" someone called me from behind.

I spun around and saw this little guy with a moustache in dark clothes and a black ski cap coming out from between a couple of cars. It took me a second to realize that the little guy was *Rachel*.

She smiled mischievously, declaring, "Hey, man!" her hands on her hips. "Well, what do you think?"

I was speechless.

"I'm going to Bailey's *in disguise!*" she whispered delightedly. "I took a fake moustache from backstage when I helped with the make-up for *The King and I*. And now, even if someone sees us, they won't know who I am!"

She beamed with pride at her idea.

"Wow," I said, still recovering from not recognizing her. She'd really surprised me, which is hard to do. I usually think that I can anticipate most people's behavior, but she really threw me with this one.

"Let's go!" she said. "Before I lose my nerve."

"OK . . ." I said. "Man."

She sat very close to me as I drove the Plymouth out of the parking lot and down the road out of the Moon-shak. I was very careful to do everything perfectly in the Super-Coupe. Driving a strange car is, well . . . strange, and I didn't want to make a mistake with Stewie's pride and joy. But something else was at the back of my mind.

"So you've been planning this for a while," I said. "If you swiped that moustache before."

She paused a little and said, "Maybe."

"Think you're pretty clever, don't you?" I teased.

"No," she said, cuddling closer, but I could tell that she was lying. And she knew that I knew that she lying. But it all didn't matter; we were *out* and together.

I kept both hands firmly on the wheel – ten o'clock and two o'clock – as I felt her next to me. I hadn't driven since the

end of June, and it felt great to be moving again. But I had to
be careful: Stewie's car had good power, and the twisty, unlit
two-lane blacktop that led to Boonesville demanded all my
attention.

Rachel turned on the radio and leaned back against me.

"Go faster," she said, and I tried to oblige. She turned up
the volume – the song was "Nowhere to Run" by Martha and
the Vandellas – and moved in closer. I kept my eyes on the
road as the forest whipped by on both sides. At that moment,
when we were free – alone, with speed and music and the
night all to ourselves – I could have, *should have* driven on
forever, to Canada maybe, and avoided so much future trage-
dy. But Stewie would have wanted his car back, and my curfew was midnight.

Bailey's itself was nothing. I mean, it really *was* a shack.
A big shack in the middle of a gravel parking lot off to the
side of Route Zero in the middle of nowhere, with neon beer
signs in the windows: "Schaefer" . . . "Rheingold" . . . "Rolling Rock." But when you walked into Bailey's, when the door
swung open and you got that first sweet/stale whiff of cigarettes and beer and sweat and perfume, when you looked into
the smoky darkness and saw the drinkers at the bar and the
bumper-pool shooters in the back and the dancers jockeying
around the jukebox blasting some prime, primal Stones, you
knew that you were in someplace special. Somewhere you
could relax and just be yourself, disguises notwithstanding.
Not that there weren't hundreds if not thousands of bars or
honky-tonks like Bailey's all over the U.S. of A. It's just that
this was *our* honky-tonk, *our* place – where we felt comfortable and could be ourselves, away from the authority of Jerry
or Harriet or any Marshak whatsoever, if only for a few hours.
And, to tell you the truth, it was the only Boonie bar that actually welcomed the counselors from Mooncliff and the other
camps in the area. Tioga, Blue Lake, Deerhead, etc. The rest
of the Boonie bars were strictly for the locals.

So when we walked in, my small friend with the moustache and I, the first thing I did was stop and scope out the
room to see if there was anyone there from Mooncliff: anyone
who might recognize me, much less Rachel, much less Rachel
in disguise. Or, for that matter, anyone who might notice that
the guy next to me was a *girl*. But, fortunately, no one noticed
me or us at all.

"What do you think?" I asked her.

"I don't see anyone," she muttered.

"OK, let's go." I put my head down and went straight for
the farthest, darkest corner of the place. At first, I held out my
hand to take hers.

"Are you out of your mind?" she hissed at me, slapping
my hand down.

"Sorry," I whispered, pulling it back quickly. "Force of
habit." Two guys holding hands would be highly suspicious in
Bailey's. It wasn't that kind of bar.

There was a vacant booth in the corner beyond the
bumper-pool table, and we went for it. I moved into one side,
and she took the other. We looked at each other, excited and
nervous, across the worn wooden tabletop.

"We made it," I said. "I think. So far."

"This is *great*," she trilled. "I can't believe I'm here." She
pressed her fake moustache back on; it was peeling off a little
at the edges because she was smiling so widely.

"So . . ." I said. "What do you think of the legendary Bailey's?"

"I think I love you," she said simply. I wanted to immediately reach across the table to hold her hands – well, I wanted
to do more than that – but I couldn't even touch her.

"Really?" I said. "That's very nice . . . Joe." She still had
the ski hat on, concealing her hair, and that stupid moustache,
but she was Rachel underneath. "I love you too," I whispered
back to her.

Which I could tell that it was the right thing to say because she practically *purred*.

"What if I came over and sat on that side with you?" she said. Even in this dark corner, the look in her eyes burned right into me. And she knew it.

"I think that could be very dangerous," I said.

Just then, a squat waitress in an apron approached our table, interrupting us.

"So, what'll you have, fellas?" she said as she dropped a basket of snack mix in front of us.

We looked straight at each other and *did not laugh*.

"Uhhh, two Rolling Rocks," I said, in a voice deep enough for the two of us that almost made Rachel crack up.

The waitress looked down at us, paused for a torturous moment, then said, "Two Rocks, it is."

She walked away from the table just before we imploded in stifled laughter. Rachel grabbed a handful of the snack mix, ate a piece, and threw a piece at me.

"Hey!" I said, catching it against my neck. I instantly ate it, whatever it was: some salty pretzel-like substance. "Yech."

She giggled, "I can't believe I'm actually here, after hearing about it all these years. After the kind of day I've had . . ." She looked away for a moment, somber thoughts suddenly clouding her mind.

"Yeah, well . . ." I said sympathetically. I didn't want to press her. If she wanted to talk about what was going on with her parents, that was up to her. She was the one under pressure; I was there to help and support her.

"I was on the phone with my mother *three* times and my father *twice*. Can you believe it?" she said grimly. "They even made me speak to the judge!"

"A judge? Wow," I said. I really did feel sorry for her. (Sorry, Your Honor.)

The waitress put the beers on the table between us, along with two little napkins.

"Anything else?" she said. "Kitchen closes at eleven. You can pay me when you're ready." And left without so much as looking at us.

I picked up the mug of beer and toasted Rachel.

"To you," I said.

"No," she said. "To you."

"To the Super-Coupe!" I said. Which satisfied us both, and so we drank carefully through the foam.

"You know," she said, wiping off her mouth. "I don't really like beer."

"It's an acquired taste," I said. "Watch your – !"

She half rubbed her moustache off, but I warned her quickly enough, and she smoothed it back on.

"Ohmygod," she said, pressing her upper lip, looking around to see if anyone noticed. "Is it still there?"

"Yes, it is," I said. "Harry."

She gave me a smirk and said, "I thought I was 'Joe.' Don't I look like a Joe?"

"Frankly, no," I shot back. "We're lucky it's dark in here, and everyone's half smashed."

"Oh, this is ridiculous," she said. "This stupid table between us. I can't stand it. Let's get out of here. Pay her, and let's go."

She got up, and I got right up with her. Fortunately, I was getting used to her sudden changes in mood and desire, and was ready to keep up with her. I dug into my back pocket and pulled out my wallet as Rachel walked away from the table. I threw some bills on the table, making sure that I left a good tip for that wonderfully oblivious waitress.

As I went after Rachel, I noticed a couple of counselors from Mooncliff at the bar whom I hadn't noticed before, a couple of the Junior girl counselors. I ducked my face, pretending to scratch my cheek, so I don't think that they saw me as I dodged around a waitress and followed Rachel quickly out the door.

The night air instantly hit me hard and cold. Where was she – in the dark?

"It *stinks* in there!" she said in a loud voice. "Yuck!" She was standing off to the side, down the steps, in the parking lot.

"Sssshhh!" I tried to quiet her.

"It smells like a smelly, old ashtray!" she said. "Why didn't anyone tell me?"

I rushed down off the porch, to keep her from talking.

"Ssshh!" I said. "That's what *all* bars smell like!"

"But that's *disgusting*! Double yuck!"

"Stop it," I said. "You sound like a girl!"

"I *am* a girl!" she said. She stripped off her moustache and ripped off her ski cap. She shook her head, sending her long hair flying in the night air. That stopped me right there: it was incredibly sexy, like something a Bond girl would do.

"Yes, you definitely are," I said and held out my hand for hers. She grabbed it, and we ran to Stewie's car. It was cold, and we needed to be together after all that wasted time, separated by that very stupid table. As I ran, I tried to reach into my pocket to get Stewie's keys, but it's hard to run and reach at the same time.

"Hurry!" she said, shivering. "It's cold out there!"

"I know, I know," I said, finally digging out the keys and looking for the right one. I thought about Marcus' crack about "raging hormones" and had to stop myself from laughing out loud.

"W-w-what's the matter?" she stammered, stamping her feet to generate some warmth.

"My fingers won't work," I said, separating the keys and trying to pick out the ignition key.

"Here it is!" I opened the driver's side door and let Rachel dive in, just missing the steering wheel. I scooted in after her and slammed the door. I jammed the key into the ignition and revved up the engine.

"It's fur-eezing!" she wailed, rubbing her hands together and moving up close to me.

"It'll heat up soon," I reassured her, checking to make sure that I had the heater on high.

I turned to her, relieved to see her non-moustached face and flowing hair again.

"It'll heat up *now*," she said.

We fell into each other's arms, and . . . and the rest is personal. Extremely personal. (The memories of those moments and moments like them are just about all that I have left to myself. Almost everything else about Rachel and me has been excavated, dissected, and displayed by the judicial system and the media, in tandem, for all the world to ridicule and/or enjoy. Can't *some* things be private anymore?) Let's just say that when we surfaced some time later, the windows of the Super-Coupe were all clouded, and we were where all lovers want to be. I didn't know what time it was, so I turned on the radio.

"What time is it?" Rachel asked.

"That's what I'm finding out."

"Do we have to go back?" she said forlornly.

I looked at her, so lovely in the faint light, and said sadly, "What a question." She knew exactly what I meant. I turned on the radio as she started to look for her shoes. There was not a lot of room in the Super-Coupe, and it was hard to see.

But then I tuned in a station and Cousin Brucie announced that it was 11:38.

"Oh, crap," I said.

So we switched into frantic, high-gear getting dressed. It was like a sped-up silent movie.

"It's OK," she said. "We're going to be late. I've already missed the C.I.T. curfew."

"No, we are *not* going to be late!" I said, starting the engine with only one arm in my shirt, but we had to get going. "I refuse to give them the satisfaction."

I hadn't missed curfew all summer, and I wasn't going to miss it tonight. And I just had a feeling that Jerry or Harriet or somebody would be there, at the Main Office, checking.

I sped all the way from Bailey's to Mooncliff. I know that I probably made some illegal moves, but I don't think I was totally reckless (though Rachel gasped once and had to hang onto the door handle on a couple of turns). The Super-Coupe screamed into the parking lot at four minutes to midnight. I slammed on the brakes, skidding in the gravel as I pulled into Stewie's spot under the trees. I should have been quieter and stealthier, coming back so close to curfew and with an illegal C.I.T., but time was tight so I had no choice. I kissed Rachel goodbye quickly and deeply, wished her good luck in sneaking back to Girls' campus undetected – she was already late for her C.I.T. curfew by almost an hour – and ran full-speed up to the Main Office, still pulling on my jacket. And I was right to do it.

As I walked into the Main Office at exactly two minutes to midnight, according to the big clock on the wall, sitting right there on the other side of the counter was Jerry, waiting; crew cut erect and wide awake. He was pretending to read the sports section of the *New York Post*, but he wasn't kidding anybody.

"Hi, Jerr'!" I greeted him happily. "Just in time!" I said as I signed in on the clipboard at 11:59.

He looked up at the clock, unsmilingly, then back at his newspaper. He seemed truly disappointed that I beat the curfew.

"See you at Line-Up," I said brightly, "In just about" – I checked the clock – "seven hours and forty-five minutes."

He didn't even smile as I waved to him, walking out. I guess I shouldn't have taunted him like that, but he was such a jerk: he almost *required* it. Didn't he have better things to do at midnight? Why be such a nitpicker/taskmaster/fanatic? It was only summer camp. Still, he was my boss. There were only two-and-a-half more weeks left in the season, and I shouldn't make things any worse for Rachel or myself. My father always told me, "Don't make things worse." I should have believed him.

Record of Events #11 – entered Sunday, 6:14 A.M.

~

When I got back to my bunk, everyone was asleep, thank goodness. It was cold, but I showered anyway. Afterwards, I remember lying in my bed, still buzzing, unable to sleep. I remember hearing a coyote in the distance, howling something that seemed very important to him. I can hear its echo in my mind to this very day.

My mind kept tossing over and over again, the same thoughts, the same worries: Did Rachel get back to her bunk undetected? Did those Junior girl counselors recognize us at Bailey's? How difficult were Rachel's parents *really*, and how much trouble would they make for us/her in the future? And how would I fit this all into my freshman year at Columbia and all that schoolwork to come?

I don't know when I got to sleep, but I must have, because the next thing I knew it was morning, and the Very Fat Doggy was throwing up in the bathroom because of all the green-and-white popcorn he ate the night before at the basketball game. I owed Stewie for use of the Super-Coupe, among other things, so I stayed back to deal with the Very Fat Doggy and his foamy emerald vomit. It was really repulsive; the last thing I needed that morning.

Of course we were late, the Very Fat Doggy and I, getting up to breakfast, so I didn't see Rachel at Line-Up. As we walked into the Mess Hall, I looked over at her table. She was there, but she was sitting with her back turned to me so we didn't make any eye contact. But it was good to see that she was there.

Just as I sat down at my end of the table, the Very Fat Doggy was constructing a stack of pancakes and drowning it in syrup.

"What is *wrong* with you? You just had your head in the *toilet*!" I yelled at him. He tried to answer me, but his mouth was too stuffed for his words to be intelligible.

"Kids have no feelings," Stewie said from the head of the table as he whacked the Doggy Bully, who had been elbowing the Smart Doggy, on the head with a spoon. "Stop that, dummy!"

Just then, from nowhere, little Esther from the Main Office scuttled up to our table and whispered something into Stewie's ear. He listened carefully, with his eyes closed, concentrating hard. We watched him listen until Esther said, "OK?" and walked away.

"*I* . . ." Stewie announced. "Have an important phone call that cannot wait." He bunched up his paper napkin, threw it on his plate, and got up.

"Hey! Dogs! Do me a solid and be nice," he said and walked quickly away in the direction of the Main Office.

"You heard him, animals!" I said, taking charge. "Be solid, and be nice."

After breakfast, I waited on the porch for Rachel as long as I could, even as I kept getting dirty looks from Estelle through her cigarette smoke.

But when Dale, from behind me, called, "Hey, is Stewie back? Who's watching your bunk?" I knew that I had to go.

All morning, I didn't see Stewie. All through Inspection and First Period down at the Nature Shak – which I was supposed to have free – he was gone. As I watched the Doggies watch Norm the Bug Guy dissect a bullfrog and make its dead legs jump with jolts from a big dry-cell battery, I was getting more and more annoyed with Stewie. Rachel's bunk had tennis

First Period, and I wanted to try to track her down there; now I couldn't.

"Where's Stewie?" asked the Doggy With Braces three times until I snapped at him.

"Shut up and stop drooling," I said. "No one knows. Turn around and watch the show."

I sat on a bench watching as the Doggies squealed with delight/disgust when Norm the Bug Guy's scalpel cut deeply into the frog's body and a jet of formaldehyde squirted across the table.

"Now, boys!" Norm cautioned them, and they instantly calmed down. He had such a good way with kids, a voice of patience and assurance. I was so far from that kind of counselor. For me, the kids were an annoyance and an obstruction. They were always *in the way* of my real life.

I heard someone walking up behind me and turned just in time to see Marcus with a big smirk on his face. He was huffing, a little out of breath.

"Hey," he said. "Here you are. Dale wants to see you."

"What?" I replied.

"At Jerry's Shak," he said. "He's waiting for you."

"Who?" I asked. "Dale or Jerry?"

"*Both*," he answered with a little too much joy in his voice. "I'm supposed to watch your bunk."

Damn! I thought, *we got caught.* I could think of no other possibility as I walked up from the Nature Shak to Jerry's. Those Junior girl counselors must have seen us and told somebody. Or maybe Rachel got caught walking back last night. I *knew* we shouldn't have gone to Bailey's, no matter what Rachel said. I know that she was upset about her parents and everything, but I should have talked her out of it. In any case, as I walked to Jerry's Shak, I knew that I was in trouble, a place I was generally not accustomed to being. At least not until I got to Mooncliff and fell in love.

I knocked on the door and stepped in. Dale was there alone, sitting in a chair, waiting for me. I could tell he was waiting for me by the grim look on his face.

"Hey, Dale," I said as I entered. "Marcus said you wanted to see me." I decided to play it cool and innocent. Dale didn't say anything at first. He just kept looking at me. Then he shook his head and sighed. He put his hands on the armrest of his chair and, with great effort, pushed himself up to a standing position. He stood there, looking at me with serious eyes.

"Let's go," he said.

He walked right past me and out of Jerry's Shak. Without saying a word, I followed him.

Dale was a big man, striding across the campus pissed off, and I had to fast-walk to keep up with him. I wanted to say something to him, but I didn't dare. I didn't even ask where we were going.

Finally, Dale broke the silence, spitting on the dry August grass, saying, "This is *exactly* what I told you *not* to do!"

At first, I thought we were going to the Main Office, but he bypassed the Main Office and headed straight for Stanley Marshak's house. This was weird: just yesterday I was standing outside Stanley's house, when Rachel was in there, and now I was being summoned there. This was like being called into the principal's office but *worse*. This was an actual job that I was being paid for.

I must have hesitated at the top of the path to Stanley's front door because Dale barked at me, "Let's go!"

I followed him down the walkway. On the front porch, he let out a deep, disgusted sigh and rang the doorbell. I couldn't even look at him in the face. Dale had been fair to me all summer; this was not a good way to pay him back.

The front door swung open, and unsurprisingly, there was Jerry, looking down on me with a sneer.

"Come on in, wise guy," he said, as Dale held the screen door open for me. Stanley Marshak's little house was by no means a shack. You walked in, and it was a different world of luxury and comfort. He had great air-conditioning and a big color TV. With its fluffy furniture and puffy carpeting, it was actually nicer than Stanley's house in Roslyn where he interviewed me what seemed like a million years ago.

There was a living room and, beyond that, an office area where Stanley was sitting behind a big desk, waiting for me. With Jerry on one side and Dale on the other, I walked in. I was trying to be completely calm and I was, until I saw that Harriet was there, too, standing in the corner, arms crossed in front of her, glaring at me in the same perfect Mooncliff running suit that she always wore. I could almost see the rays of hatred emanating from her narrowed eyes.

"Sit down," said Stanley, pointing bluntly to an armchair, catty-corner to his desk. I sat while Jerry, Harriet, and Dale took places around the room, all looking directly down at me.

"So," said Stanley, sitting back in his wide leather desk chair, smoothing one end of his moustache with his fingers. "What do you have to say for yourself?"

For a change, I was smart and kept my mouth shut. I didn't know exactly what they knew, and I didn't want to get Rachel and myself in any deeper trouble than we already were. So silence was golden, for the time being.

"*Well . . . ?*" Stanley said, leaning forward. I guess he didn't like my golden silence.

"I don't know what you want me to say," I started, sounding very humble and reasonable.

"Damn!" sputtered Jerry in the corner angrily. "We should just fire his ass! Him and all the other anti-American, peacenik punks!"

Harriet shushed him, though I could tell by her steely look that she sympathized with him. But Dale spoke up for me.

"Come on, Jerr'," said Dale. "That has nothing to do with anything!"

And it didn't! I kept my politics pretty much to myself that summer, except in conversations with friends, of course. And Rachel. The Assistant District Attorney also tried to drag my supposed anti-war feelings into the trial. All I can say about that is: if being against the War is a crime, then half the kids in this country would be in jail with me. *More than half!* End of sermon.

"Look, son," said Stanley sternly, trying to drill into my eyes with his, "you know what you did was wrong. To take an underage C.I.T. off campus – at night – to a *bar,* breaking her curfew. You know that's wrong, don't you?"

He had me; I knew he was right, and he knew that I knew that he was right.

"What can I say?" I said, simply and slowly. "She asked me to. She was upset, and she asked me to."

Harriet snorted in disgust. "Oh my God."

Stanley held up his hand to stop her. "No," he said, "let him talk!"

I had to come up with something else to say.

"That's really it," I said, looking at Stanley for some understanding. "You know Rachel and –"

"I know Rachel Prince very well," Stanley cut me off. "She is a very lovely girl, but let me tell you: coming from a broken home like she does, she has certain . . . problems."

Anger flashed through me. Who was he to talk about Rachel that way?

"Well, that's –" I started to defend her.

"Shut up!" snapped Stanley. "You were wrong! You were wrong, and she was wrong. You knew it, and *she* knew it! So don't make any . . . any –"

"Damn, we should just fire his pinko ass!" sputtered Jerry, unable to contain himself.

"But we *can't,* Jerry!" said Stanley, shutting him up again. "So stop saying that."

"*Can't*" fire my ass? What was this?

Stanley leaned toward me, making his leather chair squeak. He looked at me with deadly eyes.

"You know I should let you go, son," he said. "You were warned before, but you didn't listen. And quite frankly, I'm disappointed in you. With your background and education, I had very high hopes for you."

I hated when adults said they were "disappointed in you" – as if they really liked you in the first place, and now you *mean* something to them.

"I run a clean camp. But because of, because of – *uhhh* . . ." Stanley was talking straight to me, but he was having trouble getting out what he wanted to say.

"Stewie Thurman –" muttered Dale.

"Stewie Thurman's *grandmother*," continued Stanley. "I can't fire you."

"OK," I said nodding, pretending that I understood him.

Seeing that I was confused, Dale explained things to me: "Stewie's grandmother died last night, so he has to leave camp to go to the funeral and, apparently, deal with this big family emergency and everything, so he's leaving camp today and won't be back."

Stanley sat up in his chair, both hands gripping the arm-rests, and declared, "And, I don't care, I am *not* going to leave a bunk with *two new* counselors, even if there's only two weeks left in the season, no matter what the other idiot counselor did." He glared at me, sat back down, and picked in his ear with the nail of his pinkie.

"You are a fortunate young man," sneered Jerry to me. "To have Mr. Marshak here as your employer."

"*Very* fortunate," added Harriet darkly.

My mind was swirling with conflicting thoughts. "*My* Stewie?" I said. I had last seen him at breakfast when he got that call from the Main Office. But his grandmother *dead* and Stewie *leaving camp*? And that's why they can't fire me? I didn't know exactly what to feel.

"So how did she die?" I asked.

"Oh, who cares??" Jerry spurted. "That's not the point! The point is –"

Stanley cut him off, talking straight to me, "The point is that you're staying in Bunk 9, but only by the skin of your teeth." He pinched his thumb and forefinger tightly, in demon-stration.

I tried not to react, and certainly not to smile.

"*But*," continued Stanley. "You stay on the straight and narrow, the rest of the summer. You understand me?"

"Yes, I do," I answered promptly, adding "Sir" after the slightest pause. I didn't think that my "sir" sounded too insin-cere, but I could sense that Jerry didn't buy it.

"Now get out of here," said Stanley.

I stood right up. "Right," I said. "And thank you, Sta – Mr. Marshak."

"Thank me for what?" he said. "If the old lady hadn't'a died, *you'd* be the one on your way out of here. Not...not...not –"

"Stewie Thurman," Dale finished the thought for him.

Seeing my chance to go, I turned and left the room, my head down, before anyone said anything else to me. I didn't want to look anybody in the eye or say anything to get myself into further trouble. I walked straight out the door of Stanley's house and into the fresh air.

Record of Events #12 – entered Sunday, 8:06 A.M.

~

It was amazingly good to be outside, to get a clean breath away from all those adults, all that craziness. I walked back to my bunk as fast as I could, thinking about Stewie, his grandmother, this "close call," all that I had to fix, *and* what they might be doing to Rachel at that very moment.

When I walked into the bunk, Stewie was almost all packed up, and half of the Doggies were crying. I went over to Stewie and put my arm around his shoulder.

"Hey, man," I said. "I just heard. I'm so sorry."

Stewie shrugged my hand off his shoulder and continued packing.

"Yeah," he mumbled. "Well. It's, uh . . . a surprise." His eyes wouldn't meet mine, but I understood.

"Was she very sick?" asked the teary Redheaded Doggy, sitting on his bed next to Stewie's.

"*All* old people are sick, you dummy," said the Doggy Bully.

"You need any help?" I asked Stewie.

"Nah," he grunted. "I'm good."

The Doggies were crowding around so I shooed them away.

"Come on!" I barked at them. "Leave Stewie alone."

"Yeah!" said the Fat Doggy. "Let the Groinmaster pack in peace."

I got the kids ready for General Swim. They hardly talked, and I could hear a few of them sniffling. I wonder if they would have cried for me, had I been the one who was leaving.

A couple of the Doggies came over to Stewie with a brown bag filled with contributions from everyone for his drive back home to Massachusetts: Hershey bars, gum, Charms, strips of candy buttons, and a couple of six-packs of Nik-L-Nips.

"This is for your trip," said the Fat Doggy.

"A *CARE* package," added the Smart Doggy.

Stewie turned and took the bag from them. "Thanks, Dogs."

He put the candy into his gym bag, but the Very Fat Doggy shrieked, "No! The chocolate'll melt!" He practically dove into Stewie's gym bag, retrieved the candy, took out the chocolate, and put it in a different bag.

"Keep these separate!" the Very Fat Doggy said very seriously to Stewie, handing him back the two bags of candy, but showing him which one had the chocolate, "And keep this one out of the sun. The sun is the *archenemy* of chocolate!"

"Come on, Dogs," I called them. "Into suits! Who has 'grounds' today? I don't want to see any wet suits on the floor after we get back from swim."

"Are we gonna see you later?" the Doggy With Braces asked Stewie, who was almost fully packed by now.

"Yeah," said Stewie, without turning around. "I'll see you all later."

I could see that he wanted to be left alone. "You guys go on down to swim!" I said. "I'll be right behind you. Go on! . . . And *you*, putz, don't forget your towel again!"

When the Doggies were gone, I changed into my bathing suit as Stewie clicked the locks closed on his last suitcase and checked his other belongings in a pile on his bed.

"You sure you're OK, man?" I said.

He just sighed.

"When the next laundry comes in, I'll send you your stuff," I said. "Leave me your address on my bed."

"Good idea," he said, turning to me with a little smile.

"It's good you have the Super-Coupe," I said. "So you can take everything with you."

"Right," he said, swinging the closed suitcase off the bed and onto the floor with a thump.

"You still gonna be here after swim?" I asked.

"Yeah," he said.

"Cause you shouldn't just go without saying goodbye," I said.

He wouldn't look me in the eye. I guess he was pretty close to his grandmother, with all his stories about his grand-parents' cranberry farm. I love both my grandmothers, but I don't know if I would leave camp if one of them died and not come back even after the funeral. Maybe I would. In any case, Stewie was going.

"I gotta get down to swim," I said. "They've been on my case like you wouldn't believe."

"I'd believe it," he said with a tight smile. "Life is full of surprises."

"Yeah," I said, standing at the open screen door. "Well . . . see ya."

"Take care, man," he said, giving me a twisted smile and a little power-fist salute. "Me gotta go now."

As I turned to go, he yelled out one last thing, "Hey! I'm gonna send you some *real* cranberry sauce for Thanksgiving! Beats the hell out of that Ocean Spray crap."

I let the door slam behind me and trotted down the steps toward the Boys' waterfront. I was sorry to see him go; he was basically a good guy and a good co-counselor. And that was the last time I ever saw Stewie Thurman.

I ran down the path to the Boys' waterfront in my flip-flops, thinking how insane the last few hours had been. I hadn't even gotten to talk to Rachel, to see what *she* was go-ing through. I wondered if she got the same going-over I got, but from Estelle. As I got down to the waterfront, I saw that the kids were already lining up to sign in at the Buddy Board.

I grabbed a long bamboo pole from the rack and went out onto the dock. I found an empty space in front of Area #3 and stood with my pole as the pairs of checked-in kids dove into the water.

My head was spinning with clashing thoughts. Would they move another counselor into Stewie's spot, or would I be covering Bunk 9 all alone? That didn't seem likely; I needed some kind of back-up, handling the Doggies. Leaning on my bamboo pole, I looked over at the Girls' waterfront across the lake where the girls were having *their* General Swim. At this distance, I couldn't see clearly, but I wondered if Rachel was over there. There was so much I had to tell her. And I wanted to see how she was holding up. Why were these people so dead-set against us? It was only a summer camp; the whole *idea* of a place like this was to fall in love and have fun. Instead, they wanted to bully and tyrannize us. It was pure jealousy. I wasn't a *bad* counselor. I just wanted to be with my girl; that didn't hurt anyone. I saw how the other counselors treated their kids. Even Stewie used to whack them occasionally or snap a towel at some kid's bare butt. I never hit any of the Doggies, no matter how much they might have deserved it. It was funny how righteous Stanley got about not wanting to leave a bunk with *two* new counselors, as if he were protecting the integrity of something precious. If it was that important to Stanley not to leave the bunk with a strange counselor, I should have asked him for more money right then and there! (Only kidding.)

The whistle blew for the buddy call, bringing me back to my senses on the dock. I moved the long bamboo pole from one hand to another, shielding my eyes from the glare of the sun. As the kids started to count off their numbers, I looked down into the deep, dark water of Area #3 and saw the vague flicker of something red on the bottom. At first, I thought that it was just a shaft of sunlight, going down into the water. Then I saw that it was a kid!

Instantly, I dropped my pole and dove straight down into the black water, pushing down off the edge of the dock. I pulled down with my arms and kicked my feet to dive deeper toward the Red, but my stupid flip-flops hampered me. I kicked them off and swam deeper. There, I saw the boy lying face down on the bottom of the lake – his *hair* was what was red. I swam frantically, ripping my way through the water, down to where he was. As I grabbed the kid's wrist and pulled him up off the sand, I saw that it was the Redheaded Doggy!

Holding his arm as tightly as I could, I pushed off the squishy bottom, jerked my body upwards, and swam to the surface as hard as I could. I kicked my legs to get some force upwards. My lungs were bursting and burning. Pulling as hard as I could with my other arm, I swam up toward the light above. I wouldn't let the Redheaded Doggy's arm go, even though I wasn't sure I could make it to the surface. I was about to let it all go when I burst into the open air. I gasped once, hauling the Redheaded Doggy up out of the water. Coughing and choking, I called "Help!"

People were already in the water, ready to help me. Someone took the Redheaded Doggy away from me just as someone else grabbed me from behind and pulled me up, clear of the water's surface. I was still gasping for breath, spitting out water as someone else yanked me up the ladder and onto the dock.

Choking, I was turned onto my stomach, but I could see that they had already put the Redheaded Doggy onto his back, and Sal was blowing air into his mouth. Kids were crying, standing all around as I tried to get my breath as water and mucus coughed out of my nose and mouth.

"Get back! Get back!" someone yelled. "Give 'em room!" said someone else.

I tried to get up, but someone pressed gently on my back and said, "Stay down, man, stay down. Get your breath." And that seemed like a good idea. My sides ached and I still was spitting up watery phlegm. I had this fiery, shooting pain in my forehead and my temples, but I was OK. I was alive. I was breathing. I was breathing, and so was the kid.

∿

The next thing I knew, we were back at Bunk 9. Someone had run to get Dr. K. from the Infirmary to check out the Redheaded Doggy and me. Stewie and his stuff were completely gone, but people hardly noticed. Now the Big Topic was how I saved the Redheaded Doggy's life; Stewie's leaving was old news. Dale came to the bunk to see the Redheaded Doggy, and Sal, who actually saved the Doggy with his Red Cross breathing, showed up too.

Sal sat on the end of my bed. I was sitting up after the doctor had examined me and given me the OK. I must have swallowed a gallon of lake water because I still felt a little queasy. But all that didn't matter; what mattered was that the kid didn't drown.

"Thanks, son," said Sal to me with real sincerity, patting my leg. "You did good. I've never lost a kid, and I didn't want to start now."

"Yeah," I said. "It was kinda bizarre. I was lucky that I saw him."

"No," said Sal. "*He*" – pointing to the Redheaded Doggy on his bed – "was lucky you saw him."

Of course I should never have had to save the kid in the first place; his swimming "buddy" – the Doggy With Braces – should have been watching out for him, and truthfully, the Redheaded Doggy wasn't a strong swimmer and probably shouldn't have been passed into Area #3 in the first place. But all that didn't matter now: I was a hero.

By Evening Line-Up, word had spread all over camp so that Jerry had to call me up to the flagpole, to help with the lowering of the flag. I gave Jerry a big smile and wave. I could see that he was burning inside. Not only did I still have my job, but he also had to be *nice* to me, "the hero."

After dinner, I was besieged on the front porch of the Mess Hall by all kinds of people congratulating me. Kids, other counselors, people who hadn't talked to me all summer came up and patted me on the back or said something nice. I was humble about the whole thing; it was lucky that I saw the flash of red in the water. I didn't say that if I hadn't been daydreaming about Rachel and our situation that I might have seen the Redheaded Doggy go underwater in the first place, and no heroism would have been required.

In the midst of all the well-wishers, I saw Rachel at the back of the crowd. I hadn't seen her since last night. I had so much to tell her *and* to ask her. Was *she* OK? That's really what mattered to me.

Fortunately, the crowd saw her . . . and parted. They opened a path for Rachel to walk straight to me and give me a huge, deep, warm, wet kiss. Everyone whooped and cheered at our kiss. I was a little embarrassed, but on the other hand, I didn't care. It was almost the end of the summer, and I was kissing my girl.

"Let's get out of here," I whispered to her.

I took Rachel's hand and broke through the crowd. People still cheered and clapped as I pulled Rachel free and down the stairs of the Mess Hall porch. As we walked away, hand-in-hand and temporarily free, I saw Jerry and Harriet and Estelle, standing together, all three of them, looking our way disapprovingly. For the moment, I didn't care: I had saved a kid's life, had nearly drowned *myself* don't forget, and I had Rachel.

It was Free Play, and we managed to elude the Doggies and her girls to steal away to the Quarry. As it turned out, Rachel wasn't so good, and the Quarry was the perfect place to talk.

As we walked down the trail to the Quarry, Rachel told me how they – by "they," she meant Harriet and Estelle – had been very mean to her about her going to Bailey's with me and breaking her curfew. They'd threatened to call up her parents, which was the last thing that Rachel wanted. She had to make a special plea to Stanley *not* to let them call her parents. He finally stopped them from making that call, but she said that he hadn't been very nice to her.

"Why are people so horrible?" she sighed.

"Because they're jealous. They see us, and they're just jealous," I replied, taking her hand as we walked through the cool forest. "People are unhappy and frustrated in their lives so they have to look outside themselves, to take revenge on others."

"That's what I see my parents do," she said, looking straight ahead, her expression grim. "I'm *really* looking forward to going home. It looks like I'm going to live with my mother, but they're gonna make me go to my father's house, every other weekend, wherever *that* is."

"Why?"

"I don't know! He never liked me around the house when he lived there. Why would he want me now?"

"To punish your mother," I said.

"Exactly!" she exclaimed, gripping my arm. She had a strong, bony little grip. "It doesn't make any sense."

"No," I said. "It makes *perverted* sense. People do what they *want* to do for their own selfish reasons. Nothing is accidental."

"How am I going to get through all this?" she wondered.

I turned her around by the shoulders to face me.

"I'm going to save you," I said, looking straight into her eyes. "That's how."

"OK," she said, trying to smile. "I believe you."

It was the right thing to say, and what's more, I meant it.

When we got to the Quarry, we saw that unfortunately we were not alone. Across the water, a bunch of Boonies were partying on the cliff on the far side. There must have been at least twenty kids and quite a few cars. We could hear the radio from one of the cars, blasting across the Quarry, but I couldn't tell what the song was. We couldn't actually blame them for invading "our" space; it was a beautiful evening to be outside, and it was really *their* hang-out, *their* space.

One guy in a bathing suit stood at the edge of the rock and, to our amazement, jumped off the cliff and straight-arrowed, feet first, right into the water, far, far below him.

"Wow," I said. "That guy is out of his mind!"

"I guess that water really *is* super deep," Rachel said. "No wonder they dump all their garbage there."

Another Boonie jumped into the water – head first, in a beautiful swan dive – to the whoops and cheers of his friends.

"It's amazing what people will do for some cheap thrills," I said.

"They just want to be free," she declared. "Just like everybody else."

I spun her toward me, took her in my arms and whispered in her ear, "Someday, it'll be us. I promise. . . . Someday."

We had to run through the forest to get back on time, but we made it.

Record of Events #13 – entered Monday, 9:01 P.M.

~

Of course I should have known that Jerry, Harriet, Estelle, etc. weren't finished with us. They could have left well enough alone, but they had to prove that they had the Upper Hand. (Why do adults always have to do that?) They couldn't fire me and kick me out of camp now that Stewie was gone, so what did they do? They found a way to send *Rachel* out of camp. The second-to-last week of camp was the big Senior Trip, a five-day excursion to a bunch of different places (this year, it was the Baseball Hall of Fame, the Howe Caverns, and some other touristy sites I can't remember), and at the last minute, they decided to make Rachel a *chaperone*.

"Bastards!" I said when she told me of their plan to send her away. "Who thought of that brilliant idea?"

"I don't know. Harriet? That scarecrow Estelle?" she said bitterly. "Who knows?"

"You could refuse to go," but even as I said it, I knew that that wasn't going to happen. She was still a C.I.T. and, technically, could still be ordered around.

"Oh, I wish I could," she winced. "But when they didn't call my parents after the Bailey's thing, I promised Stanley that I'd do everything by the letter until the end of camp."

"And this is how they treat you? By sending you away from me for five days?" I said.

She had no answer for that.

"We can do it," she said with weak enthusiasm.

"We have no choice."

The Five Days Without Rachel were a big lesson in Negative Learning. I learned that I did *not* like being without her. It was one thing to miss her for a few hours between morning and afternoon activities, or not see her overnight. But to go for five days without her was both actually depressing (I missed seeing, talking, touching, etc. her) and annoying (it was completely unnecessary and punitive). There were plenty of other C.I.T.s who could have gone on the Senior Trip. They picked Rachel just for spite, to keep us apart. And I haven't mentioned all the other things they did to keep us apart all summer, like making sure that we were on different teams for the Olympics – she was a Greek, I was a Roman. *Plus* they made sure that we were on opposite ends of the climactic Apache Relay. And the all-camp Sing too. She was a Martian, and I was a Buccaneer. You should have seen her, her skin all painted green, dancing the "Martian Monkey." It caused a sensation in the camp and greatly displeased Estelle, Harriet, and all the other prudes, blue-noses, and killjoys.

I learned that not only was the world a lot less fun when Rachel wasn't around, *I* was a lot less fun. I was grouchy and impatient with the Doggies, and I didn't particularly care that I was. Dale moved Sid, from Marcus' bunk, over to us to take Stewie's place, but he proved to be almost completely worthless. He was a warm, fat body, and that was about it. All Sid did was read *Mad* magazine and steal candy from the Doggies. He was like a big Doggy himself, only he was supposed to help me watch the kids, not just lie on his bed, chain-smoke Viceroys, and pass gas. For two of the Five Days Without Rachel, it rained like some monsoon season somewhere. I had never seen anything like it; the rain came down like *nails*. So the kids were restricted all day to "bunk games," which meant sitting on their beds, reading comic books or playing quiet games. For me, it was two days of napping, brooding, and breaking up fights over *Battleship*, *Sorry*, and a coveted PEZ dispenser in the shape of Wonder Woman. Not to mention a maddening day-and-a-half long argument among the Doggies (and idiot Sid) about which superpower would be the best to possess. My personal choice? Invisibility.

With Rachel gone, I also got a new level of teasing from people.

"So, how's the horny bachelor life?" said Eddie from the Bronx as he threw an arm around me roughly on the way up to Evening Line-Up.

"It sucks," I said.

He laughed, but I didn't think it was all that funny. I especially didn't like it when Jerry, passing on the way into dinner, cracked, "Feeling lonely, hero?" He walked away before I could think of a fast comeback that didn't have a curse word attached. Something to take the buzz off the Crew Cut. It was probably best that I kept my mouth shut. He was still my boss, and it was only a few days until the end of camp. I could hang on and hold my tongue that long. But what I especially didn't like was that Jerry started punishing the Doggies as a way to get at me, giving them extra chores like "policing the grounds" around the Mess Hall or his Shak (which meant picking up cigarette butts and any little scraps of paper or trash on the ground). It was one thing to go after Rachel and me; it was quite another thing – completely unnecessary and unfair – to penalize the Doggies.

I spent two hours being talked to by Norm the Bug Guy about the cutthroat faculty politics at the Bronx High School of Science and why I should become a botany major at Columbia. Sheesh!

The only thing that made the Five Days Without Rachel somewhat bearable was that, a couple of times, I was approached by some of the prettier girl counselors. I guess the fact that I was Rachel's boyfriend gave me some kind of stamp of approval. (If Rachel chose me, I *must* have something to offer.) When Rachel was around, she monopolized my time.

But now that she was gone, if only temporarily, I was free to be approached by other girls – something Rachel would not have exactly appreciated. She would have been jealous, and I take that as a compliment.

It was on the fourth endless afternoon. I was laying on the sidelines, watching the sweaty Doggies stumble around the burnt August grass, attempting to play soccer, when up stepped Sharon Spitzer, the blonde, unapproachable swimming goddess. Towering over me, she shaded her eyes with both hands, looking down.

"Hi," she said softly. "I'm Sharon."

For most guys, that would be enough for them to declare their ever-lasting love. Instead, I just said, "Hi yourself."

She was wearing white short shorts and a little halter top. Her skin was brown and her hair was golden. She swayed over me, trying various angles to see in the bright sun.

"You belong to Rachel, don't you," she said, as both a statement and a question.

"You could say that," I replied, squinting up at her. "You could also say that she belongs to me."

Sharon gave a little snort of a laugh then sat down suddenly, right next to me in the grass, cross-legged. She was wearing silver sandals and her toenails were painted pink.

"Y'know, I know Rachel pretty well," she purred. "I live near the Princes, and my parents and her parents belong to the same beach club."

"Aren't you all lucky?" I said.

She snort-laughed again cautiously, judging me.

"Rachel is a sweet girl," she said in a way that made it sound like an insult. Sharon was a few years older than me, probably a junior or senior in college, and obviously enjoyed talking down to people. I didn't mind; I just looked at her pretty face and perfect form, and let her condescend to me as long she wanted, so long as I could enjoy the view. A girl this pretty would never have talked to me at home, unless to ask me some kind of favor like help with homework or the answers to a test.

I confess that I liked the person that I had become at Mooncliff, even if it was a big front. I really had no business being with beautiful girls.

"I agree," I said.

"I've watched her grow up," she continued. "Here, and at home."

"Good for you," I said, playing with her.

"Are you sure you know what you're getting into?" she asked, as if she knew some nasty little secret. She had a little gold chain around her neck that caressed her throat just so. I told myself that I should get one of those for Rachel.

"Does anybody?" I answered back, not giving an inch.

Sharon tossed her head, freeing some strands of blonde hair that were sticking to her brow. It was a beautiful move, similar to Rachel's head toss.

"Have you *met* the Princes?" she asked.

"No," I said measuredly.

She laughed again, a long ripple of rich-girl's laughter. She finally provoked me enough so that I had to defend myself, at least a little.

"I'm not in love with her parents," I said, sitting up higher.

"'Love'?" she repeated, a note of mockery in her voice. "Are you 'in love' with Rachel?"

I hesitated. It was none of her business.

"It's none of your business," I said. "But the answer is . . . yes." I was proud of being in love with Rachel: Why be ashamed of it?

Sharon snickered and sat back, hugging her long, smooth legs into her body. She looked me over, unabashedly evaluating me.

"She's had a lot of boyfriends before you," she said.

"Eric?" I snapped right back, knowingly. "I know about the past. I *care* about the future."

I sounded more confident than I felt, but Sharon seemed somewhat convinced.

"Rachel's lucky," she said. "Rachel Prince has always been a fairly lucky girl. But" – she stopped for suspense –"I think *you're* the one who's going to need some luck."

She rose as quickly as she'd sat down. I didn't move. Her legs went all the way up to those tiny white shorts.

"Thanks for the wisdom," I said, shielding my eyes. "... Sharrrron." I liked saying her name, drawn out like that.

"On second thought," she said, backing away from me. "If I were you, I wouldn't worry too much. Summer things never last."

She smiled, turned, and walked away, satisfied with our encounter, knowing that she got in the last zinger. She knew that I was watching as she walked away; I could tell by the bounce in her step and that perfect sway of her perfect . . . everything. She was not a nice person and yet I was still flattered by her attention. Such is the power of pretty girls. She had that in common with Rachel, that power. I was glad that Rachel used her power for me, and not against me. And even if what Sharon said about "summer things" had some objective truth, it didn't necessarily apply to Rachel and me. We could be the exception to the rule.

ᴎ

The day that the Seniors were coming back was the worst. The Doggies knew that I missed Rachel and had teased me for the first four days. I didn't let it bother me too much, but on the fifth day, it really got on my nerves.

I was walking the Doggies back from basketball, a game that they had lost to Bunk 7 – kids *younger* than they were. Dale awarded Bunk 7 free canteen at the Snack Shak while we got to walk back to the bunk across the hot campus in the scorching sun, across grass so burnt it smelled like hay.

"You blew three lay-ups, you fat can o' crap," the Doggy Bully gave the Fat Doggy a push.

"Oh, yeah?" answered the Fat Doggy, "Then why couldn't you guard Anton? He kept running past you like you were, you were –"

"Sue Storm, the Invisible Girl!" cracked the Smart Doggy. Which made everyone except the Doggy Bully laugh hard.

"Shut up, jerkwad!" said the Doggy Bully as he reached out to grab the Smart Doggy, who dodged his paw and ran for cover behind me.

"Shut up, the lot of you!" I said. "You *all* played terribly, losing to those babies! It was a total and complete group effort!"

That bit of truth quieted them down until we got back to the bunk, but then the Doggy Bully made the mistake of opening his mouth again.

"And *you're* not much of a coach either," he muttered. The Doggies giggled at that.

I was not in the mood for his backtalk and made clear, "You think my coaching taught you to dribble the ball off your feet three times in the second half? You think my coaching let Anton practically *walk* to the basket whenever he gave you a feint? You think my coaching taught you guys to miss twelve out of sixteen foul shots as a team? Don't all of you be stupid together!"

I was harsh with them, but they deserved it.

After a few sullen moments, the Fat Doggy mumbled, "He just misses *Rachel*."

The Doggies snickered and I let it go, but then the Smart Doggy added, "He just misses Rachel's *cuppies*."

I flashed with anger at that and grabbed the Smart Doggy by the back of his neck.

"What did you say, smart mouth? What did you say??" I shouted at him, bending him over, squeezing maybe a little too hard.

"Are you gonna shut your trap, or what? What?? You guys gonna say anything about Rachel anymore, everrrr???" I yelled, holding him there frozen until they all shut up, scared.

I released the Smart Doggy from my grip, and he started to sniffle.

"Now get on your beds and shut your mouths!" I shouted, and they instantly obeyed. I walked up and down the center aisle of the bunk, glowering, making sure that they knew I was really angry this time. It was pin-drop quiet. I could see the red marks from my fingers on the back of the Smart Doggy's neck. To this day, I still feel bad about doing that. Sticks and stones, etc. I should never've put my hands on him. He was a good kid, curled up crying on his bed; he just said the wrong thing at the wrong time. Sometimes there are consequences when a person says the wrong thing at the wrong time.

On the night of the fifth day, the buses from the Senior Trip were late getting back. They were supposed to get back at eight o'clock at night, but the Main Office got reports from the road that they were delayed. I was edgy all day. The Doggies asked me, "Aren't you happy that Rachel's coming back today?" I told them to shut up and mind their own business. I waited by the Main Office – in the rain, under an umbrella – until almost midnight, until the buses finally did pull in. I'd had hopes of seeing Rachel, but when it got so late, I knew that they would hustle the Seniors and everybody else back to their bunks. As it approached midnight, it seemed futile to wait much longer, but I did. Even under an umbrella, I was getting pretty wet. But I thought that even if I didn't actually talk to her, I would make sure that she saw me waiting for her. And she would appreciate that. And that seemed to be enough reason to wait out in the rain.

I didn't talk to her until after breakfast the next day on the Mess Hall porch where I waited for her. She ran to me, smiling back tears of joy.

"I missed you so much," she said softly, into my neck. I felt her sweet breath.

"You have no idea," I murmured.

We kissed just once, because there were people nearby, but it was better than nothing.

"I saw you last night," she said. "But they made us go straight to the –"

"I know, I know," I said, standing close to her.

"I really don't like to be apart from you," she said very simply, as if she were reading my thoughts. And that was *exactly* what I thinking at that moment.

"I bought you a present," she continued.

"*You're* my present," I said.

"No, you'll *like* it," she teased.

"All I want is you," I insisted.

She really liked when I said that.

"When are you free?" she purred.

"When we get our asses out of here," I said, meaning all of Mooncliff.

"No," she giggled. "I mean *today*."

"I don't know," I said. "This afternoon, *if* Sid shows up to take the Doggies to tennis."

"Well, that's when you'll get your present," she said. "I mean your *first* present. Your *real* present is gonna have to wait until tonight."

It turned out that my first present was an "I Fell In Love at the Baseball Hall of Fame" T-shirt, with crossed baseball bats inside a big heart, and the second present was private . . . and fantastic.

Record of Events #14 – entered Tuesday, 3:51 P.M.

∾

The last days of the Mooncliff summer were like a roller coaster – intense, fun, and chaotic, all at the same time. You wanted desperately to get off and yet it all seemed to end too soon. Regular activities came to a halt as the schedule was filled with special events and the preparation for them: the Scavenger Hunt; the Awards Dinner; the Masked Ball; the Burning of the Lake. The campers' empty trunks were delivered back to the bunks, and we had to start packing up the kids' stuff to be shipped back to their homes. Some Doggies had Arts and Crafts projects to complete. The Doggy Bully and the Smart Doggy wanted to finish some Red Cross swimming badges. And not only did I have my Bunk 9 responsibilities, Dale started to lean on me for extra things to do. Eddie from the Bronx somehow got poison ivy in both his crotch and armpits and was laid up painfully in the infirmary for several days, so I wound up watching Bunk 7 at times when I should have been off. Dale also put me charge of the Inter section of the Scavenger Hunt.

"I want you to do this for me. I want to beat Estelle, bad. The other guys are nice enough, but they're, y'know, *cretins*," he said. "That Dolin dude! Couldn't find his own ass with two hands and a *map*! . . . OK?"

I couldn't say no.

But for Rachel and me, the last days meant the same thing: When would we get to see each other next? When would we get to be alone? And any delay, any obstacle started to cause some friction between us. Not to mention the fact that our days at Mooncliff were numbered, and who really knew what was going to happen after that.

"I *waited* for you after lunch," she said. "I got Sara to let me off, and you weren't there!"

"I'm sorry," I said. "But I got roped into setting up the Mess Hall for the Awards Dinner tonight."

"Then why didn't you tell me?" she asked. "I would have come and helped you."

"How was I gonna tell you?"

"Send one of your kids!"

"To Girls' Campus??"

"That's not where I was waiting!"

She could become angry quickly, and only more so in these last tense days.

"Once we're back home," she said. "You're going to abandon me. I know it."

"Are you serious?" I shot back. "You're the best thing that ever happened to me."

"You'll go off to college, to Columbia. You'll be in the City and forget about me."

"And you'll be home. You'll go back to Eric."

That stopped her. Maybe I shouldn't've brought it up, said his name, but I couldn't help it. I was worried what would happen when Rachel was out of my sight, *even in the future*, and I couldn't un-hear what that girl said: that Rachel still loved him.

"What are you talking about? That's ridiculous," she said in amazement.

"I'm sorry," I said. "But I have to ask you –"

"Don't you trust me?" she said, her eyes penetrating me. "I told you that is all over. It was a joke! Over a long time ago! I love you completely – with all my heart. I told you that. I'm telling you that right now! And if that's not enough, I don't know what else to say –"

"OK, OK, OK," I said, putting my arms around her. "You don't have to say anything else."

And I silenced her with a kiss.

"All I want is you," I whispered. "I know what's good . . . and we're good. Right?"

She nodded and nuzzled against my chest. I was good at calming her down. I think that was one of the reasons she liked me. She needed calming. On the one hand, she loved being headstrong and willful. She was a spoiled, rich, pretty girl; I knew that. But I could tell that she was also scared: Scared of what waited for her at home. Scared of how her parents' troubles might overwhelm her own life. Scared of fitting back into a high school that she didn't like in the first place. And scared, I guess – I *hope* – of losing me.

At the Awards Dinner, the Doggies won a couple of honors. The Smart Doggy won an All-Around Camper Award, the Doggy With Braces won a Most Improved Camper, and the Doggy Bully won a couple of sports awards. They gave me, along with several other people, a rousing Hero's Hurrah for saving the Redheaded Doggy. (It really seemed to burn Jerry that I got such a nice ovation. I guess that some people in the Shak liked me.) But in the "gag" awards at the end of the evening, the Senior Girls who had cooked up that segment gave me – *are you ready for this? I shouldn't even say it* – a copy of the Mann Act. It got a big laugh from the counselors and another slow burn from the Crew Cut, along with disapproving looks from Harriet, Estelle, and Stanley.

"What's the Mann Act?" asked Rachel when I saw her for just the briefest moment on the crowded porch after the dinner ended, way too late for the kids.

"It's a joke, and actually wrong," I said, being bumped by somebody. "I never took you across state lines."

"Let's move it, people!" sang out Jerry, clapping his hands. "Nighty-night!"

"Nighty-night!" I said to her softly. She had two tired girls hanging on her, so I just let her go with a smile.

"See you tomorrow," she whispered.

"No!" said one of the girls to Rachel. "You're helping us pack, Rachel."

"*All day!*" said the other girl.

Rachel looked stricken as they dragged her away. "Someday this will all end," she joke-mourned.

"That's what I'm afraid of," I said as the Doggies pulled me in the opposite direction.

≁

The whole next day I spent helping the Doggies pack their trunks. What a pain. Everything annoyed me about the day, especially the incessant squabbling among the Doggies about who-belonged-to-what. At one point, I wound up tearing a big *Archie* annual comic book in half, Solomonically declaring, "I now pronounce you *both* Jugheads!"

Sid had disappeared someplace, so I was left to fill out all the trunk tags alone, which were color-coded for where the trunks had to go: Westchester (red), Jersey (orange), Manhattan (green), Long Island (blue), etc.

There were also these Camper Performance Reports that we were supposed to hand in every week, commonly called "the B.M. charts" because there was a column to be checked off, indicating whether said camper had a proper bowel movement that day. I am not kidding about this. That was in addition to all the activities that were supposed to be listed, along with a wide column for special achievements. Anyway, I hadn't kept up with the B.M. charts since Stewie left, and now I had to finish them off to hand in to Dale, who had to hand them in to Jerry. No paychecks were to be released until all the B.M. charts were handed in. So I had to sit in my bunk and make up stuff to finish them off while the Doggies packed and fought and packed and fought.

"What did we do last Wednesday night?" I called out, racking my brain for something I probably wanted to forget.

"The Haunted Campfire!" the Smart Doggy answered promptly.

"Right!" I said, quickly writing down the same thing on all ten charts spread out on the bed before me. I could get them finished before . . . before *what*? Rachel was stuck with her bunk too. There was no place to go. There was so little time left, and I was far from where I wanted to be. I should be with Rachel, getting the most out of the last days of Mooncliff and planning our first days back in the real world. Instead, I was calculating and recording the bowel movements of nameless children whom I would never see again after Thursday.

The two days before the Burning of the Lake on the last night of camp, Dale came to me with a proposition that changed things.

"How'd you like to work Close-Down?" he asked me.

Close-Down was three days of work after the campers left, closing everything up in Mooncliff that needed to be closed, putting away what needed to be put away, and essentially reversing everything that we did during Orientation. I knew about Close-Down because the other counselors had mentioned it. It was excellent pay for a few days' work and was a plum that Dale, who was in charge, handed out to his favorites.

"Me?" I said.

"Yeah," he said, putting his hand on my shoulder. "I was thinking that sometimes we weren't so fair to you about some things, so I thought if you wanted to work Close-Down, I'd be happy to use you."

"Wow," I said. "Let me think about it, but *yeah*, I could use the money! Thanks!"

I started to think about telling Rachel, about calling home and telling them that I'd be a few days late. Then I thought of something else.

I shouted after Dale as he was walking away, "Dale! How will Jerry like that I'm working Close-Down?"

Dale turned and smirked, saying, "Jerry don't run Close-Down."

I was excited to tell Rachel. On the one hand, it would postpone our getting together right after camp, but on the other hand, it would give me a lot more money for the fall; money that would help us all through the autumn and beyond.

But when I told her, I didn't get the response I was hoping for.

"That spoils all my plans!" she said, her blue eyes literally darkening.

"What 'plans'?" I asked her.

"Everything!" she said. "You don't understand. My parents won't let me go out with you until they meet you –"

"Fair enough," I commented.

"But they're not living together anymore," she continued. "So to get them together to meet you is not an easy thing. I've gotten them to agree to meet you at our beach club the day after we got home."

"Your 'beach club'?" I said, trying not to sound derisive. I already knew about their beach club from Sharon Spitzer.

"And now that's all gone for nothing!" she said, right in my face.

"I'm sorry, Rache'," I said, "but don't you see? Getting offered Close-Down is a good thing. I just can't turn down that much money for only a few days' work."

"How much are they paying you?" she asked.

I told her.

"Is that all?" she said, raising her voice. "To hell with the money! I can give you that out of my birthday money, for God's sake!"

That was a bit of a jolt to me: I knew that we came from different "worlds" (towns, income, family situation, etc.), but her disparaging comment about how much I was going to earn for Close-Down made that fact "real-er" than it had ever been before. And, truthfully, it was annoying; I'm not rich and spoiled.

"Well . . . I'm sorry," I said without feeling apologetic. "But it's a lot of money to me, and I can't turn it down. It's only a couple of days, and then I'll be able to buy you –"

"I don't want you to buy me anything!" she cut me off.

I tried to reason with her.

"Why didn't you tell me you had things set up with your parents?" I asked her.

"I didn't want to tell you until it was set," she answered. "I just got off the phone with her this morning, and it was not particularly pleasant. But I did it because I want things to be right for us when we get home."

"So do I!" I said. "That's why I can't turn down the Close-Down money. You don't realize it now, but I'm doing this for us."

She looked at me and said bitterly, "Why are you trying to spoil the last days of camp?"

We argued it all around again, with no different conclusion. We were both very stubborn people, but I wasn't going to give in. I had already promised Dale, and as I said before, I could use the money.

"I'm sorry," I said. "But there are certain things I have to do."

She turned and walked away from me, but I couldn't play her spoiled, rich-girl games, not every time. There were certain things on which I had to take a stand, at least at the beginning.

The last night of Mooncliff was the Burning of the Lake ceremony. It was the crowning ritual of the summer, symbolizing the end of blah-blah-blah, to be renewed next summer with more yak-yak-yak. Even though I knew that this was to be my one and only summer at Mooncliff – there was no way that Stanley would re-hire me even if I wanted to come back – I nonetheless felt a pang of emotion, thinking about the past eight weeks. Even though I'd had more than my share of trouble here, this place would always be special to me because, trouble or not, it was where I met Rachel.

Of course, the Burning of the Lake was not an actual fire. It was a fireworks show, set out on the swimming area floats and some rowboats that had been moved into position around the lake that afternoon. There was a big cookout with burgers, hot dogs, corn on the cob, and unlimited pitchers of bug juice, spread out in the setting sun on the hillside sloping down to the lakefront. Everybody brought a white Mooncliff T-shirt for friends to autograph with the green Magic Markers that were spread around in #10 cans. The P.A. system played Motown and Beatle songs, and everybody was pretty mellow, with the food and the scene and the sense of it all ending.

When the sun was almost completely down, the last of the light dying on the lake, Jerry tapped his microphone, and he and Harriet began the ceremony of the Burning of the Lake. With some fake-Indian drums thumping behind him as torches were being lit one by one, Jerry, wearing a very impressive, slightly ridiculous feathered headdress that hung way down his back, commenced reading the text of the ceremony. It was a corny hodge-podge of an "Indian legend" about the purification of the Spirit of the Lake to sanctify our memories and cleanse our souls for the challenges of the Harvest Season. (It was also a big fat commercial for Mooncliff, subtly urging all the campers to be sure to tell their parents that they had to come back next summer, to complete the Great Cycle of Nature or something like that.) The "text" was solemn and silly, but taking it semi-seriously was part of the fun. I looked down at the Doggies sitting on their blankets, faces just visible in the glow of the torchlight, and they were all absolutely enraptured. *"Many summers ago, when the Earth was still new . . ."*

Once the actual fireworks started to the blasting sound of recorded Sousa, with the Doggies completely engrossed, I melted away from them and drifted toward the back of the mass of campers. As the fizz of bottle rockets and storm of sparklers began shooting up from the floats on the lake, with all the shrieking and laughing and whooping in the dark excitement, I found Rachel in the deep shadows of the trees behind the crowd, where she knew I'd be looking for her. We moved together naturally and kissed deeply. I could see that she had been crying.

"I get very emotional at these things," she whispered into my neck, looking down, catching her breath softly between kisses.

"That's OK," I said. "Emotion is good. In fact, in some situations, emotion is required."

"I hate when we fight," she said. "Let's never fight again."

We kissed until she broke away and said, looking searchingly into my eyes, "I just don't want to be like my mother. I just want someone to love me for *me*. Is that so terrible?"

I saw real fear in her eyes, a deep fear, maybe for her, the deepest.

"No," I said as tenderly as I could. "It's not so terrible."

We kissed again as the fireworks exploded in the sky, with *ooohs* and *ahhhs* all around us. We held each other as Roman candles, cherry bombs, and sparkler wheels "burned" the lake. Star mines boomed in the hills, and all the kids screamed. The embers from the sparklers and the multi-stage rockets, the exploding shells and mid-air flowers flew up into the velveteen sky and disappeared into the stars.

As the whole Mooncliff population, arm in arm, sang the camp Alma Mater, whose treacly words I won't even reproduce here – and, believe me, they're worse to the tune of "Danny Boy" – Rachel and I kissed and held each other tight against Time.

"I'm scared to go home," she said, hiding in my arms. "I shouldn't be, but I am."

"We're going to be fine," I said, trying to sound as comforting as I could. "I promise you, things will be better once we're out of here: We'll be free. No Jerry, no Harriet, no schedule to obey."

"But they'll be other things –" she said.

"And we'll *deal* with them!" I assured her. "As long as we're together, nothing can hurt us."

"But what am I supposed to do when I get home," she asked. "And you're not there for three days?"

"Do everything that you have to do, and wait for me," I said. "We're going to do everything right. We're going to make this last forever."

"I love you so much," she said, which is exactly what I wanted her to say. As the last thunder of fireworks exploded in the sky, she gave me a kiss that could last me, if not forever, then for the next three days.

Record of Events #15 – entered Tuesday, 9:15 A.M.

~

The last morning of camp was drizzly, cool, and foggy, right out of a 1940s black-and-white movie. I almost expected to see Bogart in a trench coat leaning against one of the buses, a cigarette dangling from his lips, amused by the whole sorry human scene. The rain made everything more difficult. All the wet gear cluttered up the bunks and the Mess Hall, dripping on everybody and complicating everything. One stupid Doggy lost a galosh (one galosh, two galoshes?). I had the kids strip the sheets off their beds one last time. They needed breakfast – and I needed a major transfusion of coffee – but we all wanted to just get the kids on the bus and get them out of there. It was time.

Coming out of the Mess Hall, I could see the buses lined up across the baseball fields. Rachel and her bunk hadn't come out yet, but it was all too insanely busy to spend time waiting. During breakfast, the bus lists for the kids, fresh and warm from the mimeograph machine in the Main Office and fragrant with intoxicating purple ink, were handed out by Esther, and one of the Doggies thought that he was on the wrong bus. So in addition to making sure the kids had made and packed a paper-bag lunch (cold cuts or peanut butter and jelly) for the bus ride, and getting them back to the bunk for a last clean-up, now I had to deal with this misrouted Doggy.

I ran up to the Main Office, got my misplaced Doggy onto the right bus, and made it back to the bunk, completely soaked, so that when Jerry called for the Inter boys on the P.A. system, we were barely ready. (Damn Stewie for not being there!) I made sure that the Doggies had picked up all their stuff, eye-swept the floor one last time, and we were outta there.

It had not stopped raining, but it was a little lighter, so our soggy march up to the buses was a bit easier. The Doggies' spirits were high, all excited and giddy, so one last time they sang the *Rawhide* theme that gave them their name. "*Keep rollin', rollin', rollin'* . . . *Keep them doggies rollin'* . . ." And we walked fast, in lockstep, and laughed at the "*move 'em on, head 'em up, head 'em up, move 'em on*" hash they always made of that part. We didn't care. The momentum of the moment carried us up to the buses.

Organized in front of the array of monster silver buses, Harriet in a perfect green Mooncliff canvas poncho yelled through a bullhorn, reading from a clipboard, ordering "My bus captains!" and "My bus monitors!" around at high volume. They had all done this before, but it still felt disorderly. Everything was loud, with kids rushing everywhere. I checked one more time that all the Doggies had the right color-coded tags. The drizzle seemed to hold the bus fumes in the air, souring the scene. Diesel and rain: never a good combination, and so soon after breakfast. Already I heard the sound of one kid throwing up; at least it wasn't one of my kids.

I looked for Rachel down the line but didn't see her in all the mess and bustle of umbrellas and the crowd, spread across the baseball field. I wanted to go find her, but I was stuck with the Doggies with no other counselor to spell me. Sid had un-surprisingly disappeared.

"God, it stinks around here," said Marcus, sidling up next to me, dripping rain off his Mooncliff baseball cap, carrying his big knapsack.

"Tell me about it," I replied, still scanning the crowd for Rachel.

"So you're working Close-Down?" he asked, already knowing the answer. "I wish Dale'd asked me," he continued. "I could use the bread. Damn, these buses stink."

"They have to keep the motors running so the air-conditioning stays on," I said. "Otherwise, they'd get too hot inside."

"Please don't talk reason!" he said, "I'm almost past my puke-point!"

"Connecticut Bus Number One! That's *yellow tags only*!" shouted Harriet through her bullhorn. "Connecticut Bus Number One – yellow tags only! Let's load 'em up here at the first bus on my left! My left!!"

"That's me! I'm going back by way of my uncle's house in Stamford," said Marcus. "So call me, Brainiac!" he shouted, backing away. "And I'll tell you what *really* happened this summer." With a smirk, he waved and was gone down the row of buses. I was going to return one last wisecrack, but I let it go. Strange guy; OK to hang with but down-deep unhappy.

The Doggies started to nag me, all at once. They were all restless and who could blame them, standing in the rain for too long.

"When are we getting on the buses?" a stupid Doggy asked.

"When they call you!" I answered impatiently.

The Very Fat Doggy pulled on my sleeve and whispered up to me, "Hey . . . Hey! . . . I gotta go." Meaning the bathroom.

Great! "You'll have to hold it," I told him.

"New Jersey Bus Number One! Orange tags only!" called Bullhorn Harriet. "Let's load 'em up here, right next to me on my right!"

"New Jersey!" said the Doggy Bully. "That's me!"

"Good!" I said. "Go! Get out of here!" and I pushed him out of our line and toward his bus as the other Doggies shouted goodbyes. One down, nine to go.

"Manhattan Bus Number One! Green tags! You're next!"

The Very Fat Doggy pulled down on my shoulder and squealed with discomfort, "I gotta drain my lizard! *Real, real bad.*"

I turned on him and growled, "Tie a knot in it!" I looked around for someone to watch the Doggies, but no friendly face was there to help me.

"Long Island Bus Number One!" called the Bullhorn. "Long Island *blue* tags! Start your loading, Long Island Bus Number One! Blue tags only!"

That could be Rachel's bus! She was on *one* of the Long Island buses – there were three of them, the largest contingent.

The Very Fat Doggy was starting to dance in place next to me, crossing his legs. "Hey, I really-really-*really* gotta go!"

"OK!" I said, "Come with me!"

I turned to the Smart Doggy and gave him an order. "You listen for the announcements from Harriet and make sure all these guys get on their right buses, OK?"

"Yeah! Definitely!" he answered.

"Good!" I patted him on the shoulder of his wet poncho. "I'll be right back!" To the Very Fat Doggy, I commanded, "Follow me!"

I took off, hustling across the soggy grass behind the lines of campers waiting for the call to board their buses. I glanced behind me to make sure the Very Fat Doggy was with me. As I passed by the lines of Junior boys and Junior girls and their counselors, there were so many umbrellas up that I couldn't see around them. I knew Rachel had to be somewhere around there.

The Very Fat Doggy pulled on my sleeve, whining, "Where can I go?"

I pointed to a girls' bunk that was back about fifty yards from the ball field and said, "Look! Go over there to that bunk!"

"But that's a *girls'* bunk!" he protested.

"OK!" I said, pointing him to another place. "Then go over there and go in those trees!"

"That's gross! Someone will see."

"Long Island Bus Number Two!" called Harriet's bull-horn. "First call for Long Island Bus Number Two!! Blue tags only!"

"Then go in your pants!" I roared at the kid. I had no more time for kids and turned away from him to go find Rachel.

And there she was, looking for me! Our eyes met at the same time, and she rushed straight to me. She was rain-soaked and beautiful, blinking away the tears and raindrops from her eyes.

"I've been crying all morning! I'm all cried out!" she said, laughing and crying as she fell into my arms. We kissed deeply. I heard some *woo-hoos* from somewhere, but I didn't care. And I don't think Rachel did either.

"Bus Number One for Westchester! Red tags only!" went the bullhorn call. "Bus Number One for Westchester!" It started to rain harder.

Rachel broke for air. "You promised to keep the summer from ending."

"No!" I tried to cheer her. "This will be better! I'll call you tonight, and I'll see you in three days! We're going to do everything right."

"I believe you," she said passionately, trying her hardest to show me that she agreed.

"Second call for Long Island Bus Number One!"

"Oh, no!" she said, "That's me, and I'm a bus monitor! Oh, God, I knew this would happen. I gotta go!"

"That's OK," I said. "We can *do* this!"

She started to drift away from me. "Promise you'll love me forever," she said. "No matter what happens."

She kissed me once more with perfect lips, then pushed away from me.

"I promise!" I said, waving goodbye with a hand that seemed to belong to someone else as she turned and ran away.

And then she was gone, disappeared into the crowd. Just like that. Really gone. Our perfect summer ended, right then and there. And in some ways, I might just as well have ended my life, right then and there.

Then it hit me: *"No matter what happens."* Why did she say that? What did she mean? Was she already fatalistically kissing us goodbye? I wanted to run after her and ask her what she meant, and to take it back, but that was impossible. I had to go back and make sure that all the Doggies got onto their rightful buses.

And they did. At least, when I got back to the Bunk 9 line, no one was there, so I presumed that they all got onto their buses. I guess even the Very Fat Doggy found his way back from the bathroom and onto a bus.

The first bus in line pulled away . . . and then the second and the third. Those of us left behind stood and waved. I couldn't figure out which bus was Rachel's, so I waved at them all. They were all the same: silver and smelly and gone.

Esther from the Main Office, the little old grey owl, came up and stood next to me, waving a green-and-white Mooncliff pennant as the last bus finally left.

"Another summer," she chirped. "Shot to hell." Which made me laugh, coming out of the mouth of this tiny old lady. And because she might have been right.

~

For the rest of the day, Dale worked us hard, us being the dozen or so counselors who stayed back to work Close-Down. Fortunately the rain soon stopped and the sun came out, making things slightly easier. But we traded rain for humidity, so the work was still quite strenuous. We started doing the reverse of all the jobs we did during Orientation: collecting, hauling, and storing the mattresses and bedsprings; rolling up and storing the tennis nets; taking all the boats and floats out of the lake and putting them into dry dock; etc. Of course, we didn't do all those things on the first day; it was a full three days of heavy labor, and we earned every penny we got.

By the end of that first day, the only thing I could think of was getting to the pay phone outside the Main Office by 8:00 p.m. to call Rachel, just as I had promised. On our first night apart, I refused to be late for our first phone call.

And I wasn't. I was exhausted and muscle sore, but I wasn't late. Dale gave us time after a back-breaking afternoon of hauling, scraping, sanding, and painting all the rowboats and canoes for a late swim in the perfectly placid, empty lake. The lake – in fact, the whole *camp* – was somewhat weird, empty of people. It felt haunted and somehow just *wrong*.

I got up to the Main Office well before 8:00. I could see the clock on the wall through the window. The rest of the guys had gone into Bailey's after eating dinner in a corner of the big, mostly empty Mess Hall, but I begged off. I suppose I could have called her from Bailey's pay phone, but that would have been noisy and I might have missed 8:00. Besides, I didn't want to go to Bailey's without her.

I dialed Rachel's home number, reading carefully from the piece of pink stationery she had written it on, even though I had already memorized it. I practiced what I was going say if her mother answered, how bright and happy I'd sound. I'd say, *"Hello, is Rachel there?"* But I wished that Rachel herself would answer; I hoped that she'd be waiting by the phone for my call. I cleared my throat and went over in my mind the things I wanted to say before I realized that no one was answering. I let the phone ring eighteen times, I think, when I stopped counting the rings. Then I hung up.

OK, she wasn't home. Her mother – or her father – probably took her out to dinner. On her first night back, that made sense. In the wake of their divorce, I hoped that at least *one* of them would be nice to her.

So I waited there for a while. I'd give her/them some time to get back from their dinner; it was still on the early side. I could wait. I had waited eighteen-plus years for Rachel, a few more minutes wouldn't kill me.

I called four more times until almost 10:00 when I figured it had gotten too late to call. I know that if the phone
rang in my parents' house after 10:00, they would think that
it was some kind of emergency. ("*Who died?*" I can just hear
my mother saying.) So after thinking it back and forth – what
would Rachel want me to do? – I gave up and went back to
my bunk. It was cold by then. Nothing to do but go back and
crash, and rest up for tomorrow: hauling mattresses and counting days.

I thought about trying her number again early the next
morning, after a super early breakfast in the Mess Hall. But
I couldn't call the Princes' house at 8:00 in the morning anymore than I could have called at 10:00 the night before. I
wanted to make a good first impression on her mother, no matter how lunatic or hard to please she might be. Every action I
was going to take would be designed to make things better for
Rachel and me.

Dale worked us all day, taking down the beds, removing
and storing the window screens, and after that, clearing out
a meadow near the campsite on the far side of the lake. As
a "treat," Dale had a couple of the few remaining workers in
the kitchen bring us a picnic lunch in a motorboat. (It was
really so we could keep working straight through the afternoon, without going back to the Mess Hall for lunch.) But
what I really wanted was a phone. By the end of an afternoon
of clearing brush in the sun, I was half agreeing with Rachel
– *To hell with the money.*

They ferried us back across the lake in the late afternoon
in two boats. We were all pretty tired and sunburned.

"Well," muttered Big Alby as we stepped out onto the
boating dock, "Stanley is sure getting his last nickel's worth
of sweat out of us."

Nobody disputed him.

Like clockwork, I was up at the pay phone by the Main
Office just before 8:00. Dale had taken pity on us and sent
someone into town for some six-packs.

"This is only because Stanley and Jerry aren't around," Dale told us, sucking back a Rolling Rock on the front porch of the Mess Hall where the beers were in a big blue plastic tub of ice. "But you guys are earning it."

"One more day," he said. "Then, back to reality."

I admit that I was a little beer-buzzed when I dialed Rachel's number, leaning against the outside wall of the Main Office. I still had the pink paper folded tightly in my pocket, but I already had the number in my brain. Tonight, I was ready to let it ring forever.

Instead, before the first ring ended, someone picked up.

"Hello?" she answered. It was Rachel.

"Thank God!" I said.

"You don't believe in God," she replied.

"I know, but if I did, I would be thanking Him now."

She laughed, "Oh. Wait a second!"

There was about a minute of silence. I didn't know if Rachel covered the phone with her hand or put me on hold, but there was no sound for a long time. Then –

"You have no idea how much I've missed you," she exhaled with relief.

"Yes, I do," I shot back. "I called you all last night and –"

"Oh, I am *so* sorry, baby!" she said. "My mother dragged me out to dinner with *Herrrrb*." The scornful way she said his name almost made me laugh, but I didn't.

"That's OK," I said. "I just wish I had known that –"

"*I* didn't know they were going to take me out!" she said. "You think I *wanted* to go out with them? I was *dying* when it was eight o'clock, and I knew you were calling."

"I *was* calling!" I assured her.

"I *knew* you were," she said. "I *felt* you. You know that."

We talked a while longer – fortunately, I'd remembered to bring a pocketful of coins. She told me how difficult her mother was being, and how she hadn't even seen her father but was dreading it. I gave her continuous sympathy, trying to pick up her spirits and look on the bright side of things. I hated to hear her sound upset and edgy.

"I don't know when she's watching me, or when she's not watching me," Rachel whispered. "But I'm trying to make the best of it, like you said, and not get into fights with her. And I'm trying to set up the dinner, so she can meet you so we can go out. I can't wait to get some wheels so I can get out of here. But I have to handle things very carefully."

"You *will*," I assured her.

Finally she said, "I have to go. She's nagging me to get off the phone."

"That's OK," I said. "I should go too."

"You don't want to talk to me anymore?" she asked.

"No," I laughed, "I was just saying that because you had to go. I could talk to you forever."

She laughed a little and said, "Good answer."

"But really," I lowered my voice, trying to sound seductive. "I wish we could do more than talk."

"Stop that!" she giggled. "Wait till you get home."

"I can't wait," I said. "One more day. *Two* more days! I'll be home, day after tomorrow. Then we'll be in The Zone again."

"The Zone . . ." she repeated with that musical thrill in her voice. "But call me tomorrow night," she continued. "Please."

"At eight?" I asked.

"Eight o'clock. I'll be here," she said. "Waiting. I promise."

Her voice sounded warm and reassuring, so that when I hung up the phone, I stood there under the floodlight, surrounded by the cold night, thinking, *OK! This isn't so bad. I can get through another day easily because tomorrow night I'll be talking to Rachel. And I'll be one day closer to her.*

~

I got through the next day, moving the rowboats and canoes into dry dock, now that the paint had dried, but when I called Rachel's home at 8:00 that night, there was no answer. Nothing but the now-familiar sound of the phone ringing and ringing and ringing in my ear.

"This seems to be a pattern," I said out loud to no one as I hung up the pay phone outside the Main Office. On this last night of Close-Down, everybody had gone into Bailey's one last time. Now I wish I had gone with them.

I called every ten minutes for the next hour and then gave up. But I did the right thing, trying that long. That is what mattered: doing the right thing, not necessarily the result.

I made one last call to my home, telling my parents when I'd be there the next day. Probably in the afternoon, but I was dependent on Sal, the waterfront head, who was driving me home. (I was lucky; he had a big enough truck, an El Camino, so that he could take all my stuff.) My mother was embarrassingly overjoyed to hear that I was coming home tomorrow and promised me a big "welcome home" dinner out.

"Anything you want," she said. "Fried clams at Howard Johnson's. Anything!"

I said that I'd think about it and hung up. I stood there and listened to the crickets in the dark. I watched the moths hit against the floodlight over the door of the Main Office and thought about all that I had waiting for me at home. The good and the *very* good.

I was too restless to go back to my bunk – I was mostly packed anyway – so I walked around the Moon-shak one last time. It was fairly dark, but there were a few lampposts around the campus, and the sky was moon bright, so I could see where I was going. I made one long, slow circuit of the campus. I walked by the Rec Hall, all dark except for a floodlight over the big rear door. That's where I first talked to Rachel after the square dancing. I remember that she was a little suspicious of me; she was suspicious of every boy, I think. But I'd made a good-enough impression. It was in the basement of the Rec Hall, by the Snack Shak, where I first saw her, so pretty and mysterious across the room. Marcus said that she would tease me to death. Maybe she did.

I went by the net-less volleyball courts and the target-less riflery range. It was too dark to walk to the Quarry, but I thought of all our good times there. I walked around to all the places where we talked, all the places where we made love – whether physically or with our words. I heard some laughter from the staff house, behind the kitchen. There were still a few people around, but I didn't want to see or talk to anyone. I had had enough of other people for a while.

I walked down the long slope to the lake and sat on a circular bench that was built around the trunk of huge oak tree; everything else had been put away. I watched the moonlight shimmer off the rippled surface of the water, recalling how early in the summer I baited my trap for her in the rowboats with *Gatsby*. Not that I'd needed it, old sport, but I think it might have helped at the time. I would have gotten her anyway. We were *fated* for each other. I guess you would have to add to that: in both good ways and bad.

All the times we sat together by the lake, dreaming of the future, and now the "future" was upon us. I was ready to go home, more than ready. I had great things waiting for me: a beautiful girl and the beginning of an Ivy League education. Everything I ever wanted, and more. I admit that I was nervous, but I was hopeful, too, trying to think only positive things. I know it sounds corny, but this is exactly what I was feeling. Isn't that the point of this whole exercise: to be truthful? Do you want me to make up evil and dark thoughts just because of what happened later?

It was getting colder by the open water, and a little spooky. The wind had picked up for no reason, and the surface of the lake flickered with moonlight. The branches of the big tree shuddered, shaking all the leaves like tiny bells. I thought that

I heard the rustling of an animal in the bushes directly behind me. I turned quickly to look, but there was nothing to see. It could have been my imagination. Or not. Who knows, it could have been ghosts – ghosts of other Mooncliff lovers, before Rachel and me. Ghosts of lovers from summers past, whose love died in the autumn but somehow came back and lived on here. Winter ghosts. Poe ghosts. Maybe when everyone was gone, they were still around, not having to dodge Jerry and Harriet, or whoever were the Jerrys and Harriets in their day. Now they could spend all the time they wanted being together, unlike Rachel and me. We were always under the threat of someone seeing us, or having to get back to the bunk by such-and-such a time. We were never free. That was the challenge of the future: How would we be together when we were really, finally "free?"

I zipped my jacket all the way to my throat, turned up my collar, and hustled back to my empty bunk. I wanted to get a good night's sleep. Tomorrow would be the end of the greatest summer of my life and the beginning of the greatest fall.

Part II

The Fall

Record of Events #16 – entered Wednesday, 6:36 A.M.

~

The first thing I did when I got home from the eight weeks at Camp Moon-shak – after taking my things out of Sal's El Camino, thanking him, carrying them inside, and kissing my waiting mother on the cheek – was call Rachel. I walked into our house, which wasn't very big to begin with, and it seemed small and dark, compared to the expanses of the summer. The summer was all about the big outdoors; even the *indoors* were big. Now there I was, back home, and things felt different. Cramped.

I went directly into the kitchen, picked up the phone, and dialed. Nothing had changed in the kitchen: same table and chairs, same pots and pans, same smell. You would think that with having their only son away for two months my parents might have changed *something*, but no, everything was exactly the same. By the time I finished turning over these thoughts, I realized that the number had rung several times and nobody was home at Rachel's. I slowly hung up the phone on the wall in the kitchen: the same phone, on the same wall. I was somewhat disappointed that she wasn't home, but there was nothing I could do about that for the moment.

The second thing I did when I got home from the Moon-shak was sleep thirteen straight hours. I know that I had all these plans – lists of things to do, stuff to buy, friends to see – that I went over and over in my mind during the long drive back with Sal, but once I got home, all the tiredness of the summer descended into my body. Sleeping in my own bed, in

the cocoon of my own dark bedroom upstairs, made me realize that I hadn't gotten a really good night of sleep all summer.
Sleeping in a giant, drafty bunk with a dozen drooling Doggies and Stewie too, with raccoons walking just outside and
coyotes howling in the distance, isn't the way to get a good
night's rest. There were no curtains on the windows, no privacy, no quiet for eight weeks. No wonder I was bone-dead tired.

After my thirteen hours of coma-sleep, I came downstairs
feeling like somebody had hit me over the head with a baseball bat. Maybe a shower would make me feel human again,
but first I went into the kitchen to ask my Mom a question.

"Hi," I said. "Did anyone call for me?"

"Yes," said my mother, turning around from the stove
where she was cooking something. "A girl. But she didn't give
her name. She said that you would know who it was."

That made me feel better instantly. I ran back upstairs and
took a hot-cold-hot-cold-hot shower, sort of like James Bond
does, that reinvigorated me and somewhat restored my humanity. All the while my mind raced with plans. I had much to
do: Connect with Rachel. Meet her mother and her father, in
whatever order they wanted. Get myself organized for Columbia. And do all my shopping for school. I had only a couple of
days before Freshman Orientation started. Thank goodness,
I was finally "going away to college." OK, it was only Manhattan, not all that far from the Island, but I'd still be living
on campus, in the dorms. I know that some kids commuted to
Columbia and had to live in their parents' home; at least I was
spared *that*.

I came back downstairs, clean and ready for the day. My
mother read my mind and had French toast, Canadian bacon,
and the real thick apple juice I like prepared for my first breakfast home. It was one of the few good things she cooked, and
I needed fuel. I had taken the Freshman Orientation packet
from Columbia to Mooncliff, but I have to admit that I only
glanced at it once during the whole summer. I guess I had

wanted to be a different person, a less responsible one. Now that I was back in the real world, I had to attend to business.

"Can I use your car this morning?" I asked my Mom, who was pouring milk into a measuring cup with surgical concentration.

"Why?" she said suspiciously, with that parental reflex of refusal.

"You know I have a million errands to run," I said.

"'A million'?" she repeated archly.

"As many as I have," I said. "And no more French toast. Please."

"Well . . ." she said, pausing for no reason because we both knew that she had to say 'yes,' "As long as you bring me a half a gallon of milk from the A&P on the way home."

"Does the milk have to be from the A&P?"

"You know your father likes the A&P milk," she answered as if it were something I should know. And I admit that I did.

"OK," I muttered. "One half-gallon, A&P milk." I loved my parents, but I already couldn't stand being home.

I made a list of everything I needed. I figured I could buy some stuff at the Columbia bookstore, but I wanted to start with some basic things, all fresh and new, the spiral notebooks I like, pens, etc., and I could probably get that stuff cheaper out here. Things in the City were generally more expensive. Plus I had to go to the bank. There were a couple of guys from high school, Paul and Jeff, I wanted to catch up with before they went off to school (Williams and Lehigh, respectively), but they could wait. I had more immediate things to do.

I waited until after 10:00 to call the Princes' number. I figured that was a decent hour: not too early, not too late. I picked up the phone on the kitchen wall, dialed the number, and pulled the long cord into the dining room for some privacy. I needn't have bothered. On the second ring, it picked up.

"Hello," said a female voice, "Prince residence." It was a soft Southern-accented voice and definitely not Rachel.

"Hello, is Rachel home?" I asked.

"No," said the voice. "I'm sorry she's out. May I ask who's calling?"

I gave her my name and number and asked when she'd be back.

"She went out with her mother, so there's no telling," said the voice. "But I'll tell her you called."

Before I could say "thank you" she hung up.

OK, I thought to myself, *I'll do the rest of what I have to do, and I'll see Rachel later.* I told myself that I had to be patient; if I thought about all the time I *wasn't* with Rachel, I'd go nuts. Instead, I went on my errands.

The first thing I did was go to the bank. I had *two* checks: one was my regular paycheck for the summer, and the other was a separate check for Close-Down. I put the whole regular check into my savings account, and the Close-Down check into my checking. I have to say that I felt good about this; I'd wanted to come back with a decent chunk of money to start the fall with, and I did. I'm not exactly a pauper, but I'm just about the farthest thing from rich, and this was far-and-away the most money I had ever had in the bank in my entire life. I had no idea what my expenses would be, but at least I had a nest egg to start with.

As I drove around from store to store in my mother's old Ford Falcon (a car that does not deserve a nickname), it occurred to me that, if I wanted to, I could just drive over to Rachel's house. I knew the address, and I knew where the town of Oakhurst was. I had been there several times. I was even at a debating tournament at Oakhurst High, the same one that Rachel went to. I could drive over there, go into a gas station and just ask for directions. I'm sure it wouldn't be too hard to find the house; there was nothing stopping me. Nothing stopping me except good common sense. The last thing Rachel needed was me showing up unannounced, before she had time to prepare the situation. Not that I didn't want to drive over there, take her in my arms, and re-enter The Zone – with everything that meant. The main thing is that *I didn't*. Instead, I finished my errands, stopped at the A&P for the half-gallon of milk, and went home.

I was rewarded for my patience and self-control. Not more than ten minutes after I walked in the door, the phone rang. I pounced on it, feeling optimistic.

"Hello?" I answered.

"Thank God it's you," Rachel said, and I felt instantly happier and calmer. "God, I've missed your voice. I've missed your –"

"Everything," I concluded for her, and she laughed the musical laugh that I loved. I'd loved it on that first night after square dancing with Pecos Pete and the Joad family, and I loved hearing it then, over the phone.

"So how have you been?" I asked her.

"Semi-horrible," she said fake-cheerfully. "But I'm much better now."

"Me too," I agreed.

"Can I ask what you are doing for dinner tonight?" she floated.

I played along. "I don't know," I said. "What *am* I doing for dinner tonight?"

"You're going to meet me *and* my mother and *Herrrb* at our beach club and have dinner," she said. "If that's OK with you?"

"That is *more* than OK with me!" I answered eagerly.

She lowered her voice and whispered hurriedly, "You have no idea how horrible it is here, the tension. She really hates me."

"She doesn't *hate* you," I tried to comfort her. "I'm sure she's just –"

"No!" she cut me off. "You'll see."

"OK . . ." I said. "You know that *I* don't hate you."

"I don't hate you either," she said.

Just like that, we were back in The Zone. We talked a little longer. Rachel gave me the address of the beach club and a bunch of warnings about what not to talk about during the evening: the War, the Marshaks, and the divorce.

I just laughed her off, "Don't worry, sugar. I know how to handle adults."

"You've never met my mother," she said.

"Don't worry so much!" I said. "I'll charm her, and she'll relax and let you go out with me, and we'll have everything we want. Time, privacy, no Jerry, no Estelle. Just like we planned."

That made her laugh. Which is what I always wanted, one way or the other: to make her happier.

"I told you, we're going to do everything right," I said. "See you tonight."

Record of Events #17 – entered Thursday, 5:16 A.M.

~

Forget about what I said to Rachel. I was completely nervous about that first dinner at the Costa Brava Beach Club for a whole list of reasons, as you can well imagine. First time meeting the Mother . . . *and* the Mother's New Boyfriend. I know that many, if not most, teenage girls fight with their mothers, but there was something definitely strange going on with Rachel and her mother, something extra. (And maybe with her father too, for that matter, but apparently I wasn't going to meet him this time.) And it was at one of those ritzy beach clubs on the ocean – the kind of place I'd been to only once in my life, courtesy of rich cousin Ralph. But I resolved to make the evening a success. We had to get through this night in order to get time on our own.

I approached the dinner as I would a college interview. I got out my lucky blue blazer (the one I wore to my Columbia interview) with my lucky Bobby Kennedy for Senate lapel pin in the pocket, a blue pinstripe Oxford shirt, neat pants, and shined loafers. I passed on the tie; I figured that it *was* a beach club. I got myself into a frame of mind to impress Rachel's mother and *Herb*. I would be crisp and alert and respectful. It was very clear what had to be done. I would out-phony the phonies and win their trust so that they wouldn't interfere with Rachel and me.

"You look gorgeous!" said my mother when I came down-stairs, which instantly made me check myself in the front hall mirror. I was not gorgeous, but it would have to do; my appearance, I mean. I ran my fingers through my hair, trying to neaten up one last time.

"Can I take the Chrysler?" I asked her.

"Ask your father," she replied. Neither my father's Chrysler nor my mother's Ford was really new or nice, but the Chrysler was newer and nicer. And bigger.

"Hey," I said to my Dad who was leaning back in his recliner, reading *TV Guide* very close up, "You think I can have the Chrysler?"

"You think you can put some gas in it?" he replied. Which meant yes.

"Thanks, Dad," I said. "You should put your glasses on."

"Good night, college man!" he said, bringing the little magazine closer.

My Dad has a good sense of humor. He's basically a gentle man who always tries to say "yes" to me, provided I didn't screw up. That arrangement worked well for a fairly long time.

∾

I got to the Costa Brava Beach Club early, but I didn't go in. I parked the Chrysler on the side of Ocean Boulevard, in full view of the Costa Brava's illuminated entrance. I didn't want to be too early or too late. I wanted to walk into the dining room where I was supposed to meet Rachel and her mother at exactly, perversely 8:00. I timed it perfectly, despite the snotty look and slow response I got from the guy who parked the Chrysler, which was way too shabby a car for this place, and despite the snooty questioning I got from the guy at the front desk when I asked directions to the dining room.

I walked into the reception area of the Neptune Room, went straight up to the tuxedoed maitre d' at his podium at exactly 8:00, and asked for "The Capulet table, please!" Then I corrected my little joke and gave the right name. He looked down at me, gave me a brief unfriendly inspection, and passed me off to a young girl in a blue and white uniform.

"Louise, take this young man to table twenty-four," he said to the girl and went back to looking at whatever he was looking at. The girl in the uniform smiled blankly, turned her back to me, and walked away. I guessed that I was supposed to follow. Nice place, but I refused to let their attitude bother me. I followed Louise as she turned the corner, and I could suddenly see the whole Neptune Room spread before me, all blue and white – blue tablecloths and white candles and white plates, and a wall of windows showing the white, sandy beach and the wide blue Atlantic Ocean just beyond. My eyes zipped around the room full of diners, talking loudly and eating loudly, until I saw Rachel.

She was at a corner table, and she was looking straight at me, rising out of her chair with a huge smile on her face. Seeing her, I felt a charge of pleasure and excitement.

"Thank you, Louise," I said. "I see them," and I almost ran over the poor girl, getting to Rachel.

"Hello!" I practically shouted as we converged.

She greeted me with a kiss on the cheek, her hands holding me back a little by my forearms, just in case I got too close. A quick look in her eyes told me that she was nervous but hopeful.

"Hi!" she whispered. "You're late."

"No, I'm not," I whispered back. "I'm on time."

She took my hand and turned me to the table where I could see her mother and the man who sat across from her. It was a round table, and Rachel and I were going to be sitting across from each other.

I greeted her mother first.

"Hello, Mrs. Prince," I said warmly, trying not to sound insincere. "It's so nice to meet you."

I tried not to react to the sight of her face as I extended my hand, but Rachel's mother was *not* a pretty woman. In fact, with all her make-up and puffy reddish hair and mouth and fingernails and jewelry, she was quite the opposite of attractive. I'm not saying she wasn't expensively and carefully dressed, but everything about her was a little too much, and it was especially off-putting, next to the pure beauty of her daughter. It was no wonder that she resented Rachel.

"Nice to meet you too," she said, sounding completely insincere, shaking my hand with a limp rattle of bracelets. "Rachel cannot stop talking about you."

"Good things, I hope," I replied.

"You've made quite a big impression on her." She was not just looking at me; she was sizing me up.

"Mother," Rachel muttered.

"Well, Rachel makes quite an impression on everybody," I said. "You should be very proud of your daughter." I would not back down.

"Yes, I am. *Very,*" she said with a smile like a knife, not backing down to me either. "Let me introduce you to Herb Perlov."

All this time I felt the presence of the man sitting across from Mrs. Prince, but I could not, would not disengage from her. Now I could.

"Hello, sir," I said to the man sitting down. Rachel introduced me as I shook hands with Herb.

Even though he was sitting down, I could tell that Herb was a big, bony man. Balding and tanned, he leaned toward me with an aggressive smile, a hairy hand coming out of his blue seersucker sports jacket. He tried to crush/test my hand in the handshake, but I was ready and held my hand firmly in his vise.

"Nice to meet you," I lied.

Herb had bushy black eyebrows behind thick black-framed glasses, a peeling, freckled dome, and an extremely confident grin.

"Sit down, kid," he said. "Have something to drink."

"Herb!" Mrs. Prince cautioned him.

"I didn't say anything alcoholic," Herb defended himself. "Have a Coke," he said to me.

"Thanks," I said. "I will. Make it a double." Which got a tension-breaking laugh from everyone as I sat down.

I looked across to Rachel and said a private "hi."

"Hi," she whispered back to me as her mother interrupted to ask her a question.

"Rachel," said Mrs. Prince. "Tell me again what's the name of that store where you bought those ridiculously expensive boots?"

Rachel answered her mother sharply, "They were not ridiculously expensive, and I didn't even want new boots. *You're* the one who told me to go buy them." They began an uncomfortable exchange of claims and counter-claims about said boots. Embarrassed, I looked down at my table setting – fat silverware, big, mostly-white dishes painted in a nautical theme, with 'Costa Brava' in blue, and several different glasses – and caught my breath. I remembered to snatch the blue napkin off my plate and put it in my lap.

"Leave her alone, for God's sake," Herb said to Mrs. Prince. "Stop busting chops!" And he winked at me, in an "us guys" way.

"So Rachel tells us that you're going to Columbia," he said, taking the cellophane wrapper off a cigar.

"Yes, sir," I said. "I'm starting this week."

"Columbia," said Herb, biting the end off his cigar. "Good school."

"Tell him where you went, Herb," said Mrs. Prince. "Go on." Before Herb could tell me, Rachel's mother crowed, "*Harvard*. The college *and* the law school, right?"

Herb didn't say anything. He just chuckled and lit the tip of his cigar with a gold Zippo lighter.

I admit it: it *zinged* me. Harvard was a big name to drop, and she dropped it right on me.

All I could do was mutter, "Also good schools." Which made them burst into laughter, in my direction.

"I love to drop the H-bomb!" said Mrs. Prince to Herb with a little smirk. "It always gets such a great reaction."

I looked across to Rachel for comfort, but she was looking down at the tiny printed menu that was next to each plate. She looked much more grown-up than at Mooncliff, in a dress, with make-up and her hair done. She looked beautiful and uncomfortable at the same time.

"Hey," I said to Rachel. "When I called you this morning, you weren't home. Who answered your phone?"

"Oh," said Rachel as I startled her out of her thoughts. "Ella Ruth. She told me that you called."

"Is she your – ?" I asked her and Mrs. Prince.

Rachel jumped in, saying, "She comes in to help clean up and stuff, but we don't have a live-in anymore. My mother thought that the last one was stealing from her."

"I did not!" said Mrs. Prince, sitting straight up.

"And Ella Ruth doesn't steal?" I commented.

"Not so far," said Rachel, playing back to me. "But I'm sure my mother is watching her very carefully."

"It is not that –" Mrs. Prince defended herself.

Herb interrupted, "I tell you, Eleanor," – *Eleanor*! That was the first time I'd ever heard Mrs. Prince's first name! – "I can find you someone trustworthy, somebody who is bonded. And *fully* guaranteed, if you know what I mean."

"It's not about the stealing –" Mrs. Prince said.

"Oh yes, it is," Rachel put in.

"No, it's about privacy! It's about feeling comfortable in my own home," Mrs. Prince insisted. "I just got one giant nuisance out of my house. I don't need another!"

That comment stopped the conversation for a moment. I was wondering if anyone was going to mention the Princes' divorce. Now someone had.

Mrs. Prince broke the silence, addressing Rachel, "You know *Herb* was very helpful to me, during all the proceedings."

Herb spoke up, between cigar puffs, "Bernie did a fine job for you. I was just happy to be of help, reading things."

"You are always a help," responded Mrs. Prince, with a way-too-charming smile in Herb's direction that made Rachel squirm in her seat.

Fortunately, the waitress came just then to remind us what the specials were.

I had no control of the conversation; I just went wherever it was pushed.

Mrs. Prince turned to me with a cocked eyebrow as she cracked a dinner roll with her perfect pink talons. "So, has Rachel told you of her well-thought-out plan *not* to go to college?"

Before I could answer, Rachel jumped in, "At least not straight out of high school! Why can't I take a year off before I go to college?"

"For what, exactly?"

"To live!"

"You don't know how to live?" Mrs. Prince said, with a raised eyebrow. "Why not learn a little something first? *Then* you can live."

She and Herb had another good chuckle over that.

"You don't always have to ridicule me, Mother," Rachel said. She looked at me for help.

I started to say, "People have all kinds of different paths to –"

"I know a little something about education," Eleanor cut me off. "When I was head of the PTA –"

"*Once!*" Rachel said directly to me. "When I was in fourth grade, she actually did something."

Herb asked Rachel bluntly, "So what are you going to do for a year? Go work in the Peace Corps?" He reached his hand a little ways on the tabletop to pat Rachel's hand, for emphasis. "Even to work in the Peace Corps, you need a college degree. At least."

She immediately pulled her hand away from his. Which I was glad to see.

"I can just picture my poor little girl working for the Peace Corps!" Mrs. Prince said, between bites of bread. "Imagine her in Africa: 'Is there a Bloomingdale's in this jungle?'"

It wasn't funny, but Eleanor and Herb laughed as if it were hilarious. Now I've seen parents tease their kids before. My Dad sometimes teases me. But with Eleanor Prince, there was almost no affection in her teasing. It was all, in one way or another, a little hard, a little cruel. I smiled a grim smile of support at Rachel, one that said: *Let's just get through this, and we'll be OK.*

Her eyes widened with embarrassment and cried out, "*You see what I'm going through? You see? I wasn't exaggerating!*"

And she wasn't. "Come on, Eleanor," rasped Herb. "She's much too fair-skinned for Africa. Maybe the Peace Corps has a junior branch in East Hampton." Which gave rise to another duet of laughter.

For the record, the dinner itself was decent: shrimp cocktail, salmon in some whitish sauce, and potatoes au gratin. Not much better than the fried clams at Howard Johnson's that my parents splurged on, my second night home, but I guess I'm low class. Maybe that's why she hated me, because almost from the moment that I sat down, I felt waves of condescension coming from Mrs. Prince. And Herb wasn't that friendly either, no matter how much he talked and "joked." To tell you the truth, I don't think Mrs. Prince would have liked anybody Rachel brought to the dinner. For some reason, she was resolved to give her/me/us a hard time. Rachel could have shown up with Mahatma Gandhi, and they would have tsk-tsked him for wearing a diaper. Oh, there was a surface niceness throughout the entire meal, but I could tell by the time we got to dessert: Rachel and I were in for some considerable amount of trouble. I just didn't know how much.

"Daddy said that he's getting me a Mustang when I get my license," Rachel said.

"We will have to see about that," Mrs. Prince responded tartly.

"It doesn't matter what you say," said Rachel. "The judge said that he could give me a Mustang for my birthday."

"After the stunt you just pulled? I don't *think* so –" Mrs. Prince scoffed.

"He's still my father –" Rachel insisted.

"Who thinks he can spoil you –" Mrs. Prince interrupted.

"Who will do whatever he wants *anyway*!" continued Rachel. "Am I right?"

She looked at Mrs. Prince and Herb, and they looked at each other grimly, seeming to agree with her.

"I think the Court just might have something to say to Manny about that," said Herb.

Rachel laughed and said to me, "Wait till you meet my father. He's a real trip-and-a-half." I could see that she was saying that just to torment her mother, and Herb, too, for that matter. But it didn't make me feel any better, seeing what I was getting into, in the real world of Rachel Prince. And her father's name was *Manny*.

"You'll look fantastic in a Mustang," I said, privately, across to Rachel, seeking The Zone.

She smiled at me, seeking the same thing.

"We'll see what the future brings," said Mrs. Prince, as if she had already decided the future. "You have a very big, important year of school in front of you, young lady. Let's see how you do."

As we left the table and single-filed out of the Neptune Room, I managed to get behind Rachel and whisper to her, "Can I see you tomorrow?"

She whispered over her shoulder, "I don't know. I'll call you in the morning."

"I don't like it," I said. "Not seeing you."

She whispered, "Don't you think I feel the same way?"

Then she stopped and faced me.

"But *now* do you see what I'm dealing with? *Now* you believe me?"

The hopelessness in her look – and the directness of the plea behind it – touched me deeply. More than ever, I saw that she needed me. And nowhere in any of this was there any mention of Eric.

∾

In the parking lot, I prayed – and I am not a praying person – that they would bring my car *last*. I didn't need any comments – or non-comments, for that matter – from Mrs. Prince or Herb about the Chrysler. My prayer was answered when Herb's humungous black Lincoln Continental was pulled up to the curb first. When I first saw it, I swear that I thought it was a hearse. No kidding.

"Thank you so much for the dinner, Mrs. Prince," I said, trying to sound straight-on sincere. "It was really wonderful."

"Why, you're welcome," she responded as if she were surprised that I should have the manners to thank her. "I certainly hope we'll see you again," she said when we both knew that she meant the opposite.

"Oh, you will, Mrs. Prince," I answered her, taking up her challenge with a smile. "*Guaranteed.*"

Her eyes narrowed: she didn't like that I said that, but I couldn't help it. I had to show her, right then, that I was a serious person in Rachel's life.

I let the parking attendant open the front door for Mrs. Prince while I got the rear door for Rachel. (It was one of those cool, open-from-the-rear back doors on the Continental.) She gave me a *Thank-God-that's-over* roll of her eyes and whispered a quick "I love you" as she scooted into the back seat. She looked great in a dress. I was sorry to close the door on her and her tanned legs. As soon as I slammed the door, she turned to look at me through the window. I was instantly sorry that I missed the chance to kiss her – or something – but by now Herb had turned on the Conty's engine, and they were about to drive away.

"I love you," she mouthed again through the glass as the big car sped away. I waved and said the same thing. I hoped that she saw it.

I hoped that they *didn't* see the shabby gray Chrysler being pulled up to the curb for me. *But then again*, I thought, *so what if they did?* This is who I was. They were going to find out, sooner or later.

~

Some nasty aftertaste – I think it was that white sauce on the salmon but it might have been the conversation – was making me queasy so I drove to my favorite local diner, The Lexington, near the railroad station in my town, to get something to take away the bitterness that wouldn't go away. When I walked in, as I had done a thousand times during high school after some school play or game or event, I saw a couple of friends of mine, kids from my class. Not close friends, more like "say hello" friends. But they saw me, too, and called me over.

These were kids who were going to live at home while going to college, going to places like Hofstra, Adelphi, Queens, and Nassau Community ("the thirteenth grade"). I was lucky that my scholarship covered room and board as well as most of my tuition. If I had to live at home for the next four years, well, I just wouldn't do it.

I sat down with them and we talked about starting college in the next few days, about what we did that past summer, about who was doing what and where. I had a black-and-white milkshake that covered up the sour tickle in my stomach and made me feel better. But all the while that I joked and bantered with these three guys and two girls, I kept thinking about Rachel and Mrs. Prince and Herb *and* going off to Columbia. And how I was going to keep everything together and get what I wanted.

"So you gonna live in the freshman dorm?" one of the guys, Marty who was going to Nassau Community and had been in my homeroom for years, asked me.

"I guess so," I said. "Wherever they put me."

"You can have my bedroom," cracked Vincent. Which made us all laugh.

"No, thanks," I said. "I am ready to Get Out. If you know what I mean."

We all knew what I meant. Nothing more needed to be said.

On the way home, I remembered to put some gas in the Chrysler, just as I had promised my Dad. At least I had something real and specific to feel good about.

Record of Events #18 – entered Thursday, 11:17 P.M.

~

The next morning I woke up with a million things to do, including finishing packing all the stuff I was going to take to Columbia. It was good that I could leave some things at home and get them later in the year as the weather got colder; I didn't have to take everything in one trip. But as I was getting the day going – showering, eating breakfast, making lists – I couldn't stop thinking about what had happened last night: how flat-out mean Mrs. Prince and Herb were to Rachel and me. The more I thought about it, the angrier I got; but *cold*-angrier. There was no way that I was going to let Mrs. Prince interfere with Rachel and me. They obviously had no idea about love, and she obviously had no sympathy for Rachel. If she did, she wouldn't've treated me, someone her daughter obviously cares about – and Rachel herself! – in such a haughty, snide, backhanded manner. It would be insane to let Eleanor Prince determine our lives.

The phone rang. I picked it up before the second ring was even finished, pulling the phone, cord, and myself into the dining room for some privacy.

"Hello?" I said, hoping, *feeling* that it was Rachel.

"Can you meet me outside the Lord & Taylor in Garden City at one thirty?" she whispered.

"I can do anything you ask me to," I said right back.

"OK," she murmured dreamily. "One thirty." And then she hung up.

I hung up too. Short, but very sweet.

"Can I borrow the car this afternoon?" I said to my mother, who just happened to be standing there in the kitchen when I went back in to hang up the phone.

"What," asked my mother, as she was clearing away my breakfast dishes. "She calls, and you jump? You're not even done packing!"

I turned back and said, "Ma? Just leave me alone, please. You really don't know what you're talking about." Then I continued on upstairs, not wanting to get into an argument.

As I went up the steps, I heard her shout, "I didn't say 'yes' about the car!" But I knew that she didn't mean it. There was no way that I was *not* going to take the car. My mother was big on empty threats. But I generally had good judgment and never got into any real trouble. (I don't count any of the stuff that happened at Mooncliff.) She knew that I'd be ready for tomorrow. As I said, I was always a good kid.

I vaguely knew where the Lord & Taylor in Garden City was, but I checked in the Yellow Pages for the address. My family didn't shop at Lord & Taylor. It was too far away and too expensive anyway. If it hasn't been made clear before, I don't care that much about clothes and outside appearances, but if Rachel did, it was fine with me. I was there to be with her.

I straightened up the inside of my Mom's Ford. I wished that I had time to wash the whole car and maybe get my mother's smell out of its interior, but there was no time for that. On my last trip to the bathroom, I gave myself an extra spritz of Right Guard and hoped for the best.

"When are you going to finish packing?" asked my mother at the front door as I was leaving.

"I'm almost done," I said, cutting across the lawn. "Did you do the rest of my laundry?"

"What do you think?" she answered, as if to say: *Of course I did!*

"Then everything's fine!"

I got to Garden City early, which was a good thing, because Lord & Taylor was a big store, and there were *four* entrances. I parked in the lot next to the huge, white-painted
brick building and figured that, if worst came to worst, I'd
just walk around the outside, from entrance to entrance, until
I found her. It couldn't be that hard. Locking the Ford, I pock-
eted the keys and walked toward the Lord & Taylor. It was very
clean-looking, with trimmed bushes and little flowers framing
the walkways. There was a large glass-doored entrance right
in front of me; maybe she would be there. That seemed to be
the logical place. Why shouldn't logic be on my side?

I waited there ten minutes, standing in full sight of the
entrance, easy for anyone to see. I watched the well-dressed,
mostly female customers spin through the revolving doors, in
with nothing and out with big "L&T" shopping bags. I looked
at my reflection in the plate glass window, me in my jeans and
open Oxford shirt over a T-shirt. Maybe I should have dressed
better, but as I said, I don't care about clothes. I care about
people.

There was a large clock with Roman numerals on a fancy
lamppost that read almost 1:40. OK, I told myself, I'll check
the other entrances. I can't stand here any longer.

I checked the other entrances. First, the one on Franklin
Avenue – she wasn't there – then the one on the other side.
Not there, either. I decided to go back to the parking lot side;
that was the most logical meeting place. I was starting to get
sweaty now, which was a complete drag. I had to slow down.
There I was, walking in circles around a big rectangle when
I had so much to do to get ready for Columbia, so many "responsibilities" as my father would say. But instead, I was
chasing a *real* dream.

Then she called from behind me, "There you are!" And I
turned around as she jumped into my arms.

"Oh, baby, baby, baby," she cried into my neck as she held
me tightly. She smelled like sweet flowers. Her long, dark hair

felt silky against my cheek. I held her so tightly that she had to push away from me.

"You're crushing me," she said.

"I know," I answered. "I don't care."

She looked terrific in tight jeans, high leather boots, and a pink blouse that looked as soft as a cloud and very touchable. She had a nice leather purse on a strap with a golden clasp that hung from her shoulder. It was still kind of new to see her in something other than a Mooncliff uniform; she was definitely not the same girl at home that she was at camp.

"Now control yourself, please," she said. "This is Nanci Jerome," directing my attention to a girl – a big, shapeless girl dressed mostly in black – standing a few yards away from us, smiling and giving me a little wave. "She drove me here."

A large, friendly pudding of a girl with short, brownish hair, she wore black leotards that covered her thick arms and her legs down to her tan Dingo boots. She had some weird type of colorful peasant skirt wrapped around her wide waist, and a sheepish grin that kind of reminded me of Marcus.

"Well, thank you, Nanci Jerome!" I said.

"It's only 'cause Rachel nagged me until I said yes," she said with a little lisp. I tried to keep looking her in the eye, even though I couldn't help but notice how thick her legs were in her black tights below her too-short skirt. And slung over one shoulder was this giant, overstuffed brown suede purse, dangling with fringe and beads, while the other shoulder was draped in some kind of shawl. Or maybe it was *two* shawls. Even though she was in Garden City, she was dressed for Greenwich Village.

"She's very good at that," I said, squeezing Rachel's hand to keep her from saying anything else.

"That is *not* true," said Rachel. "But Nanci did save my life. She's the only one who can talk some reason into Eleanor."

Nanci gave me a little twisted smile of pride.

"Well," she said to me wryly, "Rachel seemed to be in such *agony* without you that –"

"Great!" I said. "I love it when Rachel's in agony." Which made this Nanci laugh. She understood me.

Rachel pulled a little on my hand and said, "So, Nanc', you want us back here at five?" She spoke as if she were confirming a previously agreed-to plan.

"I promised Eleanor," said Nanci, pressing her hands together in a fake prayer. "Please, let's not make her nuttier than we have to."

"I owe you, Nanc'!" Rachel shouted as she hooked my arm.

"We both do!" I said as Rachel turned me away with a whiplash pull, not looking back for a moment.

"Let's go!" she whispered. "Where did you park?"

"Where are we going?" I asked as she pulled us into a fast walk toward the parking lot.

"To the beach," she said with a look of intense happiness on her face. "I want to walk on the beach with you."

"OK!" I said, glad to be with her, glad that she seemed so excited to be with me. And the beach was an inspired idea: just what I would have suggested, if I knew we had the time. As we walked, she pressed close to me.

"So, who is this Nanci?" I asked, even as I plotted in my mind how to get to the beach from there. And which beach was closest? Probably Jones.

"Nobody. She lives around the corner from me," Rachel chirped. "Very artsy, very quiet. Goes to Pratt, two grades ahead of me. She's loved me since I was in second grade, and she was in fourth. The main thing is that Eleanor trusts her. She's older and . . . well, look at her. *And* she has asthma. But it's what let me get away this afternoon. I think, amazingly enough, Eleanor actually feels *sorry* for her."

As ever, I was pleased by Rachel's certainty about things: her easy confidence in making judgments, her ability to dismiss doubt from her mind. I wanted to absorb that determination from her.

"Would you love me if I looked like *that?*" she asked, holding close to my arm as we walked.

"You mean like this Nanci?" I asked. "Yeah. Of course I would. "

She sniffed once, in disbelief. "Sure."

"But I have to say, I'm glad you don't," I finished. Which made her snicker with satisfaction.

"Oh, you can't believe how frustrating it was last night, being so close to you and not being able to touch you!" she said, staying close to my side, tilting her head toward me.

"Oh, yes, I can believe it."

I stopped walking and spun her to me for a big, time-stopping, traffic-halting kiss. Which was way overdue. One long kiss, and everything that felt good came rushing back into my body.

"I have to *breathe*," she gasped, breaking the kiss.

"Breathe later," I mumbled and kissed her again.

Someone honked at us, or I could have kissed her there forever. Right there, on the asphalt, we re-entered The Zone.

I was a little apprehensive when we approached my mother's Ford. It was parked between a dark green Pontiac GTO and a fairly recent Mercedes Benz, which made it look even shabbier.

"That's me, in the middle," I said, trying to keep any note of defensiveness out of my voice. "It's my mother's car."

"That's OK," said Rachel, trying not to sound disappointed at the drabness of my ride. "When I get my Mustang, I'll have my own car, and we'll really be free."

"Are you *sure* your father is gonna give you a Mustang?" I asked her as I unlocked the passenger side.

"Of course he is, he promised me. Besides, he *owes* it to me," she said as she slid between the cars to get into the Ford. "And even if he didn't," she continued. "He'd give it to me just to spite my mother."

Nice people, I thought to myself as I watched her scoot into the front seat in her perfect jeans, perfect boots, perfect everything. How could Eleanor have produced such a beautiful daughter? Maybe her father looked like Paul Newman. Highly doubtful. Would a Paul Newman marry an Eleanor Prince? Then an odd, disturbing notion flashed across my mind: *What kind of a daughter did Eleanor Prince actually deserve?*

I quickly got into my side, turned on the car, and drove out of the parking lot. Rachel sat close to me. Very close. Just the way I liked it.

"It's no Super-Coupe," I said as she fiddled with the radio. "But it will get us there." I had already plotted in my mind the best way to the beach. I could cut across on Old Country Road to the Meadowbrook Parkway, which would take us straight down to Jones Beach.

"You know," she said, nuzzling in next to me. "It's only been a few days, but Mooncliff already seems like a long time ago." She was right: these crowded, gray, ugly suburban streets were a different world, so far from the green paradise of Mooncliff. So busy and meaningless. Too much asphalt and not enough Nature.

"The only thing I really liked about the Moon-shak was *you*," I said.

"Is that true?" she asked, moving away and looking at me.

"Not really," I said. "But you were, far and away, the best part."

"Well, that's true," she said. Satisfied with my answer, she moved back against my side.

"It's the only part that I want to continue," I concluded. "If I never see that place again, that's perfectly fine with me, as long as I have you." The truth is, I felt vaguely adrift in both worlds: Mooncliff and the City. The only thing that made any sense now was being with Rachel; she was absolutely real. Everything else mattered less. In fact, she was snuggling in so close to me that I lost my concentration in the cloud of her perfume and let the car weave before I caught myself.

"Hey!" Rachel shouted.

"Whoa!" I gasped.

"Keep your eyes on the road," she cautioned. "Is this how you want *me* to drive?"

"No!" I said. "You're going to be a great driver. In your Mustang. Jeez." I could just picture her, behind the wheel, like a model in a slick commercial.

"There is only one important question that's still up in the air," she said.

"What's that?"

"What color should I pick?"

We flew down the Meadowbrook, talking back and forth, as relaxed and easy as always, telling each other everything that had happened in the last few days. It was only with Rachel that I felt I could let my guard down, and I know she felt the same way.

"So," I said. "How's ol' Herrrrb?"

"Oh," she grunted. "He is *very* creepy. He's been sleeping over, and he leaves his stuff everywhere. And then I see him in the morning in his *bathrobe*!"

"Gross!" I said.

"You think so?" she laughed humorlessly. "I almost threw up my Pop-Tart, he's so hairy. And you should see the way he looks at me."

"Well, you be careful," I warned her. "Watch yourself around him, the skeeve. You tell me if he does or says anything."

"If my father found out Herb was sleeping in his bed," Rachel said. "He would kill both of them."

"Really?" I snickered.

"No," she shrugged. "Probably not. . . . Just wishful thinking."

When we got to the end of the Meadowbrook, I changed my mind at the last minute and drove to Point Lookout. It was generally less crowded there – at least it was the last time I was there, the previous summer – and the parking was easier. Even with Rachel sitting *super close* next to me, I couldn't wait to stop the car and hold her and really *be* with her.

After I paid the parking attendant, I found the furthest, most obscure corner of the lot and stopped the car.

I put the Ford into park, turned to her, and said, "Well, here we are."

We kissed, etc., for a good fifteen minutes. In fact, they were the best fifteen minutes I had experienced since the last time we had kissed, etc., way back at the Burning of the Lake. That seemed like a long time ago, and we were now in a different universe.

"We can't do this here," she said, pushing me away for air.

"Yes, we can," I mumbled and dove back into her softness.

"No!" she said. "There are kids around."

"What kids?"

"*Those* kids!" she said, pushing me away with a straight arm and turning me so that I could see the two little kids – a boy and a girl – looking in the car window.

"Go away! Get out of here! Go! ... GO!!!" I yelled, scaring them but good. It brought back the rush of feeling I had when I was yelling at the Doggies, this instantaneous release of blind anger that I subsequently regretted.

"Don't they have any parents?" I said as I watched them run away toward an open station wagon on the other side of the parking lot. "Idiots."

"Don't be so rough. They're only kids," said Rachel, pulling herself together. "Come on, take me for a walk on the beach and tell me how much you love me."

She was right to make me take her to the beach. We took off our shoes, rolled up our cuffs, and walked together alone across the sand. We held close to each other and talked about everything. One minute, she was laughing about how we escaped detection when we were in the bushes and she surprised me while I was on O.D., and the next moment she was almost in tears about how she dreaded the coming school year.

"No," I tried to encourage her. "Your senior year can be your *best!*"

"Not with everyone worrying about college when that's the *last* thing I want to do," she answered. "Already Eleanor is on me about this College Night they're having that I have no intention of going to!"

"You have to look at it as a chance to get away," I reasoned.

"Yes, I want to *get away,*" she said. "I want to get away with *you.*"

"But until we can find a way to spend more time together, you've got to try to make things work there," I said. "Don't you have any friends at school you can hang with?"

In the back of my mind, I thought: *What am I saying? Do I want to push her back into the arms of Eric, or some other guy?* Fortunately, she wasn't thinking in that direction, at least she didn't seem to be, on the surface.

"What," she snapped. "You want me to try out for cheerleading like my mother? You don't understand; I am *finished* with all the people at Oakhurst. I can't stand it anymore!"

"OK, OK," I said, holding her, trying to stop her tears before they flowed. "Don't worry! We have *each other!* We can talk every night, and be together on weekends. You can call me whenever you want. You'll see, everything will be all right."

I held her for a while, then we walked for a little longer, saying nothing. I hoped that she believed me; I hoped that I was right.

Finally, she broke the silence. "I love the waves, how they go on forever," she said. "It's so beautiful, how they destroy themselves. But they keep coming back. Just like we will, right?"

We drove back to the Lord & Taylor with her tight against my side. We didn't have to talk. I drove one handed with the

other arm around her as she played with the radio, never finding a song she liked for more than a few seconds.

"What'll Eleanor say when you come home from Lord &
Taylor with no new clothes?" I asked her. I probably shouldn't
have brought it up, but I couldn't help myself: sometimes I
have to say whatever pops into my head, especially when I'm
on the lookout for trouble.

"I'll tell her that I couldn't find anything," she said.

"Will she believe you?"

Slowly, she said, "I . . . don't . . . care."

I let that sit in the air for a while. I didn't know Rachel's
mother well at all, but I wondered if outright defiance was the
best strategy to take with her.

"Maybe you should run in and buy *something*," I suggested. "Just to shut her up."

"OK," she admitted, "You're right. I'll go in and buy
something really expensive. I have my father's credit card."

"Really?" I said. "Lucky you."

~

Nanci was waiting right where we left her. Even though I
drove at semi-unsafe speeds to get back to Garden City, we
were late.

"You told *me* to be on time, and where were you two ju-
venile delinquents?" she huffed in pretend anger, her bangle
bracelets clattering on both wrists as she posed with her one
hand on her wide hip, her giant purse on one shoulder like a
lump.

"Ha, ha, ha," sang out Rachel merrily.

In the other hand, Nanci held an ice cream cone that was
almost finished, gobbled down to the pointy little end. I gave
Rachel's hand a quick squeeze. Rachel's body was so slim and
perfect, and Nanci was so – what's a nice word? . . . chubby
– that it was almost incongruous to see them together. But I
didn't care. Nanci got us together that day, and it wouldn't be

the last time she did favors for us. But I'm getting ahead of my story and my "state of mind."

"You know how she'll be if I get you home late," said Nanci. Speaking directly to me, she added, "Eleanor Prince is not the easiest person in the world."

"I'm beginning to get that idea," I answered dryly.

"Don't worry," Nanci said to me. "I'll protect her." I liked what I saw in her eyes: Nanci really did like Rachel.

"This is my guardian angel," said Rachel, with a touch of sarcasm.

"More like a human shield," Nanci said.

"Isn't that the truth?" muttered Rachel, as if in private conversation with Nanci. They giggled together; I wondered what exactly their relationship was as Rachel grabbed Nanci by her big, round shoulders and said, "But *now* we have to go back into L-and-T and buy something, so shut up, OK?"

"But –" Nanci sputtered.

"Just go!" Rachel ordered. She turned Nanci around so that she faced the store, and winked at me.

"Not so fast! Rachel!" said Nanci, gulping air. I could now hear a little of the asthma in her voice.

"'L-and-T'?" I mocked her expression.

"Don't blame me," she said as she pushed Nanci toward the store entrance. "It's how I was raised. I'll call you tonight."

"Really?" I asked sharply, having learned to be somewhat suspicious of her phone promises.

"I *promise!*" she said. With that, she pushed Nanci into the whirling revolving glass door and followed her in the next compartment, and just like that, she was gone.

I stood there for a moment, a bit stunned at her sudden departure. I knew that she was running late and our "date" had to end, but I still wasn't ready right then for her to be gone. I felt her absence as if it were a real, tangible thing.

OK, I thought, *she's gone. I am now out of The Zone, and I have to get on with the rest of my life. Where am I? . . . And where did I park the car?*

When I got home, I got into a fairly big fight with my mother. Or, rather, she got into a big fight with me.

"Why didn't you call me? You were gone so long!"

"I wasn't near a phone!"

"How could you not be near a phone? There are phones everywhere!"

I went upstairs to escape the noise. I still had a bunch of things to do. I went to my stereo, a decent KLH system (nothing fancy but it sounded good enough until I could afford something better) and turned on some Dylan. Maybe the thing I missed most about being away all summer was being away from my music and the ability to change records/music/mood/environment at any moment. So I put on *Blonde on Blonde* as I had a million times before, but I kept the volume low, and took out the Columbia Freshman orientation envelope. I opened it and read through the material again. It was so official, and they had so many events planned. I was moving up to the big leagues, the *Ivy* League, and it was exciting. And, I will admit, I was a little scared. But at least I had Rachel here at home, on the Island. So no matter what happened, I had, for the first time, this absolutely fantastic girlfriend.

Later I went downstairs and apologized. It's always the right thing to do with your parents, even if you don't particularly mean it. I had finished packing and gone over everything on the checklist. I was in pretty good shape.

"Would you like to go out for dinner?" my mother asked.

"It's your last night," my father said. "Last night, last meal."

"Nah," I said, weighing the value of a meal in a restaurant versus the value of a call from Rachel on my "last" night. "Let's call Vinnie's for something."

"How about a large half-mushroom, half-pepperoni, extra-cheese –"

"*Now* you're talking!"

∿

I got my folks out of the kitchen quickly, after a very pleasant, memory-saturated dinner of pizza and cheese sticks dipped in marinara sauce (Vinnie's specialty). And just as I was putting the last dish into the dishwasher after cleaning up the kitchen by myself, I was rewarded with the sound of the phone ringing off the wall.

"Hello?" I said, expecting nothing.

"How soon can you get here?"

It was Rachel, whispering. She sounded scared.

"Why? What's wrong?" I asked.

"Meet me around the corner from my house. On Buckingham Terrace. Half an hour."

And she hung up.

That was it.

Instantly I went into action. I asked my father if I could borrow the Chrysler, which he agreed to after only moderate pleading.

My mother had started in with, "But he has to be there at nine o'clock tomorrow morning!"

But I countered her with, "Check-in and registration are *all day* tomorrow, from nine to three. Plus I'll be back soon."

My Dad saw reason, gave me the keys, and let me go.

I was out of there fast. I wondered what could be wrong with Rachel. Maybe she'd gotten home too late from Garden City and Eleanor was giving her trouble for that. Or maybe she'd bought the wrong stuff, or she'd bought too much. Rachel was just as nervous about the school year's starting as I was. It wasn't fair of Eleanor to upset her for no reason. But I had a pretty strong sense now that their fights occurred regularly, and there didn't have to be a good reason for them.

~

I had visualized the drive to Rachel's house many times in my mind, and now I was finally going. As I mentioned, I was vaguely familiar with the town of Oakhurst and the high school. I had sort of memorized the route to her house by studying the Oakhurst street map at our public library on one of my errands – which big streets led to which smaller streets, which led to her cul-de-sac with the embarrassingly pretentious name.

The town of Oakhurst itself was pretty ritzy; one nice little shop after another, separated by cafes and hair salons. No gas stations or chain stores in this burg. I drove down the main drag at a cautious speed, knowing that the cops in a town like this *love* to pull kids over and hassle them. Not that my hair was that long, but this was known as a fairly tight-ass town. I understood: they had a lot to protect.

I turned away from the town and its streetlights and into the neighborhood of houses, snaking through the lush streets in my father's clunky Chrysler. The deeper I drove into her neighborhood, the bigger and wider apart the houses got. I mean, I knew that the Princes were rich, but not *this* rich. I had been to nice neighborhoods before – my rich cousin Ralph's in Jamaica Estates, for instance – but nothing like this. As I drove slower and slower, tracing the path I had memorized from the map, down the long, winding blocks, seeing one mansion after another with their wide, wide lawns and tall, tall hedges, I wondered just what I was getting myself into. How could Rachel be having such a hard time in a neighborhood as beautiful as this one? At least on the surface.

As soon as I turned slowly onto Buckingham Terrace, I saw Rachel standing on the sidewalk against a huge bank of hedges, looking for me. At first she didn't see that it was me; I guess she was expecting me to be driving my Mom's Falcon. From a distance Rachel seemed to be OK, but my relief at seeing her was boosted by a good laugh: she was holding a tiny, fluffy, white French poodle with a pink rhinestone collar on a long, sparkly leash. I pulled over to the curb so quickly that I scraped my front tire.

"Hi!" I said breathlessly as I got immediately out of the car, "Are you OK??"

As I approached Rachel, her little dog started to bark angrily at me.

"Max!" she shouted at the dog, pulling back on the leash. "Stop it!"

The dog stood on its hind legs, yipping like a madman and straining to attack me.

"Hi, Max," I said to the dog, pretending to be nonchalant while staying out of the range of the little sharp-looking teeth and snapping jaws. I didn't want to seem scared of a small dog; no boyfriend should be that much of a wuss.

"How you doin', boy?" I said, reluctantly keeping my distance.

"It's a *girl*," said Rachel pulling back on the leash. "Max-*ine*."

I looked and, sure enough, it *was* a girl.

"Down, Max! Girl," I said, frustrated that I couldn't get to Rachel. "Are you OK?"

"You keep saying that," said Rachel, trying to pull the dog behind her, so that we could reach each other. "Of course I'm OK."

"On the phone you just sounded like something was wrong."

"I was *whispering*, silly!" she said. "They don't know that you're meeting me here. They'd kill me if they knew you were here."

"OK . . ." I said. "OK," comprehending that there was no crisis, no emergency. I had rushed over there, semi-panicked, for nothing. Meanwhile, the dog kept barking non-stop.

"Why don't you tie her to a tree?" I asked. "Or we can put her in the car."

"I'm not going to tie her to a tree!" Rachel answered, affronted by the idea. "But," she reflected. "We can put her in your car."

"Great!" I said, and with a quick switch, Max was in the backseat of the Chrysler, and Rachel was in my arms.

"Baby, I really thought that something was wrong," I said when we surfaced from the first round of kisses.

"Why do you keep saying that?" she said, pulling back from me.

"It was the sound of your voice," I said. "It sounded like you needed me."

"Well, I always need you, but –" she said, reaching to touch my cheek.

I grabbed her hand and held it.

"No," I said seriously. "I was really concerned. I thought that something bad had happened. I don't know what Eleanor or Herb are going to do and –"

Laughing, she threw her arms around my head and pulled me into a single kiss, effectively silencing me. It was a good, deep kiss. And kissing is always better than talking, right? She took a breath and held my face in her hands.

"Oh, baby," she said. "You are so sweet. No! I forgot to give you a good luck kiss for tomorrow. I know how much it means to you, Columbia and everything. Besides, didn't you *want* to see me again?"

"Of course I did – *do*," I said. "But I got worried."

"All you want to do is protect me."

"Well," I said. "Isn't that my job? Isn't that what a boyfriend is supposed to do?"

She smiled contentedly. "You really *do* love me, don't you?"

"You know I do. Is that so hard to believe?"

"No," she replied, but something suddenly changed in her. I could see it in her face.

She turned away from me. I wasn't sure what I'd said, but it didn't really matter. I was getting used to Rachel's emotional swings. I knew that she was under a lot of pressure, or rather, she *felt* that she was under pressure. Which is really the same thing when you think about it.

"It's just . . . I don't know how I'm going to get through this year," she said in a tired, small voice.

"What?" I said, trying to turn her back toward me. "Why? Did something happen?"

"She threatened me again," she said. "About not letting me see you if I don't take this school year seriously and apply to colleges and all that garbage that I don't want to do."

"That's ridiculous," I said.

"And Herb is always behind her," she said. "*Agreeing* with her, adding his stupid little advice. I really think there's something crooked about that guy. I really hope my father takes care of him."

I hated to see her so troubled by all these adults.

"It would serve them all right," she said. "If my father killed *both* of them."

"Don't say things like that!" I finally caught her eye and turned her around to face me. "Look, nothing is going to stop me from seeing you. *Nothing. Ever.* No Eleanor. No Herb. *Nothing.*" Which made her smile, if just a little. "We're going to get through this week, and then I'll come home, and we'll go out on Friday night, on a date," I said confidently. "Just like regular people, regular teenagers."

She paused, reflecting on the idea, sniffing back a tear. "A date? That sounds . . . interesting. Where would you like to take me?"

"Since Bailey's is too far, how about . . . paradise?" I replied.

That earned me a wide, dreamy smile from her, and another long, deep kiss. (I was getting this boyfriend thing down pretty well.)

"I really hafta go," she said. "They're gonna wonder where I am. It's not so long till Friday."

"It really isn't," I agreed with her and tried to mean it.

"You're so lucky," she said glumly. "You're going off to the City. I'm still stuck here on the Island."

"Just don't you fall in love with any of the guys at high school," I said. "Some rich quarterback, or –" I was about to say the name "Eric," but I didn't dare to. I didn't want to remind her of him.

"Don't worry," she replied. "The boys at Oakhurst are like children. They're all conceited and shallow. I don't want anyone but you."

That was very good to hear.

"Don't *you* fall in love with any of those super-smart college girls," she cautioned.

"There *are* no girls at Columbia," I countered with. "There are girls at Barnard, across Broadway, but I think they're pretty separate."

"Good," she said firmly.

We walked a few steps back toward the car before she started to cloud up again.

"I'm going to miss you so much," she said. "I hate to go back in there. I sort of hate everything but being with you. Is that wrong? I hate it when things end –"

"This isn't the end," I said, taking her by the shoulders. "This is the beginning! I'll see you this weekend, and once school gets started, we'll see more of each other than ever. And we'll be freer! No Jerry, no Estelle!"

She stood there, trying to believe me.

"So this is not an actual goodbye," I reasoned. "It's a *temporary* goodbye. Just until Friday."

"Until Friday," she repeated, trying to build confidence.

We were back by the car. Max was standing up in the back seat, her wet nose against the window, licking the glass.

"I have to go," she said. "Hell-eanor will have the cops out for me."

She reached out and opened up the rear door of the Chrysler. Max instantly jumped out and ran straight to my pants leg. I recoiled, as if she was going to bite, but she just started smelling my ankles and shoes intently. Rachel grabbed the leash and pulled her back.

"She likes to smell things," Rachel said.

"She's a dog," I said.

We stood there for a while, facing our moment of separation.

"I had no idea you were this rich," I said.

"Don't say that," she said. "And there are plenty of people richer than us."

"Which of these mansions is yours?" I asked.

"They're not mansions," she said. "They're just big houses."

"Same thing," I said.

She sighed and pointed down the block, saying, "When you go past the cul-de-sac, look across to the far end. It's the big brick house straight ahead, with the long driveway and the black door. The one that looks like a prison."

We had one last kiss. This time Max wound her leash around our legs as she sniffed my pants up and down. Then, as Rachel smiled a "goodbye" and walked away, I got into the Chrysler and turned on the engine. I did a quick three-point turn and drove back past Rachel. Rolling down the window, I waved one last goodbye.

"Bye, Max!" I yelled, which made Rachel laugh as I drove on.

I slowed down and cruised past the entry to the cul-de-sac, looking down at the end, just as she had instructed. Sure enough, I saw a huge brick house with a black door and shutters in the distance at the end of a long lawn, a perfect stretch of green.

"Some prison," I muttered. Then I sped up and got out of there.

∿

I always seemed to be leaving her. I decided to look at it as just another Five Days Without Rachel. One of my main memories of the whole thing with Rachel was the sense of constantly *leaving* her. I always seemed to be driving away from her, feeling the emptiness of missing her. Even now, in this cell, I can still summon up the feeling of that particular hurt. But at that moment, I remember feeling really positive and enthusiastic about things. It was going to be a great year – a full school life *and* a full love life. I was going to make it that way: everything playing, hitting on all cylinders. OK, I could see that, with Rachel and me, I was going to have to be the stable one considering her home life and what was happening with the divorce, etc. But we could do it. We could handle Rachel's parents. And Herb, too, for that matter. We could do everything.

But even then I was learning that everything good in this life – even a few extra moments with Rachel – comes with a price. When I got back home, I discovered that Max had peed on the floor in the back seat of the Chrysler.

Record of Events #19 – entered Friday, 9:39 P.M.

～

The next day I went off to Columbia. All my life I had been told that one day I would "go away to college," and now this was the day. OK, it was just an hour's car ride into Manhattan, and I planned to be back that Friday night to take Rachel out, but it was still a momentous day. My mother fought back tears as my Dad and I pulled out of the driveway with a full carload of my stuff, partially because I was going away and partially because we weren't letting her come to help move me in. I let her fuss over me and tell me I looked "just like Sir Laurence Olivier" (her standard compliment to me – once she had meant it; now it was our private joke). But I didn't let her come with me to help me move into my dorm; I'm not that stupid.

I'm not going to go into too much detail about my time at Columbia. Only what's necessary. They don't particularly like me over there. (I'm using *extra* fake names for them all.) They weren't too pleased about all the publicity from my trial, and they don't like the fact that I will be forever associated with their wonderful institution. Their idea of famous alumni is more like Alexander Hamilton, John Jay, and FDR, not some teenage thrill/revenge killer. Even an innocent one.

My father dropped me off on Amsterdam Avenue, just where the Freshman Orientation packet told us to. There was a long line of waiting cars. We got into the back of the line and gradually inched our way to the front. On the sidewalk, there were porters in uniform with big sleds on wheels, ready to take people's luggage away. My Dad and I got out of the car and started unloading the Chrysler.

"We shoulda taken your mother with us," he said. "She would have liked this."

"You can tell her about it," I said. "We unloaded luggage. She didn't miss anything."

A porter put some colored tags around each of my things in a very efficient way and gave me a receipt for everything. A young man in a blue blazer with the Columbia crest on its pocket told us to follow the signs for "Freshman Registration." I saw other guys getting out of cars with their fathers (or both parents). Everyone seemed excited and busy; it was a clear September day, perfect for new beginnings. So much optimism, so much anxiety.

My father clapped me on the shoulder and gave me a squeeze.

"I'm real proud of you, son," he said. I could see a little tear shine in the corner of his eye.

"Thanks, Dad," I said.

His words still haunt me to this day. They echo in my mind as I sit here in this never-ending cell/hell, trying to remember everything.

~

I'll admit that I was nervous on that first day, but it was a *good* nervousness. I had been waiting my whole life for this moment, and it had finally come. I followed the path of signs onto the campus, with a stream of other freshmen, coming up from the car line on Amsterdam Avenue. I walked with a bunch of other guys who mostly sort of looked like me: guys in jeans with their hair a little long, in long, floppy shirts, wearing different kinds of sneakers. Oh, there were a few guys in sports jackets and ties, a few large jocks (tall and/or wide), and a few black/Chinese/Puerto Rican guys, but mostly they were like me. Or, rather, I was like them.

The people in charge were very nice to us freshman as they processed us through the system like smart little sausages. One after another, we got our room assignments (with a key in an envelope) and registered for our classes, with a lunch in between. Everybody was smiling, being helpful to the freshmen. Which was the right thing to do. I mean, most of the freshmen, myself included, were pretty exhausted/shell-shocked by the end of the day. This was after moving in. I wound up dragging all my things up the narrow staircase to my room on the fourth floor of one of the older dorms, one without an elevator.

I'm not going to say too much about my roommate, any-more than I have to for the sake of my story. I'm going to call him Roommate A. If you want to know his real name, you can look it up in the newspapers. He testified at my trial, so it's all there in the transcripts. He was subpoenaed, so he had no choice in going on the witness stand. I know that he did not enjoy the experience, so I don't wish to prolong his public exposure. I'm sure that he already feels that I've ruined his chances to become Governor of New York or a Supreme Court Justice or something, but there's nothing I can do about that now. I will tell you this one thing about him and let you be the judge: he puts actual shined pennies in his penny loafers. (Now you see why I've chosen to call him Roommate "A.")

I could hardly wait until 8:00 when I could call Rachel and tell her all about this very full day . . . and to ask her about *her* first day of school. But first there was this long dinner, followed by an even longer "Invocation" in the famous fake-Greek library, full of platitudes and malarkey. Nice, in-telligent platitudes and jokey, ice-breaking malarkey, all of it well-meaning; but it still ran late. One thing I learned quickly about Columbia: these people *loved* to hear themselves talk. Once the Invocation ended, I bounded down the wide stair-case in front of the library to find a pay phone. As I walked around campus during the day, I had scoped out where the pay phones were. There were a pair of phone booths in the basement of my dorm, which I saw when I was getting my mailbox and its tiny key. I would try for them first.

My dorm was just catty-corner across from the library so it was an easy trot across the pavement to my target. I shot down the stairs to the mailroom, visualizing that at least one of the phone booths would be empty. In the Freshman Orientation packet, there was information about having a private phone installed in your room, but it was way too expensive for me. I would have to rely on the hall phone that served my whole dormitory floor and the pay phones scattered around the campus.

At the bottom of the steps, I turned the corner and walked down the basement hallway into the mailroom and, wouldn't you know it, both phone booths were occupied. I could see the little overhead lights shining down on the two guys in the booths. One guy had his back turned to the glass; the other one was holding onto the handle of the bi-fold door that enclosed him.

Damn! I thought. What should I do: wait, or try to find another phone? Maybe if I went over and stood outside the booths, one of them would get the idea that someone was waiting. That would probably be rude, to stand right outside, but still, they should know that someone was waiting to use the phone.

Just then, as if reading my mind, one of them – the guy on the right – pulled opened his door as he was hanging up the phone. Before he was out of the booth, I made my move and was in his seat, which was still warm, which sort-of grossed me out, before he was out of the mailroom.

I closed the door behind me, dropped my coins in – coins that were damp from my tight grip – and dialed. To my great relief, the other end picked up before the first ring ended.

"Sorry I'm late," I said.

"I am too," she whispered. "But I forgive you."

I was instantly glad to hear her voice. I felt my whole body *unclench*.

"How are you?" I lowered my voice to match her whisper.

"I'm without you," she said. "So how good can I be?"

"But *now* you're back talking to me," I said. "So things are better, right?"

"Yes," she said. "You're right. I like that you're right."

There was a moment of silence, a comfortable silence. We were back in The Zone.

"How was your day at school?" I said.

"Not so great," she answered dryly. "But how was *yours*?"

I was really sorry to hear her say that, so I just replied, "Interesting. Busy. The main thing is: Am I going to see you on Friday night?"

"I hope so," she said. "I *think* so. She's on the warpath. Somehow she found out about last night, when you came to see me. She says the problem is when I lie about things. But if I tell her the truth, she doesn't like that either! But – forget it – nothing's going to stop me from seeing you Friday."

"Good," I said.

She told me about her school's assistant principal who had singled her out and all the people at Oakhurst High she disliked. In a perverse way, I was almost happy to hear how much she couldn't stand all the people in her life, and how much she dreaded her upcoming year in high school. The unhappier she was, the more she was bound to me.

"And how is He*rrrr*b?" I asked, prompting a bitter laugh and a grunt.

"You're not gonna believe this," she said. "He started to move more of his stuff in. I was in my mother's bathroom and I found these disgusting little bits of hair all around the sink. And his shaving stuff was there! It's like he's living here permanently."

"No, really?" I said. *So soon after the divorce? Manny's really gonna love that!* I thought, but I didn't say.

"He's moving in," she said. "And she calls me a slut."

"She does not!" I shot back.

"Yes," she said. "And *worse*."

I felt a flood of anger rise within me suddenly. The thought of somebody being cruel, or saying something this cruel to Rachel blanked my mind for a moment. And this was coming from her mother?

"Are you there?" she asked.

"What?" I replied.

"What's wrong?"

"Nothing."

"Don't you want to talk to me?" she said, sounding suddenly insecure.

"All I do all day is talk to you," I shot back. "In my mind. All day, I think, 'I can't wait to tell Rachel this,' or 'Rachel would laugh at that.' What are you saying? You're *never* out of my mind. Never, for a moment."

She didn't say anything for a moment. Then she replied contentedly, "Good. Now, tell me about Friday night."

Record of Events #20 – entered Saturday, 5:38 A.M.

~

Friday couldn't come soon enough. After a couple of days of various kinds of orientation activities and assemblies, I started actual classes. Nine o'clock in the morning, five days a week. I had heard that, in college, schedules were supposed to be easier. Guys could stay up all night and sleep until noon, or not have any classes on a Friday or a Monday or both. Unfortunately, that didn't apply at Columbia, at least not during freshman year.

Right from the start, I realized that I was going to have to work my butt off, studying here. There was a lot of reading, for every class, and a science requirement that included a full laboratory session every week. I chose geology – "Rocks for Jocks," instead of say, "Mickey Mouse Math" or "Physics for Poets" – because it was the only science class that didn't meet on Friday afternoons. That way I would be sure to be able to get out of the City early, before the weekend rush hour began in earnest.

"You're not staying around?" asked Roommate A. "They're having a mixer with the freshman girls at Barnard."

"No thanks," I said.

"Suit yourself," said Roommate A. "More room for me."

Our room was small, so anytime the other guy was gone, it doubled one's amount of living space. In one way, I was lucky. I won the coin toss when we moved in, and *he* had to sleep on the top of the bunk bed. I'm not kidding: the room was too small for two separate beds. At night, before going to sleep, the last thing I would see was the metal web of springs and sagging mattress above me, as Roommate A tossed and turned his fat body into dreamland. I'm just glad he didn't sleepwalk. I might have gotten crushed some night.

Friday afternoon, I was out of there like a shot. I stuffed my suitcase with enough clothes for the weekend, a pillow-case full of my dirty laundry for my mother to do as long as I was there, and a lot of books for my weekend's reading/ homework. My Freshman Composition teacher (who testified at my trial and whom I will here re-name in order to protect his privacy: Professor Brilliant – he'll love that!) wanted a pa-per every Monday. This first one was only two pages – typed, double-spaced – but it still had to be written. But I had until Monday morning. Between then and now, I had plenty of time.

Going back to the Island, I had two choices. Either I could take the subway down to Penn Station and catch the Long Is-land RR out to my hometown's station, or I could take the sub-way all the way out to Jamaica in Queens and catch a bus out to the Island. The railroad way was more expensive and faster, except that there was a schedule and sometimes you had to wait. The subway-bus option was longer and cheaper, but it kept me moving and let me off just two short blocks from my house. If I took the railroad, I had to be either picked up from the station by car (which usually meant my Mom or Dad) or take a cab (too much money.) This time, I did the subway.

From years of riding in and out of Manhattan during high school, I had my New York subway-riding technique down pat. Find a corner seat, secure whatever package or piece of luggage I was carrying, get out a book, curl into a shell, and disappear into my reading. But to make sure that I wasn't bothered or hassled, I was also sure to protect my space with wide elbows and a surly look, too, like *I* might be the one with a butcher knife under *my* coat, so don't mess with me. This was unless there was a little old lady standing there. Then I would give her my seat. Fortunately, there was no little old lady when I got on the Broadway local at 116th Street.

Is there anything worse than commuting on public trans-
portation? (I mean, besides sitting in a cell, going absolutely
nowhere.) Is there anything more unpleasant than a long ride
in a bumpy, smelly crowded subway? Yes, there is: a long ride
in a bumpy, smelly crowded *bus*. But I learned to do it. Millions of people do it every day. I just never learned how *not* to
complain about it.

So I carefully put my little suitcase on my lap, opened it
a crack, and slipped out a book. I felt like a tourist, carrying
a suitcase on the subway, but I had no choice. I put my hand
in and drew out the first book on my list: Homer's *Odyssey*.
Perfect for the long trip home. I opened it to the page I had
marked and dove in.

I surfaced in time to change to the express train at Nine-
ty-Sixth Street. Sometimes, I can concentrate so hard on
things that I lose track of where I am, so I always have to be
on guard from falling too deeply into my own thoughts. That
can be dangerous, in the real world.

I had prepped my parents, telling them that I was coming
home Friday night, so they knew that I wanted use of one of
the cars. If they wanted to go out to a movie – which happened
once every five years or so – they could take the Chrysler and
leave me the Ford. Everything was planned. I would pick up
Rachel at 8:00, and we would be free . . . at least for a few
hours. That goal – *being alone with Rachel for a few hours* –
got me through the week and would get me through the rest of
my trip back to the Island.

By the time I changed trains at Fifty-Ninth Street and
again at Seventh Avenue to pick up the E Train out to Queens,
I had steamed through the Homer selections and was onto
Plato's *Republic*. Did I mention that Columbia is famous for
force-feeding the classics to their freshmen? In high school,
we got some of this stuff, but this was the real thing.

I had done this basic route, bus and subway, many, many
times during high school, escaping from the Island into the
City with my friends. I wasn't exactly an everyday dead-in-

the-eyes drone commuter, but I knew the way and could just follow the crowd, out of the subway car, up the stairs, and out to the buses.

You know from Mooncliff how much I hate buses. Well, the city buses were even worse. The diesel was fumier, the grime grimier, and the roads simply sucked. But I knew what to do: I went to the second-to-last seat in the back, barricaded myself next to the window with my suitcase, and disappeared into Plato. And I did, for a few pages of tiny print, before other thoughts started leaking into *The Republic*. Like where would I take Rachel that night? Did I have enough cash to cover the weekend? What about Saturday? Could I also see her on Saturday? I reminded myself to clean out the backseat of whatever car I was taking – probably the Ford – and to throw a blanket in the back, just in case.

My mother gave me a big welcome when I walked in the door. I admit that I was tired. I was up early that morning because Roommate A woke me with his cough. He smoked unfiltered Gauloises, if you can believe it, a habit he picked up, he told me more than once, when he did a summer session at the Sorbonne.

"How would you like to do some laundry for me?" I asked her as I trudged up the stairs with my suitcase.

"Me?" she said. "I would *love* to do some laundry for you. I haven't done enough laundry this week, and I was really hoping for more."

"Thank you, Mother," I said.

"So what do you want for dinner?" my mother asked as I got to the top of the stairs.

"Whatever you want!" I said. And I meant it. I had more important things to do than think about food.

I spent the time before my 8:00 date with Rachel showering and shaving, wolfing down some take-out Chinese food while I finished off the Plato, and cleaning out the car (yes, I remembered the blanket). I left early, wearing nice jeans, a blue-striped Oxford shirt, and my blue blazer. Before Rachel,

I never really gave much thought to what I wore or what I looked like, other than to be clean and presentable. Now I wanted to look at least *decent* for her. I couldn't let the contrast between our appearances be too noticeable. It was one thing when we both wore a lot of Mooncliff green-and-white; the real world was different. I didn't want to be the Beast to her Beauty, at least not so obviously. And, if I had another encounter with Eleanor and Herb – I really hoped that Rachel would just come right outside when I rang the doorbell and spare me – I would feel more adult, armed by my sports jacket with my lucky RFK pin in the pocket.

By then, I could get to her house in my sleep. In my dreams, both day- and night-dreams, I had already driven this way many times. All week I had been waiting to see Rachel, and the time had finally come. Through classes – some boring, some interesting – studying and not studying, sitting in my dorm room or someplace else, I would think about Rachel. I couldn't keep my mind on any subject more than a few minutes before thoughts of Rachel, fantasies of Rachel would intrude, transporting me back to The Zone. Nothing was better; nothing was as satisfying. And now we were about to be together. It was crazy, but my heart felt like it was going to burst out of my chest.

I timed my arrival perfectly, turning into the Princes' cul-de-sac at five minutes to eight. It was a good, long walk up the flagstone path to the front door of the huge brick fortress and its big, shiny black-painted door. I heard the sound of my steps, slapping on the stone. I always knew that *this* moment would come: calling for her at her house. I didn't think things would look so big and unfriendly – all black shutters and curtained windows – but I refused to be intimidated. I rang her doorbell at exactly 8:00.

I waited longer than I expected to – why wasn't she right at the door? – and was on the verge of pushing the button a second time when I heard footsteps inside, approaching. The door opened. As soon as I saw Rachel, I could tell that she had been crying. She couldn't even look me straight in the eye, but I could see.

"Come on in," she said softly, forcing a smile. "They want to see you."

"They?" I said, probably louder than I should have. As I walked in the doorway, I moved to kiss her.

"No," she said, putting out her hand. "Not here."

She took my hand and led me into the house. It didn't take more than a few moments, walking through the Princes' foyer and living room – with the big, fancy staircase leading to a balcony overlooking the downstairs and a gold-and-crystal, flower-encrusted chandelier hanging from the silver ceiling – for me to feel that there was something unnatural about the house. Everything – all the furniture, the lamps that glowed dimly, the velvet drapes that hung over the windows like vultures, the huge fireplace in the living room with a gleaming set of brass fireplace tools in a stand – everything was thick and heavy and rich-looking, all satin and silk. But as fancy and rich as everything was, there seemed to be no fresh air in the house.

"How're you doin'?" I whispered as we passed through a dark dining room that had against one wall a big breakfront with glass doors that held plates edged with gold and lots of little painted china statues of dogs in different little outfits.

She squeezed my hand and said, "Wait till we get out of here."

I squeezed back, in support. But just before we entered a big back room, she dropped my hand and pushed it away.

The dining room opened onto an enormous back room with big windows, a high ceiling, flowery, tropical wallpaper, and French doors at the end that opened to the outside patio. There was a large bar with four black barstools and another fireplace – even bigger than the one in the living room – made of rough flagstone with another set of brass fireplace tools that had horses' heads for the handles, and over the mantel a big, modern clock with spiky hands and dots for numbers hung on the wall. Set against the other wall was an enormous color TV, the biggest I'd ever seen. And at the back of the room, right in front of us, on either side of the French doors, were Eleanor and Herb, enthroned in big black leather Barcaloungers. They both held highball glasses filled with an orange liquid in one hand and something to smoke in the other – she had a cigarette, him a cigar.

"Well, hello there!" Eleanor called out as we entered. I don't think I visibly cringed, but I cringed inside.

"Hello," I said, trying to sound normal and relaxed. "Happy Friday!"

I gave them a nice smile and stood there in the doorway with Rachel. This was the last thing I wanted – Round Two with Eleanor and Herb – but I was ready to endure whatever they had in mind for me.

"Working ya hard, freshman?" cracked Herb, swirling the ice cubes in his glass.

"Yes, sir," I said honestly. "They are."

"Good!" he barked and took a sip of his drink. "Hard work is good for ya. Toughens ya up."

"You're right," I said. "It's good to be tough." I knew that my automatic agreement with him was just on the edge of insolence.

"Beats lying face down in a rice paddy!" he said with a sharper tone.

"Herb!" barked Eleanor. "Come on! Nothing about the war!" She turned to me and said, "We were just watching Walter Cronkite and he said –"

"Hey, kid," rasped Herb. "Get a load o' this! *Remote control* . . . Zenith Space Commander."

He held up this metal device and pressed a button with his thumb, which changed the channel on the big TV from across the room.

"Nice!" I said. It *was* cool, and it was the polite thing to say.

"You press your finger," said Herb smugly. "You don't even have to move. It even has a button to mute the sound. Something every woman should come with."

"Herb!" cautioned Eleanor.

"Only kidding! Only kidding . . ." Herb answered. "By the way, El', great whiskey sour."

Rachel rescued us, interrupting with "We have to go, Mother." She took my hand and started to back us out of the room.

"Did you feed Max?" Eleanor called as we were going.

"Yes!"

"Don't be late! You remember what we discussed."

"I won't be! And yes, I remember. Every word."

"Don't be such a brat, and say goodnight to Herb!" Eleanor ordered, but Rachel said nothing, turned us around, and sped us out of the room.

I called out a weak "Bye!" as Rachel practically dragged me across the dining room and the living room toward the front door. I tried to say something, but she shushed me.

"Wait!" she whispered. "Wait until we're outside."

She slammed the door behind us and instantly turned to me, almost leaping into my arms. She hugged me tightly, burying her face in my neck. It was as if she were holding on for dear life.

I held her tightly, trying to comfort her.

"Baby," I whispered. "What's wrong?"

I wanted to get her away from the house. It would be just like Eleanor to be looking out from behind the velvet drapes.

"We should go," I said, holding her away from me. I looked into her downturned eyes and asked, "Where would you like to go?"

She looked up at me with those blue-blue eyes, now wet with tears, and said simply, "Your room."

∿

I briefly thought of smuggling Rachel up to my room without introducing her to my parents, but that wasn't reasonable. It was the correct thing to do, plus they would have heard my key in the door and would have come to see who was breaking into their house anyway.

"Mom, this is Rachel," I said. "Rachel, this is my mother."

"So nice to meet you!" they both said, in absolute unison, rushing toward each other for a quick little hug. It was hard to watch, and I separated them as soon as I could.

"We're going upstairs," I said. "I want to show Rachel my –"

"Don't be rude," Rachel said, turning on me. "Your mother and I are allowed to say hello."

"Yes," my mother stood, agreeing with her. "Have you noticed how bossy he is?"

"Absolutely!" Rachel declared. "He is very bossy!"

"So, you know what you do?" my mother suggested. "Don't *let* 'im boss you!"

Rachel laughed and my mother laughed too. They were having a little fun at my expense, but I didn't mind too much.

"Can we just please stop the tag-team match – ?" I said, delicately separating them.

"There's some Baskin-Robbins in the freezer!" my mother said as I guided Rachel gently in the direction of the staircase up to my room.

"Thank you! We're fine!" I said, practically herding Rachel up the stairs.

"Will you stop?" Rachel hissed at me.

"Good night!" I said to my mother as an invitation for her to disappear.

"Good night, Rachel!" my mother called, but by then we were halfway up the stairs.

"Your mother is so cute!" Rachel whispered, trying to turn around.

"Please!" I said as I guided her into my room and closed the door behind us.

"She's like a little doll!

"What? Is there a Peasant Barbie?"

"Be nice!" said Rachel, putting her arms around my neck.

"I *am* nice!" I said, pulling her into a kiss that was way, way, way overdue.

"Can I breathe?" she gasped.

"Breathe later."

~

It was later that the real tears came. In the moonlight. We were lying on my bed when I touched her on the back of her arm someplace and she let out a little "Oww!"

I reached and felt the little rough patch on the soft part of her upper arm and she said, "Oww! Stop that!"

"What is that?" I said but she pulled away from me and covered the spot on her arm.

"Nothing!" she said, but I grabbed her and turned her arm to the moonlight; there was a dark little circle on the pale flesh of her upper arm.

"What is that?" I said, not sure of what I was seeing. "What happened?"

She looked down, not wanting to tell me.

"Eleanor burned me there with a cigarette."

"*What*?" I said, my mind briefly flashing white with anger. "Are you kidding??"

"She says it was an accident," she scoffed. "But I don't believe her."

"That –" I didn't curse but I wanted to. "She can't do that," I said. "You should have called the police."

"And then what? When she says it was an accident," she said, her eyes filled with tears that reflected the outside light. There was a streetlight two doors down from my house that burned all night. "And anyway, Herb is this big-deal lawyer.

He knows all the cops and the people in the town government. He's always dropping these big hints about his connections and who he knows. I really think he might be connected to the Mafia."

"The *Mafia*?" I repeated, thinking that Herb certainly seemed sleazy enough to be in the Mob, but that meant nothing. "How do you know?"

"I don't *know*," she said. "I've just got this feeling, just the way they stop talking about stuff when I enter the room."

"OK," I agreed with her, seeing that she was seriously worried about what was going on. "Then why don't you call your father and tell him about what she did?"

"I *should* do it," she said sardonically. "Pour a little gasoline on the fire. See how *she* likes it."

"I suppose you're right," I said, seeing her point. "But you can't let her burn you, or do anything like that again!"

"But I got my revenge," she smirked. "I took three hundred dollars from her."

"*What?*"

"She won't miss it!" Rachel dismissed my objection. "She has loads of cash hidden in the back of her closet that she never uses. My father has cash too. They both love cash."

"Well, good for them," I said. "Good for all of them. . . . Bastards. . . . Still, stealing is wrong."

She just laughed once and said, "You know I only do what I have to do, under the circumstances. You understand. The money is for *us*."

I sat there, holding her in the moonlight through the window. I touched her leg. It was sleek and smooth, like soft ivory. She took my hand and held it against her face. I caught a glimpse of the burn mark again.

"I just can't stand the thought of anyone being mean to you," I said. "*I* really feel like calling the cops on her. Or some social service –"

"Please don't!" she pleaded, holding my hand tightly. "Let me handle things. I can deal with it . . . for now."

"OK, but if she's *burning your arm –*"

"I'll get my Mustang when I turn eighteen, and I'll get myself out of there."

"Good," I said.

"I have an appointment with my family's lawyer," she continued, shifting around and sitting up. "And I'm going to find out exactly how much my grandma left me."

"Excellent," I said. "The grandma money."

Looking out the window, staring at nothing, she said, "After all these years, they still don't know who they're dealing with. I *refuse* to let them ruin my life."

She started to shake, unsuccessfully trying to hold back her tears.

I really didn't know where she was going, or what her intentions were. How bad things would get with her mother and everything. I only knew that I wanted to be with her. To help her, and hold her, and do everything that a lover and friend should do. Again, it was the obvious thing to do.

～

I didn't see her for the rest of the weekend. I spent most of the next two days sitting at my parents' dining room table, waiting by the phone and working on my first Freshman Composition paper for Professor Brilliant. Both things sucked. I didn't actually talk to Rachel again until Sunday night when I was back at the dorm.

"My father came and took me," she said. "It was *his* weekend."

"What do you mean 'his weekend'?" I asked.

"I told you," she said. "They're gonna split me sometimes."

"And you couldn't call me?" I asked, trying not to sound too put out.

"It was super early in the morning and he took me with this friend of his on a private plane to this lake in Connecticut," she said. "They didn't have a phone there."

"On the private plane?" I asked, playing dumb on purpose.

"No!" she said. "Where we went. To this stupid lake. We flew out of Islip. Then we came back. I was sick the whole time. The one good thing was that I didn't have to see Eleanor and Herb for two days."

"Is Herb still there?"

"Herb is *always* here!" she half screamed through clenched teeth. "Don't you understand?"

I let there be silence for a while. I reminded myself that no matter what I had to do (commuting, all this homework, and Roommate A), she had it worse. And, for that, she needed me.

"OK," I said. "I'm sorry."

"Don't be," she muttered. "I should have found a way. But I could *feel* you. I could *feel* you waiting for me."

"Remember Friday night?" I asked, trying to bring her closer to me even though we were on the phone.

"I remember," she said, a dreamy smile in her voice.

"That was the best part of the weekend."

"Damn right it was!" she laughed her musical laugh.

"What do you think about next weekend?" I asked.

"Can I just get through this weekend before we start worrying about next weekend?" she pleaded.

"Sorry," I muttered. "I was just asking."

"No," she said. "You're right. That's how I'm going to stay alive until I see you again."

"Call me," I said. "Whenever you want. If I'm not in class, I'm in my room. I gave you the number for the hall phone in my dorm. Use it! I could be in the library or someplace, but it doesn't matter –" My mind started to spin, thinking of the work I still had to do.

"Oh, no!" Rachel hissed. "He's looking for me."

"Who's looking for you?" I asked.

"I gotta go."

"Tomorrow night?" I said quickly. "Eight o'clock?"

"I love you so much," she whispered desperately and hung the phone up hard.

Sudden silence. I hung up my phone softly, left high and dry, worrying about what she was facing at home, worrying about this unfinished Freshman Comp paper and all the rest of the work I had to do – until the next time I could be in The Zone with her, and escape this unfriendly, pressurized world.

Record of Events #21 – entered Saturday, 9:48 P.M.

~

Things went on like this for a few weeks. Some things better, some things not. I got to see Rachel on Friday nights – glorious Friday nights when we'd go back to my room upstairs to be together. Sometimes she'd find a way to steal time on Saturday or Sunday, and we would meet secretly at the Oakhurst public library or some mall, any mall. But she always felt nervous that someone would see us together and report back to Eleanor.

I didn't ask her about Eric, nor did I detect any slip up on her part. She seemed as devoted to me as ever, and just as sure that we were going to be together when she got her "grandma money." I didn't really know whether to believe her about that; I was just happy that we were together and she still seemed to love me as much as at Mooncliff. Maybe more. I didn't detect any further cigarette burns on her, thank goodness, but her relationship with Eleanor was as rocky as ever. And Eleanor loved to put up roadblocks between Rachel and me, whenever she could.

"They don't understand why I want to spend time with someone who actually *likes* me as a person," Rachel said. "Is there something wrong with that?"

Apparently, there was.

On alternate Fridays, I had the pleasure of picking her up at her father's condominium apartment in Garden City.

Manny Prince. He *was* a trip-and-a-half. If you thought I got a frosty reception from Eleanor and Herb, you can imagine what Rachel's actual father thought of me.

"Come on in," he said with a tone of voice that said *Get the hell outta here, punk!* as I walked into the foyer of his top-floor unit in the big fake-limestone, fake-chateau apartment building.

"Why, thank you, Mr. Prince," I replied, extending my hand for a handshake that felt like I was offering my arm to a shark's mouth. "Nice to meet you."

Manny was a large, slope-shouldered man, wearing a heavy gold watch on his thick wrist and one of those white embroidered shirts with lots of pockets that they wear down in the Caribbean. I made eye contact with him as we shook hands, and I instantly saw where Rachel got her blue-blue eyes. But Rachel's eyes were alluring and warm; Manny's eyes were as cold as a threat.

"Yeah. She'll be ready in a minute," he said, crushing my fingers just enough to establish his greater strength.

"Good!" I agreed, perhaps a bit too quickly as I extracted my hand from his grip.

"Come on in," he ordered. "Sit down."

I sat down on the first thing I could find – an ottoman at the foot of a big lounger, across from the big TV in the big living room – as Manny flipped on all the lights, showing the full expanse of the room: shiny marble floors, two chandeliers, three couches, and glimmering walls hung with gold-framed paintings of flowers and what looked like the Italian coastline.

"This is a great apartment," I said.

"It's a condominium," he corrected me.

"Then it's a great condominium," I replied.

As soon as I said it, I knew that I sounded like a smart-ass. It's just that I was nervous. I sometimes think that the source of most of my smart-assedness is nerves.

Manny glared at me. I had to say something.

"Rachel says that she likes it over here," I began enthusi-astically.

I could tell he didn't believe me.

"I love my daughter," he said bluntly. "But she's like her mother: sometimes she says things that she don't necessarily mean."

Another conversation stopper. He made me long for my good buddy Herb. Fortunately, Rachel came into the room to rescue me.

"This is so annoying, Daddy," she said, still putting one last brushstroke through her long, dark hair. "I don't have any of my right things over here. They're all at the house."

With a scornful flick of his hand, Manny said, "Whatever you don't have, buy! I told you that a hundred times. Just stop complaining."

"I'm not complaining," said Rachel sharply as she put the brush into her little purse. "I'm just stating a fact! You said you wanted me to be more realistic. Well, this is realistic."

"What time are you going to be home?" Manny said, ig-noring her comment.

"What time do you want me to be home?" she said back to him.

Manny turned to me and said with deadly directness, "Have her home by midnight."

"*Midnight?*" Rachel squealed in protest. "One! One *thir-ty!*"

Manny looked at me and said, "Twelve thirty."

"Yes, sir!" I snapped back to him.

"And don't be late."

"I wouldn't even think of it," I said, and that was no lie.

I wanted Manny Prince to like me, and I had gotten off on the wrong foot. I wondered if there was any "right foot" with this tough, thick, humor-deficient man. OK, I didn't really ex-pect him to *like* me, but if his treatment of me, someone whom his daughter obviously cared for, was an indication of how he respected his only child's feelings . . . well, I felt even more compassion for Rachel than before.

Fortunately, Manny wanted to get rid of us as fast as we wanted to get out there.

"He has a girlfriend," she said as we practically raced to my car.

"How do you know?" I asked.

"I know because my father doesn't smell like Chanel No. 5," she answered.

"I bet."

"I think he's had a bunch of girlfriends, over the years."

As I was about to put Rachel in the car on the passenger's side, she stopped suddenly, turned, and gave me a sweet, soft kiss.

"Now you see why I love you so much," she said with a sad smile. "You're the opposite of everything that I was raised with, everything that I can't stand anymore."

~

She spent the next few hours in my room, trying not to cry. Not crying about school, how much she hated it, and that she had no friends there. ("They're all shallow and stupid and competitive about *everything*.") About missing me constantly, about how her mother and father *and* Herb were treating her.

"He's always around," she said. "He came into my bathroom the other day when I was taking a shower, and it wasn't an accident."

"That sleazebag!" I hissed. "You should be sure you lock the door."

"I thought I did!" she replied. "I lock my door all the time! He said he was looking for something. I never feel safe there. One or the other of them is always after me. I cannot wait to get out of there!"

"You will, baby, you will," I said, trying to comfort her, having no real solution for her now. "You just have to be patient."

"How can I be patient when they're actively *trying* to make me miserable? Like it's a game or something," she cried as the tears flowed again. "And they absolutely *hate* you because you make me happy."

I held her for a long time. She tried to keep from crying so hard that she shook in my arms. I tried to think of things to make her happy as I checked the time on my Sony clock radio.

"So how's Driver's Ed going?" I asked.

That perked her up a little.

"*That*, at least, is good! I've got my Learner's Permit," she said, drying her eyes. "And I'm going to be a *great* driver!"

"I bet you are."

"You know I have excellent hand-to-eye coordination, or whatever they call it."

"That's because you have excellent hands and eyes," I said, happy to see her cheer up a bit.

"I'm not kidding!" she laughed.

"Neither am I!" I silenced her with a kiss. Which was always a good idea.

That helped to clear the clouds for a while, or at least helped us ignore them. I could see that the burn mark on her arm was healing, so I decided to say nothing about it. Afterwards we had a little time to relax and just be together in the The Zone. I played her records and she told me all about school: stories of her ex-friends and ex-rivals. She needed to tell me things. I could see her gain strength from being able to unload her problems on me. I understood her, no matter what she said, and I was always unquestionably on her side.

One night we spent a half hour listening to "A Hard Days' Night," a song we had each heard about a million times, over and over again until we finally figured out together that John was saying, "*So why on Earth should I moan /* 'Cause when I get you alone / You know I feel all right . . ." That became a kind of motto for me later on.

"She keeps after me to do these college applications," Rachel said. "And I have no intention of going."

"Maybe you should fill out a couple," I said. "Just in the New York area. So we can be close. Go to NYU; you'll just be down in the Village."

"I have an appointment next week with this lawyer," she said. "So I'll find out then about my grandma's will."

"Good," I said. "Whatever you want to do is fine with me."

That seemed to satisfy her. I was happy to satisfy her – that was my job. But as we embraced, I couldn't help but see the pile of books on my desk, all the work I'd brought home for the weekend, work that never seemed to be finished. All this *stuff* hanging over my head, shadowing every moment of pleasure with real assignments and absolute deadlines. I naively thought that college was supposed to be fun. I'd be free of the rigid schedule, small minds, and constricting atmosphere of high school. College was supposed to be about deep discussions with learned professors, the free exchange of ideas and all that. What I actually was doing was processing homework, one assignment after another. It was *work*. In fact, it was easier being a counselor at the Moon-shak. Which brought up a perplexing thought: What did I really *want* to do? But in Rachel's arms, all these worries disappeared, if only for a while.

I got her to her father's *condominium* well before 12:30. I wasn't stupid; there was no way that I was going to cross Manny Price, especially on the first date under her father's jurisdiction.

"What about tomorrow?" I asked, whispering in Manny's echoing marble foyer.

"We'll see," she said. "Maybe I can slip away from him. But he's promised to take me Mustang-shopping."

"Well," I snickered. "I can't top that."

"When I get my car," she said. "Nothing will keep us apart."

"I always like how you think. Why is that?"

"Sssh!" she whispered. "I think I hear him!"

I knew it was time to go, again. I was *always* leaving her. There was *never* enough time together. Ever.

"Call me if you can," I said as she closed the door on me. "I'll be waiting."

~

I wound up waiting most of the next day for a call that never came. Maybe Manny took her to several Mustang dealers, to comparison-shop. Somehow, though, I think that when the time came to buy, Manny Prince would just flip open his checkbook and write a check. Or maybe pay cash. Did I mention what Manny Prince did for a living? He owned two lumberyards: one in Nassau County, one in Suffolk.

So I sat at the dining room table most of the day, grinding through my homework, just as I did in high school. "*This* is my college experience?" I asked myself more than once, sitting right where I always had, where I had longed to escape from, not so long ago. I briefly flashed on my high school friends who *really* went away to school, my buddies who went to Williams and Lehigh, who right now were probably frolicking on the quad among the fallen autumn leaves, on the way to a football game with some giggly co-eds from Mount Holyoke or Bryn Mawr.

It was better to be lost, daydreaming about Rachel (both remembering the past and projecting the future), than do what I actually had to do. Sometimes (and maybe I promised not to talk about this) I couldn't keep thoughts of our physical life out of my head. It was indeed unprofitable thinking when she was out of touch and out of reach, but I couldn't help what my brain kept circling back to: our love making. Both the little things and the other. It was fitting that I thought about

these things while I was sitting quietly at the dining room table because over time we had learned to make love quietly:
in my upstairs bedroom, in the backseat of cars, on blankets
and beach towels, and in some frankly uncomfortable places –
places which I would revisit in a heartbeat. I learned to listen
to her when she said that it wasn't the right time of the month
for us to do certain things, no problem. I was a very considerate boyfriend. In fact, we were perfect lovers, so thinking
about it somehow made the absence worse.

Finally, I gave up and went out to a 10:00 movie (*Night of
the Living Dead*, perfect for my mood) and over to The Lexington afterwards, to see if anybody I knew was there. When I
walked in, it was like Death Valley. A couple of railroad workers, an old drunk talking to the waitress at the counter, and
that was it. What the heck? I sat down and had a big Linzer
cookie and a big glass of milk. No caffeine: I wanted to be
able to go to sleep.

As I ate, I thought about driving over to Garden City, to
Manny's condominium. Not that there was any chance of seeing Rachel; she was probably all locked up in that fake chateau. It was probably best to go home, I told myself, go home
and get some good sleep, considering I still had lots more
work to do tomorrow: two papers, studying for midterms, and
the Freshman Comp paper for Professor Brilliant that was due
every Monday (it wasn't the same paper every week; it just felt
like it was). If I couldn't be with Rachel, I told myself, I would
make the best use of all that other time. The work at Columbia was tough, and there was a lot of it. To tell the absolute
truth, in high school, I was always one of the smartest kids in
the class. At Columbia, all the kids were "the smartest kid in
the class" from their home schools, and I couldn't coast. So if
I had to be away from Rachel, perhaps it was a secret bless-
ing to make me study harder. I should make peace with the
amount of time Rachel and I had together. Separation would
only make us stronger in the long run.

Confident that I was thinking maturely and productively, I finished my Linzer cookie and milk, went home, showered, and got into bed. There, I stayed awake until the early, gray dawn, telling myself lies. I missed her everyday and couldn't go for any extended period of time without returning to thoughts of her.

I will admit that I was feeling a little depressed when I got back to the dorm on that cold, drizzly Sunday night after a delayed train and having to ride with a homeless guy asleep in his own urine-soaked pants on the Broadway local. When I slogged into my room half drenched, Roommate A and a couple of the other freshmen were sitting around, talking and smoking Gauloises. I had to shoo one of them, a heavy guy named Harlan, off my bed. I disliked feeling another person's warmth on my bed, but what could I do? I had been gone all weekend.

They were talking about this mixer a bunch of them went to at Fordham on Saturday, looking for "easy Catholic girls."

"Isn't that redundant?" Roommate A remarked.

"How did you do?" I asked.

"They weren't so easy."

We all laughed, guys complaining about girls, something we all had in common.

Roommate A pointed at me with a stab of his thumb and said, "This guy disappears every weekend for home nookie. He has no right to laugh. He willingly crawls back down, down, down into the cultural sewer that is *Lawn-Giland!*"

"I'm not laughing," I laughed along with everybody, in spite of myself.

I have to say that I despise that Manhattan hipper-than-thou thing, whether they're preppies or hipsters, Collegiate or Dalton. On the one hand, I, like all good Long Island boys, couldn't wait to get the hell off the Island and its unremitting flatness, both physical and spiritual, and escape the stifling boredom of the suburbs to the Glittering City and all its glamour and potential rewards – and here I was, going *back* to the Island every weekend. Because, on that other hand was Rachel, who gave me a reason, a very good reason, the *best possible* reason to go back. Didn't the Beatles plainly say, "All You Need Is Love"? That seems to be what all this great literature I've been studying says. And if I avoided engaging in the social challenges of Columbia and competing with all these other smart guys, well, that was just a side benefit of my greater emotion.

He continued, "Did you ever get one of her calls for him on the hall phone? This tiny princess-y voice – *'Is he there?'* – I hope she's worth it, kiddo."

"Oh, she is . . ." I answered. "Kiddo."

These poor privileged schnooks, all looking for a girl, any girl. They would die for what I already had.

Record of Events #22 – entered Sunday, 11:42 A.M.

~

My hope for a positive week, anxiously nurtured through a Monday of dreary classes, vanished Monday night. I called Rachel at 8:00 sharp from one of the phone booths in the mailroom – my "lucky" booth, the one on the right – and could instantly tell that something was wrong.

"Wait a second," she said, and put the phone down for long time, at least five minutes.

She came back on the line just as I was about to hang up.

"Sorry, baby," she whispered as she picked up the line.

"What's the matter?" I asked her.

"Nothing. Everything," she said softly. "She's on the warpath. They want me to go to this College Night for Seniors. I've already been to a bunch of these stupid things, and I just refuse to go to any more."

"OK," I said. "Do what you like."

"What?" she reproached me. "You *agree* with them?"

I tried to be calm and said, "I just want you to be happy. But I don't want you to be constantly fighting with them."

"Well, you're not here!" she said, her voice raised in frustration.

I let there be a silence and then muttered, "No, you're right. I'm not."

Then there was another silence, for a longer time.

Trying to keep things going, I asked her, "So what have you been doing tonight?"

"Nothing," she said. "Sitting in my room, not doing my homework. Reading *The Group*, looking for the dirty parts."

"How are they?" I snickered.

"We can do better," she murmured.

"So just hang on until Friday and –" I said.

"I'll be happy *on* Friday," she said firmly. "When we're together. But until then –"

"Until then," I interrupted in an affirming voice. "We're both going to be positive and do what we have to do and make the best of everything. It's what *I* try to do."

"Well, you're better than me," she muttered.

"No, I'm not," I said. "I'm the same as you."

There was a pause. Then I continued, "We have to find ways to be happy when we're not together."

"*Why?*" she asked.

There was another space of silence.

"I haven't been sleeping much lately," she said. "I'm going to steal some of Hell-eanor's sleeping pills. She won't miss them. *Or* I could just give her an accidental overdose."

"Don't do that," I said. "Why haven't you been sleeping?"

"Would you just make the week go faster?" she said in a small voice.

"I'll do what I can," I said, trying to sound warm and reassuring. That's what she needed, and I tried to channel all the comfort I could through the phone. "You'll see: we're going to be *fine*."

"I know we are," she said back listlessly.

"No," I said. "We *are*! I want to hear some enthusiasm!"

"I have to go," she sighed.

"Don't do this," I said.

"I'll call you tomorrow," she said. "I love you."

And she hung up before I could get out an "I love you" back to her.

~

The rest of the week was like that: sweet-and-sour phone calls, separated by long bouts of studying and worrying. She told me that she went to the College Night with Eleanor, just as I had asked her to, but it was a disaster. ("I told you I wasn't interested in all that junk. I don't know why I listen to anybody.") She told me that the family lawyer postponed the meeting with her, which I thought sounded strange but didn't tell her that. Other than that, she said that she tried to stay in her room as much as possible, reading trashy novels ("I was up until after three in the *Valley Of The Dolls*. Jacqueline Susann is just an OK writer, but I'm learning so much good stuff about pills!") and not doing her homework.

Eleanor and Manny were also fighting over where Rachel would spend Thanksgiving.

"They don't even like me when I'm around," she fretted. "But they keep fighting over me just so they have something to fight *over*."

"Forget about them," I said. "Think about us."

"I *do*!" she said. "All the time! That's what keeps me going. My love for you."

When she said things like that, why on Earth should I moan? It made it easier to get through the week until Friday.

~

I was late getting out to the Island on Friday afternoon. I hated getting out late, having to fight the crowds on the subway, fight the crowds in Penn Station, and fight my way to a seat on the Long Island Railroad, all the while carrying my small suitcase, which made everything clumsier and annoying for me and everyone around me. The problem was that I'd had to see Professor Brilliant, and he had office hours only on Friday afternoons, from 2:00 to 4:00. How considerate. He said it was to build character. I think it just built resentment. I don't want to get into too much detail about my relationship with Professor Brilliant because he testified at my trial, but later I may have to, if I'm going to tell the absolute truth (which, by the way, I have been doing all along).

Sitting in the moving train, nodding as I gazed out the window at the grayness of the landscape, the bleakness of Queens, I realized that this was like *Gatsby's* "Valley of Ashes." That's really where I lived, in a grungy netherworld, suspended between the intimidating glamour of Manhattan and the promise of a perfect love on Long Island. No, I lived in my mind, wrestling forever with my problems as the LIRR conductor waddled through the car, droning out the stations: "Wantagh . . . Seaford . . . Massapequa . . . *Massapequa Paaarrkk.*" Nothing was ever resolved, no matter how many times I was forced to "change at Jamaica."

My Mom was nice enough to pick me up at the station, and I rushed home to grab some food, shower, change, and get to Rachel's by 8:00. I simply rejected the idea of being late. All week long, I was subject to other people's demands and timetables. *This, tonight, being on time* was something I could control. A couple of nights, Rachel and I missed our phone call. Twice she called me back on the hall phone in the dorm the next day, but I wasn't there. Roommate A took the messages. ("Girl called." "Girl called X 2.") Overall, it had been a frustrating week. I had not done well on a big geology lab test, and I was not used to getting bad grades. I admit it; it hurt my ego. That's why I was especially looking forward to seeing Rachel: we were very good for each other's egos.

I had to make a quick stop for peppermint Life Savers to counteract my mother's radioactive meat loaf, but I still got to the Princes' house before eight. I was hoping that Rachel would just be able to come right out when I knocked on the front door – no little tap dance, no insincere small talk with Eleanor and/or Herb. They seemed to want to make me pay a price in humiliation, every time that we went out. But no matter: *they* were not important – only Rachel was.

Zipping up my leather jacket because it was getting really cold at night now, I fast-walked up the Princes' long path, ready to ring the bell at eight on the dot, collect my girl, and get out of there

Bing-bong! Even the sound of their doorbell was pompous, but I didn't care. I loved Rachel, not her family. Nor her doorbell.

The door opened suddenly, but it was Eleanor who was standing there. Her face was taut with animosity.

"I'm sorry," she said. "But Rachel's grounded tonight."

And she closed the door in my face.

I stood there for a moment, my mind at first blank, then flooded with a white rage. *Grounded? What? She couldn't do that!* I don't know if my eyes were open or closed, or how long I actually stood there. My thoughts and feelings all jumbled together. It sounded like there was a jet from JFK flying overhead, but I don't think anything was there in the sky. There was just the big, silent brick mansion and me, standing outside, alone.

I was about to knock on the door and demand at least an explanation, but I realized there was nothing to explain. Eleanor had decided to escalate her war against Rachel and me, and things were now going to be different. Very different. It was one thing to hassle us a little, the way incompetent parents sometimes do in the name of "discipline," but this was outright obstruction. Hostile action.

The question was: What exactly to do? I slowly backed off the porch, looking up the wide façade of the house, the wall of brick punctuated by black shutters and draped windows. I knew that Rachel's bedroom was on the second floor because of all the times that she'd say that she had to go upstairs to get away from "them." I figured it must be in the back of the house.

Carefully and without making too much noise, I stepped over the little hedge that lined the flagstone path up to the front door and started to cross the broad lawn, to circle around to the back of the house. The grass crunched under my feet as I kept my eyes on the house to see if Eleanor – or worse, Herb – was watching me. But I didn't see any of the drapes inside the big windows move, so I kept walking. As I curved around to the side of the house, I thought that if I could see where Rachel's bedroom window was, maybe she'd be looking out of her window, looking for me. In fact, I was certain that she'd be wanting, even *expecting* me to be looking for her. She would know that I wouldn't just walk away, grounding or no grounding. I flashed on the cigarette burn on her arm and hoped that she was all right physically. No, I couldn't just abandon her; couldn't just walk away. That would be just what Eleanor would want.

But as soon as I got halfway down the path on the side of the house, where the Princes' garbage cans were all lined up nice and neat, before I could even scope out the upstairs windows, all this high-pitched dog barking started. *Max*! I forgot about the damned dog! I guess they kept her in a back room, but wherever she was, she heard me and started a huge racket. I turned and hustled back down the path to my car, running away, just like a scared little dog.

I got back to my car and turned on the motor, revving it loudly several times so that Rachel would hear me . . . (and also, to tell the truth, so that it wouldn't stall out – the Ford had trouble starting in cold weather). I sat there, trying to get warm, cursing myself for my cowardice and impotence, trying to think of what to do. I couldn't just drive away and do nothing; that was out of the question.

What I did was drive back into the town of Oakhurst, found a pay phone on a corner by the train station, and called the Prince house. It rang ten times before someone picked up, my heart pounding harder with each ring. Finally, someone picked up.

"Hello," I said calmly. "Can I speak to Rachel, just for a – ?"

"*Don't*," said Eleanor curtly. "Call. Here. Again. Tonight."

And she hung up with a slam before I could say anything. Not that there was anything to say . . . to her.

Unfortunately, it was just about what I expected. But it didn't make me any less angry or frustrated. I drove back to the Lexington, to regroup and have something to eat. I cursed myself for making the call, a call that I *knew* wouldn't get through to Rachel. It was highly unlikely that Eleanor would've let her talk to me, if she were "grounded." Still, when Rachel heard the phone ring, even if she wasn't allowed to talk, she would know that it was me, trying to break through to her. I wanted her to know that I was making the effort, any effort. The results almost didn't matter.

That's what I told myself, sitting alone in a corner booth in the Lex, drinking coffee and treating myself to a piece of seven-layer cake. I ate it just the way I used to when I was a little kid, taking the cake apart and eating it one layer at a time. I almost made myself laugh, when I realized that I was eating like a Doggy. Little kids are demented, and I was really no different.

From the corner booth, I could see everyone who came in and out of the Lex. Unfortunately, no one came in; at least no one I knew. No one to take me out of myself. I just sat there brooding, turning over the events in my mind, going all the way back to that first meeting at the Costa Brava. And even before then, even while we were still at Mooncliff, Rachel told me that her mother would give us trouble. Since then, there had been so many instances of disrespect for us – shortened phone calls, cancelled dates, sudden changes in Rachel's schedule – that it was impossible to feel anything but disrespect for the person who had such little regard for our relationship. You would think a mother would want her daughter to be happy, especially when she was going through a painful divorce. But Eleanor Prince was not that kind of mother. And with each recollection of one of Eleanor's snubs, I felt a wave of the same white rage that I felt on the front porch when she slammed the door in my face, and on my life.

So what was I going to do? *Nothing*? I couldn't do nothing; I had to do something. But what?

So I paid my check, leaving a good tip for my waitress Adele for good luck, and went outside. It was freezing cold; I could see my breath in the light from the Lex's bright marquee. I couldn't go home, so I took a middle course of action: I drove. Driving, even driving the old Ford, always took some of my tension away. And even if I wasn't doing anything productive, at least I was *moving*. The radio was still good and loud, and it was so late that there weren't many cars on the road as I blew out my frustration at eighty mph on the Southern State Parkway till I was halfway out to the Hamptons.

I couldn't stop thinking about Rachel and this grounding. What did it really mean? How long would it last? Would she be grounded all weekend? I had had a tough week at school: lots of work, lots of papers, and a couple of quizzes. Earlier in the semester, I had referred to the attractive female graduate student with a blonde ponytail in charge of the geology lab as "Pebbles," and she had heard me. It was actually a compliment, but somehow she didn't see it that way, and lately was getting her revenge on me with pointed questions and extra scrutiny. So I was really looking forward to being with Rachel that night; I needed the comfort and sympathy that only she could provide.

After a while, almost without my intention, my driving took me back to the town of Oakhurst, all quiet for the night. And like a penny nail to a magnet, I was drawn slowly back to the Princes' neighborhood. All the streets were super silent. There were no cars on the roads or in the driveways. Except for porch lights and the occasional soft light behind a heavy drape, everything was closed up for the night. I felt a slight spark of hope: maybe Max was asleep now. Maybe there would be a light on in one of the upstairs bedrooms around the back of the Princes' brick fortress – the light in Rachel's bedroom. She said that she wasn't sleeping well lately. I wonder if she did take some of Eleanor's sleeping pills. I wished she

didn't talk about killing her mother; that was allowing Eleanor's poison to enter her heart. But maybe she was still awake,
waiting for me. Maybe right that moment she was looking out
her window, expecting me to come back.

I slowed down as I turned the corner onto Buckingham
Terrace. I figured that the best strategy would be to park
around the corner from the Princes' house and approach the
cul-de-sac on foot. That way my car would not be visible from
the Princes' house. *Stealth* and *darkness* would be my friends.
Just as I started to look for a place to park in the shadows of
one of the big, sheltering trees, far away from one of the few
streetlights, my eye caught sight of something in my rearview
mirror: It was a police car! With a row of lights across the top!

My heart jumped, my foot pumped, and I sped ahead.
I nervously checked the car that was now right behind me.
Wait a second, I told myself, *that's* not *a police car*. It was a
red-and-white car from some private security company, some
rent-a-cop; not a real policeman. He was probably just cruising
the neighborhood, checking on one of his customers' houses.
Still, he scared the you-know-what out of me and I panicked,
thinking that if this guy was around, what other security
company cars could be driving around? And what about the
regular Oakhurst police? And if they're *that* paranoid in this
neighborhood – and maybe they should be – maybe I should
get out of there. I hit the gas and sped out of the Princes' su-
per-safe neighborhood, losing the rent-a-cop behind me.

And so I went home without ever going back to her house
that night, scared again, like a frightened little dog. Very
brave, very loyal. My parents were asleep when I got home,
and the house was freezing. My father – "Heat-ler" – kept it
so cold in the winter that we all had to wear sweaters inside.
By nighttime, my room upstairs was like a meat locker. So I
undressed as quickly as I could and scrambled into bed, under
four blankets. I wound up tossing in my bed most of the night,
feeling stupid and frustrated. I must have slept, but I don't
remember exactly when. What I remember was planning:

planning how to break the grounding of Rachel. At least how to get a message to her. I finally fell asleep after tormenting my brain almost until dawn, trying unsuccessfully to remember fat Nanci from Lord & Taylor's last name. If I could get to her, maybe she could get to Rachel, and we could devise something, some way to get around this ridiculous grounding. She had to live; *we* had to live. I couldn't let them get away with destroying the best thing I had going in my life. I could picture that Nanci's face, her clothes, her large roundish body, her Dingo boots, even her giant purse with all the fringe; I just couldn't for the life of me remember her last name. Of course, first thing in the morning while I was brushing my teeth, looking at my red, wrinkled eyelids, it snapped instantly into my mind: *Jerome*.

Record of Events #23 – entered Sunday, 10:46 P.M.

∿

So the next day, instead of reading Aristotle and churning out the two papers I had due, I drove over to the Oakhurst Public Library and dove into the local telephone directory that they had by the pay phone in the lobby. I found three listings for "Jerome" in the white pages and instantly I knew which one probably belonged to Nanci's family. Only one street address had one of those fake-British names that they used in Rachel's neighborhood. I wrote down all three addresses and cross-referenced them against the big street map of the Town of Oakhurst (Incorporated in 1836) on the lobby wall. Sure enough, one of the Jerome addresses was right around the corner from Rachel. I smiled: now I was getting someplace.

I drove over to the address that was nearest Rachel's. I prowled slowly and quietly through the winding streets, so as not to attract attention. My shabby Ford didn't really belong there. When I got to the streets with the fake-British names, I went even slower. There was always a chance that Eleanor or Herb might be driving around. Of course I had every right to drive on these public roads, but still, I didn't want to be seen. My mind flashed back to that ridiculous argument that the Doggies had about which super-power would be the best to possess. I remember thinking that invisibility would be my preferred power. I was right; I wished that I were invisible right then. What if Eleanor couldn't see me? Or Herb the Sleaze? Or Manny, if he was around. If I were invisible, I could walk right into the Princes' house, right through that shiny black door, and right up to Rachel's bedroom. I'd never even seen her room, but I imagined that it must be beautiful: a princess' boudoir, all soft and frilly and inviting. I could walk right up there and –

But if I were invisible, then my body might not have any substance. Then I wouldn't be able to feel or touch her.

Maybe I had better rethink this invisibility thing again.

~

I parked and approached the first Jerome house on my list. This had to be the one. It was even bigger than the Princes' house. Only this one wasn't brick. This was a giant fake-French chateau made of pseudo-limestone. OK, maybe it was real limestone; only it all looked fake, this mini-Versailles on the south shore of Long Island.

With complete confidence – I was doing nothing wrong – I walked up to the front door, painted a perfect glossy white, and rang the bell. As I waited, I looked around at the neighborhood, the wide lawns cut close as winter was approaching, the perfect hedges and the bare trees, one humungous house after another, and absolutely no people. Why wasn't anyone out on a Saturday morning?

The door opened and I turned around. It was a nurse in a white uniform – no, it was a maid. A black maid in a starched white uniform who was looking at me with dark, suspicious eyes.

"Yes?" she said, putting her hand on the doorjamb, blocking my way in.

"Excuse me," I said. "Is Nanci home?"

I waited an eternal, hopeful moment as she looked me up and down.

Finally, she said sarcastically, "And who should I say's calling?" She could hardly get out the words.

"Just tell her Rachel Prince's friend," I said brightly. "She'll know."

She snorted and said, "Wait here," closing the door flat in my face.

I didn't care. I smiled. I had found the right Jerome.

~

Five minutes later, I was inside Nanci Jerome's enormous, echoey house, following her rather large behind in jeans and her flopping moccasins up the winding staircase to her room.

"Thank you, Pauline!" she shouted to the maid in white who was disappearing someplace into the vast downstairs beyond the marbled foyer.

"Welcome!" she drawled back and was gone.

Nanci's room was big and pretty dark, with a high ceiling and tightly closed heavy satin drapes. There were posters (Janis Joplin and the Dylan one with the curly, colorful hair) on the walls and lots of taped-up pencil and ink drawings. She was burning incense, two sticks in a glass of sand, and had one small, yellow table lamp with a fringed, satin shade lit on the end table next to her rumpled bed. In the corner was one of those big slanted drawing tables, with cans of colored pencils at the top, and a swivel high chair in front. It was still daytime, but it could have been midnight in Nanci's room.

"Eleanor and Manny Prince's marriage was basically a nightmare," said Nanci, tucking her short brown hair behind her ear. "Always was. And from what I can see, their divorce isn't doing much better. Manny is basically a brute, a Neanderthal who made a little money. My parents at least have the good sense to be old and away a lot." I couldn't help but notice Nanci's heavy asthmatic breathing between phrases, like sometimes she was eating the air.

"I guess it's good they got divorced," I said.

"It's tough on Rachel, either way," she replied, sitting back on her bed, which made the mattress sink.

"The only child of two psycho parents who fight constant-ly?" I said, finding a place to sit down – a desk chair that looked pretty solid. "Not a good situation."

"Unless she can work some kind of *divide*-and-*conquer*."

"Work both ends against the middle," I assented.

"Whatever *that* means."

"Whatever it is, it sounds good and aggressive."

She laughed, "You really hate them, don't you?"

"Why shouldn't I? All they do is make Rachel miserable. It's as if they enjoy it."

"People do odd things in the name of love."

I wondered what exactly she meant by that. She was obvi-ously telling herself a private joke. I let it pass.

I complimented her on her drawings, which hung all over the walls – squiggly, obsessively detailed drawings of odd people and tilted scenery. I was polite enough to ask her about going to Pratt where she was a painting major, before I asked her for my favor. I wasn't exactly insincere in my flattery, but I knew what I was there for.

"Of course, I'll call Rachel for you," she said. "Try to break through the Great Wall of Eleanor? I'm glad to do it: *someone* should be happy in this diseased, little world."

"Great!" I said, ignoring the cynicism in her sentiment. "We're lucky you can get through to Eleanor."

"I am completely fluent in 'grown-up,'" she replied, reaching for the yellow Princess phone on her night table. I didn't say that it was because she was shaped like one, but that's what I couldn't help thinking.

"I even play canasta," she added dryly, starting to dial. "That's assuming they'll let Rachel come to the phone. I don't know why Rachel doesn't get her own phone back."

"Her *own* phone?" I asked, instantly liking that idea.

"She used to have a phone of her own," Nanci said as she dialed. "But Hell-eanor took it away."

"Why?"

"Because she could," replied Nanci, and before I could say anything, someone answered on the other end.

"Hello, Eleanor?" said Nanci in a bright perky voice, totally different from the way she was just talking. "It's Nanci! Is Rache' there?"

She waited for a moment, with her eyebrows raised, wagging her head, listening hopefully.

"OK, I understand," she said. "But I just need to talk to her for a minute. It's pretty important."

She winced a little, listening to Eleanor's response.

"I see . . . I understand," said Nanci. "It's just something *really* important I need to discuss with her about *school.* . . . Now." I liked the way she was playing Eleanor.

Nanci waited some more, listening to Eleanor on the other end, nodding patiently, while I tried to read her face.

"Great!" Nanci said, giving me a twisted thumbs-up. "I'll wait right here."

Taking the phone away from her ear and covering it with her free hand, she whispered, "She bought it."

"You're fantastic!" I whispered as she shushed me.

"Hello, Rachel?" she said carefully. "I have someone here who would like to speak to you."

With an excited grin, Nanci shoved the phone into my hands. I caught it and spoke quickly.

"Hello, honey?" I said. "It's me. Pretend you're talking to Nanci."

"Hello, Nanci!" Rachel said with a big happy surprise in her voice. "How nice to talk to you!"

"I can't believe the witch actually grounded you."

"Neither can I," she said brightly, responding to some nicer, imaginary comment.

"I *really* wanted to see you last night," I said in a lower, more meaningful voice.

"Me too!" she sounded much too chipper.

"Is she standing right there?" I asked.

"You got it," she said, relieved that I understood her circumstances.

"Do you think you could ask her for a little privacy?" I said.

I heard her voice a little distance from the phone ask, "Do you think I could have a little privacy, Ma? It's just Nanci!"

I waited a few moments, listening to Rachel breathe, watching Nanci watch me on the phone in her dark room with all the weird drawings.

Rachel came back on. "It's OK, she's gone. We just have a minute."

"Thank *goodness*! How are you?" I whispered.

"OK, I guess," she said in a low voice. "But I miss you so much, I can't stand it."

"How long is this grounding?" I asked. "And what did you do?"

"I didn't do anything! And I don't know how long she's going to keep this up. She's psychotic, and Herb is just making her worse."

"To hell with Herb!" Just the mention of his name made me flush with anger. "We have to figure out some way to get you out of there!"

"I know!" she said, exasperated that I was stating the obvious.

"Maybe we can – Maybe *Nanci* can help us!"

I took the phone away from my ear and asked/said, "Nanci, you'll help us, won't you?"

Her eyes widened, and she shrugged. "Sure."

"Great! You're terrific," I said to Nanci. Then into the phone, "Nanci says she'll help us. So make up some story to get over here. Say that Nanci is having a nervous breakdown or something, and she needs you. Say she's on the verge of suicide!"

"Thanks a bunch," muttered Nanci sarcastically, reaching for a roll of Life Savers on her night table, revealing a wide wedge of white flesh where her peasant blouse pulled away from her jeans.

"Just get her to let you come over here!" I insisted. "Tell her it's an emergency."

"I'll try," she said.

"It *is* an emergency," I said, and lowered my voice. "I need to see you."

"I know, baby," she breathed. "Me too."

And she hung up the phone.

I stood there with the yellow phone in my hand.

"Well?" asked Nanci.

"I don't know," I said honestly, handing the phone back to her. "We'll see."

She hung up the phone with a click and turned to me with a sly look.

"You wanna smoke some hash?" she asked.

~

I should say right now that, unlike what was implied in the newspapers during my trial, I am *not* a big drug user. Some guys like to brag about how much they've done, how wild they've gotten. That's not me. I confess: I'm a wimp when it comes to drugs, so the two puffs I took from the tiny pipe – blown out of the window of Nanci's bathroom – were enough to knock me for a relative loop.

Walking back into Nanci's bedroom, I felt light-headed and hopeful, suddenly optimistic about my chances of seeing Rachel.

"You spell 'Nanci' with an 'i,'" I said. "Why is that?"

"To be unusual," she said with a straight face as she flopped back onto her bed. "Nobody would notice me if I were just a Nancy-with-a-'y.'"

I liked her humor: you were never quite sure if she was being funny or not.

"You're great to do this, Nanci," I said. "Anything to give Rachel a way to get out of there. I don't even know why Eleanor wants her around; all they do is fight."

"Parents have no idea how to raise kids, for the most part," Nanci said. "The Princes are especially clueless. But Rachel is so, you know, *pretty*, that she always gets away with things."

"So, I don't get it," I said, sitting back on the high swivel chair in front of her art table. "You're all alone in this big house?"

"Pauline is here."

"Besides her," I said. "Where are your parents?"

"In Bermuda."

"Bermuda?" I cackled. "All I know about Bermuda is shorts and onions. What about any brothers or sisters?"

"I have a brother who lives in Connecticut with his family, and my sister lives in Phoenix."

"*Phoenix*? So, like I said," I repeated. "You're all alone in this big house. I know: with Pauline –"

"And my parents' checkbook."

"Wow," I said. "That sounds kind of . . . ideal."

"You think so?" she said with a twisted, knowing smile.

The phone rang. We both froze. I felt the impulse to pick it up, but it was Nanci's phone.

"You pick it up," I said.

Emptying the little hash pipe in the little ashtray next to her bed, Nanci picked up the receiver silently. She put it to her ear and said, "Hello?"

She looked down, listening with concentration. Finally she said, "OK . . . OK . . . I will. I'll tell him."

And she hung up, in slow motion.

"Well?" I asked, knowing what she was going to say before she said it.

"Forget it," she said flatly. "She's grounded, period. Eleanor said no. That's it."

"That's *it*?" I shouted, feeling that swell of anger rise within me.

"The magic doesn't work every time," Nanci shrugged her round shoulders.

"That sucks! . . . She can't do that!"

"Well . . ." she said, looking sad for me. "For the time being, she can."

"I know she *can*!" I replied. "It's just not right!"

I paced around the room, kicking at the fluffy shag carpet, looking at Nanci's drawings of imaginary insects and pebbly landscapes and her posters of Janis and Dylan, trying to decide what to do.

"Do you know what she did, to deserve the grounding?" asked Nanci, in a sympathetic voice.

"It doesn't matter what she did!" I exclaimed. "Her actions are irrelevant! They want to keep us apart because they *can*. Reason is incidental! Reason is their enemy."

I realized that I was sounding less than logical, but I was angry. All this wasted energy and opposition; all I wanted to do was spend a few hours with my girlfriend. What was so horrible about that?

"It's funny, when you first meet Rachel," I said. "You think she has everything. Looks, money, brains, everything."

"No one has everything," Nanci countered.

"If they want to break us up," I said. "This is precisely the wrong way. Morons! Don't they realize that they are doing exactly the opposite of what they want to achieve? . . . They're making a big mistake with Rachel. She's not gonna take this forever. You can push a person too far; even Rachel has limits."

"Lots of people do stupid things," said Nanci, watching me from her bed. "Just look at the world. There's an epidemic of stupidity out there."

"And that's why you stay in here and draw pictures and smoke hash?" I asked. In some ways, I had to admire Nanci. She had her own little world, all under her control, with no interference, it seemed, from anyone.

"That's *one* reason," she said, looking at me with a sly smile as she filled the little pipe with little crumbs of the hash. "It's not the best thing for someone with asthma, but . . ."

She sort of wiggled in place on the bed and said coyly, "So why don't you sit here, right next to me, and I'll light up this *leetle* bowl, just for you."

I think she was flirting with me. I don't know, maybe she was just being nice and friendly. And while I liked her, I was certainly not attracted to Nanci. Even forgetting about Rachel, which was impossible, Nanci was just not the kind of girl I was attracted to. I'm sure there was a guy out there for her, someone who liked art and a little weirdness, and didn't mind the extra poundage; it just wasn't me. And anyway, I was there for a reason: to help Rachel-and-me.

"No, thanks," I said, backing away from her and sitting up on the high chair in front of her drawing table. I spun around on it, back and forth. "I have to keep what's left of my wits about me."

Nanci started to fill the pipe with more hash from a plastic bag on her night table and said, "You know I have a cousin who works at Ultrasonic and he's gonna show some of my drawings to the manager of the Critters and I might be able to do an album cover for them."

"That's cool." I didn't really believe her, but you never knew. She could have been telling the truth.

I looked at Nanci and wondered how much I could trust her. Then I thought that Rachel and I were sort of involved with her now, and she seemed to have a good heart inside her defensive exterior, so I decided to take a chance.

"Nanci?" I said. "Can I ask you something?"

She snickered at that. "You can ask me anything you want. It doesn't mean I'll *tell* you!" She laughed, a little wheezy laugh, and that's when I noticed the little plastic thingie on her nightstand that must have been her asthma inhaler.

"Tell me about Eric," I said, trying to sound casual but watching her reaction carefully.

The mention of the name made her flinch. Which both pleased and troubled me: pleased, because I knew that Nanci had information I could garner, and troubled, because of that flinch. What if the information she had for me was bad?

"Eric . . . ?" she repeated with a careful smile, obviously stalling. "What do *you* know about Eric?"

"All I know is that I hate his guts," I said. Which made her laugh a big, hearty loose laugh.

Eric. Every time I said that name, it left a bad taste in my mouth.

When her laugh died away, Nanci looked me straight in the eye and said, "I'm sorry you know about him."

"So what's the deal with him?" I asked straight back to her.

"You have to ask Rachel about that," she answered.

"Why?"

"Let her tell you," she said. "I shouldn't say anything."

"What?" I challenged her. "Suddenly you're getting shy about expressing your opinions?"

"I don't want to spoil things," she said simply.

"Telling me the truth won't 'spoil things,'" I insisted, but she didn't respond.

I waited her out. I just sat there, looking at her until she said something else.

"Look, I like you," Nanci sputtered. "But I'm on Rachel's side. You'll have to ask her."

"So the answer is yes, he has been hanging around."

"I'm not saying anything. You'll have to ask Rachel."

By saying that, she gave me my answer.

"Thanks," I said grimly. "I suppose I can't blame him. Rachel is Rachel."

"She goes through people quickly," Nanci said. "Either she loses patience with them, or they can't keep up with her. And frankly, her attitude turns them off. I'm the only friend in Oakhurst she has left."

"Good!" I said. Perhaps it was not the most generous thought, but I wanted Rachel to need me as much as I needed her. Simple as that.

"If I were you," Nanci said deliberately. "I'd be careful. I don't think you know precisely what you're involved with."

"Thanks," I snickered. "But don't worry about me. If you want to help me, help Rachel."

I meant that too. I had no intention of "getting hurt," and I would defend my relationship with Rachel by any means possible.

"I should go," I said.

"So *go!*" she said, not looking at me.

The room looked darker than ever, with the one little bed-side light.

"Thanks for trying, Nanci," I said. "I really appreciate it."

"It was nothing," she muttered, putting the pipe down on the table by her bedside with a clank. "Literally nothing."

"Well, I should split." I hopped down off the high chair. "You know, it just hit me: Eleanor and Herb are so selfish, they probably won't stay home all Saturday night to make sure Rachel stays grounded. They'll go out after a while, and if I just wait long enough, I bet I will get to see her tonight."

Nanci flopped back against her pillows. "You really are an idiot. You know that?"

I shrugged, "What can I say? I'm just trying to listen to my heart *and* my head. Giving credence to both of them. At the same time."

"Like I said," she grunted a laugh. "An idiot."

"Everyone's entitled to an opinion, Nanci," I shrugged. "So I'll see you again soon, right? . . . Nice pictures."

And I walked out of the room, closing the door behind me. I think I heard Nanci start to sniffle. I was sorry about that; I didn't want to hurt her or anything. Maybe it was just her asthma. She reminded me of some girls in my high school: nice enough girls, but no one you'd want to go out with, no one you'd lust after, nothing special. I wanted special. I *had* special, and I was determined to keep it.

When I walked down the long, curving stairs and across the foyer to the front door, I could see that Pauline was watching me with suspicious eyes from around the corner in what looked like the dining room that had a table with maybe sixteen chairs around it.

"Bye, Pauline," I said, seeing that I didn't surprise her, not in the least. "Take care of her."

Nanci was definitely a strange girl, but there was something I liked about her. Her honesty, I think. And I liked that she was Rachel's friend. Rachel seemed so isolated; she needed all the support she could get. That's why I was worried about this Eric. I wasn't around all week. Maybe he was.

I opened the door and was outside in a moment, happy for what I had said. I slammed the door closed and trotted down off the front porch, lighthearted. I was a few steps down the perfectly manicured front walk when I realized that I didn't know where I was going.

Yes, I did. I would do what I told Nanci: I'd go over to Rachel's house and wait to see if Eleanor and Herb would go out that evening, leaving Rachel alone. I was *sure* that they would want to go out to the Costa Brava or some other swanky place. Maybe even a Mafia hang-out, if what Rachel said about Herb was true. In any case, they wouldn't stay home, even to enforce their punishment. They'd go out, and then I'd ring Rachel's doorbell and surprise her.

I walked from Nanci's house down the block toward the Princes', staying in the shadows as much as I could. I wasn't doing anything illegal and yet I felt as if I were somehow trespassing. What was a poorish boy like me doing in this fancy neighborhood anyway, scheming to steal a local princess? I didn't belong here. And yet, here I was, gliding through the shadows, staying close to the wall of tall hedges, those perfectly trimmed, impervious hedges, to get my way.

Of course I was wrong. Again. I stood outside for a long time, behind a fat tree in front of one of their neighbors' houses with a good view of the Princes' front door and driveway, freezing my butt off. Finally, I walked back to my car and moved it to a spot two houses down from the Princes', where I could just see her house and whoever went in or out. There was the risk of detection, but I needed the car heater. And finally, after almost two hours, with no Eleanor or Herb emerging to go out on the town, I just went home, having successfully killed the entire evening.

But no Eric showed up at the Prince house, and I wasn't seen by anyone. At least there were two things to be glad about.

~

I killed the next day too, plowing through my reading, knocking out some papers (a couple of which were, to be truthful, already late), and studying my notes and textbooks for some important tests coming up, including one on Monday afternoon on the Protestant Reformation – I really needed a good grade. Mainly though, I was waiting for Rachel to call me and tell me to drive over there and rescue her, even if only for a few hours.

That didn't happen. I finally gave up in the late afternoon so my Dad could drive me to the 5:38 train. That way, I could get back to my room, get some dinner, and be in place for my 8:00 call. As if Eleanor would let her answer the phone. (This is how deluded I was, but I had to make the effort in any case. It was never about succeeding; it was always about *trying*.)

My Dad drove me to the train and didn't say anything until we were almost there.

"So," he broke the silence. "How you doin', money-wise?"

"I'm OK."

"I'm sure you'll run into some cash around the holidays," he said, dropping a hint.

"I *said* I was OK." I repeated, sounding annoyed with him when I really wasn't. I was thinking about everything else.

"Well, it's funny you should say that," he said, talking louder than he usually did. My father was a soft-spoken man. "Because . . . you don't seem like yourself lately."

"I'm more myself than I've ever been," I answered, just as he pulled the Chrysler to the curb by the door to the station. He stepped on the brake and threw the car into park.

He turned to me and said straight out, "Tell me: Is this girl messing up your life?"

I just laughed out loud at that. "No!" I scoffed. "I'd say it's the exact opposite. Rachel is the best thing that ever happened to me."

"Well . . ." my father said, with his eyes looking sad and concerned. "I hope she is."

As I got out of the car and got my things out of the back seat, he tried to give me a couple of twenties, but I said, "Thanks, I'm really OK. And thank Mom for doing my laundry. I forgot."

I grabbed my stuff and had to run up the stairs for the 5:38, but I made it just before the doors closed on me.

True to my plan, I got back to the dorm in plenty of time. Fortunately, Roommate A wasn't there, so I had a little privacy and space for a while before I got my dinner and was in place at the phone booth in the mailroom for my 8:00 call to Rachel, exactly on time.

But untrue to my plan, Mrs. Prince answered the phone.

"Hello?" she said sharply, as if accusing the caller of something.

"Hello, Mrs. Prince," I said in the politest, most nonconfrontational voice imaginable. "May I please speak to Rachel?"

And before the "*L*" died in my last word, she said right back, in this overpronounced way, "Don't you understand? Do you *want* to get her into *more* trouble? Please don't call here again tonight!"

And she slammed down the phone.

"At least she said 'please,'" I said out loud, to try to make a joke of it. But it wasn't funny, not when I thought of what Rachel might be experiencing on the other end.

But it was what I expected. *At least*, I thought, *I'm not going to be surprised by things anymore.* That fake-comforting thought did not last for long.

Record of Events #24 – entered Monday, 9:11 A.M.

∾

I got to all my Monday morning classes even though I stayed up till almost 4:00 a.m. finishing two papers for Brilliant (one overdue), another one in French, and studying for three other tests – one that afternoon.

"Can't you turn off the light?" Roommate A whined from the top of the bunk bed. "Or go into the lounge?"

"Sorry, man," I said. "All my stuff is spread out here. Turn your head the other way."

He groaned and huffed, but he was turned over and snoring inside of five minutes. (And, to tell the complete truth, he never showed much consideration for me, as you will see.)

I hit my three morning classes in a row and headed back to my room to change books before I grabbed some lunch. I'll admit that I was dragging; I was a little demoralized. First of all, it was a Monday morning. And it was cold and gray. The clanking radiators hissed steam in the old dorms, but nothing got warmer. And I hadn't seen Rachel all weekend, so I felt this *void* within me, this unfulfilled need. I had gotten myself addicted to Rachel Prince; now I was having some kind of withdrawal.

As I slogged up the three flights of stairs, I couldn't help but think about what I had said to my Dad the night before, about Rachel being the best thing that ever happened to me. All my life I had gotten mostly As in my classes, and now I was getting Bs and Cs and worse. All my teachers in high school liked me, but some of these teachers seemed to take a disliking to me for no reason that I could understand. I had never been behind in my studies before. Everything had come pretty easily, but I now was in a different place. I had always been one of the smartest kids in my class, and now I was just one of the guys, and not even that. At least I had Rachel. No matter how tough my week was, there was always Rachel-on-the-phone during the week and Rachel-in-the-flesh on the weekends . . . until now. Now everything was in question: How could I wait until next weekend to see her, and would she still be grounded then? How far would Eleanor go to keep us apart? And how far would we push back, in order to see each other?

~

I couldn't get her on the phone for the next two days. Both 8:00 calls – I was staying true – failed: once Eleanor said that she couldn't come to the phone, and once Herb said "she's out with her mother. Sorry, kid," and hung up.

I didn't know what to do: Write her a letter? Eleanor would probably get the mail before Rachel got home from school anyway. And what would I say in a letter? I love you, I miss you, and I want to see you? That was understood.

Then, Tuesday night, in the middle of memorizing Mohs scale of the hardness of minerals, I got a call on the dorm phone in the hallway.

"PHONE!" Someone pounded on the door for me.

To say that my heart jumped would be accurate. It jumped because the loud door knock shocked the hell out of me, but it also jumped because I thought that it would be, might be, must be Rachel. I raced down the hallway, pulling on my Keds, hopping as I ran.

"Hello?" I said into the phone, closing myself against the wall for "privacy."

"Hello?"

"*Nanci*?" I said, instantly recognizing her voice, instantly disappointed. "How did you get this number?"

"What do you mean, 'How did I get this number?'" she shot back. "Rachel tells me everything. I thought you knew that."

Not everything, *I hope*, I thought, but I let it go.

"OK," I said. "Good for you. When did you last see her?"

"This afternoon."

"How was she?"

"Not that good, to tell you the truth."

Nanci seemed to have a lot of answers and she gave them to me: Rachel had been fighting with Eleanor over "a bunch of things; not just you." I didn't know whether that was good or bad news.

"The harder Rachel pulls away from Eleanor, the tighter Eleanor tries to yank the leash –" said Nanci.

"Why can't she just call me?" I interrupted. "Did she tell you to call me?"

"No –" she started, which dropped my heart. "I mean, *yes*! She asked me to call you and tell you to hang on."

"'Hang on'?" I repeated. "That's it? Why doesn't she call me from a pay phone at school? I'm here in my room, during the day, between classes. Why doesn't she call me then, when Eleanor isn't around?"

"You'd have to ask her that," said Nanci.

"I *would* ask her that, but I can't talk to her!" I shot back. "Do you see my problem, Nanci?"

"Heyyy," she said, in a low, long note. "You don't have to talk like that. I'm on *your* side."

I realized that there was no point in yelling at Nanci. There was really no point in yelling, period.

"She told me to tell you that she loves you, and you'll get through this."

"That's what she said?"

"In so many words."

"Well, what *were* her words?" I demanded.

"Her *exact* words?" she replied tartly. "I don't know her *exact* words. Next time, I'll use a tape recorder."

She was breathing heavily, sounding a little exasperated, and maybe she was right to be. And she did have asthma.

"OK, Nanci," I muttered. "I'm sorry – I'm just a little, uh –"

"I understand," she cut me off. "No apologies necessary. No one said this was going to be easy, right?"

Of course she was right. *But*, I told myself, *Rachel is worth it*.

Nanci and I hung up after she assured me that she'd try to keep "the lines of communication open" between Rachel and me. Which I had to thank her for. But I went back to my room – still worried, still uncertain about our future – back to my geology textbook, wishing I could become as hard inside as a diamond. Or at the very least, corundum.

But I have to hand it to Nanci: the next afternoon, just at lunchtime, while I was changing books and eating a roast beef hero with extra ketchup and Nehi grape soda from Mama Joy's at my desk, there was another "PHONE FOR YOU!"

It was Rachel.

"Hi, baby," she purred. "At . . . *last*! Do you know that song? Oh, you can't believe how much I've missed you!"

I was whipsawed by two simultaneous reactions: extreme happiness to hear from her and extreme resentment that it took her so long.

"Try me," I said.

"Aren't you glad to hear from me? . . . Because if you're mad at me for some reason . . ."

What was I thinking? Here she was, finally on the phone, and I was wasting it.

"No-no-no, I'm not mad at you, honey," I stammered. "I-I-I just need to hear from you. . . . I guess I'm just mad at myself for needing you so much."

"That's ridiculous," she scoffed.

"Yes, I know it is," I agreed. "But that's the way I am."

"Good," she said, satisfied.

I didn't know what was "good" about things, but I let it go.

"What are you doing?" I asked her. "And where are you now? I have to know everything."

She laughed that musical laugh of hers, as if nothing were wrong, and said, "I'm nowhere. I'm at someone's house for lunch."

"Whose house?"

"Nobody's."

I thought I heard some laughter – *male* laughter? – in the background, but I couldn't be sure.

"There has to be a way that I can call you and not have to go through your mother," I said.

"I was just in study hall," she said, ignoring my statement, "in the library, reading about poison. Actually, poison*s*."

She seemed to be talking to me and to someone else at the same time.

"Why?" I asked her, trying to listen deeply into the phone.

"Oh, no reason," she trilled. "Just something to do."

"And you do 'poison'?" I said deadpan, not playing with her.

"I can dream, can't I?" she sang back, laughing at something in the room.

"Listen," I said sharply. "Do you want to talk to *me*, or whoever's there?"

There was a long pause. What was she thinking? And was that the right tone for me to take? Was she mad at me now?

"If I didn't want to talk to you," she said simply. "I wouldn't have called you."

That put me in my place. What was *I* thinking, fighting with the girl I loved and missed so much?

"Sorry," I said. "I'm crazy."

"Me too," she murmured, and for a moment, we were back in The Zone.

We made plans for Friday. Tentative plans. But, as I hung up the phone, it seemed to me like everything was going to be tentative from now on.

～

Leading up to that date on Friday night, all I thought about were two things: one, seeing Rachel on Friday night, and two, everything else. No matter what I was doing, what class I was trying to concentrate on, what book I was trying to read, what paper I was trying to finish, my mind kept reflexively flipping back to Rachel. Actually, that's not really true because my thoughts of Rachel were actually subdivided into many sub-worries: How was she getting along with Eleanor and would she be allowed out on Friday? Was Herb still hassling her, and should she tell her father? And, lurking behind all these spiraling thoughts, where was Eric in all this? Was that who was in the room with Rachel when she called me?

My mind kept spinning like that, on and off, for days. Nothing else seemed to matter as much.

～

Friday finally came around. I fidgeted, dreamed, and back-tracked through my morning classes, then subway-and-bussed to the Island through the Valley of Ashes. That night, I was, as true as I could be, at the curb in front of the frightful Prince mansion at 7:58 p.m. sharp. Lucky me, she came running out the door so that I didn't have to do my Eleanor-and-Herb-Happy-To-See-You Tap Dance. But, unlucky us, Rachel had been crying, her mascara running down her cheeks.

She didn't want to go where I wanted to go (my room), and I didn't want to go where she wanted to go (a movie.)

"I don't want to go and sit in a dark room with you. I want to *talk* to you and *be* with you! Besides, haven't you've already seen *Anne of A Thousand Days* – twice? That's two thousand days."

She didn't laugh. Instead, after some more back and forth between two stubborn people, we went to Jones Beach. I thought the beach could make everything right, but we sat in the car in the parking lot, fighting for too much of the night. Fighting and making up.

"I know you're under a lot of pressure –" I would begin.

And she would cut me off with, "You have no idea what I live with."

One topic interested her and got her excited.

"I have a new hobby," she said. "Breaking up Eleanor and Herb."

Her blue-blue eyes sparkled in the light they caught from the floodlights in the parking lot.

"They're making trouble for us," she said with glee. "*I'm* going to make trouble for them."

"Oh," I groaned. "Don't get involved with them!"

"No," she said. "It's fun. She deserves it. She messes with *my* life? She knows *nothing* about how I can mess up hers!"

She machine-gunned all these stories about life with Eleanor and Herb.

"They both have these nasty, controlling tempers," she said. "Maybe it's what they have in common. . . . But anyway, it's easy to get them fighting. The other day, she threw a glass at him, but I think she missed on purpose. Still, I'm waiting for one of them to draw blood. Then I'll get my father involved. *That* will be interesting!"

I didn't like seeing her so amped up on anger and spite.

"Don't be like them," I said, reaching for her, to pull her close. But she pushed my hand away.

"Why shouldn't I pay them back in the same way that they're treating me? I mean, what do they expect? . . . And do *you* expect *me* to *deny* my experience?"

She had a point, but that didn't make me any happier. And it certainly didn't make her amorous or physically responsive. Which was always my objective. I'm sorry, but I'm a guy.

I finally made us get out of the car and walk on the beach. That made things a little better. We took off our shoes and walked down the sand, holding hands. It was romantic and everything, with the stars and the blackness and the glory of the waves, rising up and destroying themselves and all that, one after another after another. But something felt wrong. We were together, but we should have been happier.

"I'm so alone at school," she said.

I kind of liked the sound of that – no Eric – but I was sympathetic.

"I want you to have friends," I said. "Just as long as they're not boys."

"Ha!" was all she said.

Without further elaboration, there was nothing I wanted to add. *"Don't make things worse"* my father always says. I should have been content to be walking on the beach at night with the girl I loved and who loved me. I think.

I didn't ask her about her "grandma money" or if she contacted that lawyer yet. I didn't ask her about her anti-college plans. I didn't ask about when and if she were getting that new Mustang because that would have brought her back to complaining about her father. I didn't want to say anything to upset her. I just wanted to *be* with her, with no complications or shadows. Maybe that totally carefree state doesn't exist, but that's still what I longed for. The Zone.

Even though the beach is eternal – especially this beach at night, when you're alone with the black waves – I was constantly aware of the time. I knew I had to get her back by midnight. I was not going to be responsible for Rachel breaking her curfew. I wasn't going to give them another reason to punish her.

"We should go," I said.

"I don't wanna go," she said, walking close against me.

"I know."

When we got back to the car, she leaned against the fender, and I cleaned the sand off of her feet, brushing them lightly.

"Stop tickling," she squealed, wriggling her foot, but I could tell that she liked my touch. Most times, she was a very affectionate, physically responsive girlfriend. I had to make sure that continued.

I had enough time to take her home by way of Nathan's. I thought the carnival atmosphere – the people, the games, the noise – might distract her into some kind of happiness. It was a good try. She liked the ice cream sundae we shared. I liked the way she wiped some hot fudge off my cheek and licked it clean from her finger.

I tried to give her a good pep talk on the way home – how she should try to do better in school (she told me that she was flunking a couple of courses, which was completely absurd for a girl of her intelligence), how she should try to stay out of fights with her parents and lay low, how she should avoid dark thoughts and be positive about our future. Actually, it was not so different from a pep talk I needed to give myself.

When we pulled up to the curb in front of her house, we just sat there for a moment.

"I'm sorry about tonight," she said. "I don't mean to be mean. But sometimes everything that happens just gets all jumbled up. I'll make it up to you, I swear."

"What about tomorrow?" I asked her. I knew that the possibility of an affirmative answer was remote, but I couldn't help it. I had to ask. I had to make the effort.

She snickered once, bitterly. "No, she's already told me that I have to do all my overdue schoolwork tomorrow, and she's going to *check* me. She got a letter from this obnoxious assistant principal who has it in for me, so I'm really trapped. "

"Oh."

I didn't tell her that I was probably going to do the same thing, minus Eleanor's supervision.

"I'm just trying to keep everybody happy," she said. "And not drive myself completely insane. Everybody wants something."

"I'm not everybody!" I felt a chill as I said the words.

She took a long pause, then started to apologize. "I know that things weren't supposed to be this way, baby," she half whispered. "I'll try to call you, but they've been watching me all the time lately. You *know* her."

"It's OK," I said, touching her hand. "As long as we have each other, we just have to be positive. We're *young*. Time is on our side."

She looked into my eyes and said, "I don't think I can wait that long."

Then, fighting back tears, she jerked open the car door handle – I thought she might rip the damn thing off the Ford – and ran up the clattering flagstone path and into the house.

I watched her all the way. I wondered if Eleanor and/or Herb were at a window, watching me watch her. At that moment, I really didn't care.

I waited there a good long minute, looking at the house, that phony fortress, wondering what was really going on inside there, what they were doing to her.

Then I drove away.

Another night of love, shot to hell, with my beautiful, complicated, troubled girl.

～

I waited the next day for the call that never came. I tried to concentrate on the work I had – the papers to write, due and overdue, the reading to do, the tests to study for – but Rachel was always somewhere in my mind. When I was not with her, I was simply not exactly myself. Something was missing: I felt her absence as if it were a part of me, a part of me that was *gone*. And there was so much that worried me from last night. What was happening to us?

What got me out of the house was a favor I did for my Dad. He had spent most of the morning trying to fix the downstairs toilet and needed a replacement part that he tracked down at some obscure plumbing supply place that happened to be open on a Saturday. It was on Rockaway Turnpike, not too far from Rachel's. Not close, but not far. If I moved quickly, I could swing by Rachel's house. Not for any particular reason. I mean, I wouldn't knock on her door, or anything. Just to check things out. Of course, there was the risk of being spotted by Eleanor and/or Herb, but that was a risk I was willing to take.

"Try to be fast," my Dad said. "I want to have this thing put back together by tonight."

Which meant that I couldn't drive by the Princes, if he wanted me back that soon. Which was probably for the best. I could only get myself into trouble, driving over there. I could find out only two things: either nothing, or something bad.

"Don't speed!" yelled my mother from the front door as I backed down the driveway. I had the address of the plumbing supply store and the part number written down. My Dad had called first, so there should be no problem getting it and getting back.

As I drove over to the plumbing supply store, I wasn't really tempted to detour over to the Princes. This was a direct errand for my father, time was a factor, and I was glad to get out of the house. Actually, I needed a break away from my desk; I was between papers for Brilliant and had to – what was that word? – think.

It didn't take me long to get to Rockaway Turnpike. Traffic was light on a Saturday afternoon. It wasn't even a full inning of the Mets' radio broadcast from Shea. I had to hunt for the address on Rockaway Turnpike. It wasn't as far down as the airport; it was in that middle skeevy area with the all-night diners and auto supply shops and bars and gas stations and vacant lots: the real Long Island.

The plumbing supply place was in a cluster of stores between this big Greek diner and a junkyard with a fence deco-
rated with used hubcaps. As I got out of the Chrysler, I could
see a plane coming into JFK. It couldn't have been more than a
couple of hundred feet off the ground, and it was loud enough
to bust your eardrums.

There were actually a couple of customers waiting at the
counter of the plumbing supply place and I had to take a number from a machine, like at a bakery. While I waited, I looked
around at the racks of plumbing tools and the high shelves of
cardboard boxes of parts, grouped by type and manufacturer,
all labeled with part numbers and letters. Two young guys,
guys not much older than me, were working behind the counter. They didn't seem to be having too much fun, working on a
sunny Saturday afternoon, fetching one pipe fitting or another,
one flange or another, from the shelves in the back. Whatever
happened to me, I didn't want to wind up working in a place
like this: so dark, so dusty, so dead end. I certainly was not
fond of the schoolwork I had left at home, but if it led me to
a life different from *this* one, I would do it gladly. Anything
but this.

On the plus side, the guy behind the counter found me
the correct toilet part promptly, and I found myself outside
the plumbing supply store in a few easy minutes. Nothing to
do but go back home. To cruise by Rachel's house would be
wrong – on several levels. I had to concentrate on doing right
– on several levels as well.

Then I heard a voice.

"Hey, kid!"

Somehow I knew *I* was the kid being called. And somehow I instantly recognized the voice.

"Mr. Perlov!"

It was Herb, standing with a bunch of other men in the
parking lot of the Greek diner that was right next to the store.
All the men looked at me with the same neutral/unfriendly
stare. One was tall, and the other two were pretty fat, but they

all had that same intimidating look, standing around Herb. And they all had cigars and big, heavy watches on their fat, hairy wrists. Rachel could have been right; maybe Herb *was* in the Mafia.

"What are you doing over here, in this neck of the woods?" he called.

All I could think of to say was, "Buying a ball cock." Which was the actual name of the toilet part, but it made them all explode into laughter. They laughed and laughed. One of the fat guys doubled over, coughing so much from laughing.

"I don't think you can buy one of 'dose, kid!" one of them yelled, creating another avalanche of laughter. I just stood there and took it, politely. I mean, what else could I do?

"Nice to see you," I said faintly, with a weak wave, and started to walk to my car. I didn't see any need to go over and engage with them.

"HEY!"

Herb's voice stopped me in my tracks. There was a sharpness in it which commanded me to turn and look back at him. So I did.

Herb pointed straight at me with his index finger, and said – and this was the weird thing: his voice was softer and almost *kind* – "Don't be a sucker."

Then he "fired" his finger at me like a gun and snorted.

I just nodded and mumbled, "OK." At least I think I said OK.

I got right back in the Chrysler, as I heard Herb and the men guffawing again, probably still at my expense, and drove straight home without looking back. With the ball cock on the seat right next to me.

The whole way, I couldn't stop thinking about what he said.

What kind of a way is that to talk to a kid? If he wanted to say something to me, he should have said it directly, like a man. But making some kind of oblique joke in front of his goomba friends, well, that was pretty low.

"Don't be a sucker."

What did that even *mean*? There were so many different ways to take that: That I shouldn't be so devoted to Rachel? That Eleanor was so against me that my future with Rachel was nil, so why was I wasting my time? That Rachel was indeed still seeing Eric on the sly, or someone else I didn't even know about? And on and on. I didn't know which, if any, of these insinuations were true, but all of them made me feel small and defensive and taken advantage of; there was nothing good in any of them.

As if I hadn't seen it clearly before, I now saw what hateful people Rachel was living with: Eleanor *and* this guy? How could she – how could *we* – survive them? These love-killers.

The one good thing is that my father got the downstairs toilet put back together – and working – by nighttime. That was vital. I couldn't have them tromping up the stairs in the middle of the night. I needed my privacy, and I'm sure they appreciated theirs. Funny, I never even asked my parents how they felt about my going back and forth, to and from Columbia like a yo-yo, the way I wanted, without even consulting them. Maybe they *liked* having the house to themselves, with me away. Maybe they had been waiting for this day for *years*. They seemed to like having me around, but you never knew. But I couldn't really think about that; I had enough on my mind.

When I went to bed that night, no matter how I tried to banish the words from my mind, Herb's *"Don't be a sucker!"* echoed in my mind. I fell asleep quickly as it repeated and repeated and repeated in my brain, but I didn't sleep well.

My father tried to get me to go bowling with him that next afternoon, but I honestly couldn't (my never-ending schoolwork and the never-ending possibility that Rachel might call). Unfortunately, I got into a fight with my mother about it.

"Your father asks you once in a blue moon to go out with him, and you say no?" she nagged.

In a way, she was right. My father seldom asks me for anything, outside the odd errand (see above), so I should have said yes and gone with him. But I could tell that he was just asking me to go *for me* – as a way to distract me from what was obviously going on with me.

"Leave him alone!" my father said. "It was just an idea. Forget about it!"

Later, he drove me to the train station.

"I knew you didn't want to go," he said.

"I know," I said. "I actually have a lot on my mind lately."

"That's why I asked you," my father said, as if I'd proved him right. "But forget it."

When he dropped me at the station, I could tell that there was something he wanted to say to me.

"What is it?" I asked him. "The train is coming."

He hesitated. My father was always reluctant to give me advice, especially now that I was older. Maybe it was because he didn't have much of an education, and he generally lets me do things my way. And, the truth is, I had done pretty well so far. But this time he wanted to say something to me. He turned and faced me straight-on.

"You know," he said. "You have a choice in things."

That was it.

"OK," I said. "Thanks. I know that."

I got out of the car and ran up the stairs just in time for the arriving train. I really didn't think about what he said, I was in such a rush to get on the train and get back to my life at Columbia, but truly I wish I had.

Record of Events #25 – entered Tuesday, 12:16 A.M.

≁

I didn't get Rachel on the phone Monday or Tuesday night. It's semi-ridiculous how I remember every detail – every phone call, made or missed – but I'm sorry, I do. On Monday night, Eleanor said curtly, "She can't come to the phone now," and hung up, even before I could say, "Thank you, Mrs. Prince!" with the appropriate touch of sarcasm. On Tuesday night, Herb answered and said, "Sorry, but she's doing her homework. She'll call you if she finishes."

At least he had the courtesy to say, "Sorry, but." And I didn't expect her to finish whatever they wanted her to. So I was truly surprised when someone banged on my door a while later and said that I had a call.

But it wasn't Rachel; it was Nanci Jerome.

"I hope you don't mind me calling," she said.

"No," I said. "That's OK," trying unsuccessfully not to sound disappointed.

"I'm better than nothing, right?" she laughed self-deprecatingly.

"It's not that," I said, although she was right. "I just haven't been able to get through to her since the weekend." (With Nanci, "her" automatically meant Rachel.)

"I know," she said.

"How do *you* know?" I asked right back.

"I know everything."

That stopped me a little.

"OK," I said. "Then tell me everything."

"You don't want to know everything," she said. "Believe me."

But I just waited . . . waited for her to resume. Some people just can't keep their mouths shut, and if you wait long enough, they'll go on.

"It's not good over there," she said. "They've really been fighting. I've tried to help, but those are two stubborn females. Like mother, like daughter."

"Don't say that," I snapped. "Rachel is nothing like her mother."

"If you say so," Nanci cracked back.

"Well, she's not like her mother *to me*," I added, for good measure. And I meant it. "That's what she's trying to *get away* from!" I concluded.

Nanci didn't say anything. But I guess I really had no business, raising my voice to her.

I softened my tone. "So, uh, Nanci, why'd you call me?"

There was a long pause on her end. I got the feeling that she was changing her mind about her reason for calling me.

"I, uh, I just thought you might want to know *why* she hasn't been able to call you," she said. "That's all. And she told me to tell you that she loves you."

"Yeah, well," I said. "Thanks. . . . You think they'll let Rachel out for our date on Friday night?"

Nanci laughed once. "You never know," she said. "Let me work on Eleanor."

"Why do they do this?" I asked – not really asking her, asking the world.

"You know why: because they can," she answered, and that was as good an answer as any.

"Tell her to call me from school," I said. "Away from Eleanor."

"OK," she said. "I'll do that."

I waited for her to say something else.

"You should just be careful," she said.

"About what?" I asked.

"Everything."

It took me two days to get that call out of my head (and, as you can see, in some ways I never really did.) She was trying to send me some kind of message, something between her words, but I never really got it.

~

Things, I'm sorry to say, began to get worse between Rachel and me. I didn't want it to, and I don't think she did either, but it was happening gradually, and neither of us could seem to do anything about it. Oh, we still loved each other as intensely, maybe more than ever, but circumstances aggravated our situation so that on every other phone call, or every *third* phone call, one of us would say something to annoy the other. I wouldn't be sympathetic enough to her, or vice versa. I would listen for little misstatements she might make, looking for some kind of slip-up, thinking that she might reveal something, perhaps *someone else*. Or she would hear an edge in my voice that wasn't really there and take offense. Sometimes we would end a call on a bitter note. Then, the next time I talked to her, it was as if nothing was wrong: The Zone, the same as ever. But then she'd remember something I said – or didn't say – and relive the hurt. The worst stretch was when she was "late." There was quite a bit of tension between us for those few days, but everything was OK eventually. Perhaps my greatest mistake was my continual failure to read her mind.

The fact is that she was increasingly fragile, and I had to be more careful than ever with what I said to her, just hoping for a good Friday. Fridays: when we could be together and forget the whole world and everything in it. With what she was living with – Eleanor and Herb and her father and school and just about everything else – I had to be the "one good thing" in her life, no matter how tough it was.

"Senior-itis!" she said. "That's all anyone talks about. How much fun they're having, where they've applied to, and where they're going. I just couldn't be more uninterested."

"You just have to hang on, baby," I said. "Things will get better."

I had no proof for my assertion, so it just hung in the air, like a big lie.

~

This one gray Tuesday morning, on and off through two straight classes, I just couldn't concentrate. Coursing in and out of my mind were thoughts of how to stop this drift that was occurring, the rift that was happening between Rachel and me. It felt so wrong; I knew that the fundamental love was still there. It was just the rest of life – *both* of her parents, *and* Herb, my schoolwork, the distance, the not-seeing-each-oth-er-every-day – that got in the way. And that was just *wrong*. Rachel and I had something beyond special, and it would be a shame to lose it. I walked all the way back to my dorm, coming up with no better immediate plan than telling her and myself to be patient. Friday wasn't that far away . . . assuming I'd be able to see her. (This was after another weekend that she had been grounded by Eleanor.) Who knew what was going to happen? I was not in perfect control of my own life anymore. I realized that, to a greater extent than I might have ever want-ed, my happiness depended on whatever Rachel Prince did.

I got to the top of the stairs and turned down the hallway. There, sitting on the floor, leaning against the wall with her long, dark hair cascading down her shoulders, was Rachel. My heart and breath stopped. I was surprised and excited and fearful, all at once.

"Oh my God," I said as I approached her. "What in the world are you doing here?"

"Aren't you glad to see me?" she said.

"Of course, I'm glad to see you," I said, dropping my books. "I'm *more* than glad!"

"It takes forever to get here by train!" she said. "I don't know how you do it."

"Millions of people commute. It's really nothing," I said as I pulled her up from the floor and into my arms. "But I'm very glad you did."

We kissed and held each other for a few minutes, long enough to attract some attention from a couple of guys in the hallway.

"Hubba-hubba!"

"Can't you two find a *motel* room?"

"Let's go inside," I said, digging in my pocket for my room key. "Jealous bastards!"

I opened the door and let her inside. She was wearing a thick coat with a fur collar that framed her face like a snow angel. But as she swept past me, she smelled like spring.

"This is such a small room!" she trilled. "I can't believe they put two people in here!"

"Neither can I," I said. "I think they used to be for one person, but that was years ago."

"This *is* a pretty gross dorm," she said.

"It's an old school."

"Still, you'd think they would at least *try* to make it nice. I mean it *is* the Ivy League."

"That means nothing. It's all about making money, cramming two guys in here. The Ivy League isn't different from anybody else. It's still a business."

"And this is where you are all week?" she asked, looking around at the cramped, plain, overstuffed little room. "You poor baby."

"Honey!" I said, taking her by the shoulders. "What in the world are you doing here?"

That's when she started to tear up. She spilled out her story in waves of rushed talk, punctuated by sobs and choked-back laughter.

"They're making me see a therapist," she said. "I got called down to the principal. My grades completely suck. I have absolutely no interest in logarithms, not even with a math tutor. I did crappy on my SATs *again*. I keep telling them that I have *zero* intention of going to college. They don't believe that either! The applications sit there in my room, not filled out. And I'm not going to fill them out!"

I watched her standing there in my small, narrow room, taking off her gloves, her coat, her scarf, and a sweater. Her hair was a little messy and her eyes were streaked with dried tears as she did this kind of striptease in front of me. I have to admit that I felt torn between my concern for her troubled soul, which made me want to listen to and comfort her, and my desire for her body, which I missed so much.

"So why did Eleanor ground you this time?" I asked.

"Oh, that was completely ridiculous!" she exclaimed. "I got caught drinking beer at school with a couple of other girls."

"Beer?" I half laughed. "You don't even *like* beer!"

"I know!" she said. "That's what's so ridiculous! But Lydia Sherrow's boyfriend sneaked a six-pack through the fence during a very boring field hockey game, and I thought maybe it might remind me of Bailey's or something. A bunch of us got in trouble. It wasn't just me."

"But if it was everybody, that's no reason to *ground* you!"

"I know! I was barely involved!" she said. "It's so unfair. I really don't think I can stand it much longer."

"Oh, baby! Who else knows that you ditched school?" I asked.

"Nobody," she said. "Just Nanci. When Eleanor dropped me off, I waited until after homeroom, and then I called Nanci and had her drive me straight to the train station."

"Wow," I said. "Good for you."

"I was going to make her drive me into the City," Rachel said. "But she had some class that she just couldn't miss. I couldn't believe she wouldn't take me."

Of course I was beyond happy to see her, yet I couldn't *not* worry about what new crisis her class ditching would bring.

"So," she said, drawing me toward her with her soft, loving smile. "Aren't you glad to see me?"

I thought of all the questions I had to ask her: Had she seen Eric that weekend? Or someone else? Was she concealing something else from me? Should I tell her everything, even about my encounter with Herb and what he said, something I had never told her?

Instead, I moved into her embrace, ignoring all the questions swirling in my brain, and took her strongly, saying, "You have no idea."

~

I guess we were dozing afterwards when we were awakened by the sound of the door to the room being shaken roughly, and someone trying to turn the doorknob repeatedly.

"Hey! What's going on in there?"

It was Roommate A. He had used his key, but I had bolted the inside lock shut, thank goodness.

"Oh!" I stalled him. "Hey! Wait a minute, man! I didn't know you were coming back! . . . Dammit, it's my roommate. Get dressed."

"Where did you *think* I would go?" he said archly. "I *live* here!" He pounded on the door hard, twice.

"Oh, great," muttered Rachel, already hurrying into her clothes. I tried not to stare at her, even though she looked very sexy, all disheveled and loose. "What are *you* doing?"

"I'm hurrying!" I whispered, scrambling into my jeans.

"Come on!" pounded Roommate A on the door. "Zip up and open the door!"

Rachel gasped even as I snickered at his wisecrack.

"You ready?" I whispered to her as I pulled a shirt on over my head.

"Yeah," she breathed as she had herself dressed – and beautiful – almost instantly. "OK."

I pulled open the bolt and turned the lock as Roommate A burst into the room.

"Well, it's about time, dammit!" he huffed, bulling his way into the room and throwing his book bag up onto his bed.

"What the –" Then he caught sight of Rachel. "Whoa! Now who is *this*?" he said with a wolfish grin, instantly understanding the situation. "Why, freshman, I didn't think you had it in you!"

"Thanks," I said with maximum sarcasm. With no choice, I introduced Rachel and Roommate A.

"So this is why you tear ass out of here every Friday for 'Lawn *GI*-land,'" he said, looking her up and down, practically licking his lips. "Now I completely understand, you old horndog!" (Once again, Roommate "A" earns his name.)

"Do you have to stay here?" I asked. "Can't you maybe *vanish* for, like, an hour?"

"Are you mad?" he said, slamming his books down on his desk and climbing up the ladder onto his bed. "I just came back from two tests – one in calculus – and I need to rest!"

He threw his shoes down onto the floor loudly, one penny loafer at a time, and lit up one of his stupid Gauloises which filled the room with his smoke.

(Oh, do I have to tell you that I missed the Protestant Reformation test? What was I supposed to do? She was crying hysterically in my arms half the time. I wound up making some chicken broth for her on my illegal hot plate, the possession of which is the only crime to which I will gladly plead guilty.)

With no other choice, Rachel and I left my room and went down the hallway to the lounge, with its plain, stained furniture and bad TV. But at least we were alone, at least for a few minutes on the gray, uncomfortable couch.

"I really don't like that guy," I said. "He's a slob *and* a snob. I think he's used to having people clean up after him."

"Don't think about him," she said. "Think about us."

She leaned toward me, closing her eyes, wanting to be kissed. And believe me I wanted to kiss her, but first, I had something that I had to say; something I had been thinking the whole time.

"Wait," I said. "You've got to call them and tell them where you are."

"No."

The look on her face hardened as she turned away from me.

"They're going to be worried about you," I reasoned.

"I really don't care."

"They're gonna call the police, and you don't want that."

"This is such a big dorm. Maybe someone is gone," she pleaded. "And you could get your roommate to switch beds? Or I could sleep in here. You could sleep with me! It would be like a camp-out at the end of the lake! Or the Quarry!"

"Oh, baby," I said, trying to hold her closer to me. "Just hold onto me, and it'll be like in The Zone –"

"No!" she said, pushing me away. "You don't understand! I don't want to go back there! Herb has been very creepy, and I'm afraid if I go back there something might happen."

"What do you mean, 'creepy'?" I said, suddenly feeling that blank-white rage I felt on the Princes' porch begin to rise. "What's he done?" Mental pictures of that hairy sleazeball peeking in at Rachel, doing things to her, flashed through my mind, and I was infuriated. "Tell me."

"Nothing specific," she said. "I mean, he didn't rape me or anything yet."

"What do you mean, 'yet'?" I said.

"It's the way he looks at me," she said. "He leaves his bathrobe open during breakfast, and it's disgusting. And sometimes some of his greasy gangster friends come over to watch TV, and they look at me too."

"And what does Eleanor do?" I asked.

"Nothing," she said. "She laughs as usual, and blames it on me."

Then I brought up something that I had been going to let pass.

"Tell me one thing, honey. . . . What's that mark on your arm?"

"Oh," she said, trying to turn her upper arm around so she could see the back of it, to see the dark purple bruise that I saw before when we were in my room. "Is there something still there? Eleanor pinched me a couple of days ago. Hard."

I felt flushed with anger. That must've been one wicked pinch, to cause that kind of a bruise.

"You've got to call your father," I said.

"He really doesn't care," she said, waving her hand in the air.

"How can he not care??" I almost shouted, "He's your father! *Make* him care! Do you think he wants Eleanor to *leave marks* on your skin? Do you think he wants a skeeve like Herb hanging around you? I don't care if he *is* connected to the Mafia. If I had a daughter and she was bothered by some old pervert, I'd cut out his throat, with absolutely no hesitation."

It had never occurred to me until that exact point, but I realized right then that I would indeed kill for Rachel. But only if it were justified. If she needed protection, and if nobody else would protect her, I would.

~

I waited with Rachel on 116th Street for Manny to come pick her up. It was cold and dark, and we held hands as Rachel shivered.

"I'm not going to let them win," she said, shuddering against me. "I told you that at Mooncliff. I'm not going to let them control my life."

Her blue-blue eyes were shining with brave tears as Manny drove up in the biggest, blackest Cadillac I'd ever seen.

"This is good," she said. "This is going to force their hand."

"Don't let them come between us," I implored her.

She turned to me with no verbal answer, just fear, as Manny, double-parking, ripped open the driver's side door and emerged. He looked directly at Rachel, who was squeezing my hand as hard as she could.

"I had your mother on the phone *four times* today!" Manny yelled, as if he had a mouth full of acid. "You *know* how much I love *that!*"

Rachel shouted right back at him. "They're mean to me, Daddy! You know they are! She never lets me do anything! What if I came and lived with you?"

"Forget about that right now!" he cut her off, as he came right toward her. "You know that ain't happening."

From his abrupt answer, I could tell that he really didn't want his daughter. That seemed so foreign to me: my father always gave me unconditional love. (And does to this day, even after everything that's happened.)

"What are *you* looking at, smart guy?" he said to me suddenly. "You're half the cause of all this!"

Before I could say anything, Manny grabbed Rachel's wrist and pulled her away from me.

"Get in the car!" he ordered her, half flinging her toward the front end of the huge Caddy. "I have an early meeting tomorrow, and I have to deal with this nonsense!"

Rachel looked at me with desperate sadness as she moved to get into the car.

"Call me," I said directly to her, trying to send my love and compassion directly to her, one last time before she went.

"Shut up!" Manny barked, pointing a finger straight into my face. "Stay out of this."

I had to say something.

"This is just wrong, Mr. Prince," I began with.

Manny's head swiveled away from me, shouting at Rachel, "GET IN THE CAR, RACHEL!!!"

Rachel flinched and got straight into the car, rabbit-scared at Manny's outburst. Then he refocused on me.

"You listen to me and listen to me good," he said, his index finger aiming right between my eyes. He lowered his voice, for the first time. "Stay away from her. I am not kidding." His quiet tone was even more sinister. "Don't make me tell you twice."

He was trying to scare me and he did, but only by half. Outside, I might have looked terrified – he was so much bigger and angrier than me – but inside, I knew that he could never scare me away from Rachel. No one could. At least not permanently.

He slammed back into the Cadillac and drove away fast. I think she turned toward me again, to look over the backseat, but I'm not sure. It was dark and streetlights reflected off the car's back window. In any case, I was left shivering, standing there very much alone, as Manny turned a hard right as the yellow light turned red, and the big black Caddy disappeared down Broadway.

Record of Events #26 – entered Tuesday, 11:17 A.M.

∾

She didn't call me the next day. All day, through all my classes, I thought about calling her, but I didn't even know *where* to call – Manny's or her mother's. I also thought about my father's rule: "*Don't make things worse*," and how much sense it made. I should just let things cool down. I couldn't fight both Manny and Eleanor (and Herb, for that matter), at least not right now. But I tried not to get too negative about the overall future for Rachel and me. Sure, they could make it difficult for us, but they couldn't make it *impossible* for us. We would win in the end because we were younger, and we had love on our side. All it took was patience and a belief in each other. So I didn't call her the next day. I just thought about it, over and over again.

I considered what I would do when I went back to the Island that weekend. (I certainly couldn't stay in the dorm all weekend with Roommate A.) Would I drive over to Eleanor's house? Or Manny's place in Garden City? How would I find her? I could call Nanci. I could get her to find out what was going on. I could probably get her to do anything.

∾

I went to all my classes and tried to pay attention, but despite my best intentions, my thoughts keep circling back to Rachel. With everything in danger of being lost – or at least threatened – my anxious mind couldn't concentrate on anything but her.

286   What It Was Like

I thought about all the angles of our separation and how to get around the barriers that Eleanor had and would raise against us. I thought about how much worse they might be now, after Rachel's little trip into Manhattan to see me. Then I would banish those thoughts and try to think of better things. I remembered all the wonderful times we'd had together, times in The Zone. Like a kaleidoscope, my mind flashed through scenes of Mooncliff, moments of intense memory, intense pleasure. Bright mornings on the Mess Hall porch and hidden moments under the pines . . . rowing on the lake and "Honor your partner!" . . . sunsets at the Quarry. Bailey's and the backseat of the Super-Coupe. Walking with the Doggies and her girls all around us. The Burning of the Lake and "*Promise you'll love me forever!*"

In the midst of one of these self-debates, one of my teachers called on me with a direct question. I had absolutely no idea what he was talking about – it had something to do with *The Book of Job* and forgiveness – but I couldn't even fake an answer. A couple of kids snickered, and my teacher shot me a sharp look of displeasure that I well deserved.

So you'll understand that I was pretty blue when I straggled back to my room to change books during lunchtime. I had picked up my usual roast beef hero with extra ketchup and can of Nehi grape soda at Mama Joy's, figuring that I'd eat at my desk. Roommate A was usually out and I could have the room to myself. I could eat in peace, not like in the bedlam of John Jay or one of the nearby greasy spoons, and check my notes in case there was a surprise quiz – which was not out of the realm of possibility – in my afternoon's French class.

"Phone!" Somebody pounded on my door twice and shouted my name, shocking me out of my trance of Flaubert.

"OK!" I yelled. "Tell 'em to hold on!" Not that anybody would have told anybody to hold on to anything; the phone was just hanging there in mid-air, swinging on its cord, knocking against the wall. Nobody really cared about anybody else on the floor.

I raced down the hall, pulling my Keds on. The hall floor was cold. In fact, the whole dorm was cold unless the radiators went bananas, which happened sometimes, and then it became as hot and moist as a rain forest. I grabbed the phone, hoping it was –

"Hello?" I said, out of breath.

"Hello?" said a voice I could hardly hear, but I thought it was Rachel.

"Hello?" I said louder. "Is that *you*?"

"Thank God," she said, her voice suddenly more audible, as if she had just closed the door of the phone booth she was in.

"I was hoping it was you," I said. "But I was afraid to hope."

"Oh, baby," she said, the ever-present music in her voice taking on a minor key. "Oh, my sweet boy."

"I was thinking a million times of calling you," I said, even as I remembered why I didn't. "But I didn't even know *where* to call."

"It's probably good that you didn't," she said heavily. "At least for now. They want me to stay away from you. They think that you're a bad influence on me."

"That's ridiculous," I said.

"I know," she agreed. "But you wouldn't believe what they've put me through! I had to go see this family court *judge* and –"

"No! Really?" I closed my eyes, trying to concentrate on her words.

"And I have an appointment to see this *therapist*," she continued. "*They're* the ones who need a therapist! They certainly could've used a *marriage counselor*!"

She huffed one laugh, but I could tell how upset she was.

"Where are you living now?" I asked her.

"Back with Eleanor," she snapped. "Manny doesn't want me. Where else can I go? I can't live in your dorm room, and the couch in that lounge was very uncomfortable. So tell me what choice do I have?"

She sounded so forlorn and resigned, even as she tried to make a joke.

"Maybe I could live in *your* parents' house," she said. "In your room."

"They would let you, if I asked them," I said, and I meant it.

But she just laughed sadly.

"Thanks," she said. "But no thanks. I have to figure out a way to get through all this."

I didn't know exactly what to do or say, but I knew that we were at a critical moment. I didn't want to push her too hard.

"Let me help you," I said. There were some guys in the hall, passing by, and I had to turn to the wall.

"They really want me to stay away from you for a while," she said. "They say that I've developed a quote-unquote *unhealthy attachment* to you. They say that I'm obsessed with you."

"Is that supposed to be a bad thing?" I said. "I'm obsessed with you too!" She didn't respond immediately, so I prompted her. "And what did you say to them?"

She said, "I told them that I'm in love with you."

I snickered at that, but I couldn't feel anything but the edge of dread.

"You're too smart for them," I said. "The next time they say that, you can tell them that I'm obsessed with you too."

"But listen, listen, listen –" she said until I stopped talking and there was quiet. "I've decided . . ." she let that hang in the air.

"You've decided *what?*" I asked, knowing/feeling what she was about to say.

"I think it might be better," she said slowly. "If . . . we take a break from each other for a while."

I wasn't sure that I heard her correctly.

"What?" I said. "I didn't hear you. I thought you said that we shouldn't see each other for a while."

"Only for a little while," she said. "Until they stop with this torture. They're always at me. If it's not Eleanor, it's school. If it's not them, it's Herb, always looking at me. Or my father, threatening that he won't get me my car. They're always at me, and you're always at me –"

"What do you mean, *I'm* always at you?" I interrupted. (I think that's when the hall really started to tilt, and I had to lean against the wall.)

"I mean that I'm always worried about not being home for your calls," she said in a rush. "Or Eleanor not letting me talk long enough. Or trying to figure out when to call you at school, and knowing that you probably won't be there. And fighting with them every weekend to steal time with you. I get so worked up every time I'm going to see you – and I fight with Eleanor and Herb before, of course – that after I've left you, I'm wrecked. I feel . . . I feel – I don't know, I don't know – *used up* by it all. It's just too much for me. It's too much."

She started crying, and this time, I let her cry. Theoretically I felt bad for her, a girl being forced to break up with her boyfriend. Myself? I tried not to feel anything myself. I guess, in retrospect, I was starting to go numb.

"I made a deal with them," she said. "I told them that I'd try things their way for a while. My father said he'd still give me the Mustang if I 'straightened out.' Those were his words."

"What does that mean?" I asked, trying to see exactly where she was going.

"It means seeing their stupid therapist twice a week. And trying to get decent grades, finishing off my college applications –"

"You mean you haven't finished them yet?" I asked. "Not even NYU?"

"You know what I want to do," she answered back. "And it's *not* going to college next fall! Are *you* having any fun?"

"*I* have no choice! *I* don't have grandma money. It's either college or the Army for me. I'd rather not wind up face down in a rice paddy, if you don't mind." I didn't stop, "What about your grandma money? What did that lawyer ever say?"

"I never actually spoke to him," she said. "He had to cancel that meeting, and then it never got rescheduled."

"Don't you think you should, before you start making plans for your future?"

"Please don't talk to me like that," she snapped. "You sound like Eleanor."

"That's not a very nice thing to say," I responded in a calm voice.

"Well, neither is what you said!"

I let there be a long pause. Then I asked the question.

"So what does this actually mean?"

She paused – I don't know if she was choking up or what – and said, "It means not seeing you for a while."

"What about loving me 'forever, no matter what happens'?" I said, quoting her very words as she left me on the last day of Mooncliff. "You remember when you said that –"

"I remember!" she cut me off. "I didn't say that I didn't love you. I didn't say that at all."

"I'm sorry," I groped for the right words. "I just don't understand. You say you love me, yet you want to break up with me?"

"Not break up," she said. "Just take a break."

"For how long?"

"I don't know how long!" she paused. "This therapist told them that it should be a total break, at least for a while. I'll have to see what happens."

I couldn't believe the words I'd been hearing – I *never, ever* believed that she actually wanted to leave me of her own free will – but here she was, doing it, breaking up with me.

"You really think 'boys are toys,'" I said.

"Don't say that; I'm serious," she said, her voice breaking. "I can't keep going on this way. I just have to change some things."

"But why change *us*?" I demanded. "I thought that we were one of the *good* things in your life."

"I'm sorry," she wept. "But I don't know what else to do. Everyone's pressuring me, and I can't take it anymore."

"OK," I said, sounding casual as I was imploding. "Whatever you say."

"No, please don't say that."

"What do you want me to say?" I asked, closing my eyes, my forehead against the wall. "You always said that you don't want anyone to control you. Why should I think that I was any different?"

"Please, I hate it when you sound so cold."

"Tell me, Rachel," I said, my voice cracking. "After what you've just told me, what temperature am I supposed to be?"

I heard her start crying again, and I was almost glad that she was. She was doing something stupid and wrong, and I couldn't stop her.

"We were supposed to make each other happy!" she sobbed. "I thought that if I loved you enough, everything would be OK."

"Why are you doing this?" I asked, trying to break through to her rationally, but losing hope.

"I have to do something," she said, trying to keep her voice from wavering. "I can't go on, the way things are."

"OK," I said, going back to cold, resigned. "If you say so."

"Just trust me," she said passionately and finally. "Give me time, and I'll make things better. I have to go. I love you. Goodbye."

And she hung up the phone.

I have to go . . . I love you . . . Goodbye.

~

I stood there for a long time, trying to understand what had just happened. It didn't seem possible. Rachel loved me, and I loved her. Why should we be apart *at all*? Something was wrong with the world. Very wrong.

I don't remember walking back to my room. I don't remember much of the rest of that day, to tell you the truth.

I did a lot of sleeping in the days immediately after Rachel broke up with me. (There, I said it.) And when I was awake, when my mind managed to focus, I debated over my next course of action. First I had to decide if I *had* any course of action to take. "*Don't make things worse.*" Rachel was doing what she had to do; maybe I should trust her to come back to me.

But she sounded as if she were in such trouble. Could I – *should* I just abandon her? Involved with Eleanor and Herb and her father, who knows what she was facing, even in the way of physical danger? None of them really seemed to love her or care about her. I did.

But I was smart; I laid low. At least for a couple of days. I went to my classes and, on one level, paid attention to what was going on and being said. But, on another level, it was RachelRachelRachel all the time: what to do, how to get her back, how to survive until I got her back. I know now that I didn't behave normally. But that's because Rachel and I didn't have a "normal" love. We had something deeper, much deeper, and when it was gone I kind of fell apart.

"What's the matter with you?" Roommate A asked me. It was late in the afternoon. "You've been sitting there for hours. You haven't even moved."

"I've moved," I answered him. "I've moved a great deal . . . inside."

I had given her three days of this nonsense; now I was going to call her. At 8:00, our regular time. As if nothing had happened. Going down to the phone booth in the mailroom,

I recalled all the responses I'd gotten all the times that I had called the Princes' number: *"She's not home. . . . She'll have to call you back. . . . She's doing her homework, sorry!"* Of course, sometimes Rachel answered the phone herself. Maybe I'd get lucky, and it would be Rachel again this time, the way it always should have been.

I sat in the booth and pulled the door closed behind me. I dug a handful of coins from my pocket and put them on the little shelf under the phone. I dropped two dimes and a nickel in the slot – bong-bong-bong – dialed and waited, rehearsing what I was going to say, depending on who answered. Maybe I could charm Eleanor; I could give it one more shot. Who knows? Maybe she could have had a change of heart.

Instead, I heard: *"The number you have reached has been changed or is no longer in service. If you feel you have reached this number in error, please try your call again. Thank you."*

I tried the number two more times and got the same recording each time before I was convinced.

Whoa! I thought to myself as I finally hung up. *These people are serious. Changing their phone number to keep her away from me? Isn't that a little drastic?*

Not to be outsmarted so easily, I called Information.

"I'm sorry," said the operator. "That number has been changed to an unpublished number."

"What do mean 'unpublished'?" I asked, although I knew the answer.

"The customer has chosen not to have the number published," said the operator. "Can I help you with anything else?"

"No," I said. "Thank you," and I hung up quietly.

All I could do was go back to my room and think quietly about my options.

~

Over the next few days, I thought of the many ways by which I could get the Princes' new unpublished phone number. One of the kids I graduated with, a guy who sat in front of me in homeroom for six years because our last names were one letter apart, worked for the phone company. I knew I could get the number from him. Or I could pretend to be some kind of door-to-door salesman or polltaker and try to get some information out of one of their neighbors. I also knew some of the stores that the Princes used in the town of Oakhurst, and I'm sure that I could make up something, like I'd found Eleanor Prince's wallet right outside their store, and did they know her phone number so that I could arrange returning it?

Or I could do what I eventually did: go to Nanci Jerome's to flirt with her and smoke her hash in order to find out Rachel's new phone number. (I stopped things before they went too far. But, of course, she was using me too. This is one of the many reasons why I didn't testify at my trial: all this *stuff* should never have had to come out, and my testimony would have just added to the sensationalism of the whole thing. Rachel didn't know about it for the longest time. But, in a way, she's the one who practically *forced* me to do it. Just add it to the long list of actions of mine of which I am not particularly proud.)

When I drove away from Nanci's house, I was so close to Rachel that I had a hard time resisting the urge to just burst into the Princes' house and take her away with me, after apologizing profusely for my transgression with Nanci. But I never did . . . either.

The next day, when Nanci called me after finding out the Princes' new number from her mother, I thanked her and told her she was a true friend. I'm not sure that's exactly what she wanted to hear from me, but I couldn't really worry too much about that.

I debated about waiting until 8:00 to call, but I decided that was too obvious. I had to play this carefully. If the phone rang precisely at 8:00, they would know it was me. If I called earlier, I might catch them off-guard.

I don't know why I felt so confident as I dialed the new, not-yet-memorized number. I just felt that Rachel would be glad to hear from me, to know that I hadn't abandoned her, that I was still, if nothing else, her true friend.

The kitchen was clear. My parents knew that something was going on with me and gave me a lot of space. But I still pulled the long cord into the dining room after I dialed and waited, hanging in suspension as I had done so many times before. One ring, two rings. The line picked up; my heart braced itself.

"Hello?" It was a cautious *Eleanor*. My timing was wrong!

"Hello??" she said again, sounding even more suspicious. "Who *is* this?"

I panicked and hung up. Which was a stupid thing to do: stupidstupidstupid. Now she would *know* that I was on to them and had found out their new number, *and* I hadn't even *said* anything! I should have at least asked to speak to Rachel or something, and said what I wanted to say. Instead, I hung up like a fool. A fool *and* a coward.

I went back up to my room to berate myself for this bad move.

"What was I thinking?" I said out loud to myself. I sat on my bed cross-legged and bounced a tennis ball off my wall so many times that my father had to yell up the stairs, "Can you please cut that out? You're shaking the whole house!"

"Sorry!" I yelled back.

I stopped bouncing the ball off the wall and just lay on my back, tossing it straight up in the air softly, hitting nothing. I couldn't stop thinking about the bad move I had made. And what made it worse was that it was a bad move I had *planned*. Nanci told me that Rachel "clouded my judgment." Maybe she was right. I had never before gotten such mediocre grades or been on such terrible terms with my teachers or lost touch with my friends from high school; so much of my mental energy was devoted to Rachel and the maintenance of our relationship. I admit that it was tough getting bad grades, grinding through my classes, and barely co-existing with Roommate A and his phony French cigarettes in that tiny room. But there were many, many moments of true happiness with Rachel – both actually being with her and when I was alone, *thinking* about her and us – that made it all worthwhile. Didn't the Beatles just sing, "All You Need Is Love"? I believed that then (and, to some extent, despite everything that happened, still do).

Anyway, I fell asleep in the way-too-late night, after deciding that, what the hell, I was glad the Princes knew that I had their new unpublished number. Now, whenever their phone rang, they would always have to wonder: "Is it *you-know-who*?" And Rachel would always be reminded: "He hasn't forgotten about me. He still loves me."

I woke up the next afternoon (I guess it was actually the afternoon of the same day), and overnight I had come to another conclusion: I had to see Rachel one more time, in person. It wasn't fair to me, it wasn't really even fair to her, and it certainly wasn't fair to Us – to The Zone – to end things on the phone. I had to see her once more. I wanted to see her tell it to my face: that we were over. Sorry, that we were on a "break" for "I-don't-know-how-long." Not that I was going to challenge her decision. She had the right to do and to feel however she wanted. But I deserved an explanation *to my face*. I was owed that.

So I did the most logical thing I could think of: I went to see Rachel at Oakhurst High on Monday, to see her in person. I knew that I could ill-afford to ditch all my Monday classes, but likewise I couldn't just let my relationship with Rachel end on a phone call. It was eating me up, this "wrong" ending, and I had to get past it if I wanted to move on with my life.

I didn't want to go to her house – or Manny's condominium, for that matter. That would be even more complicated. And I wanted to see her as soon as possible, to get it over with now, Monday. OK, by ditching all my classes on Monday – or certainly the morning classes – I know that I was making my bad relationships with a few of my teachers worse, but I couldn't just let things with Rachel end like this. If they were going to be finished, they had to be finished correctly.

I don't think that my parents totally believed me when I told them that I had "Monday off" when I showed up super early by surprise to borrow my mother's car. They didn't fight me too much about it. They were pretty considerate of me and what they sensed I was going through at the time. (Maybe if they had been a little less considerate and a little more intolerant, I wouldn't have gotten myself into the trouble I got myself into. I don't blame them for anything I did; as I said, I was obsessed. I would have pushed back hard if they had tried to stop me and any of my carefully planned actions. I am completely responsible for everything I ever did, ever felt, and ever said.)

It was very cold that Monday morning, right before Christmas vacation, but I wanted to get to Oakhurst High early. Maybe if I could see Rachel before her classes; see her early, and get it out of the way. But I was determined to make it "official" – face-to-face. It might have been her decision to break things off, but it would be on *my* terms, in person and final. Maybe I could even get back to Columbia in time for my afternoon classes.

Unfortunately, on my semi-frantic drive to Oakhurst High in the Falcon in the early rush hour traffic, the car heater got stuck on high, so I had to keep the window open as heat poured out of the vents. I cranked open the window and turned the vents away from me, but by the time I was in Oakhurst, my body was covered with sweat while my neck and left arm were icy cold from the rush of outside air.

And I didn't leave early enough either. As I came in sight of the glass-and-steel palace of education, there were so many cars whizzing around – lots of nice GTOs and foreign sports cars – and so many kids crossing the street every which way, in the crosswalks and between cars, that I couldn't really look for Rachel and keep my eyes on the road at the same time. There was a student parking lot with cars streaming in, but a guard in a uniform was standing at the big iron-pointed gate, checking parking permits, and I didn't have one. It was getting closer to the start of school, and if I had any hope of finding Rachel before classes began, I had to get out of the car and find her on foot.

I whipped around the corner and, halfway down the block, I luckily found a parking spot in front of one of the big, old Tudor houses that lined the street. I got out of the car, locked it, and hurried down the sidewalk, joining the crowd of people moving toward the high school.

Approaching Oakhurst High School on foot, I was even more impressed by the newness and sleekness of the building, glistening in the sharp winter sun. My high school was old and brick and used-up; this building was made strictly of New Money. As I ran across the street, dodging cars, I looked at every kid – every *girl*, actually – looking for Rachel. Since it was winter, the girls had big coats on, some with fur collars turned up and heavy scarves, hiding their faces, and some girls wore hats. Rachel used to wear this little navy blue ski cap sometimes, but mostly she let her long, dark hair – of which she was so proud – flow in the wind, even if it meant being cold.

I hurried toward the majestic front entrance, looking this way and that at the rush of kids heading up the steps toward the doors. At the curb, there was a line of cars dropping off kids, including quite a few Cadillacs. Fortunately, I didn't see the Princes'. The last thing I needed was for Eleanor to see me. I stood in the middle of the stream of kids as they went up the front steps, ignoring me in the rush. All these kids seemed to be good-looking and well-dressed, so much neater than the scruffy, pimply guys at Columbia. I looked into all the girls' faces, but I didn't see Rachel. I did see more than a couple of girls who looked like Rachel: pretty, confident girls with the same long, dark hair, parted in the middle. But I didn't see my girl.

Two loud buzzing bells from the building sent everybody into a faster gear. I guess it meant just a few minutes to homeroom, and some kids still had to get to their lockers. I stood against the tide of students rushing past me, wondering what to do. There seemed to be another busy entrance on the side of the school by the parking lot; I could check there. She might be coming in from that side, but I didn't have time to decide. I had to do something quickly; I turned and joined the flood of kids going in.

Once I got inside the heavy glass doors, inside the lobby, it was warm. They had good, strong heat in there. As I walked in, I looked both ways down the hallway and saw nothing but kids: kids walking quickly, kids at their lockers, slamming them closed. Dozens of kids, all ignoring me. I had absolutely no idea which way to go to find Rachel.

Three bells buzzed, and the intensity of activity increased. More lockers were slammed. I had to do something: I saw a group of girls, pretty girls. Girls who might, just *might* know Rachel. As you know by now, I'm a fairly shy person, but I had no choice. I walked right up to them, tall girls with long hair and jewelry and soft, pastel sweaters.

"I'm sorry," I asked, trying to make eye contact with any one of them, "Do any of you girls know Rachel Prince?"

They all looked at me blankly. Pretty, empty stares that said nothing.

One of the girls, a blonde wearing a long OHS letterman's sweater, leaned forward and said, "Do you go to Columbia?"

Dumbfounded, I said back, "How do you know that?"

The girls just giggled and looked at each other, sharing some silly secret.

"Do you know where Rachel is now?"

Four bells blasted again before they could answer me.

"Do you know anyone named Eric?" I asked in a loud, specific voice, but they looked at me as if I were talking in a foreign language.

"We gotta go," the tall blonde said.

Scattering for their classes, the girls started walking away, saying goodbye to each other, and ignoring me. But one girl, a cute redhead, grabbed my sleeve.

"She has English first period, I think," said the redhead, releasing me and disappearing into the throng.

"Where's that?" I shouted. "Where is English??"

But she was gone in the rush of kids. The hallway was emptying quickly, and the classroom doors all seemed to close at once. Suddenly I was alone.

At the far end of the hallway, I saw one of those Safety Officers, like the one outside the student parking lot, coming toward me. I immediately turned and walked the other way quickly.

"Get to your class, son!" he yelled out between cupped hands. "Tiiime's up!"

I picked up my pace and got to the end of the hallway to turn a corner, out of sight of the rent-a-cop. I was thinking, "Where could the English classes be?" I probably had ten minutes when these kids were in homeroom to get to where the English classes were: wherever that was. I was getting sweaty again. I opened my collar wider and tried to get some cool air onto my neck.

I heard footsteps behind me, but I didn't dare turn around. Seeing a flight of stairs on my right, I took off and ran right up, two at a time. I just felt that it was best to get off that first floor, just in case the rent-a-cop was behind me. I mean, I still sort of looked like these Oakhurst kids. Maybe I was a little shabbier, but still, I was only one year out of high school.

At the top of the stairs, I went left and down the hall. I breezed down the hallway, checking out the bulletin boards covered with lots of colorful flyers for summer programs in Europe and sailing camps in the Bahamas. Lucky kids. I figured that this must be the foreign language area: *not* English.

I kept moving. I only had a little time before homeroom broke. If I had any chance of finding her, I had to be in the right place at the right time.

"Hey! You!" a gruff voice yelled from somewhere behind me, far down the hallway. I didn't turn around, but I knew he was yelling at me. "Stop right there!"

The bell rang, and I took off down the hallway. The doors of the classrooms flew open, and kids started to flood into the corridor, giving me cover for escape. I turned left, and there was another staircase there. I ran down the stairs, taking two at a time, holding onto the banister so I didn't break my neck.

Back on the first floor, I turned right and saw something that made my heart perk right up: a big poster of William Shakespeare's impassive, impressive face – so I *knew* that I was in the English area. Finally.

By now, the hallways were streaming with fast-walking, loud-talking kids, rushing all around me. Frantically, I looked at all the girls' faces as they passed by: no Rachel. A few *almost*-Rachels, but not the real thing. But she *had* to be somewhere in the rush of kids getting to class. I knew that this was my best, maybe my only chance to see her, and I was not going to blow it.

There! At the end of the hall, I saw a flash of blue-blue eyes, somewhere through the crowd of bodies. I took a chance.

"Rachel?" I yelled over the loud buzz of kids. "RACHEL!"

Just then, a hand grabbed me roughly by the collar and pulled me backwards.

One of those Safety Officers turned me around with a jerk of my neck and growled into my face, "Are you a student here? Lemme see your ASB card!"

I twisted out of his grip with a throw of my shoulder and backed away. He was big and wide, with a determined, angry scowl.

"Wait a minute!" I said. "Isn't this a public school?"

"Do you belong here?" the guard snapped. "Come with me, son."

I backed further away from him, one more time yelling, "RACHEL?" over the crowd's head. People started to clear away from us, watching the confrontation between the guard and me.

"I thought this was a *public* school," I said as I moved away from him, preparing to escape when another pair of hands grabbed me from behind. It was a second security guard, the one I had seen when I came into the building.

"Come with us," he said. "You don't belong here."

"RACHEL!" I yelled again as I struggled unsuccessfully to break free. The two of them got hold of me and started pulling me back down the hallway as I screamed "RACHEL!!!" one more time. "I tried! . . . I TRIED!!!"

All the kids were watching the spectacle of me being dragged away by the two rent-a-cops, but I didn't care.

"SAY SOMETHING!" I screamed, hoping that somewhere in the crowd she would hear me.

All the kids were laughing and shouting and pointing at me as I was pulled away, twisting in vain to escape the guards' strong grip. Yes, I felt shame and embarrassment, but over the din of laughter and jeers I thought I heard her call my name one last time. But I wasn't sure. It could have all been my imagination.

~

They let me go after about two hours of questioning in this tiny, windowless room without calling the police on me, but it took a lot of smooth talking and believable promising on my part. First, the guards yelled at me for a long time about trespassing and illegal entry. Then this nasty assistant principal whose name was Peevey came in. He said he "knew about" me, having apparently talked to Eleanor Prince about this boy who was "bothering" Rachel and causing problems for her and her entire family. I rationally told him that Mrs. Prince misunderstood me and my motives.

I was beyond relieved when they let me go. But, in a twisted way, for all the hassling I got, I was happy that I did it, that

I had tried to see Rachel "one last time." I remember thinking that as I drove back home to drop off the Ford before I took the bus and subway back to Columbia. By then there was no hope of making my afternoon classes, so I decided to save the money on the cheaper trip back into town. Funny, even as I was messing up my life, at each step along the way I was trying to do the right thing. I was honoring Love and my true feelings. I wasn't hurting anybody. I was trying to be honest with what I actually felt and what I thought that Rachel felt. OK, maybe she didn't feel the same way about me anymore, or she wouldn't have done what she did. At that point, I realized that things had definitely changed in some truly essential way. I had to turn a leaf and readjust my thinking. That was it: from now on, I couldn't be responsible for Rachel anymore, only for myself. Maybe it would turn out to be a good thing, after all.

Part III

What Happened Then

Record of Events #27 – entered Tuesday, 9:43 P.M.

∿

The next few months were not easy, but I got through them, barely. At first, I almost couldn't stop thinking about her, about calling her, about getting back with her, about going over to her house and knocking the door down – to hell with what Hell-eanor or Herb or anybody thought – and making things right. Every night at 8:00, I thought about a call that I didn't make. Every Friday night, I didn't drive over to Buckingham Court, to that big brick house at the far end of the long lawn. Everything I did, I did *without Rachel*.

In some ways, life was easier for me, loveless. With no Rachel in my life – make that: with no Rachel *present* in my life – I was free to do many specific things that I was previously unable to do. Like watching 8:00 TV shows precisely when they began. Like having Friday nights to myself. Like . . . that's the end of the list. Oh, yes: I had my "freedom."

Fortunately, some things were in my favor. New York, and especially Columbia, are made for the lonely. Everybody is equally lonely, everybody shut up in the dorms, especially in winter, and no one cares. So everybody leaves everybody else alone. I shouldn't say that "everybody" is lonely. I would see some people who weren't as I walked around the campus and the neighborhood; I would see families . . . friends . . . lovers. I accepted the possibility of positive human contact. But at that moment, being alone was the best way for me to survive.

The first weekend, even though I wasn't going to see Rachel, I went back home to the Island. By now, it was almost like a reflex. Roommate A had gotten used to my being gone every weekend and bragged that he had a "hot little chippy" in his weekend plans for the room. Plus I had all my dirty laundry from the week that I had gotten used to my mother doing, saving me from going down to the gross washing machines and dryers in the basement of the dorm like the other poor sucker freshmen. So I went home.

In some ways, that was the best thing to do. I could sleep later, undisturbed by Roommate A. I could stay in my room and not talk to anybody. There was food downstairs in the refrigerator. I had my stereo and my records. All I had to do was stay in my room, do my homework, and lay low. In time, I'd get over Rachel. Oh sure, I'd be blue for a while and my heart might have been technically broken, but I knew that, over Time, I'd recover from her love. I refused to let something that was once good create anything bad.

Those were good resolutions; I wish that I had been able to follow them. Instead, my sleep was lousy; there is no other word for it. And I didn't really have much of an appetite, no matter how many of my favorite foods my mother offered me. I just wasn't hungry. I couldn't keep my mind on my reading. Every second thought, every third paragraph, reminded me of Rachel. Or something about her. Or something about Eleanor or Herb or Mooncliff. I'd be studying for some test or quiz, and invariably I would come across a word or a concept that would flip my mind right back to Rachel. Say, I'd be studying for an exam on minerals and there would be a mention of "cobalt compounds" – I *couldn't not* think of her eyes. Or I'd be hammering out some mini-essays on Descartes, and there would be a section on the reality of sensory perceptions. And I would think of how Rachel felt when I held her. Not that long ago, she'd lain in the bed across the room. With me. But that was over. Would I rather have been reading Descartes or touching Rachel? What a question. I know it was stupid, but all thoughts eventually led me back to her. My mind couldn't help it. I was *sick* with thoughts of Rachel Prince.

I didn't leave my room till late that night. I think that I was afraid that I would drive over to Buckingham Court, but by then it was too late and I was too tired. I drove over to the Lex instead, just because there was no other place to go, and there are few things more comforting than a Linzer cookie and a tall glass of cold milk. On the one hand, I felt pretty pathetic, seeking consolation from a raspberry filling, but on the other hand, I knew what made me feel better. I wanted to reduce things to simple pleasures, so as not to think about anything complex, or anything at all.

"Hey, man," someone said to me, poking my shoulder. I was sitting in my favorite booth where I thought I could see everybody who came in, but I guess I was mistaken.

I looked up and it was Marty, a kid who went to my high school, from my homeroom. He was with another guy.

"Hey, Marty," I said. "What's up?"

"Nothing much," he replied. "You know this dude, Freddy Masaro?"

"Hey, man," I said to the tall, skinny guy next to Marty. I wasn't sure if I knew him or not. He might have gone to our high school, or maybe from somewhere else.

"How's life?" Marty asked.

"Life sucks," I said cheerfully

"So what's new?" Marty chuckled.

They were just standing there by my table, so I said, "Wanna sit down?"

"'K," Marty said, and the two of them slid into the booth, opposite me.

"You getting' something to eat?" said Freddy to Marty.

"Yeah," answered Marty. "Let me think about it. What is that?" He pointed to my plate.

"Linzer cookie," I said with my mouth full, spraying crumbs all over the tabletop.

"Nice!" he said. "I think I'll have a chili dog and fries. Maybe *cheese* fries!"

"Make that two!" said Freddy, slapping the tabletop in a quick drumbeat.

"So how's Columbia?" asked Marty. "I figured you'd be halfway to law school by now."

"Not quite," I muttered. The last thing I wanted to joke about or think about was *more* school.

"Freddy goes with me to Nassau," said Marty.

"How is that?" I asked them.

"High school with cigarettes," said Freddy.

I laughed, "I know what you mean."

"Hey," said Marty, "You want to come to a party tomorrow night at Freddy's house?"

"It's not really a party," said Freddy. "It's just a bunch of people hanging out."

"OK," I said, finishing my milk and belching. "I'll think about it."

"You should come hang out with us," said Marty. "It'll be fun."

"'Fun,'" I repeated. It sounded like a foreign word, an unknown substance. "Lemme think about it."

～

I spent the next day, sleeping, waking up, working some, and then sleeping again. I didn't call Rachel, didn't drive over there – nothing. I should say nothing *physical* because I spent the whole day with Rachel floating in and out of my thoughts. Even when I resolved myself to "Stop thinking about her!" – that *was* thinking about her. She tormented me with her absence.

Finally, as if to punish myself for ruining my day – OK, I did knock off a paper for Brilliant and did some distracted studying – I decided to ruin my night as well by going to that party at Freddy's house. I figured that a night with those losers would thoroughly depress me, even worse than losing Rachel. (I shouldn't call Marty and Freddy "losers." They were nice guys; *I* was the loser.) But I couldn't stay in the house anymore, especially when my mother urged me to come downstairs to watch "a very exciting *Mannix*."

Freddy's big basement was crowded with kids, both boys and girls, and no one I recognized. It had a ping-pong table, a loud stereo, and a table full of cans of beer and soda and boxes of cold pizza.

"His parents aren't home," Marty shouted in my ear over the pounding, loud Cream. "So don't trash anything."

"I won't," I yelled back.

Marty laughed. "Right. I forgot who I was talking to." He patted me on the back and walked away.

Left alone suddenly, I went and grabbed a beer from the table. No Rolling Rock like at Bailey's. I took a Budweiser and found a place to sit in the corner. I could watch the doubles ping-pong game from there while I sipped the sour Bud and wondered what the hell I was doing in Freddy Masaro's basement.

"Why are you sitting in the corner?"

A girl's voice jarred me out of my thoughts.

"What?" I looked up and there was a girl, standing in front of me. A girl wearing wire-framed glasses who looked familiar.

"Hi," she said, taking a sip from a Bud. "Why are you sitting in the corner?"

"Because it's comfortable," I answered. "And I can watch the ping-pong game, and it's in the corner."

"You don't remember me . . . Amy Hendler? I helped put up posters for you when you ran for student council vice president."

"Oh, yeah," I pretended to remember her. I went to a very large high school and it was impossible to know everybody in your grade. "I lost."

"I know," she said.

There was a pause in the conversation. Amy was wearing a peasant-type dress, and she smelled like that sweet-dirty-hippie smell.

"I thought you went off to Harvard or Yale or someplace like that," she said.

"No, Columbia."

"Oh . . . I'm going to Adelphi, but I'm thinking of transferring to Albany State."

"That's probably a good idea," I said, taking a sip of the Bud. "Smart to get your ass off the Island."

"Yeah, you're right," she shrugged. "But you never know about things. It's not so bad here. Sometimes I don't think it matters *where* you are, it's *who* you are. And luck. Luck is important."

I thought about how I used to be lucky, and how things had swung in the other direction.

"But, even so," she said. "Eventually I think that luck evens out."

"You know," I considered her words. "I think you could be right. At least I hope it does."

She stood there in front of me, shifting her weight and moving the beer to her other hand.

"How do you know Freddy?" she asked.

"I don't," I said, taking another sip. "Actually, I guess I know him through Marty. You know Marty?"

"No."

I suppose at that point a normal guy would have put a move on Amy Hendler. She knew me and seemed to like me. She wasn't any beauty, but as you know, neither am I. I could have asked her about Adelphi, or if she liked the Hendrix that was playing, or if she wanted to challenge the team playing ping-pong in the next game, or if she'd like to go someplace else (like the backseat of my car). Only I didn't say any of those things. In fact, I didn't say much of anything. I let her stand there in front of me until she shrugged her shoulders and walked away.

I know I was stupid, but that was the way I felt. These kids were really no different from me. They were going to school, living their lives, trying to get by and maybe have some fun. But in that crowded, noisy, airless basement, vibrating with "Spanish Castle Magic," I couldn't have felt more removed from the normal human race. I felt dead inside without Rachel, simple as that.

One more bad beer and I went home, not really feeling any better for having wasted the rest of the night. But at least it was late enough to go home and get directly into bed. I figured I'd shower in the morning. As I got undressed, throwing my clothes on the chair next to my desk, I remember thinking that I actually did that girl Amy a favor by not getting involved with her.

"Luck evens out."

And as I fell asleep, I could still smell Rachel's perfume, deep, deep, deep in my pillow.

Record of Events #28 – entered Wednesday, 5:58 A.M.

~

The good part about breaking up with Rachel was that I was free to experiment. If my life was to be changed, I could change it completely. Clean slate. I went through entire days without talking. Because I didn't have to talk to Rachel at 8:00 every night, I was free not to talk to anyone at all. I found that there was power in silence. I didn't have to lie about anything, or talk my way around the ups-and-downs-and-end of our relationship. I didn't have to imagine possible encounters with Eleanor Prince, and how I would craftily ridicule her without her even knowing it. I didn't have to waste a moment's thought on Herb, or his goombas, either, for that matter. (I never got a single good feeling from that guy, and I was proven to be right.) So for long stretches of time in the weeks that followed, I didn't talk to anyone. In the street and in the stores, I could just nod and smile. I briefly thought of getting cards made –"I AM MUTE" – but that would have been cheating. It was more of a challenge to get through the world without speaking. I could pick things out myself in a store or point to things on a menu. I didn't have to talk when paying for things. When people said "Thank you," I could just smile my "You're welcome." Maybe they would think I was a tourist or an alien; partially right in both cases.

The longest I went without talking was 104 hours. I finally had to break my Talking Fast (*haha*: pun intended) when Brilliant asked me a direct question in class, and I had to answer. Needless to say, I needed to do well in that class. By dumb luck I had read the material just before class and gave a correct, even semi-eloquent answer. He smiled at me, nodded with approval, and went on with the lesson, extending my answer. Funny, for a moment it was like the old days in high school: me, nailing the right answer and getting strokes from the teacher. There's nothing like the threat of Academic Probation and Loss of Scholarship to focus the mind. (Oh, did I neglect to mention that official "pink" letter from the Dean of Freshmen that I had received?)

The one "good" thing about Rachel's dumping me was that I was forced to put more time into my studies. For so long Rachel had been the most important thing in my life, that everything else was, if not insignificant, certainly less important. What I got from Rachel – acceptance, inspiration, and a sense of fulfillment – was supposed to be the end product of my education. But with Rachel, I had those things already. Every time I was with Rachel, I experienced complete happiness, both giving and receiving. At least that was how I remembered it.

Night after night, I sat in my dorm room, at my desk, in a pool of lamplight, and studied hard. I was behind in almost every class, so I threw myself into my course work with a combination of enthusiasm and desperation. Even "Rocks for Jocks." For a while, it was a relief to get out of myself and get lost in Dante or Montaigne or Kant. But then I would come across some word or concept – like "earthly paradise" or "the sublime" or "obsession" – and my mind would involuntarily flip back to Miss Prince. And briefly I would disappear into The Zone. The Zone we lost. No, not "we" – The Zone that *she* threw away. I know that her family life was super difficult. Some only children are coddled by two permissive parents; others wind up being victimized by two vindictive ones, especially when there's a nasty divorce going on and there's a mother's disgusting, lecherous boyfriend living in the same house. But, hey, life is tough all over. I gave her my unconditional love, and she didn't know what to do with it. But all this rationalizing didn't help: there was no happiness for me without Rachel Prince. I was "infected" with her love, and there was no cure. Had she ruined me forever? And at the end of these mental excursions I would find myself sitting back at my desk with an open book in front of me, my mind would clear, and I would think, *I've got to do well in this class. I've just got to!* If my grades got so bad that I lost my scholarship, I would be totally screwed. No way my parents could afford the full tuition at this place. Which put more pressure on me.

One night I was sitting at my desk, deep into reading Edmund Burke on the French Revolution when a small black spider crawled slowly across the floor. I got up and stepped on it. It didn't belong in there.

"Sorry, Charlotte," I said. And as I wiped off the bottom of my sneaker with a tissue, I couldn't help but think of Eleanor Prince.

Just then I got a "PHONE!" pounded on my door. Funny, I hadn't gotten a call on the dorm phone for weeks. I was starting to enjoy my regained anonymity, and now another call.

"Hello?" I said cautiously.

"Hi."

It was Nanci Jerome.

"Oh," I said in the same cautious voice. "Hi, Nanci."

"You don't sound glad to hear from me."

"Should I be?" I asked. I somehow knew that her call would not be good for me, but I didn't hang up.

Nanci paused before she said simply, "You know she misses you. You must know that."

This was the last thing I needed to hear.

"Then why doesn't she call me?"

"She can't."

"Then she doesn't miss me that much."

I let the silence sit there on the line. I really had no business being curt with Nanci. She wasn't the one who broke up with me.

"I'm afraid she might do something drastic," Nanci said finally.

"Like what?"

"Like I don't know," she said. "You know Rachel."

"Then you shouldn't say something like that," I countered. "She did what she wanted to do. Now she has to live with that decision. We all have to. I am."

"She still loves you," Nanci insisted.

"Don't tell me that," I said. "Tell her."

"You're a cold-hearted bastard. You know that?"

I just had to laugh at that.

"It's getting really bad over there," Nanci continued in a darker tone. "Eleanor hit Rachel, and Rachel even hit her *back*. It is *not* a good scene."

"Do yourself a favor, Nanci. Don't call me again," I said and hung up.

The last thing I needed or wanted was reports of how Rachel was doing without me. I had enough trouble learning to live without her, without backsliding and unnecessary echoes. Not that I didn't care about her: I couldn't help that. But I had to try to take care of myself first. And I have to confess that I wasn't doing that well, trying to forget.

Sometimes I just had to get out of my room, away from my studies and thoughts of Rachel, away from Roommate A and his cigarettes, away from no-thoughts-of-Rachel, to walk the streets of New York. That's one good thing about Manhattan: at any time of day there is always someone else awake, someone else walking the streets, someone else going through something worse than you are. At least that's what I saw when I prowled Morningside Heights almost up to Harlem, then down to the river, and through the West Side to Central Park. I went down to the Hudson many times, but I never jumped in. I developed quite a relationship with the Hudson River. I walked sometimes till I thought my legs would fall off. Twice I walked down to Times Square at 2:00 a.m. to get an Orange Julius. That's another great thing about New York City:

you can get an Orange Julius at 2:00 a.m. (In fact, I wish I had one right now; it's a mighty satisfying beverage.) You are completely free to join the sleepless, the homeless, and the psychotic roaming the streets at all times of the day or night in perfect, timeless free-fall.

I walked through areas where I thought I might be mugged. Hell, I half hoped that I might be mugged; that would have solved a lot of problems. I didn't court trouble, but I didn't avoid it either. I walked in straight lines when and where I wanted to. I jaywalked when and where I wanted to. I walked against traffic down Broadway for a couple of blocks, causing a couple of close calls and a ridiculous argument with a Pakistani cab driver. I only did that once, walking against traffic. I really didn't want to endanger anyone else. My indifference to human life was strictly a private matter.

I held a fairly steady conversation with myself, weighing the pros and cons of past actions, how I would have changed things that were now, of course, impossible to change. I mentally relived the first walk to the baseball backstop, my back still sweaty from square dancing . . . the long, lost walks during Free Play, when we told each other everything . . . the rowboats on the lake, beating against the current. Bailey's and the Super-Coupe, sunset at the Quarry, and Sharon Spitzer telling me *"Summer things never last."* Even the Five Days Without Rachel. With my Mets cap pulled down so that I could see the pavement and not much else, I ran these internal movies over and over in my mind: changing the dialogue, changing the endings, feeling the smooth stones that I kept in my coat pockets, amusing myself by muttering tongue twisters like "turmoil, turmoil, turmoil" and singing "So why on Earth should I moan, why on Earth should I moan, why on Earth should I moan," over and over again.

One time I must have been talking out loud to myself because this homeless guy in the street came up to me and yelled, "Shut up! . . . Who made *you* God?"

It was on a grimy side street off Amsterdam Avenue where a lot of the social service agencies and flophouses are. I was walking down the street, minding my own business, and this guy just jumps into my face and starts screaming.

"Who made *you* God? . . . Who made *you* God?" he shouted at me, right in my face.

At first I was terrified. He was big in his grimy tan overcoat, and the whites of his eyes were yellow. He stood in my path, swaying and shouting. I tried to move around him but he blocked me with a surprisingly quick sidestep.

Fear flashed several alternatives across my mind: Retreat? Run around him? Punch him in the stomach and *then* run?

But instead I just rose up and yelled back at him, "NO – who made *you* God??? Go on! Who made *you* God?"

I gave madness for madness, and he – glory be – was frightened. He visibly flinched, frightened of *me*. I don't think anyone has ever been frightened of me in my entire life, but he was. His eyes flickered with the recognition of something, I don't know exactly what – perhaps the threat, perhaps the acknowledgement of a kindred spirit – but he turned his gaze from mine and, seeming to shrink inside his overcoat, slunk away from me, back toward his cardboard bed, hidden in a doorway behind some garbage cans.

I walked on, triumphant.

Now I ask myself . . . Was I different? Had I really changed inside? Had I actually been *damaged* by my relationship with Rachel? Was I "crazy-in-love" with her? How could that be, when all I had were good memories? OK, some of them might have been enhanced in the light of retrospection, but everyone does that. I thought that all I needed was love. I guess the Beatles were wrong.

No matter how far I walked or where I went I couldn't shake the continual, recurring questions: How did Good become Bad? How did I fail to protect what was dearest to me? How did I let Rachel get away when all I wanted to do was keep her? What could have been more important to her than keeping us together? Did I not understand her at all? How could I have been so wrong – about so many things?

I was on Central Park West now, walking back uptown, passing the Museum of Natural History. I thought I heard someone call my name. I looked up and saw only the statue of Teddy Roosevelt on horseback. There was another high-strung dude; I think he went to Columbia too.

Then someone suddenly grabbed me by my shoulder, yanking me backwards, trying to turn me around. Instinctively, I jerked away from the force, not knowing who was trying to hold onto me. Had the homeless guy followed me? Some cop? Was it Teddy himself?

I whipped around and saw a big kid there with a wide smile on his face, giving me this enthusiastic "hello." I had no idea who this kid was as he grabbed my hand and shook it vigorously, but he looked vaguely familiar. He might have been one of my cousins from New Jersey, the ones we almost never see, but I wasn't sure.

And there was this woman standing behind him, this big, lipstick-mouthed woman, talking a mile a minute in my face. The kid was grinning, grabbing me by the shoulders and shaking me happily. But it wasn't until he screeched, "I told you so! It *is* the Assistant Groinmaster!" that I realized it was one of the *Doggies*.

"You were Jonathan's favorite counselor!" the woman was saying. "He talks about you all the time!"

I pulled back from them, but they kept advancing. I watched her mouth move and kept looking at the kid, trying to figure out why he looked so strange.

"He always talks about how you saved the Klein boy from drowning," she said. "He even wrote a composition on you for his honors English."

"That's very nice," I said, trying to say nothing.

"I got an A minus on it!" the strange Doggy said, still closing in on me. "Are you going back to Mooncliff next summer? I am. Dorny is. We all are."

That's when I realized that it was the Doggy With Braces, seven months older – and now, *without his braces*! And he'd had a growth spurt: he was damned near as tall as me. And his face was a different shape. He was even uglier and more ungainly than before. No wonder I didn't recognize him.

"Because of you," the woman said. "He's been reading real books. Not those awful comic books."

The woman, presumably his mother, pulled me away from the kid and whispered in my ear.

"Jonathan respects you so much," she said, smelling of Listerine and something else. "Do you think you could say something to him? He's been giving his father and me such a hard time lately. Say something to him."

I looked at the woman, her pleading, piggy eyes, and the Doggy With Braces Without Braces, all hero-worshipful behind her, and I thought: how ridiculous. Asking *me* for advice? Me, as I was crashing and burning? But then I actually thought of something to say.

"Come here," I said to the Doggy as I conducted him away from his mother. He let me guide him by the arm as I turned him around to face me.

With my hands on both his shoulders, I looked into his gleaming, trusting, dopey eyes and said, "Everything is temporary. Repeat that to me."

"Everything is temporary," he said back.

"Everything is temporary," I said again, burning my gaze into his brain.

"Everything is temporary."

"Good," I said, releasing him. "Now, get your ugly face out of here."

He grinned, laughed, and hauled his mother away down the sidewalk. Turning back, he called to me one last time.

"Hey!" he yelled. "So are you going back to the Moonshak?"

"Never in a million years!"

Who would have known then that the last laugh would be on me?

∾

I slept for about twelve hours when I got back to my dorm, body and mind exhausted, but in a good way. Even Roommate A's thunder-fingered typing and cigarette smoke couldn't disturb my sleep. When I woke up, I took my quasi-Bondian hot-cold-hot-cold shower that made me feel even better. I went in with two guys on a large pizza and ate three huge slices with pepperoni. I was stuffed and ready to go.

I sat down, knocked off two overdue papers for Brilliant, and made up a bunch of other work. I had the classical music station on my clock radio on low, and I listened *through* the pure, comforting music to concentrate on my work. I didn't realize it then, but it was as if a fever was breaking. After a long, dark period of time when everything was about losing Rachel Prince, twenty-four hours a day, seven days a week, the spell was slowly ending. I had lost her: the story was over. The air was clearing.

Of course, this happened over a space of weeks. It wasn't just suddenly, *"Hey! I'm over Rachel!"* But one day, coming back from French class, I saw this poster from a new movie with this very pretty, dark-haired French actress that someone was thumbtacking to a bulletin board in the hall. As I passed, I thought, *wow, that girl looks a lot like Rachel*, and I didn't feel a twinge of pain. Then I realized that the miracle had happened. I had been healed, cured of Rachel Prince.

∾

Things started to get better for me in several ways. My grades improved; my sleep improved; my relations with Roommate A and my parents improved. I paid attention in class and learned more. I found that I could work straight through 8:00 p.m.

without a pause whatsoever. Of course, my sex life wasn't as good, but I could live with that for a while. When my sex life was great, the rest of my life wasn't so hot. Someday, I told myself, I would find a way to combine the two.

One thing I do remember is something one of my teachers said. Actually, he quoted a very smart man – Goethe – putting words in the mouth of the devil Mephistopheles in *FAUST* who said: "All theory, dear friend, is gray." That really hit me hard. I had found out that everything I thought to be true was reversed. True love made me miserable; heartbreak was better than love. I guess that's what's called getting an education. Negative learning. Maybe the best thing is to live day-to-day, and not necessarily try to overthink everything all the time.

That worked for a while, long enough for me to start to re-gain my strength. I even went to a freshman mixer. Of course, I just stood along the side and drank (the official punch and some smuggled-in rum), but I didn't dance with anyone. I talked to a girl for a bit in the line for punch. She was cautious; I was defensive. It was pointless, just like the encounter with that girl Amy in Freddy Masaro's basement. Even though I was technically "over" Rachel, there was still an emptiness in my heart. So when I talked to this nice, short, smart blonde, she could tell that I wasn't really all there. I was still lost, in The Zone but *alone*. Rachel had hurt me, and although I felt I was basically "healed," I didn't want my stitches to reopen. So I went back to the wall, danced with myself for a while, and left in a semi-contented state of mind. Someday, I would fall in love again, and it would be better. I would do things right next time.

~

So it was, of course, on a perfect spring day, weeks later – blue sky, cherry blossoms on the trees, and I had just gotten back an A on a very tough French test – when I was crossing 116th Street to get some lunch between classes, and I heard her call my name. It was that same voice – the joyous, seductive *musical* voice that hooked me the first time we ever talked, on the walk back from the Rec Hall after what's-his-name and his square-dancing family. My heart paused, and I turned around, and there she was, blocking the sidewalk: Rachel, as beautiful and defiant as ever, with her blue-blue eyes and her perfectly tossed dark hair.

"I told you I'd come back to you," she said. "You didn't believe me."

At first, I didn't say anything. Intellectually, I felt ice-cold to her, yet my body was drawn to her like a magnet. I experienced the actual physical force of her *pulling* me toward her, but I held back.

"What are you doing here?" I asked.

"I *drove* here," she said proudly, stepping to the side to show me a ridiculously beautiful new red Mustang convertible.

"So you finally got your Mustang," I said. "You always said you would."

"A car means *freedom!*" she swept her hand across the hood luxuriously, like a model in a TV commercial. "Real freedom. For *us*."

"There is no *us*," I said.

"That's up to you," she shot back with a tight smile, confident, yet a little needy at the same time too. She waited for me to run to her, but I wasn't going to. At least not immediately.

"What would you have done if I hadn't come along here?" I asked, trying to play it cool.

"I was going to wait another twenty minutes," she answered. "Then I was going to go up to your dorm room. Don't worry, I was going to find you."

She was so damn beautiful.

"Why did you come back?" I tried to find some resistance inside. "I was just beginning to –"

"I *told* you I had to get some things in order," she talked over me, coming closer. "Like letting things calm down. Like getting my Mustang. Like getting their *confidence*."

I watched her come toward me, working her magic. She was wearing this filmy, fluttery blouse and tight jeans.

"Things are better now," she continued. "I got them to trust me. I'm seeing this therapist, who is not so bad. *And* I've got them ready to let me see you again!"

"And that's why you're here?" I held firm.

"I told you," she said artfully. "There were some things I had to get in order." She got closer and closer. "You have every right to say 'no' to me," she said simply. "But I'm here because I love you. And I always have."

She was straight in front of me, her eyes locked on mine.

"I know what I want," she said point-blank.

Then she kissed me deeply, as if nothing had happened, nothing at all, and in a few moments, we were back in The Zone. Right then, *right then* I was lost, even if I didn't know it myself.

"Let's go up to your room," she whispered. "And I'll tell you everything."

~

Fortunately, Roommate A was out so we had a long time to be together. As she told me everything that had happened to her in the past few months, I couldn't believe how much I missed her. Just watching her mouth move and her hands talk, playing with her hair or touching a button or something on her girlish blouse, was like a movie to me. She was trying to be upbeat for me, trying to wipe away any hard feelings I might have had. Rachel always thought that she could charm anyone out of anything, especially me.

"I can't believe we're finally together, after all this time," she said. "Back in The Zone."

"The Zone," I repeated.

"It hasn't been easy," she said softly. "Being without you."

"That was *your* choice," I said back.

She looked down, picking at the lint on the blanket on my bed, not wanting to meet my gaze.

"You don't know what I've had to go through," she said. "You don't know how hard it was for me not to call you every day."

"Then why didn't you?" I said coldly, trying to hide any sympathy I felt for her. I wasn't going to make it easy for her; at least not *too* easy.

"I had to get everything clear!" she insisted. "I had to get them to stop suspecting me of everything! You have no idea what I've had to do. I had to get everything in order."

"And is everything in order now?" I asked sharply.

"OK," she said with an impish smile, "How about this, for a start? They're going away for the weekend, this weekend coming up. To visit some friends in the Hamptons. One of Herb's Mafia friends, I think. They've been fighting like animals lately, as bad as with Manny. So, how would you like to come over and spend the weekend with me? You and me, all alone, just the two of us, in my house. We can sleep in my bed. We can do . . . anything you want."

She looked down modestly, trying to conceal any sense of power she felt over me. I think she could tell that I was drawn in by what she was saying. She knew that I still cared for her, but if that wasn't enough for me, not yet, she offered something more.

"OK," she said. "Then how about this? You come over this weekend for a session of strip poker. With me and Nanci."

"Strip poker with you *and Nanci?*"

"She'll do whatever I tell her to," she said confidently. "In fact, I'll give her to you. As a present. You can do whatever you want to her. And me too, if you're extra-*extra*-nice."

"Are you kidding?" I asked her.

"I want to make you happy," she said. "I *owe it* to you."

She turned my face to hers.

"Listen to me," she said confidentially. "Things really are going to get better. Soon," she insisted. "You have to believe me. I have real plans for us."

I certainly wanted to believe her, but I was rightfully wary.

"I don't know what to believe," I said. "I shouldn't admit this, but you really hurt me. I shouldn't allow myself to be hurt by anyone again, even by you. *Especially* by you."

"Please?" she begged, taking my two hands in hers. "You're all I want. All I've ever wanted. All I've been working for. *Please*? I promise to be good, and everything . . . I promise."

She leaned forward to kiss me. Our lips joined, and everything in the room started dissolving, just as it used to, as I took her down. How could I not? I had been so lonely and empty inside. How do you say "No" to Love? The answer is "You don't."

I made her leave early, so she wouldn't face too tough of a rush hour back to the Island. Actually, I was impressed with the confidence she had in her driving ability. Driving in Manhattan was a huge challenge to me, and I had been driving for a lot longer than Rachel. The cab drivers are merciless, there are potholes all over, and the bike messengers are completely insane.

"You'll be proud of me," she said as we walked to her Mustang, parked on 116th Street. "I'm a very good driver. I learned on Eleanor's giant, ugly ol' car, so driving Candy is no problem."

"'Candy'?" I asked, anticipating the answer before she said it.

"It's my name for my Mustang, silly," she said, holding tight to my arm as we walked. "The name of the paint color is *Candyapple Red*, so don't you think that Candy is an appropriate name?"

"It's not appropriate," I said as we approached the blaringly red little convertible. "It's perfect."

"I wound up getting the convertible," she said reflectively. "I think that was the right thing to do."

I had to laugh at her. She was so innocent in some ways: complaining about her horrible parents even as they showered gifts on her. Yet I believed – and still believe to this day – that her parents (*and Herb*) were bad people who did bad things to her. What exactly those things were and how long they went on, well, some of it we'll never know. But it was obvious that they felt guilty about the way they treated Rachel. They *had* to give her things like Mustang convertibles to make up for the hell they made her live through.

"Drive carefully," I said. "You'd be better off going up to the Triborough Bridge and taking the Grand Central to the Van Wyck and down."

As she was taking her keys out of the purse that hung from her shoulder, she said, "I know of only one way to get back home, and that's through the Midtown Tunnel, and that's the way I'm going. Don't confuse me."

"There's more traffic that way," I said, knowing somehow that she wouldn't change her mind. "The Long Island Distressway, World's Longest Parking Lot."

She sniffed a laugh, ignoring me, and opened the door of the Mustang with her jangly set of keys. It was truly a beautiful car. Deep red paint, shiny black leather interior, bucket seats.

"Black leather seats," I said. "Don't they get hot in the sun?" I sounded like *my father*.

"Yes, they do," she said, tossing her purse across the seat. "But they *look* so cool that it's worth it. Now, give me a kiss."

She turned to me pertly, expecting me to be right there, ready to adore her. And I have to admit that I was. I took her in my arms and kissed her, feeling how soft and frail her body was. I pulled her closer and kissed her harder until she pushed me away.

"Not here!" she said, getting into the driver's side. "Save it for the weekend."

"The weekend," I repeated.

"It'll be like old times," she said. "But better. We'll have our freedom and *everything*. Just as we always wanted."

Her eyes sparkled with confidence. She seemed a little smug, as if she had just won some secret battle.

"You knew I'd take you back, didn't you?" I asked her, not really wanting to know the answer (I already knew that), but feeling that I had to ask it.

She thought for a moment, weighing her words as I've seldom seen her do. "Let's just say I know what we had . . . and I know where I want us to go."

"OK," I let her be mysterious. Some things about Rachel were never going to change. But I couldn't help it: I liked that once more she was planning for "us."

"See you Friday," I said. "Like old times, but better." And, after making sure that she was safely inside, I slammed the door closed.

I watched her through the window as she turned the key in the ignition and revved up the sweet roaring engine. Very methodically, she checked her rearview mirrors and put the car into gear. She didn't look at me at all, concentrating on her driving. I was proud of her as she gave me a quick wave, put her hands back on the steering wheel at "ten-o'clock-and-two-o'clock," yelled "BYE!" and drove smoothly away.

She left me standing there, in the middle of 116th Street, waving goodbye. I stood there, feeling strength and oxygen running through my body. My mind was spinning with pleasure and a sense of satisfaction. I had survived and "won" – Rachel had come back to me.

Record of Events #29 – entered Thursday, 9:07 P.M.

~

It felt strange and slightly dangerous to ask for a ticket to Oakhurst at the Long Island Rail Road counter in Penn Station, instead of my hometown. A weekend at the Princes' mansion, a couple of days of illicit love between expensive sheets with my new/old girlfriend, and who knows what kind of games, starting with strip poker with *two* girls: just what I needed after a fairly dark time in my life. It was both slightly scary and every guy's dream about to come true.

I had my small suitcase filled with books to study for finals, but I felt pretty confident, as I was caught up in all my courses, that I could devote plenty of time to play this weekend. I had started to make more direct eye contact with my teachers, and they seemed to be responding better to me, just like old times in, dare I say it, high school. I let them think that it was their superior teaching that was leading to my improvement as a student, and it worked. Getting Rachel back was the icing on the cake.

She was waiting for me in the parking lot of the Oakhurst train station, leaning against the door of the red Mustang, like the All-Time Suburban Wife of Your Dreams. Tight jeans, tight blouse. Sexy smile, sexy pose. She knew she looked great, a fact confirmed by the big grin that I couldn't keep off my face.

"How was your day, honey?" she asked, in a soft, Doris Day voice.

"I'm exhausted," I said, playing along. "I need a drink."

I walked up to her, dropped my suitcase on the gravel, and kissed her deeply, picking right up from where we left off on 116th Street.

I released her and said, "You look fairly amazing."

She knew she did. I had seen it before, how she used her looks as a weapon. On me and others. But she never looked so confident, so serene. Maybe she was genuinely happy to have me back.

"OK," she said. "Let's go home, lover."

I liked how she looked behind the wheel of her Candy. She had already girled it up with a string of beads and crystals hanging from the rearview mirror and flower and peace-sign decals on the dashboard.

She gunned the engine and turned on the radio: some noisy acid rock came on. (Great sound, of course, in the Mustang.) She immediately turned it down and said, "Find us a love song."

I did as I was told.

"This is the beginning of a new era," she stated with quiet confidence.

I liked how she was sounding: a little vague, but resolved. She had definitely changed some in the time we'd been apart. She seemed a little more reserved than before, a little more self-aware. Maybe it was because of this therapist she'd been seeing. Maybe she had grown up a little.

"I am . . . completely . . . focused," she murmured, carefully driving out of the railroad station parking lot.

I found the beginning of "Blackbird" on WPLJ, and promptly turned it up. " – *singing in the dead of night, take these velvet wings and fly . . .*"

"There you go!" I said proudly. "One love song, as ordered. Your wish is my command."

She actually sighed with pleasure and started singing along, off-key, with McCartney. She certainly seemed happy to be back with me. And I certainly liked being back with her. I could even feel the blood in my veins circulate faster. She created energy and excitement all around her, and I was happy to be there again, in The Zone. But this time, I resolved that I wasn't going to be "a sucker," if indeed that's what I was.

~

The Princes' house looked bigger and more magnificent than ever at the end of the long green lawn, far back from the street at the end of the cul-de-sac. It never failed to amaze me, how this peaceful-looking fortress could contain such poisonous feelings.

"My father likes his privacy," she said, driving slowly through the crunching gravel of the driveway on the side of the house. "Or rather, *liked* his privacy. He really liked being far away from people."

"It's a beautiful house," I said truthfully. "At least from the outside."

"I hate this house," she said, stating a fact. "And I'm gonna get out soon. It's time."

"Good," I said, and didn't question her further as she pulled the car around to the garage in the back.

"A *four*-car garage?" I said, impressed. I realized that I had never been around to the back of the house. It had a huge backyard with a big patio and barbecue and what looked like a whole lawn area that I couldn't even see all of.

"Hey. Check *this* out," she said, pulling a little metal device from the console of the Mustang. She pressed a button on the little box, and one of the garage doors, the one closest to the house, started to rise, all by itself.

"Cool!" I said, and it *was* cool, listening to the slow grinding of gears as the door disappeared upwards.

When the garage door was fully open, Rachel let up on the brake and rolled the Mustang into place.

As we came to a stop, I saw a white Cadillac parked on the other side of the garage.

"Wait a second," I said in surprise. "Isn't that Eleanor's car?"

"Don't worry, silly," Rachel said with one of her musical laughs. "Eleanor and Herb are away for the weekend, thank God, and they took *his* car. We are *all alone*."

And with that, she put on the parking brake and turned off the engine. The silence was a relief.

"Ah," she said. "A moment of peace. Finally."

She turned to me with a warm smile, "This is what I've been waiting for."

Then the dog started to bark.

"MAX!"

~

We went into the house through a door in the garage, into a laundry room, and finally into the kitchen.

"Max!" Rachel kept yelling at the dog as she scampered around my legs, sniffing me, barking, threatening to, but not actually biting me. I shuffled in, carrying my suitcase, using it as a shield against the dog.

"Max! Don't you remember the most important person in my life? I don't get this; she's really very friendly," said Rachel as she put her keys and purse on the marble counter by the sink. "Come on, Max . . . Maxine! In here!"

She snapped her fingers down low at Max, who loved her mistress and followed the finger-snaps back into the laundry room, where Rachel immediately shut the door.

"Thank goodness!" she breathed. "I love her, but sometimes I wish there was a button to turn her off!"

"Sometimes I wish *people* were like that," I said.

"Me too," she agreed, locking the laundry room door and taking a deep, dramatic breath. "Now we can relax."

I had never seen her bedroom. In all the time we had been together, she had never taken me up to her room. (It wasn't her fault, really. Eleanor never made me feel welcome in this house.) But now she held my hand and walked me up the stairs to her bedroom, up the fancy staircase with the big balcony overlooking the foyer and the giant, ugly chandelier hanging in the middle of it all. She didn't say a word: she didn't have to.

She opened the door to her room and let it swing wide for me to enter. It was, of course, like a princess's boudoir. White furniture, sheer lavender curtains and bedspread, perfumed air, soft light glowing from the little lamp by the bed.

"I didn't know that you had a *canopy* bed," I walked in slowly and quietly on the thick, creamy shag rug, "but I might've guessed."

"It's been waiting for you," she said behind my back.

When I turned around, she was already unbuttoning her blouse.

∿

The whole weekend began just like that: like a dream – in and out of her bedroom. I admit it, I was grateful to be near her again, to touch her body, smell her smell, everything. As I've said before, I know what's good.

Afterwards, she brought us tea with some fancy cookies from England on a tray, with a flower in a skinny vase balanced on the corner.

"Do you like tea?" she asked as she settled back onto the bed.

I sipped a little bit of the hot liquid, "Not really."

"Come on!" she said. "Tea is good! Cultured people drink tea!"

"I *do* like cookies."

She laughed at that. She looked pretty when she laughed, when I could catch her in an untroubled moment. But then – I couldn't help myself – I asked her a question.

"By the way, I meant to ask you," I said, reaching for a second cookie. "Did you ever talk to that lawyer? . . . About your grandma money."

"Yes," she said. "As a matter of fact I did." And she took a sip of tea.

"And what did he say?"

"He said several things."

"Such as?" I was instantly wary: she was being so measured in her responses.

"Well," she said and took another sip of tea. "He said . . ."

I think she was using the tea sips to give herself time to think.

"He said that it turns out . . . that I don't get my grandma money until I'm *twenty-five*."

"No!"

"That my dear mother somehow had the terms of my grandmother's will changed, so that I don't get anything until I turn twenty-five. And she can still control it even then since she's the exec – exec –"

"Executor?"

"Exactly," she put her teacup down in its saucer with a clank. "My father doesn't care. He'd give me the money now. Anything to shut me up. It's Eleanor."

"It's always Eleanor," I said. I didn't want to add fuel to her fire: it was just the truth.

"I know," she said, smoothing out the bedspread. "I know, I know, I know."

"Well that's a disappointment." I played it safe, understating the matter. I knew that she was counting on that money for her after-high-school, non-college plans.

"So what are you going to do?" I asked sympathetically.

"I'm not exactly sure," she said slowly. "But I'll tell you one thing."

"What's that?"

"I'm going to have to do something."

~

Later, as it was getting dark, Rachel showed me all around the house, drawing the curtains as we went. I had never seen the den or the office or the guest suite or the kitchen or the butler's pantry or the finished basement before.

I said "This is *huge*" so many times that she finally had to say, "Stop saying that! It's just a house!"

"I know," I said. "I'm just saying."

"I don't care about all this!" Her voice echoed through the far reaches of the basement. "Don't you understand? I just want *out*! . . . It's so close I can *taste* it."

I didn't say anything back, seeing that while some things had changed, some things had not. She was still holding a great deal of anger inside; I had to be careful, if I didn't want to lead her into areas of dangerous thinking.

"Come see this," she said. "If you want to see something."

She led me back upstairs and into Eleanor's large bedroom, with its flowery fabrics, heavily carved furniture, and overwhelming odor of expensive perfume.

"Doesn't it smell in here?" said Rachel. "Like dead flowers or something. I keep telling her to air it out, but it doesn't help."

"Jeez," I mumbled, looking around, feeling the solidness of the thick, chiseled wooden post on the corner of the bed and smelling the sweet, thick air.

"Look in here," she said as she vanished into a doorway.

I followed her into a closet, an enormous clothes closet with shelves and drawers and double-hung racks of blindingly colorful dresses all around the walls. And row after row of blouses and Capri pants and scarves and belts in a jumble of patterns and fabrics, enough to make you slightly dizzy.

"This closet is bigger than my bedroom!" I said truthfully, looking all around. "Who needs this many clothes?"

There must have been a hundred pairs of shoes on little shelves, taking up one whole corner of the closet.

"She thinks that she has secrets in here," Rachel snickered.

I have to say that it felt creepy, being in Eleanor's closet. I didn't want to be this close to anything about that woman, much less her underwear, her brassieres, and her smell.

"Come look at this!" said Rachel, walking out of the closet as suddenly as she walked in. I followed Rachel across the room. I could tell that she really enjoyed trespassing on her mother's territory.

Rachel went into an adjoining bathroom – all pink tile, gold fixtures, and fluffy pink carpet – and slid open the mirrored door on the medicine cabinet above the pink marble sink.

"You want to get high?" she asked, picking up pill bottles from the little shelves and shaking them. "Some uppers? Speed kills . . . time. Maybe some downers in case you can't sleep because of the pills you took before? Maybe something in-between, in case you get a little touch of menopause that turns you into a raving lunatic? . . . I should have put poison in one of them a long time ago."

"Don't be silly," I said. "Besides, you'd get caught."

"No, I wouldn't," she said. "I would switch out the powders. Eleanor's a candidate for suicide anyway. No one would be surprised."

"You should stay out of there," I said, not liking to be in Eleanor's bathroom. The air was moist and heavy, as if the windows in there, too, hadn't been opened in a very long time.

"Why should I?" said Rachel, closing the medicine cabinet. "I'm sure she looks through my stuff all the time."

She walked back into the bedroom, saying, "I can just hide things better. She's smart, but sometimes she can be so stupid. Fortunately."

I followed her out, saying, "Come on. Let's get out of here," but Rachel went straight to another door on the far side of the room.

"This is the old closet that she gave part of to Herb, the creep," she said as she ripped open the door and dove into the far reaches of the closet floor. Hanging above her, I could see a row of men's suits and sports jackets and lots of white shirts that looked like they'd come straight from the dry cleaner's.

"Look at this!" said Rachel, turning around, waving a big black gun up in the air.

"Hey! Put that down!" I yelled, alarmed at the sight of the revolver that looked absolutely huge in her hands.

"You know I know how to handle a gun!" she scoffed, admiring the gun from different angles.

"Be careful!" I said.

"I *am* being careful!" she said. "I'm being *very* careful. I've taken it out before. And I know how to put it back so he never catches me."

She looked closely at the gun, turning it around to see it from different angles. "I think it's a thirty-eight."

"Is it Herb's?" I asked.

"I told you he was in the Mob," she said with satisfaction.

"Please put it back," I said.

"Here!" she held it out to me, "Feel it!"

"No," I recoiled.

She put one foot up on an ottoman and posed with the gun placed at her hip and said, "You think I look like Faye Dunaway?"

"Better," I said, reaching to take the gun from her. "Much better. I don't like blondes. And I'm no Clyde. Why don't you put it back?"

She turned and held the gun high, trying to keep it away from me.

"No, let me hold it for a while!" she demanded. She really seemed to want to keep the gun, and I instinctively knew when to retreat.

"OK!" I said, my hands raised. "Just be careful, and then put it back."

She pivoted and aimed toward the far corner of the room.

"Ka-CHKK!! Ka – CHKK!! Ka – CHKK!!!" she shouted, shooting at nothing. "Take that, Sharon Spitzer!" she yelled, blasting her imaginary target twice more.

"You really want to shoot Sharon Spitzer?" I asked, my eyes never leaving the gun.

"Well," she paused. "You said you didn't like blondes . . ."

She put the gun down on the dresser – thankfully – and oozed into my arms for a long kiss. (I think the gunplay excited her.)

We kissed for a very long time as she molded her body to mine.

In a moment of breathing, I murmured, "Sharon Spitzer once told me that summer things never last."

"Well, she was wrong," Rachel whispered between kisses. "I'm glad I shot her."

~

We ordered in Chinese food that night.

"Why go anywhere when the whole idea is to be together?" she reasoned, and I agreed with her.

"We get delivery people all the time," she said. "That's what they're for."

She handed me the menu and said, "Pick out what you want. Order anything. Eleanor left me the cash."

"Well, that was nice of her."

"It's the only thing good about her," Rachel shot back. "She certainly doesn't *cook*."

"Do you like spare ribs?" I asked her, looking down the list of soups, entrees, and chef's specials.

"I like whatever you like," she said.

"Right answer," I responded. "Even if you don't mean it."

That made her laugh.

"You think it's easy? Being this perfect?" she trilled as she drew the menu out of my hand. "OK. Leave everything to me."

~

We ate in the big back room with the hot, tropical wallpaper, in front of the big TV, next to the big rough-stoned fireplace. Everything about this house conspired to make me feel small and poor, but I resolved not to let it bother me. I had every right to be myself with Rachel, and now that I had her back, there was no reason to change.

We ate until we were stuffed. (I have to say that her take-out Chinese food was much better than the stuff we got from House of Chang, and it wasn't just because it was different. I know what "better" is. At least I was learning.)

I played with the controller for the giant TV while we ate. It was a very cool toy and saved lots of walks across the wide room, to and from the channel selector, going back and forth between *The Brady Bunch* and *High Chaparral*. My father would absolutely flip over a thing like this.

"Do you want any more pork?" Rachel asked me, carrying in one of the little white cartons from the kitchen.

"Is that a leading question?" I had to joke. I mean, her comment was just sitting there, in mid-air.

"Oh, you rude boy!" she gasped, faking outrage. "Can't a person say anything anymore?"

I had to laugh at her. It was good to put her on the defensive, where she had me so often.

"Yes, Rachel," I said. "I would love more of your pork."

With a smirk, she forked more pork onto my plate and said, "Say when."

"When."

And she stopped.

"Thank you, waitress," I said. But as she turned and walked away, I had to add, "I always tip my waitresses."

She laughed and said, "You better!"

∿

I helped Rachel clean up the kitchen. It had *two* sinks, *two* ovens, and a refrigerator the size of a small bank vault. I was good at wiping the counters off. My father was fairly fanatical about crumbs – "You wanna draw *bugs?*" – so I learned to be a good counter-wiper like him. I was also showing off how domestic I could be for Rachel, just as she was showing off for me, rinsing off the dishes and putting them neatly in the dishwasher, everything just perfect. Maybe someday we could just live like this, like normal people, with no conflict from the outside. We could just be ourselves, a couple in our own place. Maybe not this grand, but our own. Someday.

When we finished with the kitchen, we went back to the big room with the television and cuddled on the couch all the way through the end of *The Name Of The Game* and something called *Bracken's World*.

All day I hadn't mentioned anything about her promise (though I thought about it all day). Now was as good a time as any to bring it up.

"So," I started casually. "Did you talk to Nanci today?"

"What do you mean?" she said. "I talk to Nanci every day. Almost."

"So," I said. "Did you set her up for tomorrow night? For, uh, you-know-what?"

"That depends on what you-know-what is," she answered with a sharp cackle.

"You know what I mean," I said, moving closer to her on the couch. "*You're* the one who suggested it."

"What –" she said, turning to face me. "I'm not enough for you? Just me alone?"

"You're enough for any guy," I said positively. "In fact, you're too much! But in a *good* way."

"Too much what?" she goaded.

"Too much everything," I answered. "Too pretty, too smart, too sharp, too sure of yourself, too everything."

She considered what I said and liked it. As you can see, I was getting much better at love-talk, this time around. The thing is, I really meant it. Or else I would have added, "Too much trouble."

But, honestly, getting her back made me feel *great*, and I didn't want to question or upset things. So I ignored the obvious.

"Well, I gave Nanci a general hint," Rachel said. "But really, she'll do whatever I tell her to."

"Everyone is your slave?" I teased her.

"Not *everyone*," she smiled, turning away from me because I teased her with the truth.

"'Boys are toys'?" I floated into the air.

She sputtered a little when I repeated those words – *her* words, which I first heard repeated on the lake at Mooncliff, bobbing in a rowboat.

"You know I never forget a thing," I said.

She looked at me shyly and pleaded, "But you only remember the *good* things about me, right?"

And with that charming, sly smile slicing through me, what else could I say but "I try."

"Promise? You've been so good and understanding," she said. "About everything. So I'm going to give you a present."

"Good, I love presents. When?"

"Tomorrow night," she said in a low voice, coming closer. "With me *and* Nanci."

"What exactly might this present entail?"

"That's up to you. It's whatever you want to do. Let's give her what she deserves. She's so damn nosey, and so in love with you."

"She is not!"

"Oh please!" Rachel crowed. "That cow moons over you – or *moos* – every night. I can tell by the way she talks about you. Why shouldn't I let you have your way with her?"

"You're not jealous?" I asked her, still skeptical.

"You don't love her, do you?"

"Absolutely not!"

"So?" she shrugged. "Then I give you permission to use her for a night. I'll *give* her to you."

"Why are you doing this?"

"Because I think you might like it. Don't boys like stuff like that? . . . And because she deserves it. And because I've put you through a lot. I know."

It was nice to hear her say that.

"Then afterwards," she continued merrily. "You can be my slave."

I had to laugh at her, she was so willful and wild. She might have matured some, but she was still Rachel.

~

We slept in her canopy bed that night, our first night together in a real bed.

"This is what I've dreamed of, for so long," she said, her head on the pillow close to mine. "You don't know how much I've needed you all this time."

"Yes," I said softly. "I do."

"Good," she said firmly. "We're going to have fun tomorrow. Promise."

"Whatever you say," I answered. The promise of "fun" from Rachel was something to contemplate in a leisurely manner.

She snuggled up close to me, falling asleep after a few minutes, and, rather than snoring, she was *purring*. She looked so young, her face all relaxed and angelic in the almost-dark.

After a few minutes I slipped my arm out from under her pillow without waking her, before my *arm* went to sleep.

I remember looking up at the lacey fringe of the canopy as it cast strange shadows on the wall, thinking how good things were. *All things come to he who waits*, I told myself as I fell asleep. But somewhere in the back of mind was a kernel of Worry, just waiting to sprout. I could never just "be happy." I always knew that at any moment, somewhere, something could go wrong.

Record of Events #30 – entered Friday, 6:43 A.M.

~

That Saturday started out as one of the greatest days of my life. It ended quite differently, but the beginning was fantastic.

Rachel brought me breakfast in bed. Blueberry pancakes! In a sun-filled room, propped up on pillows, with a kiss for starters.

"It's the only thing I know how to make," she said, putting the tray over my lap. "And coffee. And tea. And I know how to pour Tropicana."

The whole day, I was happy and nervous at the same time. It was so forbidden for me to be there. We stayed inside all day because Rachel said she wanted to, but I also knew it was so that no one, no neighbor, even with the houses so far apart, would see me there and report back to Eleanor. Rachel seemed a little tense and distracted during the day. Yet sometimes she would giggle to herself.

"Why are you giggling?" I asked her, after I caught her for the third time.

"I'm...happy that you're here," she said, her eyes shining clearly.

"And you're not worried that Eleanor will find out that I spent the weekend here?" I had to ask.

"No," she said casually.

"Liar," I caught her.

"OK, you're right. But I'm going to do what I want," she declared. "I can't let her run my life. Not anymore; now that I have you back. Some things are worth the gamble."

"Sounds good to me," I said, trying to sound supportive, seeing how serious she was.

I wondered if she took any of Eleanor's pills but didn't ask her. I didn't want to upset anything.

"It's a gorgeous day out there," I said, looking out the back window at the Princes' backyard. It was maybe ten times as big as my folks' backyard. My father would have loved the huge barbeque grill and patio.

"It's gorgeous in here too," said Rachel, flashing me a look at her naked shoulder under her silky robe. (Did I mention that she stayed in her robe almost the whole day?)

"OK," I said. "You win."

We played the Young Marrieds all day, lots of time in bed, snacks in bed, and playing around in bed. We would go for long periods of time when neither of us said anything, and it wasn't uncomfortable for a moment. It was just . . . nice.

Nonetheless, I was already starting to think about what time I would have to get out of the Prince house tomorrow, in advance of Eleanor and Herb's return, and how to remove all trace of my presence before I left. And of course, all day, I never forgot about my schoolwork: that was a constant curtain of worry hanging behind my every thought, the cloud in every blue sky.

But no matter how skittish I felt inside at times, I still managed to ignore my misgivings and "force myself" to have a beautiful time in all this Prince-ly luxury. But I could tell that something was bothering Rachel, too, something deeper than I had seen before, despite all her vows of independence, defiance, and emancipation. Something was on her mind and was keeping her distant.

"Can you just tell me, what are you nervous about?" I finally had to ask her.

"Nothing," she said.

"That's not true," I replied. "Not even the little card game you've set up for us tonight?"

"Don't be silly."

"Eleanor and Herb aren't coming home tonight, are they?" I persisted, thinking that was the thing most likely to worry her.

After a pause, she said, "No, of course they're not."

"Are you sure?" I pressed her.

"No! They are definitely not coming home tonight! I wouldn't have brought you here if they were going to be around. I'm not deranged. When I'm ready to deal with Eleanor, you'll be the first to know."

"So why do you look so preoccupied?"

"I'm not preoccupied; I just have a lot on my mind. Aren't I entitled to my own thoughts?"

"I guess so," I admitted grudgingly.

She gave me a quick kiss on my cheek, chirped, "Good. You're sweet to worry about me," and walked out of the room.

She always thought that she could just charm anyone at any time and escape the consequences of having to explain herself. And she could.

~

I spent a lot of the rest of the day playing pinball on the *two* pinball machines that Manny had in the basement. It was an excellent substitute for thinking. Of all the luxuries that the Princes possessed, I think it was the *two* pinball machines – one cowboy-themed, one baseball-themed – that impressed me most. There was less of a thrill in winning an extra ball – since all the balls were free anyway – but I got over that quickly. After I conquered both machines, I went upstairs to find that Rachel was asleep in her bed. That made me feel somewhat relieved; at least she wasn't taking Eleanor's speed.

I tiptoed out and decided to go back downstairs to try to do a little studying, but something, some suspicion, made me take a detour into Eleanor's room. I opened the door and walked into the same heavy perfumed air, the same smell of "old." But I was relieved: I looked on the top of the dresser and saw that the gun that Rachel had been playing with was gone. She must have put it away. Good.

I went downstairs and checked out the Princes' stuff in the living room: lots of knick-knacks and ashtrays and more dog statuettes, and very, very few books. Only what looked liked Book of the Month Club Main Selections, all in a row, all seemingly unread. Books as furniture – call me a snob, but that's pathetic.

But I have to say that it was very comfortable there. The big black leather Barcaloungers in the big backroom were so deep and enveloping that I fell asleep in one of them, watching the Mets win on the huge Zenith, with Max asleep in my lap. By then, she was my best friend. I didn't mean to fall asleep, but Tom Seaver was cruising, and the sun made the room so warm and cozy. I daydreamt what it would be like to have a house like this, all these rooms, all these *bath*rooms, all these deep, dark closets. It took a lot of money, a lot of work, a lot of something. Lumber yards, huh? . . . And I couldn't help but think about what Rachel had planned for that night. Strip poker? With Nanci *and* Rachel? *OK,* I remember thinking to myself, *that might be fun.* I wasn't sure I would know what to do when all the clothes started to come off, but I told myself not to worry. I trusted that Nature would take over. Nature and Rachel.

When I woke up from my Barcalounger coma-sleep, I took a shower. This was before Nanci came over. I mean, wouldn't you've? Rachel let me use one of the guest bathrooms, which was nicer than any bathroom in my house. And I have to admit that the Princes' towels were extremely fluffy.

As I was drying myself off, Rachel opened the bathroom door a crack and peeked into the still-steamy room, "What do you want on your pizza?"

I'm proud to say that I didn't even flinch when she opened the door.

Calm as cake, I said, "Whatever you want, sugar. As long as there're mushrooms . . . And pepperoni . . . And extra cheese!"

She laughed and closed the door with a click.

It felt good – and odd – to feel so at home at the Princes. What would Eleanor – *and* Manny, *and* Herb, for that matter – say if they knew I was there all weekend? And knew what we were planning? I couldn't wait for the night to arrive. I was nervous, but in a good way. I was ready for a good time.

~

"Should we wait for Nanci?" I asked as I helped make up trays for the pizza.

"I guarantee you she'll've eaten," Rachel said. Not maliciously: matter-of-factly. "Besides," she added. "There'll be leftovers. We'll never eat all of this."

I got down some glasses from a cabinet and some napkins from a drawer.

"You already know where things are," said Rachel admiringly. "I don't even have to tell you."

"Sorry," I said.

"No! That's what I love about you! You don't have to be told things."

That struck me funny.

"Well, that's one way to put it."

"That's why we belong together," she said calmly, as if she were stating a known fact. I loved when she said things like that – it's what I had been waiting for, all those long, lost, lonely weeks. Love definitely beats No-Love, by a Mooncliff country mile.

~

We ate the pizza in front of the giant TV, watching one of my favorite movies from when I was a kid: Errol Flynn in *The*

Adventures of Robin Hood featured on *Million Dollar Movie*. But I had never realized that it was a *color* movie! When I saw it as a little kid, we had a black-and-white TV at home, so I assumed that the movie was too. It was even better – if, oddly, somewhat more fake in color.

Rachel loved it as much as I did. (I haven't even bothered to write down all the instances when our taste in things was completely congruent, from *Gatsby* on. We loved almost all the same things, except when it came to the Beatles. She was a "Paul" person while I was obviously a "John" person, but that made sense. She went with "cute" and I went with "smart.")

"Do you want anything else to drink?" Rachel asked as she took a second slice of pepperoni. Did I mention that the Princes had cases and cases of soda in the garage? Coke, Fresca, Orange Crush, Canada Dry ginger ale, Hire's root beer. Everything it seemed, but my beloved Nehi Grape.

"Later I'll make some whiskey sours, and we'll get Nanci drunk," she said. "Eleanor has the greatest recipe, supposedly."

During a commercial, Rachel, feeling frisky from all the Sherwood Forest swashbuckling, picked up the metal poker from the set of horse-head brass tools by the flagstone fireplace, next to a basket of cut wood.

"They used to teach fencing at Mooncliff," said Rachel as she assumed the pose of a swordswoman, using the poker as her weapon. "I don't know why they stopped it. I really liked it. . . . Lunge!"

She showed off her fencing moves in quick succession. "Parry one . . . parry two . . . riposte! Advance . . . retreat . . . *lunge!*"

She straightened up and said, "I love sticking people. It's like ballet, but deadly."

"Wow," I replied. "You are lethal."

"No," she said, wiping a wisp of hair from her forehead, "I just want to rob from the rich . . . and keep it all for myself!"

She made me laugh.

"Come back and watch the movie," I said. "What time is Nanci coming over?"

"Be patient," said Rachel, leaning the black poker against the flagstone. "She'll be here soon. And I think we might have a little surprise for you."

"I bet you will," I agreed. "Come over here."

Rachel giggled and resumed her place beside me on the couch. I held her close to me. She felt small and warm in my arms.

"You've been jittery all day," I said.

She snuggled into my embrace, "Not jittery. Excited!"

Then she pushed herself away from me.

"You don't know how long I've been planning things," she said. "Starting with getting you back. And then, *tonight*. I'll have Nanci."

Her eyes sparkled with the thoughts running through her head. I loved to see her so alive and enthusiastic.

"This weekend is the beginning of everything. Everything is falling into place," she continued. "I've gotten Eleanor to trust me. See how she went away this weekend? And I have you back. And now we'll get Nanci."

I wondered exactly what she was thinking. In some ways, I didn't want to know. I was just happy to have her back and happy to see her making plans for us.

"Soon I will have you forever," she said. "And have everything I want."

Suddenly she jumped up from the couch again.

"Oh! I forgot to make the whiskey sours!" she announced, slapping her forehead and practically leaping over the coffee table on her way to the bar in the far corner of the room. "My head is not screwed on today!"

I watched her as she disappeared behind the bar and then came out with a few decks of cards and a carousel of poker chips, which she plunked on the counter.

"Here are these!" she said before going behind the bar again.

I saw the cards and poker chips and I thought to myself: *This is* really *going to happen. Strip poker, with two girls.* I had better keep my cool, maintain the Steve McQueen inside, and try not to make a fool of myself.

"I know how to make these," announced Rachel as she lined up the ingredients in front of her: a couple bottles of different liquors, a big glass pitcher, and a little jar of maraschino cherries. "Right after I lock Max in the laundry room."

"I'll be right back," I said and went upstairs, taking the steps two at a time. I had to prepare for the night as best I could. I went straight into the bathroom and brushed my teeth – and tongue – hard. I had had the pepperoni too.

I splashed water on my face and dried it with one of the Princes' perfect towels. I combed my hair and checked myself in the mirror. Too late to shave, but my beard isn't very rough anyway. I looked OK for a "beast." Maybe this could be a night of pure fun. Me and *two* girls? Why not? I'm young, and it's spring, and I'm back with Rachel. Maybe this was a good night for growing up and controlling the situation – not have the situation control me. I had been down-hearted for so long. Now, for a change, it was time to feel *up-hearted.*

Then the doorbell rang. Nanci had arrived. The festivities were about to begin. My first impulse was to run downstairs and get the door, but then I controlled myself, remembering to be "cool."

Let Rachel get the door and let them get themselves set up downstairs, I told myself. I'd wait and make a grand entrance in a few minutes. Funny, I don't think of myself as being so calculating about how I appear to other people, but this was a special occasion. I didn't want to mess up tonight, not with everything going so well, and not with *two* girls. I had enough trouble handling one.

After a few minutes of letting them wait, I trotted down the stairs and fast-walked toward the backroom. Nanci and Rachel were standing there, in the hallway, waiting for me. Nanci, in her standard Greenwich Village gypsy rags with black leotards underneath and the same giant purse with the fringe that she always carried; Rachel, in perfect jeans, perfect blouse, perfect little shoes, looking like she'd stepped out of the pages of *Vogue* or one of those other fashion magazines I don't read.

"Here we are!" sang out Nanci. "Your two favorite girls!"

I saw Rachel shoot me a look and a secret smile that said, *See?? I was right about Nanci's feelings for you.*

"And right on time!" I answered jauntily. "It's Saturday night, the 'rents are gone, and it's time to have fun."

I walked up to Nanci and kissed her on the cheek, then pivoted to Rachel and kissed her on the lips. And stayed there an extra beat.

When I pulled back, I saw that I had surprised Rachel – with *both* kisses.

Good, I thought to myself. *It might be better not to be on the defensive tonight.*

"We have a surprise for you tonight," said Nanci. "A big one."

Rachel's eyes met Nanci's for a millisecond, and I could see that they did have something planned for me.

"So I hear," I said. "I'm fairly excited."

"Don't get too excited yet," said Nanci. "It might not be what you expect."

"That's what makes it a surprise," I said. "I get it."

"I hope you do," Nanci shot back.

"But before we do anything," said Rachel, leading us into the backroom. "We have to drink some of these whiskey sours."

"*Whiskey sours!*" exclaimed Nanci, walking toward the bar and plopping her purse on one of the bar stools. "That is practically *senile*! My *parents* drink whiskey sours!"

"*Everyone's* parents drink whiskey sours," Rachel scoffed. "But this is Eleanor's special recipe."

"It's from her Lucretia Borgia cookbook," I cracked.

"Come to think of it," said Nanci. "My parents usually drink martinis. *'I've had tee many martoonies!'* My father actually says that."

"Your father is a great wit," I commented.

"Please don't insult my father," said Nanci, her face suddenly solemn and serious.

I was instantly stopped. It was just a joke. I didn't mean to offend Nanci. I didn't even *know* her father –

"Only kidding!" brayed Nanci, breaking into a big guffaw. She and Rachel laughed big at my sudden embarrassment.

"You should see your face!" tittered Rachel.

I let them laugh at me and said, "I'm sorry if I didn't want to make fun of your father."

They kept laughing. I could already see that they were going to gang up on me that night. You know: teasing and tormenting the one boy. I understood. I could have expected it. They had me outnumbered, two to one, and anyway, I think we were all three of us nervous. But I thought, *OK, I'm ready for them – for whatever they throw at me.* Because, after all, I *was* the only boy.

"Why don't we drink up some of these drinks?" I said. "Rachel slaved over them."

That made Nanci cackle.

"Rachel? Rachel slave over something?" she crowed. "Rachel slaves over nothing . . . except her appearance."

This time, *I* was the one to snicker. It was good to see Rachel on the receiving end of Nanci's joke. But I saved her anyway.

"Oh, come on, Nanci," I said. "Don't you think Rachel is a *natural* beauty?"

Which made Rachel smile widely and say, "Thank you, sweetheart."

"I think we better drink up then," I said, reaching for one of the dripping-wet, icy glasses of orange liquid. I passed one glass to Nanci.

"*Drink* up?" cracked Nanci. "Before I *throw* up!"

And I gave another one to Rachel, "These look delicious, Rache'."

"I sincerely hope they are," said Rachel. "I can read a recipe, I think."

I took the last one for myself and as I took a long sip off the foamy top, Nanci said, "He just likes the cherry."

I managed to swallow the first sip without it coming out of nose, but not by much.

"It tastes like fruit juice," said Nanci.

"Fruit juice with a kick," I corrected her. "And absolutely delicious."

"Let's toast!" said Nanci, holding her glass up, getting between Rachel and me.

"Good idea!" said Rachel. "What shall we drink to?"

"Honesty!" said Nanci immediately.

"Uh-oh," I said. "That sounds dangerous."

"Are you afraid of the truth?" Nanci challenged me.

"Me?" I replied. "I'm terrified!"

Rachel laughed, enjoying the sparring between Nanci and me.

"Then, honesty it is!" said Rachel, her eyes dancing with danger.

We clinked our cold, sweating glasses and toasted, "To honesty!"

"And *trust!*" Rachel added. "Trust is important."

"Trust too," I agreed.

Rachel was on edge, almost glowing with excitement. I could tell that it was going to be an unforgettable night, no matter what happened. These girls were ready for who-knew-what.

"So," said Nanci to Rachel, "should we tell him our surprise?"

I looked back and forth between them: something *was* going on.

"You mean something beyond *strip poker*?" I asked.

Rachel connected with Nanci and overruled her, "Let's start the cards first. Then, we'll . . ." What she left unsaid, said a lot.

"Are you sure?" asked Nanci.

"Yeah," she said, picking up the cards and rack of poker chips from the bar. "Let's play a couple of hands. Then we'll see what develops."

"Why are you being so mysterious?" I asked Rachel, who danced away from me.

"Girls are supposed to be mysterious! You haven't figured that out yet?" she sang out, leading the way to the coffee table. "Bring your drinks!"

"It keeps you on your toes," said Nanci.

"But what if I don't want to be on my toes?" I asked her.

She snickered, "Oh, you love it!"

And, at that moment, she might have been right.

"Come on, children!" Rachel had already set up on the couch and was shuffling a deck of cards.

"She seems to know what she's doing," I said to Nanci as we walked across to the couch.

"You think so?" asked Nanci.

"We'll see," I said.

"Stop it, you two!" said Rachel sharply. "No ganging up!"

I just had to laugh at that, thinking that's what they were doing to me, as I put my glass down on the coffee table – a big rectangle of sparkly black marble with this edge of sparkly white marble – with a clank. I dragged a big square ottoman to the other side of the table, across from the couch as Nanci sat down next to Rachel.

"OK," said Rachel, shuffling the cards. "You guys know the rules?"

"Go over them again," said Nanci, sitting down carefully on the couch next to Rachel. But no matter how softly Nanci sat down, her weight pushed Rachel up on the other end of the cushion. I could see that Nanci hoped that no one would notice, but she saw that I did, and we both looked down.

"I love this table! It's straight out of Miami Beach!" said Nanci, running her hand on the slick marble. "The Ladies' Powder Room at the Fontainebleau, if I'm not mistaken."

"Eleanor," sniffed Rachel, as if that one word explained everything. "OK," she continued, shuffling the cards again and quite adeptly too. "Forget about that. There's one pair, which beats two pair, which beats three of a kind, which beats a straight, which beats a flush, which beats a full house, which beats four of a kind, which beats a straight flush. And there's a royal flush, which is ace-king-queen-jack-ten of the same suit."

"OK, Rachel," I agreed. "Except all of that, *backwards*."

Realizing what she had said, she burst into giggles, blushing a little at her error of ranking the hands in reverse order. She liked to be perfect, especially in front of Nanci, whom she generally felt was beneath her. In a way, it was always good to see Rachel make a mistake. It made her more human, and more vulnerable: it made her more like me.

Nanci said, "I'm not talking about the rules of poker, Rachel. I happen to be a very good poker player. I'm talking about the rules of *strip* poker."

That made us all pause. And we all took sips of our whiskey sours. Which were tasting better and better.

"Well," said Rachel. "Not that I've played it before –"

"I should hope not!" I cracked.

"But I think," she ignored me. "We should start by anteing up a shoe."

"A shoe?" echoed Nanci, with some trepidation.

I could see that both of the girls were a little nervous, so I gave them an out.

"What do you say we play some hands of *regular* poker?" I said. "Just to get warmed up."

"Good idea!" both girls said at the same time, with the same enthusiasm and relief.

We played two hands, and I won them both.

"I like poker," I said. "This is a good game."

"Don't be so smug," said Rachel. "Just because he gets a little lucky."

"I'm a *lot* lucky," I said. "I mean, just look around."

"Wait," said Nanci. "This isn't fair. Even if he loses, he wins."

"What do you mean?" asked Rachel.

"Guys have it made," said Nanci. "He can't lose, no matter what happens, no matter what, you know, *clothes* come off. You know what I mean: If a girl has a lot of sex, she's a slut. If a guy has a lot of sex, he's –"

"Lucky," I finished her sentence, with a satisfied smile.

"So what exactly are you saying, Nanc'?" asked Rachel. "Do *you* have a lot of sex?"

Nanci immediately blushed.

"No, that's not what I'm saying," she stammered.

"I didn't think so," Rachel snapped back instantly. "No offense."

I didn't like to see Rachel be so sharp with Nanci, who was by no means defenseless. I just liked to see Rachel's sweet side come out, not the other.

"You're just stalling!" I interrupted. "The both of you."

They looked at me, innocently.

"Of course, we're stalling," said Nanci.

"What did you think?" Rachel added.

"Then ante up a shoe," I said.

"What?" said Rachel.

"Ante up a shoe, big mouth!" I demanded.

That straightened her right up, sitting there on the couch, Rachel, in her perfect creamy-white silk blouse and jeans.

Then a big Dingo boot landed smack in the middle of the table, surprising both of us.

"It's time to play, children," said Nanci, smilingly serious, pointing to her bare foot, with its wiggling toes.

"You are on," I said, pulling the black Ked off my right foot. (One Ked? Two Keds?)

I tossed it on top of Nanci's dusty old boot, and the two of us watched Rachel delicately remove an elegant black slipper with a golden buckle (I'm sure it was some famous brand) from her foot and place it on top of my sneaker.

"Perfect," I said, looking at the three shoes: each shoe seemed to be a pretty fair representation of the owner.

"Who deals?" asked Nanci.

"I will," I said, grabbing the deck of cards from the top of the coffee table. The Princes had nice, new, slick cards. Just broken in enough.

"Who needs more whiskey sour?" asked Rachel, getting up from the couch.

"We all do!" said Nanci. "Obviously."

I snickered; she was right.

"OK," I announced. "Draw poker, deuces wild."

Rachel came back to the table with the icy glass pitcher of the orange liquid.

"Where's your glass?" she said to me.

"Right here," I said.

As she refilled my glass, our eyes met briefly. Her look asked me: *Is this what you wanted?*

I just smiled and said, "Watch it. You're going to spill."

I saved her just before she overflowed my glass.

"Thanks," she whispered.

"OK," I said, putting down the drink and picking up the cards. "Let's play some strip poker. Whoever has the worst hand has to strip, one piece of clothing at a time."

I dealt out the five cards each for draw, flinging the cards on three sides of the pile of shoes. I've played my share of cards over the years – gin rummy and Go Fish with the Doggies, honeymoon bridge with my Mom, and, yes, lots of poker with my high school friends – so I felt pretty comfortable dealing.

"Jacks or better to open," I said. "You're to the left of the dealer," I said to Nanci.

"Sorry," she said. "I can't open . . . So to speak."

"Me neither," said Rachel. "And is everything going to be a double-whatever-you-call-it tonight?"

"Yes," I said. "Everything will be a double-whatever tonight." Looking down at my hand, I saw that I had nothing either. My high card was a ten!

"OK, throw 'em in," I said, tossing my cards onto the table.

The girls followed suit.

"OK, your deal, Rachel," I said.

Instantly, she scooped up the cards and said, "New game."

"What do you mean, new game?" I asked.

Rachel popped the deck in her hand and started dealing. "Draw poker. Deuces, one-eyed jacks, and suicide kings wild."

"'Suicide kings'?" repeated Nanci derisively. "And what exactly are they?"

"It's the king who stabs himself in the head," said Rachel, finishing the deal. "The king of hearts. The king who kills himself for love."

"What a moron," I said, picking up my cards. That's when I realized that both girls were looking at me.

"Don't look at me," I said. "I'm no suicide king! And I bet a Ked."

I slipped my sneaker off my other foot and flipped it onto the pile.

"Wait!" said Nanci, fixing her hand.

"No 'wait'!" countered Rachel. "Bet your boot, or fold your cards."

Nanci paused and looked down at her cards, considering.

"My boot should be worth *two* raises," she said, taking off her other Dingo boot and placing it on the table. Rachel and I had to move our whiskey sour glasses back from the ever-growing pile.

"OK . . ." Rachel intoned, focusing intently on her hand. "I'll see your very smelly boot" – she slipped her other little black shoe off and put it on the table –"and raise you a ped."

Like an idiot, I said, "What's a ped?" But when she showed me what it was, I realized that my mother wore them, too, for under her little shoes.

"That's not much of a piece of clothing," I said, looking at the little fleshy socklet now on top of the pile, looking like the shed skin of some reptile.

"Just you wait, sweet thing," said Rachel to me in a slightly lower voice that was exciting. Of course, I had seen her undergarments before and knew exactly what she meant.

"You know," I said. "I think we need you to make another pitcher of that, that, whatdayacallit, that –"

Then Rachel and I both realized that it was – *"BUG JUICE!!"*

We laughed and laughed, thrown instantly into The Zone by a Mooncliff memory. In fact, the whiskey sour mixture was almost the exact same color as the orange version of bug juice.

I glanced over to Nanci to see how she was taking this, seeing us having a little "couple's" moment, but I couldn't read her face. She wasn't smiling, the way she had when she saw us together a long time ago in front of Lord & Taylor, but she wasn't hostile. She was just . . . neutral. Distant.

"It's just a Mooncliff thing," I said.

"So I guessed," said Nanci, abruptly turning to Rachel. "So, Rachel, do you think he's ready? Should we tell him *our* surprise now?"

"Hey, maybe!" said Rachel.

Nanci shifted her body to one side and got up off the couch with a big side-roll, saying, "And while you make more of the 'bug juice'" – she made quotation marks in the air with her fingers – "you can tell him who else is coming tonight."

That perked my ears right up.

"Who else is coming?" I asked, suddenly concerned. Someone else wasn't in the deal.

Rachel was walking to the bar with her back to me, carrying the almost empty glass pitcher, and didn't answer me.

"So who else is coming??" I repeated.

Following Rachel across the hard, polished floor, Nanci slid a little on her one-sock-on, one-sock-off feet as she picked up her big, fringed purse from the barstool where she left it on her way out of the room. Plus, she might have been a little tipsy from the whiskey in the sour.

"Don't say anything too clever," Nanci said, "I wouldn't want you to waste your gems." Drinking brought back her lisp too.

Finally, I had had enough.

"OK, you two. Stop teasing me right now!" I insisted. "Who else is coming tonight?"

Rachel said nothing, but Nanci quite simply announced, "Eric."

Record of Events #31 – entered Friday, 8:15 P.M.

~

What can I say? I was stunned.

"I don't get it," I must have mumbled.

"You will," said Nanci cheerily and left the room.

I looked over at Rachel, who was standing at the bar, refusing to meet my eyes, as I heard Nanci trudge up the stairs.

"What is this?" I asked.

"What?" said Rachel, pouring liquor from a bottle into the glass pitcher.

"Don't say 'what' so innocently!" I said, raising my voice. That stopped her.

"You've used this Eric thing to tease me ever since we met," I said.

"What are you talking about?" she said, pretending to be innocent.

"I know you've seen him," I said, walking toward her. "I'm not stupid. You're very pretty! Guys are after you. You get bored. I understand that."

"What are you saying?" she said, putting down the bottle on the bar.

"It's why I have a problem trusting you one hundred percent," I said.

"What do you mean, you have a problem?" Rachel repeated, her face open with surprise and disappointment.

"You broke up with me once," I said. My thoughts were rolling now, and I was unable to stop. "So there's this shadow over everything –"

"What shadow? You don't know what I've had to live through –" she interrupted.

"Always this 'Eric' hanging in the wings –"

"Would you stop talking about Eric!" she shouted, slamming her fists on the bar. "There is no Eric! 'Eric' is a joke, an old joke. There *was* an Eric, but he moved away from here. In the sixth grade!"

"Wait a second: What do you mean?" I said, flat-out stunned by what she was saying.

"Oh, sure, I loved Eric – in sixth grade! Nanci did too. Every girl in the school did! He was gorgeous. He looked like Ricky Nelson. But he moved to New Jersey. We cried for a week. But that was a long time ago."

"But what about all the letters you got at Mooncliff from Eric?"

"Oh, please!" said Rachel, bringing her hands together briefly in prayer. "Sometimes Nanci used to sign her letters to me 'Love, Eric' – *as a joke*! The girls in my bunk read the letter and thought there was this guy named Eric who loved me. So I just let them think it."

"But why?" I asked, my mind spinning back to those first mentions of Eric. "Just for fun?"

"What?" she shot back. "You didn't lie to the Doggies? You didn't mess with their heads? They looked at my personal letters! Do you think I owed them the truth about anything?"

My mind started reliving all the comments and hints about Eric – what exactly she had said, and what other people had said. I couldn't have concocted the entire thing.

"Really, baby," said Rachel earnestly. "'Eric' has been a joke between Nanci and me for years! He was like a character we made up! The ideal boyfriend! When we were little, we used to have sleepovers and take turns pretending to be Eric. At camp, I would sign *my* letters to *her* 'Love, Eric!' It wasn't anyone *real*!"

"Then why did Nanci say that you were seeing Eric?" I asked.

"Because she *was*."

We both turned around and saw Nanci standing there, all in boys' clothing. A white shirt and striped tie, dark pants, and a dark sports jacket. She even had her short dark hair combed over and slicked down, like a little boy's haircut.

"Ta-daa!" said Nanci with a delighted smirk across her face, making a clumsy little bow forward from her waist. She looked like an enormous little boy. I saw that she had dropped her big purse in the corner. Little boys don't carry big purses.

Both Rachel and I looked at her, stunned.

"Are you out of your mind?" said Rachel.

"What?" replied Nanci, turning around in place, showing off her clothes. "You don't like my Eric outfit?"

"Why did you tell him I was seeing someone named Eric?" said Rachel directly, walking straight toward Nanci.

"It was just a joke!" protested Nanci. "Just to keep him on his toes and in love with you. 'Boys are toys!' Don't you remember? There was nothing wrong with him thinking there was a rival out there. Not if it made him love you even more."

"But it wasn't true!" said Rachel. "Why would you do that? That's disgusting! You were our friend."

"I'm not the one who broke up with him, Rachel," said Nanci. "That was all your doing."

By now, I admit my mind was spinning; I didn't know whether to be angry or grateful. Angry at Nanci for lying, but grateful that there was no Eric. And I couldn't believe I'd heard "boys are toys" again, this time out of Nanci's mouth.

Rachel was half in tears. "But all the help you gave us, all the phone calls you made –"

Finally, I spoke. "Yeah, all those phone calls."

"I was just helping you two stay close!" said Nanci, backing up. "I did everything for you. I drove you places. I gave him your messages."

"But why would you make things up?" demanded Rachel. "You know what I was having to deal with, with Hell-eanor!"

I could see that Nanci/Eric was sweating, on the defensive.

"But I was *helping* you!" Nanci said. "You see he's your lapdog, just like you wanted."

"Helping? How?" shot back Rachel. "How were you helping? By planting doubt in his mind?"

"Listen," I got between them. "Hold on for a second!"

"I don't know why you're so upset, Rachel. You *love* Eric!" Nanci reasoned. "When we were little and had sleepovers, we used to take turns being Eric."

"Maybe that's what you really love!" Rachel shouted back. "Being Eric! You loved getting under the covers with me! You probably miss those days."

"No," said Nanci back. "Maybe it's *you* who needs real *girl* love, not me!"

For an instant, I thought that Rachel was going to hit Nanci or something, and I wanted to stop anything like that from happening.

"Wait!" I said, making space between the two of them. "Nanci. I don't understand why you said what you said –"

"I told you what I thought –" she sputtered.

"That is completely ridiculous –" Rachel cut her off.

"Stop it!" I shouted. "Can we just *stop* for a second?"

My loud voice made them both step back a little.

"I don't know exactly what happened, exactly what went on –" I continued in a rational manner, but Rachel interrupted me.

"Nanci, how *could* you – ?" Rachel fumed.

I put my hand on Rachel's forearm and held it firmly.

"Can we just hold on?" I said, slower and louder.

The girls paused, breathing heavily.

"Maybe now isn't the time we should relive the past," I said, suppressing my own zillion questions for moment. "Let's just take a second –"

"And play more poker!" snapped Rachel. "*Strip* poker."

Her eyes flashed with the dare.

"Come on, 'Eric,'" she taunted Nanci. "Let's play for real. Now! This'll be fun. You'll get what you deserve. But you better start playing better, or he's going to see your naked body. I don't know if he's ready for that."

I could see that Rachel's comment really hurt Nanci, the way she flinched, the tears that momentarily filled her eyes. But Nanci was not going to admit that she was hurt.

"OK, Rachel," said Nanci. "Let's play."

She sat back down at the coffee table and shuffled the cards, breathing a little heavily.

With all the tension in the air, I didn't know if that was the best thing to do, but we all sat back down at the coffee table. And we all took long drinks from our whiskey sour glasses. I dealt from the deck that Nanci had freshly shuffled.

"Draw," I said. "Deuces wild."

"What about suicide kings?" asked Nanci as she picked up her cards as I dealt them.

"You're not supposed to pick up your cards until they're all dealt," said Rachel.

"Who says?" snapped Nanci.

"Those are the rules of poker," replied Rachel.

"Well, I go by my own rules," said Nanci.

"Your play, Nanci," I said. "Or Eric. Or whoever you are. How many do you want?"

"Wait a second!" she said. "Let me look."

She studied her cards, then looked at both Rachel and me.

"Two," she said as she tossed two cards into the middle.

I dealt her the two cards and asked Rachel, "How many?"

"Three," said Rachel, which elicited a confident grunt from Nanci.

I gave her the three cards and said, "I'll take two too. Two, also."

I discarded my two bad cards and looked at my hand. I kept a pair of tens and a king, and I drew another king and a three. Two pair. That could win. These girls were not very good poker players . . . thank goodness.

"Now what?" said Nanci.

"Whoever has the worst hand has to strip," I said.

"What about betting?" asked Rachel.

Both Nanci and I yelled, "No!" Which, I guess, indicated the relative strength of our hands.

"Let's just play these out, Rache', OK?" I said.

"OK," she said. "Whattaya got?"

It turned out that Rachel won that hand with three fours, beating my two pair and Nanci's pair of aces.

"Low hand strips!" ordered Rachel, pointing at Nanci. "Let's go!"

There was a big, cruel smile on Rachel's face as she sat back to watch Nanci take something off.

Nanci screwed a crooked smile on her face and, with that side-shake of hers, rolled up to a standing position. She stood there, in Eric clothes, looking down on us. Then she took off her sports jacket and dropped it in the middle of the table. It didn't reveal anything.

"That's a start," said Rachel maliciously. "But soon, we'll have you buck-naked and jiggly."

Nanci was startled by that, and so was I. I knew very well Rachel's capacity for mockery and vengeance; she had had to develop those "skills" to survive in that house. But I felt there was something new and nasty brewing here. Nanci had stepped over a line, and Rachel was going to make her pay for it.

"I have to tinkle," said Rachel, suddenly standing up.

"'Tinkle'?" chirped Nanci, derisively.

"I'm sorry," said Rachel primly. "But that's what I was taught to say. Do you prefer 'urinate'?"

I could tell from the distinct way that Rachel was trying to pronounce her words that she was getting buzzed from the whiskey sours.

She stepped away from the coffee table and walked toward the little bathroom – excuse me, the "powder room" – in the corner of the room by the bar.

"You two guys talk amongst yourselves," sang out Rachel. "Play with your whatever, your *selves*."

She skipped away from the table, nimble on her little feet, and disappeared behind the bar and into the "powder room."

I instantly turned on Nanci.

"What the hell is wrong with you?"

"Nothing's wrong with me," Nanci replied with frost in her voice.

"Why did you tell me she was seeing this Eric?"

"But she *wasn't*, was she?"

"But why lie to me?"

"It wasn't about *you*," she defended herself.

"OK," I said, forcing her to look in my face. "If it wasn't about me, then it was about Rachel. What do you have against her?"

Nanci looked down at the men's tie laying on her belly and smoothed it. The men's clothes – they must have been her father's or brother's – looked extra-baggy on her, and she knew it. Her masquerade/joke might have been backfiring on her, but she wasn't deterred: she fought back.

"I know that Rachel is beautiful," Nanci said, with reason in her voice. "She is smart and funny and attractive and all that. She is a very . . . *magnetic* person. But she is a very troubled person, getting away with things her whole life, and, ultimately, I think she's a dangerous person."

"You know what?" I said. "Finally . . . I think you're just plain jealous of her."

"Me, jealous?" said Nanci with a snort. "Hah!"

"You live vicariously through her," I went after her. "You sit all alone in your room with your drawings and your hash – and you wish you *were* Rachel!"

"That is nonsense!" said Nanci, her eyes beginning to fill with tears.

"Then why do you spend so much time around her?" I nailed her. "Why is that? Tell me that!"

Rachel came out of the powder room, the sound of the toilet flushing behind her, so I don't think she heard anything of what Nanci and I said. At least she didn't act that way when she came back to the table.

"I should have put on more layers of clothing! That's for sure," she said impishly, sitting down on the couch. "Who wants more whiskey sour, and who deals?"

Rachel lost the next hand, though it didn't seem to bother her as she slowly and sexily slid out of her jeans. She turned around as she inched the jeans over her hips and down her legs. Then she gently stepped out of them and kicked them aside, showing off her legs. It was months after summer, but she still seemed to have a tan, a healthy color in her skin. (To tell you the truth, I seldom saw her bare legs in this much light.) She was left wearing silky pink panties, with a little bow in the front.

"There!" she said sitting back down, her face glowing with excitement, for the game and for whatever she was planning to do to Nanci. I knew that look in Rachel's eye. Something was going to happen, but I didn't know what.

Nanci lost the next hand. She tried for a flush and missed.

"Strip!" ordered Rachel, taking another drink of the bug juice.

Not removing her eyes from Rachel's, Nanci/Eric stood up with her roll-move and undid her black, baggy men's pants – the belt buckle, then the button, then the zipper – and let them fall to the floor. There she stood, on her pale, chubby legs, like piano legs, topped by the big, wide triangle of her white panties.

No one had to say anything.

I made sure to lose the next hand. I didn't want to get too far ahead – or behind – in the "race" to undress. I smiled to myself as I broke up a pair of aces and wound up losing my shirt, literally. But as Nanci said before, even if I lose, I win.

By the time we played a few more hands, we had finished most of the second pitcher of bug juice, and Nanci and Rachel were down to their bras and panties. My mind was spinning happily; I didn't know where the night was going, and Rachel and Nanci were building to some kind of big fight, but honestly, I really couldn't care all that much because there was all this girl-flesh in front of me, right *there*.

"Change of game!" called out Rachel as she quickly dealt out another hand of draw poker.

"You can't do that!" scoffed Nanci, tucking her too-short hair behind her ears.

"Sure, I can!" said Rachel happily. "My house – my cards – my deal. Instead of betting clothes, this hand we bet *kisses*!"

I shot a look at Rachel and saw the mischief in her eyes. She was making up the rules as she went along, but that didn't seem to bother her. Or me. I could see how excited she was, and though I wasn't sure in which direction her excitement would lead us – to something good or something bad – whatever way she went, I was going along for the ride. I was just happy to be back with her. I remembered those pink panties with the little bow.

"Whoever loses . . . has to *kiss* whoever the winner says," said Rachel, gathering up her cards greedily.

We looked at our cards, contemplating them and the new rules.

"I'll take two," I said, shooting a quick smile to Rachel.

She dealt me the cards and said, "This will be the first boy Nanci's kissed in ten years. Other than her relatives. No offense."

"I kissed your father," said Nanci, looking down at her cards.

"You *what*?" said Rachel.

"You think you know so much, Rachel," said Nanci with a smirk. "But you don't know everything!"

"You're lying," said Rachel, going back to her cards.

"Your father put the moves on me before he moved out," said Nanci, looking directly at Rachel, who recoiled as if she had been slapped.

I tried to head off an explosion.

"She's just saying that to upset you," I put in, but Nanci cut me off.

"What do you know, Mr. Ivy League?" she shot back. "You're still looking for Eric to come walking in!"

"I wouldn't bring that up if I were you!" I said, sitting straight up on the ottoman and pointing right at her face. "How many cards do you want?"

"Four," said Nanci. "I have an ace."

Rachel snickered derisively, "I'm not going to say anything about *that*," and dealt the cards in front of Nanci.

"Straight flush!" screamed Rachel when she won. "I guess my luck is finally turning."

"I wouldn't bet on it," said Nanci sourly.

"Luck evens out," I pronounced. "It's one of the laws of nature."

"OK, loser," said Rachel, addressing Nanci with savage delight. "Now you have to kiss him" – she waited a malicious little moment, and added tauntingly – "unless you want to kiss me more."

Nanci said, "Rachel, why are you being so horrible tonight?"

Rachel snapped back with a laugh, "Just be happy I invited you over here. You're lucky that I let you into my life. Or else you'd be stuck in your room with your hash, your inhaler, and your art."

Nanci flinched and stammered back, "You *let* me into your life? Are you – you don't know how much of a joke that is."

"So why don't you kiss *me* instead of him?" said Rachel mockingly. "That's what you really want."

Rachel's eyes sparkled with malice as she watched Nanci. I really didn't know what to think: Was Nanci really in love with Rachel all along? It never occurred to me, though I'll admit I'm kind of an innocent on these things. It might seem hard to believe now, but it's the way I was then.

"No," said Nanci curtly. "I'll kiss *him*."

I think Rachel was a little jolted at how fast Nanci snapped back her answer.

Nanci got up from the couch, swaying to her feet in her big, white bra and wide, white panties. Her flesh was pink and a little blotchy. She turned toward me with a smile.

"Don't be shy," she said as she came toward me, working her way around the table. Out of the corner of my eye, I could see Rachel, watching us intently.

I stood up from the ottoman as Nanci closed in on me. She was breathing heavily and trying not to show it.

"I should have brought my inhaler," she said with a twisted smile.

"Don't you take it everywhere?" I asked, seeing how big she was before me.

"Not everywhere," she said. "Sometimes I forget it."

She was right in front of me now.

"Kiss her!" said Rachel. "Go ahead. She needs it."

Nanci leaned toward me, closing her eyes. I had no choice but to kiss her.

"Feel her if you want to," Rachel said. "You *know* she's soft and gooshy."

Nanci kissed me harder, forcing herself toward me. I felt her fleshy, wet fish lips. I started to draw back.

"Don't go —" Nanci muttered, trying to pull me toward her.

"You can touch her," whispered Rachel. "Go on. She'll be grateful."

Max started to bark like crazy in the laundry room.

"Shut up, Max!" Rachel yelled, getting up from the couch.

"Please —" breathed Nanci into my face. She kissed me again and held me. She tasted different from Rachel.

"Do what you want," urged Rachel. "She won't mind. You're doing her a favor."

Nanci cringed, but she kissed me harder, holding me closer. I felt her skin against mine. The dog kept barking.

"Shut up, Max!" Rachel said, going someplace out of my sight, maybe to see about the damn dog.

Nanci kissed my neck and held me tight to her. She seemed to be all over me, the way I was all over Rachel. Her belly pressed against me.

"Come on," whispered Nanci. "You remember. Be my toy."

She gave me another deep kiss, and I had to kiss her back.

"Get her!" said Rachel from somewhere. "Kiss that fat cow."

"Ow!" said Nanci, pulling away from me, hit by something. "What are you doing??"

I pulled back from her and saw that Rachel, with the fireplace poker in her hand, had just poked Nanci in the butt.

"It's my cattle prod," said Rachel with a fierce smile, holding the tip of the poker up toward Nanci's face. "Go on, kiss him again."

"Stop that, Rachel!" said Nanci, pushing the tip of the fireplace poker away from her and rubbing her behind. "You're drunk, and you're –"

"Right!" laughed Rachel. "You're kissing him, *wishing* it were me! I see it in your little piggie eyes."

I didn't know if Nanci was going to cry or throw something at Rachel. By then I had the feeling – more than a feeling, a *dread* – that something bad was going to happen, and there was nothing I could do to stop it. It was like a boulder, rolling downhill, and if I put my body in front of it, I would have been crushed.

"Take off your bra," said Rachel, pointing the fireplace poker at Nanci's chest. "Let's give him a good laugh. Then we'll talk about those giant grandma panties –"

"*WHAT THE HELL IS THIS?*"

The voice came from the entryway to the back room, and we all turned at once.

Like a nightmare, there was Eleanor, standing there in a fit of rage.

"WHAT IN THE NAME OF HELL IS THIS???"

I looked over at Rachel, and she was as surprised as I was.

"The first weekend I leave you alone – the very first! – and look at you!! And what the hell is *he* doing here??" Eleanor pointed at me with a long, red fingernail as she walked straight at Rachel. She was wearing a purple whatdayacallit – *a pant-suit* – with this very loud, flowery scarf, and her hair was all done up fancy, and she walked like an angry man, spoiling for a fight.

Rachel stood her ground, though I could tell that she was super shocked, and we had been drinking all that bug juice, which made us – at least me – a little woozy.

"W-W-What is *he* doing here?" Rachel parroted, "What are *you* doing here? You weren't supposed to be back until tomorrow! And where's *Herb*?"

"Herb? Herb can drop dead," sneered Eleanor. "Is where Herb is. That piece of gahbage just dropped me off and left."

"Hah!" Rachel stifled a laugh.

"What's so funny?" said Eleanor. I could swear that Eleanor had been drinking, too, the way she was slurring her words.

"Nothing," said Rachel. "So what happened?"

"We had a big fight, right in the middle of the bar at the Maidstone Club fuhgodssake," ranted Eleanor. "A place I've always been dying to go to! And right in front of all these ritzy Hamptons people. I am finally finished with him and his crap! Tomorrow he's going to come and move all-a his junk outta here!"

"Good," said Rachel, and I smiled warily, watching how she played her mother.

"Don't say 'good,'" Eleanor practically sprang at her. "You didn't answer me: *What* is *he* doing here?"

"He's here," Rachel said firmly, standing her ground. "Because I invited him here. That's what he's doing here."

"Did I or did I *not* give you explicit instructions not to have anyone over?" Eleanor practically spat in her face. "Not when I wasn't home. Except for Nanci."

"Yeah, well," said Rachel, stalling for some strength. "The truth is . . . I didn't think you'd be home. I thought you'd be gone all weekend with your *boyfriend*."

"Boyfriend, my ass," said Eleanor. "I'm never gonna see that creep again, believe you me."

"Good!" said Rachel.

"STOP SAYING 'GOOD!'" shouted Eleanor, getting closer to Rachel. "You are in big, big trouble! Bigger than you know."

Rachel stood her ground, still holding the fireplace poker. I think she held onto it to give herself a feeling of support and force. Eleanor was taller than Rachel and was asserting her dominance over her daughter. In fact, Rachel seemed on the verge of weakening at Eleanor's onslaught, but she fought back anyway.

"The fact is, Mother," said Rachel. "The fact is that I'm entitled to see who I want, where I want, when I want. I'm eighteen, and you can't stop me. You have no right."

"No right?" snickered Eleanor, her hands on her hips.

"Yes! No right!" Rachel shouted back.

Eleanor laughed, "Look at you! Talking about rights – in your underwear."

"Better than you look in yours," Rachel shot back at Eleanor with a tight smile. "A *whole lot* better."

That stopped Eleanor for a moment, so Rachel attacked.

"Maybe Herb wouldn't be after me all the time if you didn't look like *this*," said Rachel, pointing with the poker at Eleanor's body. "In fact, he told me that he can't stand to touch you. You should see the faces he makes behind your back!"

"You little tramp!" Eleanor hissed. "Well, maybe it's just because you can't keep your clothes on in front of him. I keep telling you to close your robe, but you can't help but try to flash your little boobies and –"

376   What It Was Like

"At least they're not down to my knees!" Rachel shot back.

Eleanor gasped with anger. "You ungrateful little snot-nose!"

"'Ungrateful'?" Rachel yelled. "Tell me, Eleanor, what exactly am I supposed to be grateful for? For ruining my life? For going out of your way to make my life miserable, like it was your hobby or something? And when I find a boy who's kind and decent and not one of these country club –"

Eleanor shook her head scornfully, cutting her off, "I give you everything, and look what I'm left with. I've always known what you are: a selfish, unfeeling, unloving –"

"You're looking in the mirror, Eleanor!" Rachel sang out derisively. "The mirror!!"

"I stayed with your father for almost twenty years for you!" Eleanor said the word "father" like a curse word, just the way Manny said "mother."

Rachel wouldn't take any of it, shouting back, "That wasn't for me! That was for *you* – and your American Express card! *And* your Diner's Club card! *And* your Master Charge! And the bills from Saks and Lord & Taylor –"

Eleanor interrupted, "I see that you have no problem spending money."

"And who taught me to spend money?" Rachel said, right back in her face. "All you ever could do for me was *buy things*. The only love you *know* is money."

"You never turned it down –"

"It's all I had!!!"

They both stood there for a moment, taking a breath, like two fighters between exchanges. Quite frankly, I was frozen. It was so ugly, so horrid. I sort of knew it was like this between them, but not this horrible. I looked over at Nanci. Tears were streaming down her face.

Eleanor looked at me with cold, angry eyes. I thought she was going to say something to me. Instead, she turned on Nanci. "How could you let this happen?" Eleanor spat at Nanci. "What's wrong with you?"

Nanci stood there, shaking in her bra and big, white panties.

"What?" Eleanor lashed into Nanci. "You lost your pea brain for a weekend?"

Nanci stammered back, "I'm sorry, it happened so fast."

"I thought I could trust you," Eleanor muttered. "You're as useless as she is!"

"Don't say that," wept Nanci. "I was gonna tell you, but –"

"Just be quiet!" Eleanor snapped.

"Please, Eleanor," said Nanci in a small voice, "I can't do this anymore."

"Just shut up," said Eleanor, taking two steps toward Nanci.

Nanci backed up, sniffing away her tears, "You were supposed to be gone all weekend. I try to do things right. I try to listen to you –"

"Shut up, Nanci!" implored Eleanor.

"I'm not perfect," sniveled the big girl, heaving her weight from one leg to the other. "I can only do so much."

"What are you talking about?" said Rachel to Nanci in a very steady voice.

Nanci cried in a tiny voice, "I try to do what you want –"

"Be quiet, Nanci!" ordered Eleanor. "Right now."

"What is going on?" asked Rachel, looking back and forth between Eleanor and Nanci, sensing that they'd been concealing something from her.

Nanci sniffed up her tears and said, "You think you're so smart, Miss Rachel Prince. But you . . . simply . . . aren't."

"Tell me what you're talking about, Nanci," demanded Rachel.

"I'm sorry, Eleanor," said Nanci, wiping off her cheeks. "But I can't do this anymore. It's been driving me absolutely crazy."

"*What* has been driving you absolutely crazy?" shouted Rachel.

"Tell her, Eleanor," said Nanci.

"You've already said too much, thank you very much," huffed Eleanor.

"What are you two talking about??" demanded Rachel.

"Well, Rachel," Nanci started, stifling a smile. "It's like this. You know how you and I hang out and talk all the time, and you tell me everything you do –"

"Well, not *everything*," Rachel interrupted.

"OK, not everything, maybe," Nanci accepted. "But we talk a lot. And you tell me a lot."

"Sooo . . . ?" asked Rachel fearfully. "So what exactly are you saying?"

Eleanor answered for her, "She's saying that she tells me everything you say. Nanci, you might say, works for me." She smiled triumphantly, her arms crossed in front of her. "I pay her a little every week, and she tells me everything you're doing, everything you're thinking, everything you say. Ev-er-y-thing."

I couldn't believe what I was hearing, and I could see that Rachel was completely dumbstruck. Things were spinning out of control, and yet I felt frozen and powerless to stop them. What was I going to say to them: *Stop being your true selves*?

"Rachel – ?" I called to her, but as she turned to me, Eleanor snapped – "YOU SHUT UP!" shocking the room into a moment of silence.

Then Nanci faced off against Rachel.

"It's so funny," Nanci said with a cruel smile. "You said that you *let* me be in your life? Babe, I'm *paid* to be in your life! It's not a lot of money, fifty a week, but it helps. My parents can sometimes be real pissy about my expenses. So after you go to school, I come over here, or Ellie comes over to my house –"

"*Ellie?*" I thought.

"And we talk all about you *all morning*," Nanci continued with savage delight. "I tell her every little detail about your life. Everything you tell me, I tell her. And we laugh about you. We make fun of you and all your antics. Your pretensions, your silly plans –"

"Not to mention your great love," Eleanor interrupted eagerly. "For this grubby little social climber." And she pointed to me.

Nanci rattled on with an almost ferocious glee, "We sit around my kitchen, drinking coffee, for *hours*. You might not know this, Rachel, but you are a source of amusement to a great many people. Even Pauline jokes about you!"

"What did she call Rachel?" Eleanor asked Nanci. "The Princess – The Princess of Pretend?"

Nanci and Eleanor laughed loudly at this memory.

"My favorite," said Nanci, gulping her laughter. "Is when she said" – and this was in a grossly fake Southern accent – "'*Mizz Rachel is about as deep as a puddle. But she think she's Niagara Falls!*'"

They exploded with guffaws as Rachel stood there, stunned and humiliated by what they were revealing. She still had the fireplace poker in her hand, and I could see her gripping it by the horse-head handle tighter and tighter as she became more and more overwhelmed by the twin attacks from her mother and her friend.

"What else did she call her?" asked Eleanor, her face merry with malice. "Miss –"

"Miss Easy Pants."

"MISS EASY PANTS!" shrieked Eleanor, laughing and swaying.

Nanci closed in on Rachel, saying, "Everything you ever told me about what you and he do in bed, every time he got to second base, and third base, when you were *late*, *everything* – *she* knew about it."

"You little tramp," sneered Eleanor. "I always knew you couldn't keep your legs together."

My whole body started to tense up.

Nanci got real close to Rachel and said, "I've had to listen to you condescend to me all these years. You don't hear how you sound, Rachel, but you really are a horrible little person. It's good you're seeing that therapist. Though I doubt that you'll ever become a truly nice person. *No offense.*"

I didn't know if Rachel was going to cry or going to hit one of them, or both. I should have reached for the fireplace poker earlier, and gotten it out of her hands, but I didn't.

"To tell the absolute truth, dear," said Eleanor. "*Nanci* is the daughter I should have had, she's the one I deserve. She is so smart and so talented."

"You don't have to say that, Ellie," murmured Nanci with what was clearly false modesty.

"Oh, and one more thing," said Eleanor sharply to Rachel. "Next year, you're going to Nassau Community, and staying right here with me, where I can keep an eye on you. Nanci even helped me fill out the application for you. She can forge your signature almost perfectly."

"Thank you," gloated Nanci.

Rachel was starting to breathe deeply, trying to hold back tears.

"More therapy will help you, Rachel," said Eleanor.

Rachel stood there, shaking. She sobbed, "I wish I had never been born."

Eleanor snapped back at her, "Well, that makes two of us, baby."

Rachel answered back harshly, "Anything that came out of your body would have to be evil."

With an instantaneous flash of her hand, Eleanor slapped Rachel across the face, hitting her across the cheek almost like it was a tennis forehand, swiveling Rachel's head straight around.

And that's when it happened: in a flash of rage and pent-up revenge, Rachel swung the fireplace poker, *whack*, right across the side of Eleanor's head, hard. And, in one motion, giving out this deep, almost animalistic cry, she struck her again on the back of the head as she fell to the floor.

Eleanor crashed face down, *wham*, onto the hard wood and didn't move a muscle. Not even a twitch. She just lay there where she fell. One last choking sound gurgled from her throat, then total silence.

No one said anything for a long, horrible moment.

Rachel, breathing hard, sobbed, "She asked for it. . . . She really did."

All three of us looked down at Eleanor in the purple pant-suit on the floor, not moving. We were afraid to do anything.

Nanci finally moved. She walked slowly, silently over to Eleanor and knelt down next to her. She tried to listen for some sign of breathing, then put her ear to Eleanor's back for a moment. Then she reached around to feel by her nose and face.

"I don't think she's breathing," said Nanci in a scared voice. She moved around the body and scrunched down on the floor to look into Eleanor's face.

"She's not breathing!" Nanci said, shaking Eleanor's body a little by the shoulder. There was no response.

Nanci shook her again, but Eleanor did not move at all. Nothing.

"You killed her," said Nanci.

I looked at Rachel. She was still holding the poker. It seemed as if it had become part of her arm or something.

"Rachel?" I whispered.

She said nothing. I think she was in shock, or something. She was licking a scratch on the edge of her hand.

"She – she was a good woman," Nanci wept. "And you killed her."

Silently I thought, *No, she wasn't*, but that was neither the time nor place to say it, now that there was this strange, new presence in the room: Death. Actual, real Death. And it froze us all. But only for a moment.

"You . . . you . . . evil, little –" Nanci raged, suddenly springing up from the floor, straight at Rachel.

She grabbed Rachel around the throat with both hands and slammed her straight up against the wall. Rachel's head made a thudding sound against the tropical wallpaper. In a crying frenzy, Nanci stood Rachel up hard against the wall and started to strangle her.

"You killed her!" screamed Nanci into Rachel's face, just a few inches away. "YOU KILLED HER!!!"

Rachel's face started to turn red as she tore at Nanci's hands, trying to pull them off of her throat. But Nanci, while not that much taller than Rachel, was about twice her weight, and she used it all to press against her neck.

"You stupid, evil – !" Nanci growled as she forced her hands tighter around Rachel's throat, standing her up higher and higher against the wall.

I have to admit, to no honor on my part (and do I really have to say that now, again, for the millionth time?), that I stood there virtually paralyzed through all this madness. I couldn't believe what I was seeing, almost from the moment that Eleanor had come in. It was all a living nightmare. On the one hand, it was mostly *their* fight; on the other hand, I should have done *something*.

Anyway, finally, I snapped back to the moment, found my legs, and ran to try to break them up just as Nanci heaved and took a big, asthmatic gasp, letting up momentarily on Rachel's neck.

Rachel instantly sprang back at Nanci, grabbing *her* around the throat and forcing her back across the room. Rachel lunged at Nanci and bit her hard on the cheek. Nanci screamed in pain, as they grabbed at each other's throats, struggling and spinning across the room. I jumped aside as they whipped around twice, then both of them fell to the floor, with Rachel on top of Nanci. They landed hard, very hard, onto the flagstone hearth by the fireplace. The back of Nanci's head cracked audibly against the sharp edge of rough flagstone. The sound was loud, juicy, and final.

Slowly, slowly, slowly, Rachel pulled herself up off of Nanci's body.

Nanci was lying on her back, her head at an odd angle up against the edge of the stone. Her eyes were open, but she didn't seem to be seeing anything. Her mouth was partly open, but she didn't seem to be breathing. There was a big bite mark on her cheek where Rachel had bitten her when they were fighting, and her arms were up over her head, palms facing up, as if she had surrendered to someone. There was a little trickle of blood that had started flowing slowly out from under her head. And she wasn't moving at all.

Rachel stood over her, looking down.

"I think she's really hurt," Rachel said.

"What should we do?" I asked, my mind blank.

Rachel thought for a very long moment, and then said, "I think we. . . let her die."

She turned to me and explained, "She betrayed me. And you. She was with Eleanor all along. Can you believe it? . . . This fat, disloyal pig . . . I was her only friend, and she betrayed me."

I looked at Nanci's body . . . and Eleanor's body, not more than twenty feet away from hers. It felt unreal. I had never seen a dead person before, much less two. Much less one killed by my girlfriend, and the other by Fate or Bad Luck or My Own Inexplicable Inaction.

I don't think I've ever heard "silence" like the silence that was in that room, at that moment.

Then Rachel spoke again.

"Why didn't you help me before," she asked. "When she was trying to strangle me?"

"What?" I said, a beat behind things; my mind still on the floor, with the bodies and the blood trickling, inch by inch away from Nanci's head.

"I'm sorry," I said. "I don't know: I just froze. I just . . . couldn't move."

Rachel suddenly bent over from the waist, gasping for air. I thought that she was going to throw up or something, but it was like she was choking.

I rushed over to her – at first, my legs felt powerless and slow – but I got there just in time to catch her as she pitched forward. I caught her arm as she slumped, and held her up, pulling her into my chest.

I held her tight. She was trembling, and so was I.

"What are we going to do?" I muttered into her dark hair, holding onto her so that we both didn't collapse.

We held each other for a very long time. Rachel felt small in my arms, as if she were trying to turn herself inside out and somehow vanish. Then, her whole body seemed to be become harder, more concentrated, in my embrace.

"'What are we going to do?' . . . I know what we're going to do," she said in a very even voice. "We're going to do what we *have* to do. To save ourselves."

I held her away from me, at arms' length. She was looking down; then she looked up at me directly.

"We're going to take their bodies out of here, and we're going to get rid of them," she said as if she were seeing the future. "And we're going to save our own lives."

I wasn't sure that I heard her correctly.

"We're going to take them out of here and drive them to a place where they'll never be found," she said.

"And where is that?"

"The Quarry," she said simply.

It took me a moment to connect her words to my memory of the Quarry itself.

"I've actually thought about this," she said, her eyes not focusing on anything: she was all in her daydreams. "How I'd get rid of Eleanor if it ever came to this."

I let her go on.

"I knew it could happen someday," Rachel said. "Not 'knew' so much as *felt* it could. If she didn't kill me first. There were nights when I swear I thought she was going to do it. Stab me, or something. You know about the cigarette burns. But there were the slaps and the pinches, all the time. *All* the time."

I think I said again, "What are we going to do?" but I'm not exactly sure of that fact.

Rachel walked a couple of steps and looked down at Eleanor's body.

"I can't believe this," she said. "This is . . . this is . . . *poetic justice* is what it is. This is what she got from pushing me and pushing me and pushing me, my whole life. It was what she . . . deserved."

Her tone suddenly intensified. "And then when she said that she had a big fight with Herb tonight! And a lot of people saw them! If she disappears, they're gonna blame *him*. He's a violent guy. It's almost too perfect."

"'Disappears'?" I repeated the word, not sure I wanted to follow her meaning.

"There are those swamps by the airport," she considered. "By Kennedy. That's where the Mafia dumps dead bodies, isn't it?"

"I don't know," I said. "I think so," not really thinking at all.

"But that would be too obvious," she said. "And too close to here. No, it has to be the Quarry. Just where we saw those Boonies dump all that stuff. You saw it! Stuff gets dumped into the Quarry all the time! No one cares. We'll just take them up there, and they'll just be . . . disappeared."

"'Disappeared,'" I repeated.

She tried to sound confident, but I wasn't sure of anything at that moment.

"Don't you see? The best thing is to get them far away from here! Far *far* away from here," she said in an urgent voice. "If we do this right, right now, no one will catch us. No one will evereverever look for them up there. No one will find out."

"And what happens when people come looking for Eleanor here?" I asked.

"We play dumb," she said. "We don't know anything."

"And what about *Nanci?*"

"No one cares about her!" Rachel scoffed. "Her drunk parents don't care about her! That's why they're always traveling someplace. I was her best friend, and you saw how she treated – no, sorry – *Eleanor* was her best friend. . . . So they disappeared *together*! We know that *Pauline* knew that they were involved."

Rachel was getting more animated now, thinking out loud, trying to get some sense of action into me. I admit that I was still in some kind of mental fog. Rachel saw that my eyes were straying, looking at Nanci's body on the floor by the fireplace.

"She *betrayed* me! And betrayed you!" Rachel said passionately. "All of our secrets, all of *your* secrets, she told to Eleanor. And Eleanor probably told them to Herb! Doesn't that just disgust you, to think that Herb knew all our secrets?"

I thought of Herb's raspy, knowing *"Don't be a sucker!"* in the parking lot of that Greek diner, and it made me heartsick.

"And she pretended to be my friend!" Rachel continued scornfully. "She'd work me up and get me to talk *against* Eleanor. *She's* the one who told me to ditch class to go see you. She drove me to the train that day! I think she *wanted* us to break up – no, more than that: she wanted us to really crash and burn."

"Crash and burn," I repeated.

"*She's* the one who kept the whole Eric thing going, just to make you jealous, just to put a wedge between us. ... What kind of a person is that? To give your whole life to revenge?" Rachel wondered.

We looked down at the two bodies. There was a pool of blood on the floor under Nanci's head, but it had stopped spreading. Eleanor's body just lay there.

"What are we going to do?" I repeated.

Right at that moment, we had a choice – *I* had a choice. We could have called the police, told them what happened, thrown ourselves on their mercy, and taken the consequences.

Or I could have listened to Rachel.

"I know what I'm *not* going to do," she said passionately, just inches from my face. "I'm not going to stay here and wait for the police. I'm not going to let my life be ruined. I'm going to do something to save myself. I am not going to let her win. I'm going to *fight* for my life, now that I'm free of her. And I am *not* going to any jail either, I'll tell you that. I've *been* in jail all my life. No, we're going to get these bodies out of here, we're going to clean up this place, and we're going to drive them far away from here. We're going to drive them up to the Quarry and dump them, and we're going to get away with this."

I don't think I ever heard her sound so sure of anything as long as I'd known her. In a way, this was the *realest* Rachel I'd ever seen.

"We've got to save *us!*" she said, grabbing my arm the way she did when she felt strongly about something. "And we can. We can!"

I stood there for I don't know how long – a few seconds? my whole life? – not wanting to think, wanting to go back in Time, be invisible, anything but what was actually happening.

"What do you want to do?" asked Rachel. "Leave them there until they rot?"

"I didn't say that," I said. I didn't say anything for a long moment. I don't know if I thought this explicitly, or if it was just in the back of my confused, shattered mind, but at that moment I had two choices: either walk out of that house, go to the police and tell them what Rachel had done, or stay there and help her conceal it.

"We'll do this properly," she insisted, penetrating me with those gorgeous blue-blue eyes once more. "We'll do this properly and then we'll be free forever. Free forever! You and me. Just as we always wanted."

So I stayed . . . and did what I did.

Record of Events #32 – entered Saturday, 4:44 A.M.

~

This was the plan. We would put the bodies in the trunk of Eleanor's Cadillac and drive up to Mooncliff – me, driving the Caddy, and Rachel, driving her Mustang behind me. We'd dump the Caddy in the Quarry and immediately drive back home in the Mustang. Put it all a couple hundred miles away and under water, and everything would be gone. Disappeared. As simple as that.

We got dressed and went into action.

"Watch out! Max is out!" yelled Rachel. "He'll track the you-know-what all over!"

The you-know-what was already all over the floor. Well, not all over. Actually, there wasn't that much, considering that there are eight pints of blood in the average human body. More useless *Jeopardy* knowledge.

Rachel had gone to the laundry room for cleaning supplies and accidentally let Max out. And, sure enough, the dog came running in and went straight to Eleanor's body. She had started to sniff at the leg of Eleanor's purple pantsuit when I scooped her up, well before she could sniff her way up the body.

The little dog turned in my hands and actually tried to nip me – the first time she had done that since that first walk on Buckingham-whatever-Terrace – but I held on. She squirmed and yipped. Maybe the animal in her sensed what had happened in the room, maybe not. But she was very squiggly and resistant as I ran with her back to the laundry room.

"Great," said Rachel, standing in the kitchen with a mop, a roll of paper towels, and a bucket filled with all kinds of cleaning supplies (Lestoil, Clorox, and a big bottle of Mr. Clean) as I whisked past with the wriggling Max. "Thanks."

I dropped Max gently onto the floor of the laundry room, said "Stay, Max!" as she scampered away, and shut the door behind her.

"Good dog," I said to myself, taking a breath.

A lot of what happens from here on in is, I confess, horrible. There are many other words for it, but "horrible" is an accurate start. It's what I would have said at the trial, if the Assistant D.A. had been smart enough and had gotten the chance to get it out of me on the witness stand. I don't really know why I'm saying it all now. I think it's because, finally, I have to.

I walked back into the back room, and Rachel was already on her knees, using paper towels to mop up the blood that had pooled around Nanci's head. Smart girl, she had on a pair of big yellow Playtex Living gloves to protect her hands. I saw that she was working quickly and methodically.

I said, "Be careful." Which was kind of a stupid, unnecessary thing to say, but she let it pass.

Without looking up at me, she said, "OK. What do you want to do with *her*?"

I knew she meant Eleanor.

"Well," I said. "Didn't you say we were going to put them in the trunk of Eleanor's Cadillac? I mean we're not going to sit them up in the backseat, right?"

I walked a little closer and looked down at Eleanor's body, still on the floor, still very dead. I hadn't really looked into her face. Her head had been turned away from me, face down on the floor when she landed, and I hadn't seen her face . . . until then.

She was never a pretty woman, to say the least. I think that was part of her hatred of Rachel: sheer jealousy. But in Death's odd kind of mercy, even with her face half smushed against the floor, she looked almost pretty. Her face was certainly relaxed, not screwed up and sour from the toxic feelings inside her. Whenever I met her, she always seemed bent on saying something cutting, something "witty." At least at that moment she seemed to be at peace.

"Where are the keys?" I asked.

"Give me a minute," she said, still kneeling by Nanci, wiping the floor with another paper towel and deliberately, with both hands, putting it into the big brown paper grocery bag that she had stood up next to her. Already the room smelled like bleach and ammonia combined. At that particular moment, it was a great smell.

I didn't want to rush Rachel or make her nervous, but I knew we had a lot to do before we got out of there that night, in terms of making things clean and presentable. And that was only temporarily: I knew we would have to do a lot more cleaning up once we got back. But if we really were going to dump the Cadillac in the Quarry and not be seen, we had to get there well before daybreak. According to the big, ugly clock over the mantel it was 10:45 p.m. I figured that we had about six hours before dawn. The drive was about three hours. We could definitely make it but only if we moved quickly and intelligently.

Everything I'm going to say from here on in makes me look bad. I mean, worse. I know that. I'm sorry, Counselor, but it's too late to stop now. Keep reading.

"We should put them in something," I said. "To carry them out to the car. So we don't track anything around here. Anymore than necessary."

Rachel straightened up for a moment and agreed, "You're right."

She carefully removed the Playtex gloves and carefully laid them on the edge of the brown paper bag, making sure they would stay balanced there, and not fall or touch anything. Then she sat back on her heels and sprang up to her feet, all in one motion.

"There's something in the garage, I think," she said.

I followed her out of the room toward the kitchen, where we could get out to the garage.

"How're you doin'?" I asked her.

"Good," she said, not turning around.

I didn't say anything else to Rachel. As long as she seemed "OK," I didn't want to open anything up by asking her anything other than what was absolutely necessary. *I* certainly didn't want to think too deeply about what we were doing: I just concentrated on *doing it*. And she didn't say anything either.

As we entered the kitchen, Max started to bark.

"Shut up, Max!" said Rachel as she opened the door to the laundry room, blocking the dog from leaving with her leg. "Stay!"

I scooted in behind Rachel and closed the door, keeping Max inside.

"Good dog," I said as I followed Rachel out the other door and into the garage.

It was cold in the garage. Well, cool. It was April, the cruelest month "breeding", and nights were still T.S. Eliot-chilly. It would be really cold up at the Quarry, but I put that thought out of my mind for the moment as I walked around Rachel's Mustang. Eleanor's big white Cadillac was parked on the far side, against the wall, waiting for me.

"I wish we didn't have to have the lights on," I said, worrying about who might see us from outside. Not that there were any neighbors nearby, but still, I was worried about *everything*. Which was the correct way to be.

"How are we gonna see?" Rachel countered, and she was right, of course. It was a dark, dark night out there.

Still, I thought about all the private security "rent-a-cop" cars I saw driving around her neighborhood at night, but kept that thought to myself. If someone came by, we would have to deal with that.

"There!" Rachel said, pointing to an upper shelf. "Those big canvas things."

I had to get a ladder, set it up, make noise, and take time, but I climbed up to where Rachel had indicated. Thank goodness there were no houses right near the Princes'; no pain-in-the-ass neighbors to see or hear anything going bump and scrape and bang in the night.

"These?" I asked, touching a piece of stiff, cream-colored canvas.

"Yeah!" she said. "Get those down!"

I pulled hard and two big things fell off the shelf, but they weren't that heavy. They were made of canvas and almost floated to the ground. I climbed down as Rachel was unfolding one of them.

"These are the covers that go over the loungers outside," said Rachel. "During winter."

She spread out one of the canvas covers; it was about eight feet long and three feet wide, open on top but with sides, to keep everything in.

"These are perfect!" I said. "Let's go."

We took the two covers back inside, through the laundry room, kitchen, and dining room. Nothing had changed in the back room. Eleanor and Nanci were exactly where we left them, not that I had expected anything else. But it would have been so nice if their bodies had miraculously vanished. No such luck. Not that we deserved any.

"OK," I said. "You take this one over by Nanci, and I'll deal with Eleanor."

I could see that Rachel was completely ready to defer to me on how to do what we had to do.

"OK," I repeated, trying to think, trying not to look like I was stalling, trying to stay in control of the situation for Rachel's sake (and, yes, Counselor, I know what I'm saying). "Help me lay this out."

After Rachel put one canvas cover by Nanci, she helped me unfold the other one next to Eleanor. It was stiff and crinkly, but when we got it open, it made a perfect vessel for moving what we had to move. Which were "bodies."

I knew I had to touch Eleanor, to move her into the pocket of canvas. I don't think I'd ever touched her, except for that first insincere, bony handshake at the Costa Brava. I looked down at her on the floor, mesmerized by her limp, loose-angled body, her half-hidden face, and by Death itself, still right there.

"Hell-eanor...Hell-eanor...Hell-eanor...Hell-eanor."

Four times I think I said her name. I don't know if I was apologizing, or trying to exorcize her evil soul, or saying a prayer, or conceding victory.

"Go on, baby," Rachel urged. "We have to do this."

Carefully I leaned over and took hold of both of her ankles, one at a time. She was wearing nylon stockings under the legs of her pantsuit, and her narrow ankles felt slippery in my grip. I moved her legs over onto the canvas while Rachel held it in place with her foot. Then I moved up to Eleanor's upper body. She was sort of on her side, sort of face down, so I had to change her position. That's when I saw the other side of her head, where Rachel hit her. It was all smashed in and creased with blood in her reddish hair. I think I saw a little bit of her brain, but then I made myself look away. I had already seen too many things that night that I knew I would want to forget. This was just one more.

Without trying to look too closely at what I was doing, I transferred Eleanor's upper body, holding her under the armpits, onto the canvas. I looked down at the floor under Eleanor as I moved her. No blood on the floor, but that didn't prove anything.

"You're gonna have to wipe over here after we move her," I said.

"I'm gonna wipe down *everything*," she said. "Believe me: *everything!*"

I looked at Rachel, and she seemed well-resolved and in control. Good for her. And good for me. I was going to need a focused Rachel to get this thing done.

When Eleanor was safely inside the canvas, I said to Rachel, "You should go get the car keys and get the trunk open."

"Right!" she said firmly. "I'll go get 'em."

She turned and walked straight out of the room.

I reached down and shifted one of Eleanor's legs, to get her more centered in the canvas. Then I tugged at the canvas. It would slide easily on the floor, but would that be a good idea? Shouldn't we carry her and not leave any traces of canvas thread or anything on the floor?

"Here!" sang out Rachel, jingling Eleanor's huge key ring with the black, shiny leather handbag in her other hand. "You wouldn't believe how much this purse cost . . . almost a thousand dollars at Bendel's!"

That's more than my father makes in a month, I thought, but didn't say. I stayed with the plan.

"OK," I said. "Go into the garage and open up the trunk of the Caddy. And tie Max up someplace. We have to go through there."

"Where should I tie her up?" Rachel asked.

"I don't know. It's your house. Find someplace!" I raised my voice a little, for the first time, I think. I saw the cold look on her face.

"You don't have to shout," she said and turned, walking back out of the room after dropping the thousand-dollar handbag on the floor.

"Sorry!" I said as she left, but really, I couldn't care too much about the tone of my voice at that very moment. Of course I cared about Rachel and how she was going to get through this, but for now I had to decide how to deal with Nanci.

I walked over to her body, lying against the fireplace stone. I tried not to look directly at her. She was still in her bra and panties. She was so big and smooth and pale. There looked to be some blood still under her head, but Rachel had cleaned up a lot. We'd have to do more when we got back, but it was a start.

I unfolded the other cover next to Nanci. She was about twice as wide as Eleanor. She'd fit in the canvas, easy, but carrying her might be another thing altogether.

"OK, what's next?" asked Rachel, coming back into the room with a determined spring in her step.

"Let's move Nanci into this," I said, standing by the canvas. "Then we'll take both of 'em out to the garage. OK?"

"Whatever you say," she said earnestly. "OK, baby?" I could see that she felt bad about yelling at me before, when she left the room, and wanted to make amends.

"Yeah . . . OK, " I nodded as I walked around to Nanci's head. "You take her feet."

Rachel took her place at Nanci's feet, splayed wide on the floor. Her body was wide and very still. I could see that Rachel froze when she started to bend down. She blinked, tried again, and still couldn't bend down.

"Wait," I said. "Let me do that."

I stepped down to Nanci's feet, and Rachel moved out of the way.

"Thanks," she murmured softly. "I can help, but I don't want to touch her. Is that all right?"

"Yeah," I said. She suddenly looked a little weak and lost. I didn't want her to come apart.

"Stand back a little," I said.

I stooped down and, one at a time, grabbed each of Nanci's fat, fleshy ankles. I think it was my imagination, but her body already felt cold. Colder than normal.

First the left leg, then the right leg, I lifted over the side and into the bottom of the canvas cover. Then I scooted back to her head.

I got a grip under her arms, in her armpits that were cold and moist, and hoisted her top half into the pocket of canvas. Or, let's say, I *tried* to hoist her. She was one heavy girl, and

I could barely move her off the ground. I slid her more than lifted her.

"Here," I called to Rachel. "Please! Help pull this under her."

Rachel quickly knelt down and pulled the canvas under Nanci's body that I was just able to get a little bit off the floor. It took a couple of tugs and grunts, but we got her into the canvas cover and pulled the sides up all around her.

I looked down Nanci's large, fairly shapeless body, so still.

"Now I see why she wore so many clothes," I said. "To cov –"

"Don't – !" Rachel cut me off. "Please. Don't say anything. Let's just get them in the car."

"OK," I said. I tried to clear my mind and be logical. "Put all her clothes in here. Her boots, her purse. All traces of her. Put her whiskey sour glass in too. *Everything*."

"How about the cards?" Rachel asked. "She touched the cards."

"The cards," I agreed. "Everything."

I got the whiskey sour glass, figuring out pretty easily, by position, which one was Nanci's, and picked up the cards while Rachel got her clothes and other things.

She dropped the clothes in delicately alongside of Nanci's body and put the boots at her feet. Then she picked up the big, fringed purse that Nanci always carried from the corner where "Eric" had dropped it.

"Nanci Jerome's famous suede purse!" said Rachel ruefully, holding it up like some kind of rare specimen. Then she walked back to the canvas cover and dropped it in.

"She still might have some clothes upstairs," Rachel said. "But I could explain those away. If I had to. 'She slept over last week.' There."

I put the whiskey sour glass in and tossed in the deck of cards lightly on top. The cards scattered and slid all over Nanci's body and clothes. I could see one card on top, right at the peak of her belly, almost covering her deep, dark navel: it was, I swear, the King of Hearts. The Suicide King.

"We have to move, baby," said Rachel. I guess I must've been looking at Nanci, daydreaming or day*nightmaring*, before she snapped me out of it. "It's getting late."

I didn't want to look again at the clock with no numbers over the mantel, but I knew that she was right.

"Right," I said. "Let's move Eleanor first. She's lighter."

"The one good thing about her," Rachel muttered, walking over to Eleanor to take her place at the foot of the canvas. How quickly could Rachel recover her Rachel-ness!

"OK," I said, going over to Eleanor's canvas and getting set.

I got a good grip on the two corners by her head, purposefully not looking down at Eleanor's body.

"You ready?" I asked, seeing that Rachel, copying me, had the other two corners tight in her fists.

"Yeah," she answered.

"OK," I said. "On three. One . . . two . . . three!"

And we both lifted the canvas up – it was surprisingly, pleasingly light – and started carrying it out of the back room.

"Great," I said as we shuffled the canvas as quickly as we could across the room, inches off the floor. "You OK?"

"Yeah," Rachel grunted, though I could see by the stretching in her neck cords and arms that it was a heavy carry for her. Rachel was strong, yes, but that's only strong *for a girl*.

We were out of the back room and halfway through the dining room when the telephone rang, scaring the hell out of both of us. I hate to say it, but we dropped Eleanor.

"Who is *that*??" I said.

It rang again, sounding even louder, resounding from the kitchen to the living room to the back room. They had phones all over the house.

I looked at Rachel. Her eyes were wide and glistening, blinking widely.

"Don't answer it," she said.

It rang again. We didn't move a muscle.

"Who do you think it is?" I asked her.

It rang again.

"Herb," she said.

It rang again.

"Then *definitely* don't answer it!" I said.

It rang again.

"I bet he's calling to apologize," I added.

Rachel said, "He's going to have a *whole lot* to apologize for when they think he killed Eleanor"

"Ssshh!"

It rang again. Wouldn't it stop??

"What if he comes over here?" I worried. She looked back at me with fear and uncertainty in her eyes.

"He *better* not come over here!" I said, right on the edge of panicking when it suddenly stopped. It didn't ring again. We waited a moment . . . no more rings.

"We better move," she said. "Fast."

She couldn't have been more right. We picked up Eleanor in the canvas and took her the rest of the way at double-speed, through the kitchen and into the laundry room.

We put Eleanor down as Rachel opened the door to the garage.

"You OK?" I asked when she regained her grip on the corners.

"Yeah," she huffed, "let's go."

We had to bend Eleanor a little to get her out the door and down the two steps to the floor of the garage, but we did it pretty easily. We had to carry her around the Mustang, and that made things tight.

"You should move this," I said grunting, meaning the Mustang. The weight of Eleanor swayed side-to-side and we bumped her into the garage door, but we got her past the Mustang.

"Wait!" gasped Rachel, putting her half of Eleanor down.

I put my half down too. Eleanor was pretty heavy, even for me, and Nanci would be even worse. We might have to *drag* her.

"OK," she said after a couple of breaths. "I'm ready."

We picked up Eleanor and carried her the rest of the way over to the Cadillac – Eleanor's beautiful, white Cadillac – with the trunk wide open, and put the canvas down on the cement floor.

"I'm gonna move my car," she said. "And open things up."

"Good," I replied.

I took her hand.

"You're like ice," I said, feeling her freezing fingers with both my hands.

"I know," she brought her other cold hand up to mine. "Don't worry. I'm fine."

"Me too," I lied.

I took her freezing hand in mine, and we ran back into the house to continue doing what we were doing, trying to think carefully and not think about it at all, both at the same time.

"I'll get my car keys," said Rachel as we went back through the laundry room.

"Where's Max?" I asked.

"Maid's room bathroom," she said, running ahead of me and through the kitchen.

I heard her run upstairs while I walked through the dining room to the back room, thinking that I didn't even know that there *was* a maid's room, much less that it had a bathroom.

The back room looked like a battle zone. Not that I've ever been in a battle zone, but I can imagine. The room was super quiet, as if Death had sucked all the life out of the air. Hanging over the whole room, over Nanci laid out in the big, tan canvas cover, was a palpable cloud of Nothing. Stillness. No life.

But I had to walk into this void, and do what I had to do, for Rachel.

I looked around the room. There was so much to do: Nanci to move, everything to finish cleaning up. We had to get everything ready for the long drive up to Mooncliff and then *finding* the Quarry because the only way to drive into the Quarry was from the Boonie side, through the forest, not from the Mooncliff side, the side that we knew well. With two cars. *And* two bodies. What the hell was I doing?

"OK," said Rachel, bouncing back into the room with fresh energy. "Let's keep moving."

"Right," I agreed.

"I'm gonna go get my car out of the way," she said, jingling the keys in her hand.

"Good idea," I answered.

"You finish up in here," she said, "Then we'll move her. And *then* we'll get out of here."

"Another good idea," I said as she turned and left the room again.

I looked around for more things to clean up. All of Nanci's stuff seemed to be in the canvas with her. I saw Eleanor's expensive purse on the bar and went over to get it. When I picked it up, it was surprisingly light, made of this very nice black lizard or alligator or something, with bejeweled clasps at the ends. It was really a fine piece of leatherwork, much fancier and more delicate than anything my mother had ever owned. I carried it over to Nanci's open canvas and was about to drop it in when Rachel came back in.

"Don't worry," she said, a little out of breath. "I took all the money out."

"Oh," I said. "Good." I guessed.

"Let's move her," said Rachel, approaching Nanci. "Then I'll clean up the rest, and we'll get out of here. We should already be on the road."

"I know," I said, taking my place at the head. "Come on."

I grabbed my corners, and Rachel grabbed hers.

Rachel said, "She looks so –"

"Don't!" I cut her off. "Please?"

"I was just going to say that she looks so pretty," said Rachel calmly. "That's all."

I had already seen too much that night, too many things I wouldn't want to remember: dead Nanci Jerome's pretty face was just one more of them.

"Ready?" I said. "On three. One . . . two . . . three!"

We hoisted Nanci in the canvas and started to carry her, but I could barely get her off the ground. Rachel's end, hardly at all. Nanci had to weigh over two hundred pounds: all those layers of clothing concealed quite a lot of person.

Rachel cursed. "What a load."

"OK," I said, regripping the canvas. "Do your best. We'll slide her if we have to."

"We have to," said Rachel, grabbing onto the corners of the canvas and lifting.

It was a relief that the canvas was good and thick because we had to drag, bump, and bounce Nanci into the garage over many different surfaces. If it had torn, I don't know what we would have done.

We finally got her into the garage and plopped the whole thing next to the Caddy, next to Eleanor.

"I wish we didn't have to have the lights on," I said, breathing hard. I was sweating a lot by now, but the cool air in the garage felt good on my skin.

"I told you . . . no one's going to see. We're *behind* the house," she said, breathing hard, too, her hands on her hips, bending over a little. "I don't know what we would have done if we hadn't had these covers."

"We would have done something else," I said, regaining my strength. "OK, let's open this door, and we'll get Eleanor in first."

"How are you gonna lift Nanci in?" Rachel asked.

"Just show me how to open the door, and I'll deal with Nanci later."

"I'll get the door," said Rachel walking away from me, back toward the door to the laundry room, "but we still have more cleaning up to do."

"I know!" I said, my voice echoing across the mostly empty garage.

Rachel said, "Sssshhhh!" just as I spoke, and she was right. I was waaaay too loud. The whole idea was to not attract attention, and there I was, not watching my big mouth.

"You're right!" I shout-whispered. "Sorry!"

Rachel got to the wall and flipped a switch. Behind me, the garage door behind the Cadillac abruptly jerked open and started to rise with a grinding of gears and pulling of chains that scared the hell out of me. Talk about being quiet!

Who knows who heard or saw what was going on? The lights, the noise at this time of night. We were so vulnerable, so easy to see. Fortunately, we were around the back of the house, or it would have been over (earlier) for us.

"OK," I said. "Let's do Eleanor first."

I got by the head of Eleanor's canvas, and Rachel took her place at the foot. I could see out of the open garage door: the black night was out there, waiting for us. We were just at *the beginning* of this madness.

"Ready?" said Rachel, her hands set at the corners.

"Yeah," I said, gripping the canvas.

"On three," Rachel said, usurping my job, but it was OK if she wanted to. "One . . . two . . . three!"

We raised her up and carried her around to the back of the Cadillac, wobbling and shuffling along the cement floor of the garage until we were right in front of the open trunk.

"Wait," I said, when I saw how high the trunk was, over the big chrome bumper. "Put her down."

We put her down quickly.

"What?" asked Rachel.

I looked into the trunk. Fortunately, it was, as I expected, huge. We would have no trouble fitting both canvases in there.

"Let me do this," I said.

I took a position at the middle of Eleanor's canvas and, in one motion, just picked the whole thing up in my arms and put her into the trunk. She was heavy as hell, but it was the only way to get her over the trunk gate. Rachel and I, wrestling two sides back and forth, would never have done it so smoothly.

I grunted hard as I dumped her in not too gracefully, but she stayed inside the canvas, and nothing fell out.

"Wow," Rachel said. "You're strong."

"You know that," I said to her semi-modestly as I pushed Eleanor's canvas toward the back of the deep, deep black-carpeted trunk, one side at a time.

"But now I do need you for Nanci."

Rachel groaned once. And she was right. Sorry, but we needed a *forklift* for Nanci.

It wasn't pretty, the way we got her into the trunk, and it took several attempts. I finally had to prop her top half on my knee while Rachel hoisted the bottom half onto a Flexible Flyer sled we had turned on its side. Then I could leverage her in, over the trunk gate. As I said, it wasn't pretty, or fun, or anything I want to remember. But the important thing is that we got her in and nothing fell out. No extra points for style.

"Thank God!" huffed Rachel as we finished tucking in the edges of Nanci's canvas, and pushing her all the way in next to Eleanor. They fit in easily, but it took some effort.

"Huge trunk," I gasped as I stood back, finished with this task.

"What do you think?" asked Rachel.

Catching my breath, I looked around. The garage floor looked pretty clean. I was sure that we must have left fibers and stuff as we dragged them to the Caddy – I didn't know anything about criminology then – but it looked pretty good in the light from the two bulbs on the ceiling in the middle of the night.

"Let's go take one more look," I said. "One last clean-up, get our stuff, and get the hell out of here."

"Excellent idea!" said Rachel.

"Turn off the light," I said, and she did just that.

As we fast-walked back through the house, I couldn't help but add, "We have a long way to go tonight."

"No kidding," she said with the same sense of dread in her voice that I felt in my gut.

Once we were back in the backroom, Rachel went straight for the cleaning stuff – the bucket, ammonia, Clorox, and paper towels – that she had been using before.

"Let me give it one more shot," she said, snapping on the rubber gloves. "Now that I can see everything."

With Nanci and Eleanor out of the room, it looked much emptier. But still, in a way, it was already haunted. I chose to ignore the ghosts. I made myself busy, picking up the other glasses and the pitcher of bug juice, and taking them back to the bar.

Rachel was scrubbing all the areas she hadn't been able to see before we moved Nanci.

"Try not to spread it around," I couldn't help but say.

She sat back on her heels and said, "I am trying my best."

I knew I said the wrong thing. I walked over to her and from behind, I could see that she had tears in her eyes.

"I'm sorry, honey," I murmured, putting my hand on her shoulder. "I know you're –"

"It's just the ammonia!" she declared, shaking my hand off.

"OK," I said, letting it go. I didn't want to push her. I needed her to be composed and controlled if we were going to do this insane, risky thing.

But I had to ask her another question.

"Rache', lemme ask you something else: Do you know how to get to Mooncliff? I mean, what roads and bridges?"

That stopped her paper-towel wiping.

She turned and looked up at me. "Yes. I mean, sort of."

"Well, which is it?" I said trying to keep my voice from tensing. "'Yes' which means yes? Or 'sort of' which means no?"

"Well," she said, trying hard to sound certain. "*Yes,* I *sort of* know the way. I've been *driven* there a million times over the years, and I think I could recognize the roads, but no, I can't tell you the exact names of the exact highways and everything! I mean I know you take a couple of bridges –"

"OK-OK-OK," I said. "This is what we'll do. I think I know the roads. I'll take the lead, and you'll follow me."

"That's what I was hoping you would say," she jumped to her feet and threw her arms around my neck, making sure that the rubber gloves didn't touch my back at all. What else could I do but put my arms around her and hold her tight, one more time? She was trembling with fear and adrenaline and need.

That's when I saw the fireplace poker with the horse's head, the one she used on Eleanor, lying on the floor by the wall. How I had missed it, I don't know. Maybe I hadn't *wanted* to see it.

I gently pushed her away from me and turned her toward the poker on the floor.

"Don't you think we should take the you-know-what with us?" I asked her.

"Oh, yeah," she said, somewhat absently. "Good idea."

I waited a moment and finally said, "Do you want to pick it up?"

"What?" she snapped. "You don't want to touch it? You don't want to leave your fingerprints on it?"

"No, I –"

"Fine!" she said, going to pick it up. "You're right. I guess it's my responsibility."

You guess? I wanted to say, but I didn't. Because I was being a loyal boyfriend.

"And I have the gloves on, right?" she said, picking it up carefully off the floor.

She looked at the spiked tip of the poker and then turned to me.

"How did *both* of them die?" she asked, with this look of pain and wonder on her face. "Isn't that just . . . astonishing?"

"We have to go," I said. "If we're going to do this."

"Wait a second," she said. "You haven't kissed me in forever. I think I need a kiss."

She looked small and frightened, transformed from that
confident, forceful, vital girl at that square dance.

"Here," I said, drawing her in for a long, numb, hopeless
kiss, while she held onto the *murder weapon* in one hand, but
didn't let it touch us.

It was the most unromantic kiss of our lives, and yet it was
necessary at that moment, to keep us going. A killer's kiss.

I took her hand and said, "Come on. Let's put this in the
trunk, make a final list, and then we gotta go."

"Whatever you say, baby," she said. "I totally trust you."

We ran out to the garage, almost lightheaded with excitement and terror, carrying the fireplace poker, the bag of used
paper towels, the rubber gloves, everything we could find that
might need throwing. On some level, I knew that we were
doing something "crazy" and trying to find logic and order in
it was doomed to fail from the start. But something crazy had
happened: *two* deaths. Maybe "crazy" was the only way we
were going to get out of it.

I flipped on the garage light – I had no choice – and we
took the poker over to the open trunk of the Caddy. I didn't
look at the two bodies face-on, wrapped in the two canvas
covers, but I knew they were there.

Rachel stood in front of the open trunk and looked straight
in.

"Is there anything you want to say to them?" I asked Rachel.

She thought for a moment. Then she said simply, "No."

She stepped forward, deliberately placed the poker into
the trunk, and stepped back.

"OK," I said. "That's it."

I walked forward and put the rest of the stuff in. I went
to slam the trunk closed, but just before I brought the heavy
thing down, I caught sight of Eleanor's eye, staring at me

through a dark crease in the canvas. Her "vulture eye" was most certainly dead, but I could see as clear as starlight that its owner was going to want revenge. Quickly I slammed the trunk closed, good and hard. Another thing to forget, even as I planned the next step.

"Come on!" I said to Rachel, who was still looking at the closed trunk.

"Right . . ." she muttered. "Sorry."

I took her hand and we raced back into the house. I made sure to turn off the garage light.

As soon as we got inside, Max started barking again. It was the last thing we needed. More noise, more attention.

Rachel said, "Please shut up, Max!" Then she turned to me, "I have to go upstairs, one more time."

"OK, do whatever you have to do, but we have to go. Do you have any paper and a pencil?"

"What?"

"Like a legal pad, or some typing paper. A spiral notebook. Anything. And a pen!" I added.

"Why?"

"I'm going to try and write down the directions on how to get to Mooncliff."

"But aren't I just going to follow you?" she asked, her voice tightening with real alarm.

"Yes, but I'm gonna try to write them down too. You don't have a map, do you?"

"A map?" she said.

"Yes," I repeated. "A road map. Of New York State. You know? Where we're going?"

"No," she said, "I don't think so."

I cursed.

"OK. Just get me the paper and pencil. And change: lots of change. For both of us."

"What do you mean, 'change'?" she asked.

"Change!" I said, raising my voice without meaning to. "Quarters! Dimes! Nickels! We're going to be going through,

I think, two maybe *three* toll booths, and we want to go through the *automatic* lanes, so no toll taker will be able to identify us."

"Wow," she said. "You're right. That's brilliant."

"No, it isn't," I shot back. "It's simply necessary. We must leave no tracks, no trace of our trip up there. Nothing at all! We'll take them up there, dump them in the Quarry, and –"

"They're disappeared," she finished my thought.

"Exactly."

∿

I sat down at the dining room table with the pink stationery and purple pen that Rachel gave me – it was all that she said she could find – took a deep breath, and tried to remember the way to Mooncliff. (Once I got to Mooncliff, I was pretty sure that I could find the Quarry from there. But first, we had to get to Mooncliff.)

I sat there, eyes closed, and tried to clear my mind in order to visualize the way to Mooncliff. Actually, to visualize the *map*: the actual road map – the blue and red squiggles on the green, thin, hard-to-refold paper. I closed my eyes and tried to see Long Island from above, from where we were on the South Shore. I knew that I could get to Rockaway Turnpike from there, which would get me to the airport, to JFK, and then I could get to the Van Wyck from there, which would take me up to some bridge – the Whitestone, I think – which would get me to the Bronx and off the Island. My father had a New York State road map – in fact, a bunch of roadmaps – in the glove compartments of both the Chrysler and the Ford. They gave them away at Shell stations. A lot of good they did me now.

I tried to remember the trip that Dad and I took up to Cooperstown a few years ago, to the Baseball Hall of Fame (where Rachel went on her Five-Days-Without-Me as chaperone on that stupid Senior Trip: the T-shirt she got me still exists), and recall the way we drove. I could just *see* it: getting across the Hudson on some bridge. And that would be the *second* bridge. And then there would *have* to be signs for the New York State Thruway. And that would lead me to Route 17, which was the way into Mooncliff Land. I *knew* I could find it. Whether Rachel could stay behind me the whole way was a whole other question.

I started to write down everything I remembered, as fast as I could, purple on pink.

"I'm ready," she said.

I looked up. She looked fresh and revived, in a new blouse with her purse hung from a strap on her shoulder, ready to go.

"Do you want one of Eleanor's uppers?" she offered, shaking a little pill bottle in her fist. "I don't think we want to fall asleep, driving there. And back."

"Did you take one?" I asked.

"Yes," she said. "And I advise that you take one too. Or three."

"No, wait a second –" I said, troubled by something else, something it took me a few seconds to resolve.

"Did – did you put on make-up?"

"What?" she said.

I repeated, "*Did . . . you . . . put . . . on . . . make-up?*"

I knew the answer to my question, but I wanted to hear what she said.

She looked me in the eye and said, "I'm sorry, but it makes me feel better. . . . Yes, I washed my face and hands, *and* combed my hair, *and* put on a little make-up. Is there something wrong with that?"

"No," I said, not knowing what else to say.

"So," she said. "Can we go now? . . . Please?? We don't have much time."

I stood for a moment, stunned. There she was, right in front of me, trembling with urgency. Her life was totally in my hands. She had made an enormous mistake, but I had to try to help her. Nothing I, or anyone, could do now would bring Eleanor and Nanci back to life, but maybe I could save Rachel. She's the one I loved and who loved me.

~

"I can hardly read your writing," she said, trying to read my directions in the bad overhead light of the garage, even though I had printed out her copy as neatly as I could.

"Then just follow me." Ready or not, we had to go. "I'll go slowly. If you need to stop, flash your brights. If *I* need to stop, I'll flash my right directional three times, so you'll see me."

"Don't worry, I'll see you," she said, reassuring me (and herself too). "Just don't go too fast."

"And remember, if we get separated, we're looking for the Route 17 exit off the Thruway. The Harriman exit. If we get separated, just wait for me after the Harriman exit. It's all on the paper."

"I know," she said. "You told me that already."

"And you're all locked up, and Max has food and water?" I asked.

"Would you stop worrying about the dog?" she said.

"You're right," I said, taking a deep breath, trying to clear my head in the cold night air.

I had two of Eleanor's pills in my shirt pocket. I didn't take one, but it was the smart thing to take them with me. We had hours of driving in front of us – there *and back* – besides what we were going there to do. I didn't even want to *think* about that.

"Do you have Eleanor's keys?" I asked, putting out my hand, looking at the huge white car with the dark cargo in its trunk.

"Here," she slapped the bulky, clanky key chain into my palm like a nurse handing a scalpel to a surgeon.

"You know," I said. "I've never driven a Cadillac."

She tried to stifle a laugh, but it came out, that musical laugh of hers.

"Sorry," she giggled. "But that is so – so – perfect."

I had to ignore her: it might have just been the pills.

"After you're done laughing, you think you can just help me back this monster out?" I asked.

"Sure," she trilled, trying to control her laughter.

"OK, I guess this is cool," I said uneasily, trying to get comfortable in the oversized driver's seat of Eleanor's Caddy and get a sense of the huge car's dimensions. The interior smelled like Eleanor's overripe, perfumed closet, and I wanted to change the air as quickly as I could, but all in all, it was the biggest, plushest, nicest car I'd ever been in. Standing outside my door – it took me a minute to find the switch that put down the driver's side window – Rachel quickly showed me where things were: how to work the lights and the directionals and the heater/air conditioner, how to move the *power* seats and the mirrors, and how to work the radio. There was one of those new 8-track players. It looked strange and cool, but Rachel told me to forget about playing it.

"All she has is Percy Faith and Montovani," she jeered.

"OK," I said. "Then we're outta here."

I turned on the engine, which inside the confines of the garage sounded like a Boeing 707 revving up for take-off. Then after I made sure that Rachel was clear of the car, I put it into gear, let up on the parking brake, and rolled out of the garage super slowly, checking the mirrors to make sure that I wasn't close to hitting anything, inching out into the middle of the night. I made sure that my headlights were off too. I didn't want any of the neighbors – or anyone around, some idiot walking a dog – to see us, and there was just enough light from the garage light and the moon.

Then Rachel turned out the inside garage light, and things got instantly darker, but there was still enough light to see by as my eyes adjusted. I waited, cringing, as she lowered the open garage doors, the chains grinding loudly for what seemed like forever. Then it was blessedly quiet. Then I heard the Mustang's engine turn over, and she *revved* the engine – twice! I should have told her not to, but I figured that she would have enough sense not to. Then, she turned on the Mustang's headlights, which made me even more nuts: the last thing we needed to do was attract attention to the house.

I frantically waved to her through the windshield to turn off her headlights, but she didn't see me. She just waited for me to take the lead, which was the plan. There was nothing to do but put the Caddy in drive and lead the way out of the backyard.

I rolled extra-slowly down the extra-crunchy gravel driveway. I was sure grateful that Manny Prince liked his privacy and there were no houses right around us, but I was still nervous as anything. It was late, but it was a Saturday night, and while there didn't seem to be anybody around right now, on the streets or awake in the houses, you never knew. . . . The headlights from Rachel's Mustang shone off the Caddy's rearview mirror and into my eyes. I wish she had followed my example and driven with the headlights off at least until we got clear of the house, but she didn't. We were in separate cars, and I had to trust that Rachel would have some sense and not do anything foolish for the whole, long way up to Mooncliff.

And so I turned out of the Princes' driveway in Eleanor's big, white, comfortable Cadillac and began the longest ride of my life.

Record of Events #33 – entered Saturday, 8:11 A.M.

~

Out of Rachel's perfect, silent neighborhood, I led the way, driving ever-so-carefully, stopping completely at every stop sign. Eleanor's Cadillac had a ton of power, so I had to go lightly on the gas pedal at first. Also, the brakes were very tight, and it took a few tries to get used to their stopping power: the car was so many thousands of pounds heavier than my mother's Ford or even the Chrysler. But jam down too hard on those brakes, and I'd be scraping myself off the inside of the windshield. Plus, I didn't want to have the things in the trunk rolling around and becoming undone. "Things."

When I got to the main drag in Oakhurst, I stopped at the first traffic light. Rachel was right behind me. I looked in my rearview mirror: she was there, right on my bumper. She could see that I was looking for her, and she gave me a tight little wave, then put her hands back on the steering wheel. She looked so good in that red Mustang. Candy. I tried not to think of what we were doing as the light turned green.

As I drove through Oakhurst, I kept trying to visualize the roads we were going to take to get to Mooncliff. I was pretty sure that once I got to Mooncliff, I could find the Quarry. We – by we, I mean people from Mooncliff – got to the Quarry by the trail from the end of the golf course, but other people, the Boonies, got there from the county road that ran between Boonesville and the next town over, a next-to-nothing hamlet called Loomis. There was some kind of a trail off that country road that went through the forest to the Quarry. We saw those

414   What It Was Like

Boonies who dumped garbage in the Quarry leave by that trail in a truck. There had to be access to it from the main road. I was sure that once I got up there, I could find it

I picked up my speed once we got to Peninsula Boulevard because I had to. There was some traffic on Peninsula, and I had to go the prevailing speed. To crawl along would make me stand out, and that's the last thing I wanted to do.

Again I checked my rearview mirror. Rachel was right behind me: perfect. She just had to follow me, and I had to try not to get too far ahead. I realized that my heart, which had been racing like mad since . . . well, *since* . . . was just beginning to slow down. I put my hand on my heart, and I could actually *feel* my heart beating through my shirt. I felt the two pills in my shirt pocket; I was glad they were there, "just in case." I took a couple of deep breaths and tried to relax. We had a long way to go, and I had to be absolutely in charge of the situation *for Rachel*. I was in the lead. I was the one who knew the way. Besides, I think I had enough adrenaline rushing through me to last for hours.

We headed down Peninsula. Again and again, I tried to see the map in my mind: Peninsula to Rockaway, past Kennedy, to the Van Wyck. The Van Wyck to the Whitestone Bridge, across the Bronx, which would somehow lead to the Thruway, and then upstate.

I looked behind me: Rachel was there, same as before, same spacing. Good.

For the first time, I felt relaxed enough to turn on the radio. Before, I didn't want to think about anything but getting on the road to where I was going and making sure that Rachel was behind me.

First thing, as soon as I turned on the radio, an antenna zoomed up automatically from the hood on the right side. Straight up into the air, at least three feet. And the radio reception instantly came in, strong and super clear. There must have been extra speakers in the back, and maybe even in the doors, because the sound was so enveloping. And, wouldn't you know it? Eleanor had on one of my Dad's stations.

Fairy tales can come true . . . It could happen to you . . .

Sinatra. My Dad gave me long lectures on the glory and importance of the man he called "Frankie" or sometimes even "Francis Albert." Really. And not just the songs and the singing, which are actually pretty good, but Ava Gardner and *From Here to Eternity* too. He was my Dad's generation's Dylan. So, of course, I had to turn to another station instantly. I didn't want to think about my Dad, or anything further than the road ahead of me, and Rachel behind me. I changed stations quickly and found some loud, stupid rock and roll. That immediately calmed me down.

Somehow the Mustang was now three cars behind me. (I shouldn't have let myself get distracted by the radio and all the dashboard lights.) But I signaled right, as we were coming up on Rockaway Boulevard, and checked to make sure that Rachel had seen me, even though she was going to be trapped at the red light. I looked back over my right shoulder, through the back window, and pointed vigorously with my finger, telling her to turn right.

Someone honked me – *beep-beep* – and I had to drive on. As I accelerated, I saw in my rearview mirror that Rachel had turned her right directional on: she had seen me. So I sped up and made the right onto Rockaway and immediately got over to the right side and slowed down super slow, so that she could catch up to me. I dawdled in the right lane until . . .

There she was! Coming around the corner. Great – she was right with me. I kept a slow pace until she fell in behind me. In the rearview mirror, I could see her give me that fast, *do-you-see-me?* wave that she gave me before, and I knew we were together. Then I sped up. Driving too slowly would be as conspicuous as driving too fast.

There was a lot more traffic now. We were getting near the airport, and there was always a lot of action near Kennedy:

people coming and going, twenty-four hours a day. I had to go faster and blend in with the flow of cars. I saw an enormous silver jet ahead of me, just taking off, cutting over Rockaway Boulevard and rising into the sky. How I wished I could be on that plane, no matter where it was going! I looked in my rearview mirror and didn't see the Mustang. In a flash of panic, I checked my side mirror, and there she was. In the center lane. The better to keep an eye on me, I think. I also thought that she wanted to go faster. I could see the cars stacking up behind her because she had to go slower than I was going. So I sped up. The Caddy has power in reserve, and the car surged forward with just the slightest pressure from my foot. Nice. And she was right behind me. We were on this wild, real-life amusement park ride – part house of horrors, part tunnel of love – and we couldn't stop now.

There was the turn-off for the Van Wyck coming up, which would take us to the Whitestone and get us off this damn Island. That was a good sign: the further we got from the Prince house, the better I liked it. I flicked on my signal, saw Rachel move in behind me, and drove on. We made the transition fairly easily. We were moving north on the Van Wyck, starting to cut up through Queens at a good clip. This was great: if this were rush hour, we'd be at a standstill, guaranteed. Instead, I had to keep my eye on the speedometer to stay under sixty-five. This engine felt like it could have done *a hundred-and-sixty-five*. I saw why people liked Cadillacs. Lots of room, lots of power, lots of comfort, a great radio, and a sense that you were safe inside, with the whole world locked out. Plus a huge trunk that could hold . . . anything.

All I had to do was keep the Caddy between the white lines and make sure that Rachel was behind me. She had my directions, which were proving to be surprisingly accurate, but it's hard to read purple-on-pink in the dark, in a moving car. The best strategy was to keep her in my mirrors and leave no doubt in my mind.

There was no reason for anyone to stop us. These were two entirely respectable, even enviable cars: a big, new white Caddy and a sharp, new red Mustang. Both cruising down the highway in perfect condition. People in the cars we were passing could look at us and think, "Wow. Those people must be really lucky."

When I saw the first sign for the "Bnx-Whitestone Bridge," I was so happy that I wanted to beep the car horn, to make sure that Rachel saw it. Lots of traffic now, but we were moving well, linked by an invisible wire of love. Even if a car or two would get between us, I would keep her in view, in one of my mirrors. Sometimes she would have to change lanes, or pass someone. I had to go around some idiot, who must have been drunk or something, going thirty-five miles an hour and weaving, endangering a whole bunch of cars, but Rachel saw everything, got around the drunk, and stayed with me.

We were really moving now. When I finally caught sight of the bridge at the end of a long curve in front of us, I could almost feel myself breathe easier. I felt in the armrest in the door for the buttons that controlled the power windows. There were quite a few of these little metal switches, but after some trial-and-error, I found a way to open the driver's window just a couple of inches, enough to imagine the smell of the ocean air to try to clear my mind. Anyway, I felt good as I went onto the bridge, the big towers in front of me, the black water of Long Island Sound below, and the red Mustang behind me. We were *finally* getting off Long Island.

As I moved toward the exact-change lane that was furthest to the right, I got my coins ready. (I had put my coins in my shirt pocket earlier: the other one, the one without the pills.) I briefly lost sight of the Mustang, but I had to keep my eye on the road. It would not have been a good thing if I crashed into a tollbooth.

I rolled slowly through the narrow opening at the booth and threw my change into the metal basket. The Caddy was so damn wide that I kept thinking I'd scrape the sides on some-thing, but the automatic gate flew up and I got through.

I turned to my left, to see where Rachel was. No Mustang. And on my right, parked on the side, were a bunch of police cars – and several cops standing outside their cruisers.

For a moment, I flashed: *What if Rachel's abandoned me? She could just drive off and leave me with what was in the trunk. Then, all the blame would shift to me! I was the perfect fall guy: the daughter's no-good boyfriend! Maybe I should just drive over to those cops right now, rip open the trunk, and tell them everything that had happened – everything!*

A car horn blasted loudly: there was someone right be-hind me. I looked left – there was Rachel, a couple of lanes over, looking straight at me. The car horn blasted again. I had to go; I jammed down on the gas pedal and shot ahead, throw-ing my head back against the head rest, zooming past the cops and away from the guy on my bumper.

I surged in front of Rachel and rocketed down the road, shaking off any doubt or hesitation, back in the lead. I bore down on the highway in front of me, trying to put that milli-second of uncertainty behind me. What was I thinking? Ra-chel and I were in this together. I had to believe that we could get away with this. If Herb had some kind of mob connections, it would be believable that he could be involved in a murder – especially if he and Eleanor had had a public fight that very night. But what about Nanci? Say she got in the way? It was too much to work through at that moment. And to face facts, I couldn't *undo* what had already been done. We were already in so much cosmically serious trouble – *serious* serious trou-ble – that all I could do was continue what we were doing and try to make the whole thing go away.

~

I kept a steady speed going straight across the Bronx. To-gether we made the tricky transition to the New York State

Thruway. It almost looked like we were going to drive onto the George Washington Bridge, looming in front of us, but I faithfully followed the signs, and we exited onto the Thruway, going north. I was fairly sure that this was the right way to Mooncliff – I *had* to trust the signs – but I was still nervous as hell. After all, I didn't want to stop and ask anybody anything. The whole idea was to be invisible.

We caravanned up the Thruway for a long, long time, over the Tappan Zee Bridge and north into Upstate New York. By now, there were fewer cars on the road, and my driving was slightly more relaxed, considering the cargo. It was mostly just trucks and the two of us. After a while, I could drive with one hand on the steering wheel. I realized that for the first hour or so, my hands had been positively *epoxied* to the wheel by anxiety. Now, out in the country, I could ease off a little. The Caddy was big and quiet and squishy. Eleanor's radio got great reception, and for a while, it was like driving in a moving concert hall. Then, I would remember what I was doing, shudder, and step on the gas.

I was sure that Rachel would remember that we turned off the Thruway at Harriman for Route 17. Right before we left the house, I told her, "Route 17. Remember Route 17. The Harriman exit." And she had it written down anyway. But as we got closer, I slowed down and signaled a good half-mile in advance of the exit so that she couldn't miss it. And she didn't; we exited together.

Without being too obvious, I tried to hide my face when I paid the toll taker at the exit booth: no exact-change lanes here. I was hoping that Rachel would think to do the same, but it would be hard for anybody – especially some dead-end guy in a dead-end job in the middle of nowhere in the middle of a lonely Saturday night – not to notice a beautiful girl in a hot red Mustang convertible, if anyone ever asked him about it. Talk about candy.

We were on Route 17; it was just a straight shot to Mooncliff and the Quarry and getting this thing over with. At least the first part of it. I was already thinking about what we were going to do and say when we got back to Rachel's. I had to ease up on the gas when I found that I was doing almost eighty on an open stretch of empty, easy-to-drive road. The Cadillac was so quiet that I vanished into the intricacies of my plan. The last thing I needed was to be stopped by some bored, curious, brave highway patrolman. That's when Rachel started flashing the Mustang's headlights. It took me a moment to remember that this was our sign to stop, our distress signal. As I just said, the last thing I wanted to do was stop; that could only attract attention. But she kept blinking the lights so I had to do something. The highway was pitch-dark, there was no one around, and the shoulder was pretty wide on this straightaway by a wide, dark meadow. I had no choice: the Mustang's lights were still blinking, so I figured that she must have had a reason. So I put on my right blinker and pulled off onto the shoulder.

Bumping heavily, I ground through the gravel, stepping down steadily on the brake to slow the heavy Caddy down. I had to practically stand on the brake to get it to a real dead stop. When I checked my mirror, Rachel was pulling off right behind me. I got out of the car.

It was good to step onto solid ground, even onto this gravelly, slippery asphalt. I stretched my body and looked up. The night sky was black with a million stars, pin-pricked into the velvet. I smelled that moist, new-mown grass smell of the country, and it threw me back to Mooncliff.

Rachel ripped open her car door, just as a car passed in the right-hand lane *waaay* too close for comfort for me. But Rachel seemed to ignore it, slamming the Mustang's door and running toward me. I could see that she was crying, with her purse flopping against her side by the shoulder strap.

"Oh god, oh god, oh god," she sobbed into my neck as she clutched me tightly. "Please hold me! Just hold me! I'm so scared!"

I put my arms around her quivering body and tried to comfort her.

"Oh, baby," I said softly as she trembled in my embrace. I held her tight, worried about her and worried also that someone was going to see us.

She pushed away from me and cried, "I was gonna drive off the road! I was going to smash into a –"

"Don't say it!" I said, pulling her close to me. "Don't!"

"I shouldn't have done it!" she sobbed. "No matter what they did, it was wrong to hit them like that. Nanci was an accident, but I hit Eleanor. I did. Hard. And she was wearing the Hermes scarf that I got her for Christmas!" She fell against my chest, breaking down in wordless sobbing.

I held her and rocked her gently, all the time afraid that some highway patrolman or pain-in-the-ass Good Samaritan would come along and start asking questions, all the while wondering what the hell "*Err – Maze*" meant. I realized that I didn't even have the registration for the Cadillac if someone asked me for it. Maybe it was in the glove compartment, or maybe it was in Eleanor's purse, in the trunk. I certainly didn't want to have to look for it there. I wanted to get back in the cars and get on our way.

But I held her close as she cried. A few cars were passing us. I could see the drivers slowing down slightly to stare at us as they went by.

"Let's talk about this later," I said gently but with some urgency in my voice. And sympathy.

"I don't want you to hate me," she wept. "For getting you into this. I couldn't help it. It just happened. I wanted it to happen, but I didn't mean for it to happen this way. It just happened. It wasn't supposed to be this way."

I looked into her eyes and told her the truth, "You know I'd do anything for you."

Her tears held back for a moment, and she said nothing, grateful and pitiful beyond words.

"Let's go," I said.

She turned silently and went back toward the Mustang. I got back in Eleanor's Caddy and got us back on the road to finish what we started. I refused to think about what had just occurred; it was too late for thinking.

~

It wasn't long before I started seeing Mooncliff-Boonesville-familiar landmarks: Billboards for the Old Pocono Inn and fishing boat rentals and the racing season at Goshen. Propane sold here. Ruby's Bed & Breakfast. Rachel was steady behind me as we pulled off Route 17. Now I really had to concentrate and try to remember those few rides in Stewie's Super-Coupe and the Mooncliff bus on these look-alike country roads that got us to Mooncliff. I slowed down at the exit and willed my memory to recall something/anything. Rachel was right on my bumper; I had to go *some* way. I turned left.

After a few hundred cautious yards, I saw a billboard for the Memorial Day Festival at the Boonesville Regional High School, "Home of the Spartans," and I knew that we were going in the right direction.

Every turn seemed more and more familiar as I grooved along the winding, two-lane blacktop, with Rachel following behind through the absolute-pitch-black night. It was as if I were being magnetically *drawn* back to Mooncliff. (Funny, if I ever actually showed up at Mooncliff, Stanley would probably have me arrested for trespassing or at least have me escorted off the grounds. Can you imagine what he would think if he knew what we were doing now?)

I sped up a little, to avoid more thinking. Somehow, I *knew* these roads. Bailey's was around there somewhere. If I got to Mooncliff, I knew I could find Bailey's from there. Of course, we were going to the Quarry ... and immediately back to the Island. We couldn't let anybody even *see* us around there, especially in these two fairly conspicuous cars. We would just do our business and go straight back to Rachel's house: to clean up more and decide exactly what to do next. Like how long should Rachel wait until she called the police – or Manny first, maybe – and say, "My mother is missing." It was too horrible to contemplate; I was living an open-eyed nightmare, yet I felt that I had to go on with it. I had to follow through with what we'd started and somehow try to make it right. Eleanor and Nanci were gone; all I could do now was try to save Rachel.

With every sign on the side of the road – for the Kandy Kitchen, for the monthly Rotary Meeting at the American Legion hall, for "Bait – 100 yards ahead" – I knew we were getting closer. Then I saw a green-and-white "Camp Mooncliff – ½ Mi. Ahead" sign, and my spirit felt a jolt of joy. To make sure that Rachel saw it, I beep-beeped the Caddy's horn lightly. Once I was at the front entrance of Mooncliff, I felt pretty sure that I could find the fire road into the forest that led to the Quarry. At that moment, "pretty sure" was the best I could hope for.

I pressed all the switches in the armrest and opened all the power windows. The smell of Mooncliff came flooding in: clean, cold, fragrant night air that kicked me into a new level of alertness. I told myself that I should probably take one of the pills in my pocket for the drive back. *I* would drive the Mustang back to the Island, not Rachel, so I couldn't let myself fade. We still had so much to do. I turned off the radio; the reception was lousy anyway up there, and I had to concentrate. I could *feel* that the entrance to Mooncliff was somewhere around there.

There it was! The big Mooncliff entrance sign – in all its green-and-white, log-framed glory! I gave another tap to the horn, for good luck and to make sure that Rachel saw it. She beep-beeped the Mustang horn back to me as we drove straight by the entrance and on to our *real* objective.

I slowed right down and tried to imagine the landscape of Mooncliff from overhead: an eagle's-eye view. If the entrance was *here*, and the entrance road led back *that way*, that meant that the campus was set *this way*. I mentally flew over Mooncliff, over the Mess Hall and the flagpole, over the ball fields and the Rec Hall, down to the end of the pitch-and-putt golf course, down the old railroad trail that led to the Quarry. I tried to *see* where the trail wound through the forest to the Quarry, which should be . . . *that way* . . . someplace down this stretch of highway.

I went even slower now, looking for the break, any break, in the trees. Rachel was right behind me: too close. I put my hand out of the window, palm down, to tell her to back off. I *had* to find the trail before we passed it. If not, we'd have to double-back on the other side, and then we could really be lost. We could wind up searching this dark edge of the forest forever, or at least until morning, and then we would be seen. We couldn't let that happen.

I turned on the Caddy's brights and slowed down almost to a crawl. It *had* to be somewhere along there. Boonies used this road all this time; there had to be a way in. Rachel started to flash her headlights, but I couldn't stop. I knew we were someplace close, but if we couldn't find the way into the Quarry, we might as well have been a thousand miles away. And I still had Eleanor and Nanci in the trunk. But what if Rachel was having another crisis? I was starting to – I don't want to say – panic, but I was losing my ability to focus on the road *and* the forest's edge *and* what might be going on with Rachel behind me. My hands gripped the steering wheel tightly, but they were starting to shake.

Rachel blew her horn at me twice and kept blinking her headlights, distracting me even more, *and* potentially attracting attention if someone should come along, which was the last thing we needed. We *had to* find this place *now*, or we were totally screwed. Finally, when she wouldn't stop blinking and honking, I had to stop the Caddy and lean out the window to tell her to be quiet.

"It's back there!" I heard her yell over the hum of the Caddy's engine. "It's way back there on the right!"

I gave her a "thumbs-up" to show her that I heard her and made a stirring motion with my index finger in the air, signaling to her that we should turn around. Thank goodness that she saw the trail into the Quarry (assuming that she saw correctly). Thank goodness that *one of us* did.

Rachel led the way, driving back down the road, crossing over, and bumping down onto the shoulder. The entrance to the fire road was behind a guardrail, and it was set way back from the shoulder of the road and under the trees at the edge of the forest. I don't know how I missed it. Slowly, she steered the Mustang *around* the guardrail, off the paved surface, and into the opening under the trees. I watched her as she navigated the way deliberately, bouncing and pitching through the high grass. I simultaneously watched her *and* the road behind us, looking both ways, hoping/praying that no one was coming. For the time being, we were OK: blackness in both directions. The only light in the night came from us and the stars far above.

The Mustang disappeared into the forest. Slowly, I rolled the Caddy off the shoulder, onto the grass, and immediately scraped the bottom of the car loudly on the jagged edge of the asphalt. I gave the car more gas, dragging it over rock, my teeth grinding agonizingly from the grating sound. But I rebounded with a roll, back onto the grass, and followed Rachel onto the track through the opening and deep into the forest.

The Caddy bounced and jolted me along the weed-choked trail, still on that house-of-horrors-tunnel-of-love-ride-to-oblivion. I could see Rachel's red taillights a ways in front of me, so I knew the path was bending to the right. I could just feel it: we were almost there. As the Caddy jounced and scraped along the trail, I tried not to think about what was being tossed around in the trunk, just a few feet behind my head. And suddenly I had one more terrible thought: What if there was *another couple* at the Quarry? Or several couples, just like we saw that day, swimming and diving off the edge? OK, it was very late, after 3:00 a.m. according to the clock on the Cadillac's dashboard, and cold outside, too, but there still could be lovers like Rachel and me, Boonies who needed a place to be alone. It was cheaper than a motel and twice as romantic. Of course, we weren't exactly there for romance. So for those last few yards of trail, I felt this awful dread: What if someone was there? We just couldn't allow ourselves to be seen. I didn't want to have to explain anything. What could we say?

Suddenly, the trees ended, and we were in the clear. Rachel's car was ahead of me, with the open night sky and the huge expanse of the Quarry spread wide in front of us. But most importantly, no one else was there. We were completely alone. No other cars, no other couples. Finallyfinallyfinally, we were here. It was just us, the Quarry, and the vast, empty black night.

Record of Events #34 – entered Sunday, 5:43 A.M.

∿

"We made it," I said to myself as I turned off the Caddy's engine and slumped over the steering wheel: thankful for getting there, thankful for being alone, and thankful for the silence.

After a moment I pulled myself up, got out of the car, and closed the door. Everything was quiet around me, except for some forest sounds and the faint buzz of some cars in the distance. I saw the Mustang, but I didn't see Rachel.

"Rachel?" I called softly. "Rache'??"

I heard footsteps behind me, and I turned quickly. There she was, walking back from some bushes.

"I had to pee," she said. "I had to pee for the last hour."

"Good idea!" I said and ran off to the bushes.

"Thank God I had some Kleenex!"

When I got back to the cars, Rachel was standing on the edge of the Quarry. I could see nothing but immense, dark, open space beyond her.

"Be careful!" I said and walked up to stand next to her.

"It's still so beautiful," she said, gazing out on the full scope of the Quarry, eerily just visible in the starlight: the rough boulders and tall pine trees all around, the sheer walls of cut bluestone, and the dark water far, far below. At least a hundred feet. Across the water, I could just make out the little clearing and the flat boulder where we'd sat when we approached the Quarry from the Mooncliff side.

I pointed it out to Rachel. "That's where we used to sit. That's where we saw Bambi's mother, remember?"

"But now we're *here*," she said, pulling my hand down. "You know we have to do this."

My God. It hit me again. The reality of what we were doing there. Throughout the long drive up, I tried to keep out of my mind *the reason* for the trip. Now that we were there, there was no way to avoid the fact. Not that I liked Eleanor Prince one bit, but she was a human being. And Nanci? Poor Nanci Jerome. I actually did like her, and I thought that she liked me: So why did she do such bad, weird things to me and to Rachel? Rachel, her friend, whom she supposedly liked for so many years? And if she didn't like Rachel, then why did she hang out with her? And why did she rat us out to Eleanor? Continually? And break confidence after confidence? That was unforgiveable. Maybe not a killing offense, but it was a wrong thing to do. Hurtful *on purpose*. Still, for everything, at that moment if I could have wished them both back to life, I would have. In a broken heartbeat.

"Come on!" Rachel said. "The sun's gonna come up soon. Where do you think is the best place?"

"'The best place'?" I repeated.

"To dump the car over the edge!" she said. "Don't forget what we're doing!"

She shook my arm and looked at me in the face, to jar me back to the present, a present I didn't want to be in.

"We can't *unkill* them now," she said. "What happened, happened. We just have to make the best of it now, right? Come on! You have to save us!"

"You're right," I said vaguely, not really hearing her clearly.

"Stop thinking, and *focus*!" she said then she walked closer toward the edge. "I'm trying to remember . . . What about over here? It's all deep, isn't it? It's just a big junkyard under there, right?"

"I guess so," I said, reluctantly thinking about what the next steps were.

"I bet if we can get it to go off the edge right here, the water's deep enough that it'll just fall in and sink and disappear," she said. "What do you think?"

"What do *I* think?" I echoed. "I think we should do what you say." My mind was so filled with contradictory thoughts that it went almost blank. So many horrible choices presented themselves to me, including jumping off the edge myself, that I could make no choice at all.

"This is right where those Boonies jumped off, right?" she said. "So we know that it's deep here. . . . Are you listening to me? Please?"

"I'm listening," I said.

I was thinking how far down it was, all the way to the water. The first light of dawn was just edging up over the hills, and I could start to see things more clearly. The Quarry was bigger than I remembered it; the drop from this end to the water looked enormous. The Boonies who jumped from a cliff of this height to impress their girlfriends were absolutely wacko. But if they could jump from this height and not hit bottom, it should be deep enough to swallow Eleanor and Nanci, the Caddy, and maybe this entire night.

"You should get a big stick," she said.

"What?"

"To push down on the gas pedal."

She mimed a stabbing gesture with both hands. I understood what she meant.

"You don't want to go over in the car *with* them, do you?" she said.

"No, I don't."

I walked over to the edge of the clearing, to where the tall trees began. It was still hard to see things on the ground clearly. I stumbled around, looking in the grass, searching it frantically like an animal. I kicked around some leaves and found a thick branch lying on the ground by an old log. I pulled it up and shook the dirt off of it. It was about the size of a hockey stick but a little heftier. I stripped a couple of twigs off of it and felt its weight. It would do.

I walked back to the cars where Rachel was standing.

"Do you know what you're doing?"

"No," I said, but I kept moving.

At this point, it was as if I were watching myself do these things: Slowly, methodically, and devoid of emotion I went back to the Cadillac, put the branch down on the ground, and got into the car . . . turned on the engine with the ignition key, with Eleanor's giant key ring dangling and jingling . . . pressing down on the foot brake, I took off the parking brake and shifted the car into drive . . . I opened the car door a little ways, so that I could see the ground . . . gently, I let up on the foot brake, letting the car roll forward, toward the edge of the cliff . . . "BE CAREFUL!" Rachel yelled . . . playing the brake, I inched the Caddy forward slowly . . . Rachel shouted again, "WATCH THE EDGE!" . . . When the car was about ten feet from the edge, I pressed down on the foot brake, put the car in park, and put on the parking brake.

Through the open door, I said to Rachel, "Do you want to look in the trunk one more time?"

"Why?" she asked.

"To say goodbye."

Shaking her head, she said, "Uh-uh. I said my goodbyes a long time ago."

"OK."

I watched myself lower all the power windows, two at a time. I opened the door and let it swing open as wide as it could go. Carefully, I got out of the car, dashed back to where I had set down my big branch in the wet grass, and ran it back to the Caddy. Super carefully, I placed the branch into the car until one end of it rested against the gas pedal: the smell of gas poured out from under the Caddy until I thought that I was going to pass out.

"*Do it!*" shouted Rachel.

Moving like a ghost or Fate or anybody but myself, I released the parking brake with my hand and carefully reached under the steering wheel. Holding my breath, I shifted the car into drive and pulled back as it started to move – I grabbed the branch and stabbed down on the gas pedal with it.

The Cadillac instantly shot forward as I spun away, inches from the back wheel, tumbling in the dirt. I looked up just in time to see the car go over the edge. Rachel darted forward as I scrambled to my feet, running up next to her. She clutched my arm with both hands as we looked down just as the Caddy hit the water with an enormous crash-and-splash. It sounded like a bomb, the impact echoing around the Quarry, again and again and again and again.

Then . . . silence.

We looked down. It was still kind of dark at the water's surface far down below us, and it was hard to see, but when the splashing cleared, we saw that the Caddy's back end *hadn't gone all the way under the water*. The car stood there on its front end, half-in, half-out, with its fins sticking straight up in the air, well above the surface, not moving at all.

"Ohmygod," Rachel whispered. "It's not sinking."

I waited for the car to start to sink, but it didn't.

"It must have landed on top of something," I said, not taking my eyes off the Caddy, its shiny chrome bumper glimmering in the dark, as it stood there above the water. "A boulder . . . or something . . .

"I opened the windows," I continued. "It should fill up with water, and then sink."

She squeezed my arm even tighter.

"It's *got to!*"

"Everyone can *see* it!" Rachel whispered. "What are we gonna – ?"

"Just wait!" I told her, putting my hand on hers.

We held our breath and, just as I had planned/hoped, the Cadillac slowly, slowly, slowly started to pitch forward as the car gradually filled with water. We both leaned forward, as if we could help it fall over.

"Go! . . ." said Rachel. "*GO!!!*"

And finally the Caddy tipped forward with a splash – roof down, wheels up – floating for a long moment on the water, listing back and forth, then disappearing into the blackness. A cloud of enormous bubbles came up to the surface and burst, one after another. We watched as the water gradually re-leveled and became absolutely still. Everything became calm again; nothing protruded above the waterline. No tires, no bumper, no fins: nothing.

"It's gone," said Rachel. "They're gone . . . *She's* gone. . . . I can't believe it."

I believed it. I started to shiver. I don't know if it was the cold air of dawn or what.

"You're shaking," she said, turning me by my arm. "Here, hold me."

"Can we get out of here?" I asked.

Rachel turned my face so she could look straight into my eyes and said, "Now I know that you truly love me."

"Yes, I do," I said, not wanting to think about anything. "Now can we get out of here?"

She wouldn't move, holding me by my arms. "We'll get past this, baby," she said. "And everything will be all right. Now that *she's* gone, we'll be free."

"We *have* to go," I pleaded, not wanting to hear any more of her plans. "Do you want me to drive?"

"No," she said. "I want to. You've done everything."

"Yes, I have," I said. "I've done everything. I was your lapdog. Just like I've always been."

"Oh, don't say that!" she said, grabbing me by the arm. "Don't you believe anything Nanci said! You know she was a liar and always was really against us!"

"I suppose so," I said, unable, as usual, to forget anything.

"No 'suppose so'!" she said decisively. "Come on! We've got to get home. We don't have much time. We've got to give that floor another good scrubbing. The cleaning lady comes on Monday. I wonder if Max would lick –"

"OK-OK-OK! Can you please just stop for a second!" I implored her.

"I'm sorry," she said dispassionately. "But didn't you say that we had to keep moving? Mr. Ivy League is never wrong."

She pivoted and walked away from me, toward the Mustang. Wasting no time, I ran and got in the passenger's side.

"OK, let's just go," I said, as I settled into the seat. It was pretty light now. People would be starting to go to work, and trucks and cars would be on the road. Wait, it was *Sunday* morning; people would be going to *church*. We definitely had to get out of there.

She slammed her door closed and put her key in the ignition.

"This never happened," she said confidently, turning on the engine, flipping on the headlights, and shifting into gear.

She gave it gas, made a wide circle, and found the trail in the dark trees that would lead us back through the forest, and away from the Quarry forever.

"This never happened."

The Mustang rode low to the ground, and Rachel scraped the bottom as we dipped down into the deep ruts of the trail, even worse than the heavy Cadillac. I thought I saw the reflection of some animal's black eyes in the light cast by Rachel's headlights. She swerved the car and the bottom scraped again, making a ripping sound.

Finally, I said, "Do you want me to drive?"

"No, I don't," she said, sounding annoyed. "I can drive perfectly fine. Didn't I follow you all the way up here? Which wasn't the easiest thing in the world. You're no great driver yourself."

"It was a brand new car," I protested. "One I had never driven before."

"I know," she said tartly. "You'd never driven a Cadillac before. You told me."

I didn't say anything as we slowly rambled along the bumpy trail.

"The thing is," she continued. "We're in this together now – like in The Zone. And this will keep us together forever."

I knew that she was right about that, but The Zone never felt like this before.

"If we just keep our story straight," she said. "We'll be fine."

"And what *is* our story?" I asked, my voice sounding far away from me.

"She never came home," said Rachel firmly.

"'She never came home,'" I repeated.

"Anybody asks us anything," she said. "She never came home. '*I don't know what you're talking about.*' All the way on the drive up, I rehearsed what I'd say. What *you'll* say."

"Then how did her car disappear?" I asked.

Rachel paused.

"OK," she recited innocently. "She must have come home for her car, but I never saw her, Officer.'"

Through the trees, I could see the highway coming up in front of us. We were almost out of the forest now.

"You've been thinking about this for a long time, haven't you?"

She just smiled and watched the road. "From now on, everything is going to be much, much better."

She looked sure of herself, gripping the wheel. I wanted to believe her, but I couldn't help thinking about what we'd left behind, under that black water. And back at her house. And everything.

"Be careful when you come out," I said. "I don't want anyone to see us."

"No one's going to see us," she said. "We . . . are . . . invisible."

She gave the car some gas and rolled up to the end of the trail. It was light now. The first rays of the rising sun were filtering through the trees. The dawn of a new day: I could definitely use a new day.

We looked both ways out onto the highway. No one seemed to be coming, either way.

"I think we're good," I said. "Go."

Rachel gave it gas and spun some gravel as she drove from the end of the fire road across the shoulder. She steered around the guardrail erratically and onto the road with a big bump, but she made it.

"There!" she said when she got the Mustang up onto the blacktop. She floored it, and the Mustang took off, fishtailing down the road.

I took a big, deep breath. I couldn't believe it. We actually were finished. This horrible task, something that seemed so insane and awful to do, was over.

But as we drove away, I felt no real relief. My life had changed, and nothing would ever, ever be the same again. The morning light was beginning to burn through the early mountain mist, and I was just beginning to realize how bone-tired-exhausted I was, inside and out. Maybe I should take a hit of that speed.

"So where do you want to go for breakfast?" Rachel asked. "How about some Atomic Brittle at the Kandy Kitchen?"

For a moment, my mind blanked.

"Are you *insane*??" I said, turning in my seat to her.

She just laughed at me. I should have realized that she was joking, but it really wasn't a time to joke, was it? I felt all hollowed-out inside, and she was driving her Mustang happily down the highway, as if nothing had happened.

"Don't you have any heart?" I asked her.

She looked straight ahead and said, "Oh, baby, baby, baby . . . You know they cut that out of me a long time ago."

I saw a tear form in the corner of her eye. But it would not fall.

After a moment, she said firmly, "But it's just like you said: *just* like you said. 'We're going to do everything right.'

You said that a long time ago, and I believed you. I believe everything you've ever said, and you were right all along. And now, for the first time, I feel free. Really free."

She was laughing and crying at the same time.

"This is what I've been waiting for. I won't have to worry about Eleanor yelling at me, or trying to control every inch of my life. And *Nanci*! That ungrateful pig, *spying* on me the whole time, after all I did for her! Can you imagine? And Manny? He's actually going to be happy! I mean, he'll be shocked, at first, of course. But when he realizes that he's not going to have to pay alimony anymore to that witch . . . Dammit, I might get to trade this in for a Corvette!"

She drove on, tears streaming down her cheeks, speeding up and taking the curves with ease.

"You'll see," she said, her voice breaking with bravado. "We'll get through this: we'll forget about this, people will forget, and we're going to be all right."

I felt a deep emptiness inside, where there used to be what I thought was the purest love, and said, "No, we're not."

That's when I looked in the side view mirror on my door and saw what I knew I was going to see eventually, but not really so soon: a police car was following us. At first glance, I thought it was my imagination, but no, it was real.

"There's a police car behind us," I said.

Rachel flinched.

"No," Rachel said. "He's not following us. I'll slow down a little."

She let up on the gas pedal, and the Mustang died a little.

"They can't be after us," she said. "We can't be seen in The Zone."

But the cop stayed right behind her. He was definitely on our tail.

"You know I can lose him," Rachel muttered, and she pressed down hard on the gas.

Instantly, the Mustang surged ahead, and Rachel gripped the wheel harder, taking the curve of the highway

"Don't!" I said. "Just pull over."

"No!" she said, leaning forward into her driving. "You don't know how fast I can go in this!"

I checked in my side view mirror: the police car had turned on his lights, blinking all across the top of the car.

"Pull over, Rachel!" I shouted. "Please! You've *got* to!"

I reached for the steering wheel, but she swerved the car, throwing me back against my door.

I rolled down my window, turned around, and stuck my head out of the window. The wind whipped against the back of my head as I saw that there were now *two* police cars behind us, both cars blinking wildly.

"Pull over, Rachel!" I shouted.

"I can't!" she cried desperately, and drove even faster, thrusting down on the gas. "I can't let her win! I'm *not* gonna die!!"

I was thrown back into my seat with a thud. There was only one thing to do: try to stop the car myself. But as I reached over to try to grab the steering wheel from her, the oddest thing happened. From out of the forest, a huge deer bolted across the highway, right across our path. I remember several things occurring simultaneously, but almost in slow-motion. I braced myself, knowing that we were going to hit the deer *and* that it was the same white-faced deer – Bambi's Mother! – that we saw at the Quarry during the summer. I remember thinking, *what a strange coincidence*, as Rachel screamed "I love you!" and there was the sound of squealing brakes, smashing glass, crunching metal, and then nothing: absolute, total, perfect blackness.

That was the first ending.

Record of Events #35 – entered Tuesday, 4:45 P.M.

～

I woke up in a blank, white room I don't know how many days or weeks later. It took me a very long time to wake up and focus my eyes, and even longer to realize that I was in a hospital. Nurses came and went, but I couldn't speak and nobody would tell me anything.

At first I could not move. Everything – my mind, my senses, my memory – was frozen. My body felt sunken into the mattress. I thought that I was paralyzed, but then realized that I could move my head and my upper body a little.

I think I had some casts or something on my legs, but when I tried to move and look, I felt that my left leg was attached to something at the foot of the bed. Painfully, I raised myself, little by little, onto my elbows and saw that my left ankle was handcuffed to the post of the footboard of the hospital bed. I fell back against the mattress, exhausted and defeated and disgusted with myself beyond measure as I remembered *everything*.

Then two policemen came to see me. They wore suits, but they told me that they were policemen, so I believed them. An older one and a younger one.

"Your girlfriend's dead," said the older one with a lifeless voice that I will never forget. "She went through the windshield. You got lucky and were thrown from the vehicle."

When I heard that, my heart broke . . . for good. But at the same time I was glad that Rachel wasn't going to have to endure what I was going to have to endure.

"*Lucky . . .*" I either thought or mumbled.

"We know what you did," he said. "We found the car at the bottom of the Quarry. Long Island detectives went over your girlfriend's home and your parents' house with a fine-tooth comb. They found everything except for the money."

"What money?" I said. And what did *my parents* have to do with any of this? Nothing!

"'What money?'" he repeated sharply. "How about the two grand we found in your girlfriend's purse and the other four grand that's missing?"

"What four grand?" I said.

"And there's some jewelry missing too," he continued. "The victim's jewelry box was ransacked."

"What jewelry?" I said, my head spinning. "I don't know what you guys are talking about . . . honestly."

"'Honestly'?" the old cop repeated with a huff of a laugh and a sour smile.

At that moment, I knew that no one was ever going to believe me and my side of the story. Ever.

The younger cop said, "First, we're gonna take your statement. Then you can see your parents. They're waiting outside."

That's when I felt a new kind of pain: deep, deep, ineradicable *shame*.

"Don't," I mumbled.

"What?"

"Don't let them in," I whispered. "Don't let them see me."

"Sorry, punk," said the older cop. "Live with it."

∿

I don't want to talk about what it was like when my parents came in to see me at the hospital, that first time. I'll just say what I told them – and what is true:

"*I didn't kill anybody.*"

Even as I said it, it really didn't make me feel better. The words felt like cold ash in my mouth. It was the truth, but my actions were nothing to be proud of. I should have – I don't know – *known* that Rachel was going to do something to Eleanor, and stopped her. I should have done something when she was fighting with Nanci. Instead, what I did was help her conceal the two deaths. I was loyal to Rachel instead of to any normal code of morality, and it was simply wrong. I put blind love above common decency, and that's really not a good love, is it? What we did *dishonored* our love, and to this day that still makes me sad. Very, very sad.

It was the first time that I ever saw my father cry. I had seen my mother cry a whole bunch of times, but to see my father cry was . . . well, I was discovering new lows by the hour.

A doctor came and told me that both my legs were broken: compound fractures of both fibulas, both tibias, and my right femur. I also had a severely collapsed lung and several crushed ribs.

"Does he have to be attached like that?" my mother asked the doctor, pointing to the handcuffs that chained my ankle to the bed.

"I'm sorry," he said. "Sheriff's orders."

"He's not going to run away with two broken legs," my mother said louder.

"I'm sorry," the doctor repeated. "But that's what I've been told."

"Stop it, Ma," I said. "It's all right." The handcuffs actually were uncomfortable around my ankle, but I already knew that it made no sense to ask for what I wasn't going to get. I remembered the stony looks on the faces of those cops, a look that was soon to become quite familiar to me.

I was in the Towanda State Hospital for a long time, learning to walk again. I was kept in the prison ward, handcuffed to my bed whenever I wasn't released for physical therapy, some test, or some other reason like an operation. I had five. My legs were pretty well smashed in the accident, and my right lung was damaged, too, so my energy level was low at the beginning. I wasn't getting enough oxygen so I couldn't build my strength back up, but I couldn't build my strength back up because I wasn't getting enough oxygen.

My surgeon was a dry, old guy with a very thick German accent.

"You're young," he said when he showed me the before-and-after x-rays on the light board in his office. "Theoretically, you should have a complete recovery."

I wanted to tell him, "All theory, dear friend, is gray," but I didn't. I kept my mouth shut and did all the physical therapy as hard as I could. Whenever they uncuffed me from my bed, I was down in the Rehab and Fitness Center, trying to learn to walk again. And I did. Today I don't walk with much of a limp, and I'm working on it every day. No one would ever know that my legs were once smashed to pieces on a highway in the middle of nowhere on the last drive ever with my one true love.

I don't want to talk too much about the trial; there was enough of that on TV, in the newspapers, and on the radio. It was all so humiliating, day after day, to be so exposed to public disgrace, but then again, Eleanor Prince and Nanci Jerome were dead, day after day, so I had no right to object to getting what I deserved.

By then, I had been moved down to the Nassau County jail. For a while, I was in the medical wing. Then they moved me to "protective custody." Fortunately, I was not put in with the regular jail population. By then, I was the famous "Ivy League Killer" and prey for anybody who wanted to get some notoriety by killing a famous killer.

What I actually was, was an accessory to murder. They charged me with murder in the first degree because there was evidence that Rachel had planned this whole thing for a long time. There was no evidence that *I* knew about her plans, but that didn't seem to bother the Assistant District Attorney.

Before the trial, my first lawyer and my parents got this psychiatrist who was an expert on trials to examine me. We talked for a very long time. (He was a smart guy, though not as smart as he thought he was. But, then again, *who is*?) He's the one who told my lawyer and my parents that they shouldn't put me on the stand, that I shouldn't testify on my own behalf. My first lawyer felt that since there were none of my fingerprints found on the poker – and there *were* Rachel's, as well as traces of her blood (I guess from that scratch on her hand) – that proved that I didn't have any contact with the murder weapon (which was the truth). Add to that, Rachel's bite marks on Nanci's cheek and Rachel's previous statements and behavior, he felt that would establish "reasonable doubt," enough to convince a jury that I had nothing to do with the actual killings.

I would have told the jury outright that I didn't hit anybody, with anything. I would have told them the whole damn story. But they didn't let me testify, which they tell me is not so unusual in cases like mine. Often defendants in murder cases just have to sit there and take it in silence.

How did I stay silent during my trial? I had to, that's how. I sat at the table and tried to look innocent, whatever that is. My first lawyer told me time and time again not to make any sour faces, and I did my best. I sat there stone-faced while the prosecution called, one after the other, Stanley Marshak, Roommate A, and Professor Brilliant to the stand, boom-boom-boom, to testify what a bad counselor, roommate, and student I was. Just for fun. Just to make me look like a complete maggot. They tried to depict me as some kind of sullen, subversive rebel, when I was the most obedient, most follow-the-rules kind of kid my whole life. Except with Rachel.

To my shame, I allowed my first lawyer to put Rachel on trial. He put on several witnesses who testified how "troubled" and "disturbed" she was. Her therapist testified that Rachel suffered from "adolescent depression and security concerns." She said that Rachel occasionally burned herself with cigarettes. I *knew* that was a lie. Or I thought I knew it. And it turned out that Rachel had seen some kind of child psychologist from when she was nine until she was eleven. The psychologist had passed away two years ago, but they subpoenaed the notes from his treatment of Rachel, which revealed "empathy issues." There was testimony from a boy at Oakhurst High who said that Rachel had actually said that she planned to kill her mother and tried to talk him into helping her. When he refused, she supposedly said, "That's OK. I know someone who can help me." When the Assistant District Attorney asked the boy if Rachel had mentioned the name of the person who might help her, my first lawyer strenuously objected, citing "hearsay" and some other things, but the Oakhurst boy had gotten out my first name, and the damage had been done.

It got even worse when the Assistant District Attorney started doing some improvisatory arithmetic as he was stalling for time and mentioned Rachel's age and mine and the words "statutory rape" in the same sentence. All hell instantly broke loose: my lawyer jumped to his feet in vehement objection, the crowd went completely ape, and the judge had to send the jury out of the courtroom. Later, everyone was directed to forget everything that the Assistant District Attorney had said. How can a person forget something that they've heard – really? The bell had been rung. More damage.

The trial was filled with lies, and it took all my self-control not to jump up out of my chair and "object." But I had my lawyer to do that; I had to trust him. Still, it churned me up inside, to hear falsehoods and willful misinterpretations of the truth, day after day. Part of growing up is realizing how much of life is filled with lies. Did I mention that someone told me that when Stewie Thurman left Camp Mooncliff early at the end of camp because his grandmother had "died", *that* was a big lie? It turned out that Stewie just wanted to get back to his stupid college because he had been called up from the junior varsity to the varsity football team. He arranged a fake phone call and used the old "dead grandmother" lie to get out of his Mooncliff contract early. You cannot trust anybody in this world!

Also, the prosecution made such a big deal out of all this money and jewelry – stuff that I didn't even know about – that Rachel must have taken from upstairs, or even before. They found some of it in her purse: cash and some of Eleanor's jewelry. But I wouldn't be surprised if Manny or Herb ransacked the place once they realized that Eleanor was gone, took everything, and tried to pin it all on dead Rachel.

As if I would kill for money! That was the most absurd allegation of all. I sat there at the defendant's table, not moving a muscle, as they lied. I knew deep, deep, deep in my heart that whatever I did, however misguided, I did for love.

The morning the verdict was read I wore my lucky blue blazer, the one I wore to my Columbia interview and that first dinner at the Costa Brava with Eleanor and Herb. They had confiscated my lucky RFK pin long ago, as a potential weapon. I always changed from my orange jail uniform into street clothes before the court proceedings, so that the jury wouldn't be prejudiced against me. Sure.

The courtroom was packed with spectators, eager to see me fry. Supposedly, people were selling their places in line outside to get in to hear the verdict read. There were all the regulars – reporters, photographers, my parents, ordinary/nosey spectators, and the ever-present Manny Prince.

Manny sat in the first row behind the Assistant District Attorney for the entire trial. He looked at me with such hatred in his eyes – I could almost *feel* his stare burn the back of my neck – that the judge had to caution him about prejudicing the jury. I can't say that I blamed him, but it's a shame that he never seemed to care so much about his daughter while she was still alive. Other than buying her that damn car.

Herb came to the courthouse once, but he was mobbed by reporters – pun intended – both coming in and going out, so that he never came back. At first, a couple of the newspapers had played up the angle that Herb might have been involved in the murders someway, and that I was doing a "hit" for some-one. The theory was that Eleanor had been killed in revenge for some recent killing of some other Mafia girlfriend from some other "family" in New Jersey, but that idea died away after a while. On that one day that Herb did show up, he sat in one of the back rows on the aisle, on the prosecutor's side, as far away from Manny as he could get. From what I under-stand, they never exchanged a word.

Nanci's family – the Jeromes – were maybe the saddest case of all. (Except for my parents, of course.) They were quite a bit older than my folks. Mrs. Jerome was enormous; prob-ably like what Nanci would have looked like in thirty years. She wore a black dress as big as a tent to the trial almost every day, a mink stole, and a string of pearls the size of grapes. Ultra-skinny Mr. Jerome looked like he'd stepped out of a Brooks Brothers ad, with his pin-striped suit and matching silk tie and handkerchief. He used a cane to help him walk and had a big strawberry for a nose. The two of them took about a half hour to walk up and down the aisle to their seats, right behind Manny, right behind the prosecution. Once my father tried to say something to them, but he was rebuffed in quite a nasty way. I can't say as I blame them: there was nothing really to say. But they shouldn't have been quite so dismissive to my Dad.

Only once did one of Nanci's siblings come to the trial – the brother who lived in Connecticut. He looked just like his old man: thin, conservatively dressed, and alcoholic. Her sis-ter from Phoenix never even came to the trial at all, not once. For some reason, that made me extra sad. If I had had a broth-er or a sister and they got murdered, I certainly would come to the trial every day. I'm fairly certain that I would have been in that first row every single day, right next to Manny Prince, wanting – no, *demanding* – vengeance.

When the jury came in, I knew immediately that they had found me guilty. My first lawyer told me that if no one on the jury looked at me when they walked in, the verdict was bad.

And sure enough, not one of them looked at me, and the verdict was guilty of murder. In the second degree.

When the court clerk said the word "guilty," I didn't cry. Other people behind me cried, but I didn't. I mastered my emotions even as my heart sank into the Earth. I was going to save my tears for later and not let myself be photographed crying. That's just what the newspapers would have liked. And I was going to be strong for my family, the family that I had destroyed. Make that three families: I guess I had destroyed the Princes and the Jeromes too.

Some people on the other side of the room cheered. The Assistant District Attorney and his staff were happy; they "won," even if they didn't get their First Degree verdict. My first lawyer put his arm around my shoulder and said not to worry, that we would immediately appeal. I can't say that I was really surprised by the whole thing. Three people were dead, and somebody had to pay for it. (I'm sure the jury held me responsible for Rachel's death, too, even though I wasn't driving the Mustang. I mean, why not?)

After I was found guilty, in some ways, all the excitement was over. No more trips to the courthouse. The press was already moving onto the next big story, the next murder. I got lucky: some guy named Charles Manson and these hippie-followers of his chopped up some people in Hollywood, knocking me right off the front page and out of the public focus. This was good because it finally reduced the daily humiliation that my parents suffered, so long as my trial was on the front page. And now I was old news, small potatoes; I had only "killed" three people, and Eleanor Prince wasn't any Sharon Tate. So thank you, Mr. Manson.

I've been in the Nassau County Jail all this time, but they're going to move me upstate soon, before any appeal can be filed. The only question is whether it will be Attica or Sing Sing. The difference in the driving – forty miles to Westchester vs. 350 miles to the middle-of-nowhere Upstate – would have a real effect on my parents' lives. To visit me up there, those long drives would kill my mother . . . so to speak.

I've had a couple of visitors since I've been here. My parents, of course, though I had to tell my Dad to stop my Mom from coming. I could see that it was too hard on her, especially when there were a lot of nosey, rude reporters and photographers outside. And my first and second lawyers and their staff: all very nice people. They were extremely understanding during this whole thing, from my arrest right through to the verdict. But the one visitor I never contemplated seeing was Manny Prince.

I didn't expect any visitors that day. I had been found guilty and was just another prisoner, waiting to be moved to another place in the system. The moment I saw Manny sitting behind the plexiglas partition in the Visitors' Room waiting for me, I could have walked out and refused to see him. But I didn't. I sat down and picked up the phone on the wall that connected us.

"Hello, Manny," I said.

"Hello, smart guy," he said back to me with a smirk on his face. He was wearing one of those silly, expensive, embroidered Caribbean shirts with the pockets that he liked.

At first, we just looked at each other. I suppose he had the right to gloat over his victory, but I still felt sorry for him.

"I assume they checked you for weapons," I said.

"Yeah," he said. "They search you real good in this place."

"Tell me about it," I said sarcastically.

Another pause while we looked at each other. He was "free," and I was not, but there was something very strong and very odd that almost *equalized* us.

"What are you doing here, Manny?" I asked.

"Nothing," he said, looking straight at me with the blue-blue eyes that Rachel had inherited.

"You want to see me suffer?" I asked. "Does that make you happy?"

"Yeah, it does," he snapped back. But then he became reflective. "No . . .I don't know how I feel. I wish they coulda given you the chair. Then this whole thing would be over."

"Sorry, Manny," I said. "I'm still alive."

He seemed more pathetic than I was, and certainly more pathetic than my Dad. But then I realized that it was because my father's only child was still alive, and Manny's wasn't.

"Rachel said you had a new girlfriend," I said.

"Yeah," he shrugged. "That's finished."

"I know how you feel," I said.

He shot me a dark look, and there was another silence between us.

"What do you *want*, Manny?"

He leaned forward, toward the scratched plexiglas that separated us, and whispered into the telephone after a long pause.

"I know it was her."

"What?" I said.

His eyes burned into mine, just as Rachel's had so many times, and he snarled, "You think we were monsters, her mother and me. The worst parents in the world. Right? . . . You have no idea what it was like to try to be a parent to Rachel, no idea. You don't know what we went through with her. You know how many doctors we saw, how many specialists? From the moment she was born, she was not an easy kid. Beautiful and bright as anything, but never easy. Always trouble. Eleanor and me, we fought like hell over her, what to do with her, how to deal with her tantrums, her moods. We were at the school every other week with her when she was young. She was always difficult, always headstrong, always . . . impossible. Why do you think we broke up? We *wanted* to have other kids, but we were afraid to. We couldn't handle *one* Rachel, forget about *two*! Our marriage never stood a chance, trying to raise her. ... OK, so maybe we weren't the greatest parents in the world. But we did our best. And we did try to protect other people from her."

"So now you're gonna tell me that's why you and Eleanor wanted to keep Rachel and me *apart*?" I said. "For my own good?"

"Partly . . ." Manny said. "Partly."

I didn't say anything. Couldn't say anything. Even if what he said was true, it was all too sad to contemplate.

He looked down, then looked up with despairing eyes, and continued, "OK, that's what I wanted to say . . . I know it was her. I know that she led you on, that you just followed her, doing what you two did. I know what she was really like. I always thought that something like this could happen some-day. She was a beautiful, beautiful girl, but there was always something . . . something wrong."

"Then why didn't you say anything at the trial?" I asked.

He leaned in closer and whispered viciously into the phone, "What was I gonna say? Something to *help* you? You were *there*, smart guy, and you didn't do *anything* to save those two people. You just did whatever she wanted you to do. So you *got* what you deserved."

I could have answered him in a million snotty ways. Instead, I just told him the truth.

"What can I say, Manny? I loved her."

Smiling sadly, he shook his head and muttered, "What an idiot . . . what a waste."

I laughed once, bitterly, and said, "That's what my Dad thinks. Only he doesn't say it."

"Well, he *should* say it," Manny snapped. "And more than once."

He smiled sadly and then sat back. "I saw your father in court. He seems to be an OK guy."

"He is," I said. "You'd like him. You have a lot in common. Both of your kids are dead."

"Don't you say that!" Manny shot back. "Rachel's dead, and you're alive."

That was a fact I couldn't challenge.

"So . . ." Manny continued, shifting in his chair, back and forth. "What else I came here to say was" – he stopped moving and looked straight into my eyes – "*dammit-to-hell!* I forgive you."

Then he slammed down the phone so hard on the wall that I thought he would break it, got up out of his chair, and walked out of the Visitors' Room. I didn't even have time to hang up the phone or say goodbye. And I never saw Manny Prince again.

∾

My excellent new lawyer came to me with excellent news today: I am being sent to Sing Sing, not Attica. Yes! A win for our side! I'm not sure why that happened; I think he pleaded some kind of "hardship" or something. Anyway, the System somehow worked in my favor. (Thank you, Your Honor.) It will be much easier for my parents to visit me now and cry more often in person. I don't want to think about how often my mother cries at night. There are certain things that I can no longer think about.

∾

I saw my father one last time before they moved me upstate. He had gotten friendly with some of the guards – did I mention that my Dad was the nicest, sweetest guy in the world? He thought that if the guards knew him personally, they might go a little easier on his son. That's how he thought: even as I ruined his life, all he was concerned about was me.

"Your mother wanted to come," he said into the phone, sitting across from me. "But she was too – what – overwhelmed lately." He gave me a shrug and smiled through the smudged plexiglas barrier. The entry processing for visitors – the personal searches and the waiting, the waiting, the waiting – took more than an hour sometimes.

"I can see why," I said. He seemed more tired than I had ever seen him before. The fluorescent light in the Visitors' Room sucked the life out of anyone's face, but I had never noticed how *old* he looked. "How are *you* doing?"

"Oh, I'm fine," he said. "Your mother's on that Metrecal diet again, so guess who's starving?"

I tried to laugh, seeing that he was trying to cheer me up.

"Stop at Vinnie's on the way home," I said. "And get yourself some cheese sticks. You deserve 'em."

"Food here sucks, I bet," he said, repeating what I had told him many times before.

"You have no idea," I said. "They make Ma look like Betty Crocker."

Dad laughed, "And how are you sleeping?"

"OK," I lied. But then said truthfully, "Sometimes it gets cold at night, but all that could change when I go to the new place, so what does it matter?" I couldn't bear to say the name Sing Sing.

"You want me to, I'll call 'em up in advance and tell 'em to keep it nice and warm up there," he said. "Maybe they don't know that they're dealing with *Heat*-ler here."

It made me laugh *and* it made me sad to hear my Dad say that. Happy to hear him use our family nickname for him, the one he so hated, just to try to get a smile out of me, and sad, to think of home.

I had to say something or one of us might start to cry; I couldn't stand that. I know that he wouldn't want to cry in front of me.

"Remember when Mom was the class mother in my fifth grade class?" I said, letting the memory rush back. "And it was Halloween? They made this big party at school, and Mom came dressed up as a witch, with a big black hat and an orange face and her front teeth blacked out?"

My mother, a shy woman, had *never* done anything this flamboyant or theatrical before. Before *or* since.

"She visited all the other classes and scared all the little kids, but in a good way. She was the hit of the school."

I had been at a new school that year, and I think she wanted to help me fit in. I was so surprised that she would do that; I didn't realize at the time that it was all for my benefit.

"No, I don't remember that . . ." he said, with a sad smile, his eyes misting over. "But it sounds terrific."

"It *was*," I assured him, wanting him to remember something that fine, something from so long ago, when things weren't so messed up, before I had ruined everything. "She was really something."

My father blinked and looked up at the ceiling. He started to say something, stopped, then started again, "You know we wanted to have other kids, but it turned out that we couldn't. Your mother went to a couple of doctors."

I looked into my father's eyes clearly, saying, "I didn't know that. I mean, I coulda guessed but . . . Who would want to have just one kid, especially if it turned out to be me?"

"Don't say that!" he said right back, gripping the phone tightly, looking straight at me. "This was just one crazy thing. You've been a good kid your whole life. A good son. . . . What I'm saying is: if we just had to have one son, I was glad he was you."

I wasn't going to cry; that did nobody any favors. I held tight to my feelings and refused to cry, even though I was crumbling inside at the sight of this brave, beaten man. And I couldn't help but think about the Princes, with one child, afraid to have a second one, and my parents, with one child, *unable* to have a second one. And I thought how cruel and unfair and ironic this world can be – to everyone. No one gets out alive.

"I should have known that something was going on –" he declared.

"Please don't start that –" I cut him off, not wanting to hear him try to take responsibility for something that wasn't his to take.

"I wasn't really being a good parent," he continued.

"Don't say that!" I heard my voice get louder. "This has nothing to do with you!"

But my Dad just paused and laughed lightly, shaking his head sadly as if I didn't, and never would, understand. But that's OK: he didn't understand me either. We loved each other imperfectly, I'm afraid. But then again, no love is perfect. I'd thought that I had a perfect love with Rachel. And, in a horrible, doomed-from-the-start way, I did.

"Is there anything else I can bring you?" he asked.

What did I really want? "There's only one thing that I really want," I said. "And you can't bring it to me."

"What is it?" he wanted to know.

"The jukebox at Bailey's," I said softly, holding on to one last teardrop.

He didn't know what I meant, and I couldn't explain it to him.

Record of Events #36 – entered Thursday, 8:48 P.M.

~

They moved me a couple of days ago with a bunch of other inmates, in a high-security bus with cages on the windows and chains on our legs. It's hard to walk when your feet are shackled – especially when both of your legs have been broken – but I guess that's the whole idea. I got to see highways and cars and people in the outside world. The bus even drove on some of the same highways of my own "great escape" that was depicted in maps in the newspapers. Everything I saw wounded my heart, but I was not going to show any emotion. Not in a bus full of murderers. I guess that would have to include "me."

People in other cars passing us looked up at the bus with expressions of disgust and curiosity: Who were those evil guys in that bus and what did they do to be caged up like that? Where were they going? And wouldn't we all be better off if that bus drove off the Throgs Neck Bridge and drowned everybody inside? A fair question – one that I contemplated as we crossed the bridge. I craned my neck and looked through the caged window across the water to the Whitestone Bridge. That was the bridge that Rachel and I "escaped" on when we were driving up to the Quarry with those "things" in my trunk. That's where I had that moment when I was tempted to pull over to those cops on the side of the road and confess everything. But I didn't, and that was a long time ago. And remember: "All theory, dear friend, is gray."

"Ten minutes, ladies!" the big guard in the front seat, next to the driver, yelled back to us, shackled to our seats in the cage behind him. I looked out of the window, through the heavy black grill, drinking in the last views of civilization that I might see for a long, long time. Trees, houses, stores – simple things looked exotic and unreachable. Who knew when I would next ride in a bus, or any vehicle? Would my next ride be in an ambulance, or perhaps a hearse? Such was my rosy future, my glowing prospect.

They herded us, clanking in leg chains, off the bus at the Sing Sing Correctional Facility, a maximum-security prison operated by the New York State Department of Correctional Services. As you get close to Sing Sing, you can see the Hudson River, just as you can from Columbia (at least in winter, before the leaves grow in). Same river, different institutions: both renowned molders of young American men. They processed us, yelled at us, tried to scare us – and in my case, certainly succeeded. But I've learned that I can pretend to be anything now: brave, tough, psychotic, dangerous, normal. I can even pretend to be an everyday, golly-gee, teenage-type person, as you have just seen (starting on Page One of "The Summer" – hahaha.) I think I can survive this.

∿

Now that I've been in prison for a while, I'm actually better than I've been in a long time. Things aren't so crazy. I know exactly what's expected of me here. I've befriended my cellmate (armed robbery) by proofreading his letters to *his* lawyer, so that I don't feel threatened twenty-four hours a day. Unlike at Columbia, where I felt pressure *twenty-four hours a day*. That may be the best thing I can cling to: there is no homework in prison.

One thing about being here at Sing Sing: I'm back to being the Smartest Kid in the Class. Except I hear that there's this old math genius in another cell block whom they call "the

Professor." He helps other guys with their appeals and court motions in exchange for cigarettes, better food, etc. He supposedly was an accountant for the Flying Dragons, this major Chinatown crime family, in for wire fraud and torture. Strange combination, unless he tortured someone with a wire. These Asians are getting into everything.

I exercise almost constantly, doing push-ups on my cell floor. In many ways, I'm stronger than I've ever been before. My legs are almost completely healed, just as that surgeon said they would be. Because of the inherent danger in a place like this, I've found that my senses have become sharpened. I'm out in the general population now, but I'm learning how to take care of myself, among these monsters. I'm always "looking over both of my shoulders at the same time." When fear is real, when paranoia is justified, the primal senses take over. The Hunter-or-Hunted mind resurfaces. It's called self-preservation, and it's really a wonderful thing. It's kept me going through some pretty difficult times.

There was one good outcome from my trial: because Eleanor was Herb's girlfriend and he actually *was* involved in organized crime, I was befriended by members of a crime family that was the *enemy* of Herb's family. They figured if I was messing with Herb, I had to be a stand-up guy. They gave me protection and a lot more. Of course, I never told them the truth, but by then I was very good at that.

I've almost been beaten up and have been punched a couple of times since I've been here, but I haven't been raped. That is my major achievement since the time of my incarceration; I'm not kidding. This is what I've been reduced to: animal survival. But I accept it. In the yard, in the shower, around the corners, in the shadows – no matter what my new friends in the waste management business can do for me. This is my everyday world for twenty-five to life. Isn't that insane? But, in some bizarre way, my everyday world is the same as it's always been: a life lived inside my head, with all my broken dreams and memories, imaginary triumphs and past injustices, flickering past constantly, ready to be relived and perfected. Nothing has changed in that sense: I'm still a prisoner of myself. But I finally got to escape Long Island after all, although not quite in the way I had imagined.

They let me have a couple of books in here, and, just to be perverse, I took some of my Columbia books. The Montaigne essays. He says, "The most certain sign of wisdom is cheerfulness." Oh Michel, how am I supposed to be cheerful in here? In here where the racket never stops, and there is the constant threat of violence. All my life I wondered what I'd be when I grew up. A doctor? Or a lawyer? Now I know: I grew up to be a convict.

Actually, the noise in this cellblock isn't so bad. Not as bad as the Nassau County lock-up. I can shut out this noise. Sometimes I wad up pieces of toilet paper and stuff them in my ears. I have to wet the paper and squish it up well because it's kind of scratchy. But when I put the wet wads in my ears, it feels kind of cool and tickly, and I'm more alone, more inside. This cell is really not much smaller than my dorm room shared with Roommate A, and this one my parents don't have to pay for, except, of course, as ordinary New York State taxpayers. Not to mention that this room has its own toilet and sink, right there, at the foot of the bed. How convenient.

I know I'm being watched in here. That's the whole idea, isn't it? Being watched by guards with guns because I'm a danger to society. Being watched because I might kill again. Isn't that foolish? There was only one Eleanor Prince, one Nanci Jerome, and yes, one Rachel Prince – and they're all gone. I have no other "enemy" or "adversary." I've always been a peaceful person. In fact, I'm peaceful right now! . . . That is verging on a joke. But here, in this cell, I am going to have to find some kind of peace, some way to survive. So that if I get out – *when* I get out, I must stay positive. I NEED MORE PAPER!!!!

Record of Events #37 – entered Saturday, 6:15 A.M.

~

To some people, I'll always be the Ivy League Killer, the Kid Who Killed His Girlfriend's Mother and Friend, the weird Leopold-and-Loeb-type kid who was in the papers for a while in that circus of a trial. I know I'll never get beyond that with some people. Maybe not even with myself. But life goes on . . . doesn't it? And you never know about things in this absurd/tragic world: The Mets just won the World Series. Really! In 1969. They beat the Orioles in five. *The Mets!? Won the World Series!* And a man, an astronaut, actually walked on the moon this past summer. So truly anything is possible.

They're going to be turning off the lights soon, so I have to end this for now. But I know that I'll wake up tomorrow, and everything will be the same. Nothing will have changed in here, except for one more day off my sentence.

I never thought that my life would end this way, scribbling in a little room, running my thoughts, around and around. In a small, cement rectangle. All corners, and no escape. There is only one serious question: How to live your life and not waste it? But I won't even get to try to answer it, because from now on I will have to live *prison* life.

I'm back to where I was at the beginning, talking to myself, with no one listening. Even in a cell like this, I'm going to try to find a decent life. Van Gogh painted a cell like this, and it was beautiful. There must be a way to see this cell as if van Gogh painted it. There must be a way to see the beauty in everything. Damned if I know what it is, but I'm never going to stop searching for it. I know it's out there/in here, waiting to be discovered, waiting to be felt.

Maybe I'll be a late-bloomer, if and when I get out of here. I'll still be in my forties. Maybe I'll find a cure for cancer. Of course, I'd probably have to go back and do pre-med to do that, and I guess that's not in the cards. Too much science. OK, maybe I'll be the *patent lawyer* for the guy who finds the cure for cancer. Do they let convicted felons become lawyers? They should: the acorn doesn't fall so far from the tree.

One of the best things I've read since I've been in here was that when Jonas Salk found the vaccine to prevent polio, he refused to patent it. He left it open to anybody to make it, to help stop polio. He could have made a zillion dollars if he had patented it and charged just a little for each shot. Instead, he gave it away, for the good of humanity. Wow. That is a good, pure thing. I need to believe in good, pure things right now. I need to believe in mercy and charity and helping others. I need to believe in the goodness and worth of living, and at the same time, watch my back every day, for the approaching knife.

Maybe I'll be a writer. After all, I've had a lot of practice here, in various cells, filling up these notebooks, trying to tell the truth just as my excellent new lawyer asked me to. But if I ever get out, I'll tell other people's stories, stories of some of these guys I've met here and in the Nassau County lock-up, stories that are a million times sadder than mine. They say there's this famous writer who comes here and gives a writer's workshop, but no one can remember his name. Who knows? It's better than working in the kitchen or the laundry, and it would get me out of this damned box.

They just put out the lights. Now I'm writing in shadow, from memory and with hope. Hope that'll I'll be able to read this in the morning. Hope that someday someone will read it, the Parole Board, or my judge, or The Judge, somebody/anybody who'll understand. Who'll understand and maybe even forgive.

Every night I ask myself: How did a pure, innocent love such as ours lead to such a terrible end? I'm still working on that one. If she had just *asked* me to help her get rid of Eleanor, well, first I would have tried to talk her out of it. But after that, who knows? I might have helped her anyway. And I would have found a way where we wouldn't have gotten caught, that's for damned sure.

Record of Events #38 – entered Sunday, 12:03 A.M.

~

I lay in my hard prison bed at night, trying to see what I'm writing, believing and not believing where I am. I can't really breathe in here; you know that I like to breathe. And I am reaching new levels of Negative Learning every day, beyond what I ever thought possible.

I listen to my heart – b'thump . . . b'thump . . . b'thump. I relive all the mistakes I've made in my life, the mistakes I made with Rachel, the mistakes made at the trial, the mistakes made *that night* when all of our lives ended. I replay every episode, pick at every wound, pick at every word, and I am still not satisfied. But when I finally close my eyes at night, I still see her face, those blue-blue eyes, that Mona Lisa smile . . . and it makes me happy inside. I never got a chance to say goodbye to Rachel, so I say goodbye to her every night. I can't help it: after everything that happened, I still love the girl who ruined my life.

I close my eyes, and just like that, I'm back in The Zone. I hear her final, passionate, desperate "I love youuuuu!" right before the crash, echoing in my brain – or did I just make that up? I stay very still, withdraw into my purest self, and try to recreate something real, something basic: what it was like to be in love with Rachel Prince.

But as I told the Doggy Without Braces, everything is temporary. So why on Earth should I moan? I memorize these walls every day and every night, and I try to see beyond them. I try to see all the way to the stars, to that same infinite Milky

Way that I saw at Camp Mooncliff "many summers ago, when the Earth was still new." I think that I can make myself believe anything, even that I'll get out of here someday, and that my luck will eventually even out. Maybe I'll get the chance to live a decent life, the life of service and generosity that I should have lived. I honestly don't know. Maybe the best thing for everyone is to just forget about me. Pretend I'm already dead, that I just "disappeared" like Eleanor Prince and poor, fat Nanci Jerome.

I know that my excellent new lawyer is going to hate what I've written, but I can't help it. People who read it are going to say I'm just a self-dramatizing teenager, looking for another chance he doesn't deserve. I say, so what? I've bet on the truth, and the truth shall set me free. Someday.

In any case, thank you, Counselor, for all of your encouragement and support. Me gotta go now . . . before I make things worse.

I guess it's way too late for that.

Publisher's Note

The above manuscript was deemed inadmissible and never accepted as evidence in Case No. 1004-70, Second Judicial Department, Appellate Division, Supreme Court of New York State.

Defendant X was released on 2/3/10 after serving almost thirty-five years in various penitentiaries around the country.

He is currently living in the western United States, under an assumed name, with a new identity. The writer reviewed the galleys and has approved this edition of his manuscript.

Acknowledgements

I want to thank Nancy Cushing-Jones for her unfailing good advice in many areas. I thank Lou Aronica, Aaron Brown, Barbara Aronica-Buck, and everyone at The Story Plant and Perseus Distribution for their work in helping bring my book into this world. A special thank you to copy editor Nora Tamada for improving this book in many ways, large and small. I also want to thank honest Laurie Horowitz, Kate Klimo, Eva Charney, Marsha Clark, Alan Blumenfeld, Susan Pile, Wendy Winks, and Jonathan Jackson (early readers of the manuscript who encouraged me). A particular thank you to my big brother Bruce Robinson for his lifelong support, friendship, and jokes. I also want to much-more-than-merely-thank my son Jesse and my daughter Daisy for helping give meaning and joy to my life and being inspirations to me every day. Please put me in a nice home. And I want to thank Mary Elizabeth Shutt for practically everything else.